"You're in the crosshairs, Alexa, a hunted prey in a small arena. What do you plan on doing?"

"I'm sorta winging it as I go." She checked the compass, then directed him another mile. "Stop the car."

Killian obeyed. "I'm coming after you, you know that."

Only her gaze shifted. "I'm looking forward to it." Then suddenly she leaned close to his handsome face, touched his jaw. It clenched beneath her palm. He was furious and she suddenly admired his control. "You should have put a bullet in me, Killian."

Killian was snagged, by that voice, those serious green eyes penetrating any wall he put between them. She was damn righteous and determined for such a little thing, and the chips were stacked so high against her, he knew this wouldn't end pretty. He'd get her. He'd drag her back to American soil in a body bag or by the hair, but he'd get her. It almost hurt to know that.

"I won't waste a second chance."

"For what? It's over for you, wildcat."

The tenderness in his voice slayed her, had her reaching for something she could never have because true emotion was so absent from her life, her work; Alexa hungered for it." Not today," she whispered.

BOOK YOUR PLACE ON OUR WEBSITE AND MAKE THE READING CONNECTION!

We've created a customized website just for our very special readers, where you can get the inside scoop on everything that's going on with Zebra, Pinnacle and Kensington books.

When you come online, you'll have the exciting opportunity to:

- View covers of upcoming books
- Read sample chapters
- Learn about our future publishing schedule (listed by publication month *and author*)
- Find out when your favorite authors will be visiting a city near you
- Search for and order backlist books from our online catalog
- Check out author bios and background information
- Send e-mail to your favorite authors
- Meet the Kensington staff online
- Join us in weekly chats with authors, readers and other guests
- Get writing guidelines
- AND MUCH MORE!

**Visit our website at
http://www.kensingtonbooks.com**

NAKED TRUTH

Amy J. Fetzer

KENSINGTON BOOKS
KENSINGTON PUBLISHING CORP.
http://www.kensingtonbooks.com

KENSINGTON BOOKS are published by

Kensington Publishing Corp.
850 Third Avenue
New York, NY 10022

All Kensington titles, imprints and distributed lines are available at special quantity discounts for bulk purchases for sales promotion, premiums, fund-raising, educational or institutional use.

Special book excerpts or customized printings can also be created to fit specific needs. For details, write or phone the office of the Kensington Special Sales Manager: Kensington Publishing Corp., 850 Third Avenue, New York, NY 10022. Attn. Special Sales Department. Phone: 1-800-221-2647.

Kensington and the K logo Reg. U.S. Pat. & TM Off.

ISBN 0-7582-1104-X

First Trade Paperback Printing: August 2005
First Mass-Market Paperback Printing: February 2006
10 9 8 7 6 5 4 3 2 1

Printed in the United States of America

*For the Men and Women of
Operation Iraqi Freedom.*

*From the fire teams in the trenches
to the contractors helping to rebuild
to the generals in the command center.
Your bravery, courage, and valor
have left its mark in history.*

Thank you for your sacrifice.

Amy J. Fetzer

One

Killian Moore was getting screwed.

He could feel it, like that split second moment before a car crash when time slows to a breath before impact. You know it's coming and there isn't a damn thing you can do about the rank smell of shit about to hit the fan.

He should have never answered the door, and kept right on with his plan to grill a steak, drink beer, and clean a weapon. Except he didn't, and found the deputy director of the CIA on his doorstep.

Looking like a soccer mom.

Not that the carefully styled image wasn't cute in a weekend at Martha's Vineyard sorta way. Neat, preppy clothes, pricey sneakers, a noisy charm bracelet. Even those ridiculous footie things with the pom-poms on the back. He almost wondered if she'd power-walked her spry little ass over here to deliver whatever couldn't be said in her office. That is, if he hadn't seen the bodyguard and staff car parked in his driveway.

The last woman to show up at his door unannounced was an AWACS pilot on her way to Iraq. They both knew why she'd hunted him out and he'd let her vent her fear on him with mind-blowing sex before she walked off to war.

Needful sex. He'd done the same himself once or twice.

That didn't explain the woman sitting across the table from him now, taking in the sun like it was a drug. She sipped a beer, talking about careless things like flowers and the Zen of backyard fountains. But the deputy director of covert operations coming to him instead of demanding his appearance at Langley was enough to send up an artillery barrage of warnings.

And Killian wondered just how much dancing she was going to do before she dipped. He gave her a healthy nudge.

"The point of this visit?"

She turned her attention on him, smiling softly. If it had been anyone else, he'd have thought it was genuine. But she wasn't anyone else.

"Yes, I suppose it's time I told you why I'm here."

"I didn't think it was for my steaks." He gestured to the leavings of their meal spread around them.

"No, but thank you, it was very good." She gave him a smile you saved for a kid who'd drawn you an exceptionally bad picture when you were hoping for another Michelangelo.

Killian laced his fingers over his stomach. He had all the time in the world, this week. "Just what do you want from me?"

"We need to hire your team."

Need, Killian thought. *Not want.*

She slid her straw tote bag forward, lifting out a file. Like every woman he'd known, her handbag was never out of her sight. She'd arrived with it tucked under her arm just as he'd thrown a two-inch porterhouse on the grill. Seeing as she wasn't going to leave, and he liked his steak rare, he'd invited her to join him. Killian was a washout in the kitchen, not a good thing considering his age, but other than turning an MRE into a feast, the man-pit of grilling was where he excelled. His ego'd like to stand up and growl that he excelled with women, but then, he hadn't had anyone in his bed except his neighbor's cat in a long time.

Depressing as hell. But then, Killian's line of work didn't invite *sharing*.

When she looked to be waiting for an answer, he said, "I don't agree to a thing till I hear the details." And confirm them himself.

"Don't you have to consult with your men?"

"No." He didn't explain further. Killian didn't lead his team, he steered. His buddies were the best the military had to offer. Retrieval experts. An assortment of talented men who, at one time, were obligated to follow direct command orders. Now, working in the private sector, they took jobs when it felt right. Good causes paid well. His men trusted him to select the jobs and he trusted them with his life. Dragon One had earned the right to pick and choose the contracts.

Unless the chopper payment was due.

She offered the file.

Killian wiped his hands, and pushed aside his plate before taking it. She sipped beer, bouncing her crossed leg as she waited for his reaction. He didn't give her one, keeping his breathing even, his face expressionless. There was so much blackout in the files, it took Killian three minutes to read most of it. And what he couldn't decipher had a distinct odor.

She wanted him to find an NOC? Jesus. Might as well be bin Laden. "Not exactly your average retrieval, Madame Director."

"If I thought this mission was average, I'd send our people."

He looked up. "You already did." He could tell by the Intel.

She didn't even try to appear shocked. "Yes we have," she admitted after some stalling. "And obviously failed."

Deputy Director Lania Price stood, gathering plates and flatware, and Killian was about to tell her he'd take care of it, but something was making her nervous enough to play Dolly Domestic. He looked back at the file, flipping through pages that were too vague to make it worth reading. His gaze caught on the agent's photo. Auburn-haired, big eyes, a definite ooh-rah on the sexy scale, but other than that, there was only a thumbprint and retinal scan. No background, nothing but a couple of scars and marks to identify the body. He glanced at her name. Alexa Gavlin. Deep covert operative meant a difficult snatch and grab. The whole thing stank.

"There's not enough information here." But then, that's the way it was with a nonofficial covert officer. NOCs did what they had to, and rarely reported details other than completion of an assignment.

She looked back at him. "That's all I can give you."

"No, it's not, but we'll get back to that." He put up a finger to stop her from interrupting. "Why is it so necessary to bring this one in now, Lania?" He liked calling her by her first name. It reminded her that she was in his home begging for his help on something that the CIA attack dogs couldn't handle. Killian and his team had a one hundred percent success record, yet he knew when it was time to stack the cards in his favor. This was one of them.

"Several reasons. My superiors believe this agent is a viable threat to national security."

Her superiors were the director, the National Security Advisor, and the president. "And you don't?"

"No, I agree completely." She moved from the patio table through to the kitchen as she spoke. "She's failed to make scheduled contacts for two weeks."

"That's not all that unusual." Another reason Killian didn't want the job. Spooks were a pain in the ass. The hitch was—you couldn't trust them. They were trained liars. Just like the woman doing chores in his house. "Or she's dead and your problem is solved."

"We're aware of that possibility. We've tried tapping her assets, but no one is talking. She's ours because she's talented." Price came back for more dishes. "She assumes appearances, any accent, and speaks several languages well enough to get by."

"And you let her go NOC?" Killian scoffed. "Then come crying to me when your ghost goes off the reservation. What'd she do?"

Lania's soft "June Cleaver" expression took on a feral gleam. Score one for Dragon One, he thought as she went to the kitchen again.

"All I want is for you to bring her in."

No questions. He got it. It wasn't happening, but he got it. "Say I do find her, then what?"

"She'll get a fair hearing."

Killian doubted that and shut the file. NOCs didn't get anything but shafted. "And if she's crossed and I can't bring her in?"

She stilled, and through the patio doors he saw her hesitate as she set the last of the dishes on the counter. Her head fell forward, sandy brown hair neatly restrained in a barrette decorated with a gecko that matched the print of her skirt. "We want you to retire her from the active list."

She had to be kidding. "No."

Her anger was quick and sharp as she faced him. "You don't get it, do you, Marine, we—"

"I'm not a Marine anymore," he cut in viciously and shoved the file back at her. "No deal."

She bulldozed ahead without taking a breath, and he half expected her to lean down and poke his chest. "She's a danger to active operations, and national security."

"Christ, if you think I'll jump on this 'bring the spy in from the cold for God and country' shit, you pegged the wrong man."

Price's cheeks pinkened, the only sign she was furious. "It's your duty."

Killian leaned forward, his tone soft and deadly. "Don't think for a minute you can tell me what my duty is, Lania. I owe you *nothing.* I'm a private citizen now." He glanced at the file as he sat back. They had too much history, ugly history, yet Price was just a bit too eager to drag him into this, and he wondered what the truth was behind this agent, then thought, they probably didn't even know. Kinda hard to keep up a web of lies, even when you did it for a living.

"This Alexa Gavlin means nothing to me. And neither do the needs of the CIA. But you knew that before knocking on my door." He paused for a heartbeat. "Don't let it hit you in the ass on your way out."

"I'll double your usual fee."

"You can't afford me." But that told him they were desperate. And scared.

"I'm authorized to give you half right now, and I don't want your team, I want only you."

He arched a brow. "Come again?"

Price stared him down. "We don't want any outside influences to limit our options. We need someone on the inside right now, and since you left Colombia under a suspicious cloud, you have a certain *respect* in the cartel that's essential for this."

Killian felt the noose tightening, yet said nothing, slipping his favorite Cuban cigar from the case on the table as he waited patiently for her to scramble.

"It would take weeks to set up covert ops and get someone on the inside. You have the advantage. You were a part of the cartel." His eyes narrowed. "Undercover of course, but as far as they're concerned, you're still one of them. Haven't they contacted you in the last couple years?"

She knew the answer already or she wouldn't have asked. "Careful, honey, you're not putting yourself in my good graces." Casually, he nipped the cigar tip and wet it. "I risked my life to get that deep for the DEA, and then some mole in *your* house fucked it up." *And I lost everything,* he thought, lighting up and taking a long calming drag.

He needed it, because if ever he considered hurting a woman, this was it.

Price didn't confirm or deny it.

But that Op got his friends killed. Killian nearly bit through the cigar just thinking about the ambush that wiped out half a joint task force operation with the CIA, military, and DEA. Two bodies had never been found, but since he was the only one on the inside, he was the fall guy. That day took lives and his reputation. And his Marine commission. He couldn't bring back the dead, but he'd do just about anything to get his rep back. Just about.

"Let's be clear on this." Killian patiently steepled his fingers, the cigar smoke wreathing his head. "You want me to hunt her down and bring her back. If we can't get to her, I sight down a high-powered rifle and put a bullet in her head." He met her gaze. "Have I forgotten anything?"

She tucked a loose strand at her nape as she said, "No. That's correct."

He shook his head, lowering his hands. "You people are not putting any more blood on my hands."

"Yes, well, there is enough of that there already, isn't there?"

His eyes went flat. "Get out."

"If you want that file to remain smothered, Moore, you'll do it."

So, that was the real heart of this gig. "You forgot 'or else'?"

She looked him over. "I didn't forget. I just didn't have to say it."

Hell, he'd walked right into that one. "Why should I give a damn?" Smoking, he propped his feet on a nearby chair, patient for the trump card.

She met his gaze, all pretense vanishing, and the magic card flipped out and sparkled. "I have it on good authority that Gavlin was the Intel leak."

Every muscle in him locked instantly, hard and pumping his blood, yet his gaze never left her as she handed him another file. This one was marked *Eyes Only*. Hers. He didn't take it and she dropped it on the table in front of him.

"That's some carrot you're dangling, Deputy Director," he said, his look as cutting as he could muster without leaving her bloody on the ground. If she lied, there was no place she could hide. "I know this is a real stretch, but you're backing this up with real proof?" His gaze slipped pointedly to the *Eyes Only* file. "And before you answer, remember I *will* extract everything I need from her."

Price sent him a snide look, the gloves off. "She was

on the ground and in position at the time, privy to a great deal of information from both camps. She had the opportunity."

"So did I. Motive?"

"Money. Playing both sides, saving her own neck, who knows? When you find her, ask her."

There wasn't any question about that, he thought.

She didn't expand, then said, "At present, Gavlin was last in the company of a very dangerous man, Lucien Zarek."

Killian's eyes flared. Polish, rich, and a deadly arms dealer with international ties and body count whenever he was spotted. They couldn't have thrown this woman into a darker den.

"I see you understand our dilemma. Zarek isn't known for his humanity."

Neither are you, Killian thought, and saw what others saw, what the news media saw: the deputy director of operations, a soft-spoken wholesome version of Rumsfeld. Iron under all that preppy and perfume. It wasn't all that attractive.

"She'd infiltrated Zarek's life deep enough to be a frequent guest of his compound. Her disappearance, and that Zarek's been out of sight just as long, speaks well for it."

They've gone underground. "Enough that you come here to blackmail me."

She looked offended. Killian knew that just wasn't possible. "I'm paying you and giving you the opportunity to capture the leak."

Killian inspected the glowing tip of his cigar and heard only one word: Opportunity. Find Gavlin and he'd find the truth. "Does the other side know about her?" If Gavlin's cover were blown, death would not be merciful.

"We can't say with any certainty."

Hell, that was a pat for-the-press answer. "You suspect treason." It wouldn't be the first time.

Her eyes narrowed, filled with a strange spark that left Killian wondering over her relationship with the spy. Yet she admitted to nothing. "Gavlin is a definite liability. If she's alive, she knows that and she *will* expect you. She's been out there for a very long time. Alone. Granted, it's how she works best, but given the circumstances . . . she's so far out that the only way to deal with her is to retire her, quickly."

"Jesus, you people say that with such goddamn ease."

She shrugged, smacking a bug off her bare arm. "This is national security."

"This is *murder*."

"Some problems are best dealt with the swiftest solution," she said coldly. "The good of the whole, Moore, remember that? And since when did you care so much?"

"If I didn't care, I wouldn't be doing what I do. I'd be fishing in Bali right now with a sarong clad hottie giving me one helluva blow job."

Price didn't bat a lash. "Give me Gavlin in under twenty-eight days and I'll hand over your files. Wipe the slate clean and I'll make certain those who should know it, do."

Like his father, he thought bitterly. His old commanding officer? "Why twenty-eight days?"

"Any classified information she knows will be altered by then." She tipped her head. "Take the Op, Killian. You know you want it." Prim, like a teacher dictating homework assignments.

"How do you figure?"

"Besides the files I'm keeping handy . . ." He practically snarled at her and she waved the beer bottle as if he hadn't. "You're a patriot. You understand the threat and know which side plays well with others. *And* the price of keeping the scales tipped in our favor." Tossing back the dregs of her Michelob, she grabbed her bag and stood. "I'm giving you the chance to get the person who destroyed your life and got those men killed." She slipped out a check and let it sail across the glass table to him. "Do we have a deal?"

Killian didn't touch it. "I won't put a bullet in her head for you."

"Fine, then." She adjusted the tote on her shoulder and met his gaze. "Break her neck. It's cleaner."

She turned away, walking through his backyard to the gate in the rear where a driver waited patiently for the past two hours. Killian watched the cold-blooded bitch go, and pitied any kids she might have. Probably would grow up with major issues in the touchy-feely department. He looked down at the file, and the photo, hating the woman for dragging him back into the kind of work he'd avoided. Dirty work. A sweeper. He preferred his uniform, an MP5 with the established enemy in the crosshairs. Not all this cloak-and-dagger shit.

Killian rubbed his face, wishing to God he'd never answered the door, then without a choice, he drained his beer, slid the check into the file, and stood. He went for the phone, connected the scramble line, and hit auto dial. Max Renfield picked up on the first ring.

"And you say you have a life," Killian said.

"Yeah, I do, and you're interrupting it."

"We have a problem. Round 'em up."

"Jesus, *now*?"

Killian heard the definite erotic coos of a woman in the near background and sighed, disgusted.

This just topped his day.

Max was getting laid while he was accepting orders to capture a rogue spy and kill her.

Colombia
Day 14
0645 hours, Zulu

Alexa stirred and knew two things.

The sun was cooking her skin.

And she was compromised, her cover blown all to hell.

Oh, yeah, and she was naked, too. With bugs crawling over her.

This is so not going to be a good day, she thought, letting the creatures wiggle across her breasts. Mostly because she didn't have the energy to flick them off. Breathing was an effort.

Cautiously, she opened her eyes, the lids fried by the sun and stinging. Tall canes surrounded her, blocking some of the sun. But not enough. She blinked several times, then tried moving her toes, then her fingers. Her back and rear were numb so she knew she'd been here a while. Wherever *here* was.

She took her time moving, first her arm, then her knee. Bugs crawled in spots even a man hadn't been in a while. Mentally she was screaming *eww* but it was forgotten when it took her several minutes to roll to her side, even longer before she could sit up. Her brain sloshed in her head, her tiny world tilting. She was still for a while, her head down, arms on her bare knees.

My life sucks.

She looked up. Naked in a cane field. With no clue how she got here. Was she still in Colombia? The Southern Hemisphere?

Waiting till her brain stopped dancing in her skull, she ripped a cane stalk from the ground, peeling back the papery hide and sucking on the raw sugar. She groaned at the sudden damp feel of it on her lips and tongue, gnawing like an animal. After a few seconds, she was raking her teeth across it, craving food and water. Pitching her third, she knew it was time to split. Snakes loved the cane fields and she was damn lucky she wasn't on the snack menu already.

She rose to her knees, parting the canes. Then it hit her. The rank odor. About a second before she saw a bare foot. Ashen and still.

Oh, shit.

Instantly she scrambled back, pain and cane fronds tearing across her skin. She breathed through her mouth, willing her heart to slow down. Then she moved forward, anticipating the horror as she parted the stalks again.

Dead black eyes stared up at her. *Jesus.* Santiago. Her relay contact.

Her gaze moved over his naked body. It wasn't hard to find the mortal wound. A knife protruded from his chest. Her knife.

Alexa fell back, holding her head, her eyes burning. *I didn't do that, I didn't!*

But, *my knife, my knife,* kept echoing in her brain. She looked at the body again. Blood had settled along his back. He'd been here for a day at least, by the smell, a lot longer. She didn't recall seeing him recently. She hadn't made contact since—her thoughts stopped abruptly. When? Did it matter? Her cover was trashed and Santiago had paid the price.

Someone's going to pay, she thought, and pulled the knife from his chest, dragging it across the ground to clean it. Her options for concealing it were nil, but she needed some defense.

Struggling to her feet, she used a cane like a staff, the knife to slash her way through the sharp fronds. In the distance she saw a road, but other than that, there was nothing for miles except cane fields. And blinding heat. Her body ached, her skin screaming for lotion and water. A bath, too, she thought, when she got a whiff of herself.

She walked, thinking her ass was shaking too much, her boobs were sore, and all those oil massage treatments Zarek had lavished on her had been a complete waste of money. Her body was sunburned, covered in bites and cuts that had stopped bleeding a while ago and had already started to heal. *I've been here for two days, at least.* Santiago's stay was still up for debate.

Her only concern right now was putting one foot in front of the other and hoping it led her to water. The sun beat relentlessly, sending vapor waves up from the road as she reached it. Standing naked in the sunlight should have felt good, but Alexa recognized she had more vulnerabilities than just her bare skin. Without clothes, money, and her passports, she was a prisoner in this country. With someone holding onto enough hostility toward her that they'd stripped her and left her for the snakes.

Why not just kill her?

Had to be Lucien Zarek. It was just his sort of twisted game.

She was suddenly wishing for the pool in his compound, and last evening came with bright clarity. Arriving in a limousine, dinner, Lucien looking too damn good in summer white. Coquille Saint Jacque—Zarek's French chef was an artist—a good Chardonnay. Lucien's hands on her while they danced. His mouth on hers. Strolling into his bedroom.

Then it stopped.

She pried through her memory, but her brain felt heavy in her head, her thoughts foggy and colliding. Only fractures, like a flickering movie. Had she completed her assignment and retrieved the information? Obviously not or she'd have been on the first plane out of here. But when was that? Needles of panic pushed up her spine again. Considering her present state, it wasn't last night.

But it *felt* like last night.

She stared at the dry cracked road, and tried to recall the last time she'd reported in after that night in the compound.

And couldn't.

Oh, crap. She was missing more than her clothes and the realization set in. Hard. She was in major trouble. Did she make contact with Santiago before he was killed? Was the Company looking for her? Had she even done her job?

She put the brakes on her confusion and assembled thoughts in neat order.

Okay, okay . . . Alexa Gavlin, 337-86-9981, born in South Carolina, orphaned at sixteen, recruited into NOC program at eighteen. She had no ties, no lost loves. The Company liked it that way. Made you expendable. The last thirty years filtered through her mind, the things she'd done that she wasn't proud of, to the triumphs. Till she was assigned to get proof that Lucien Zarek was dealing weapons.

That was sort of a given, she thought, walking slowly. He was an arms dealer, but gun dealing with Colombians meant little to the CIA. There were so many guerrillas and drug dealers trading and buying weapons, it was hard to keep track of who wanted to annihilate whom this week. A few crates of grenades and stolen assault rifles wasn't a concern. ATF and Colombian regulars would take care of it in joint operations. It was when the dealers grew cojònes and moved outside their realm that the CIA stepped in.

Her sources said Zarek had gone big league. Just how big, was her job.

Yet one thing struck her like a hammer. How could she remember who and what she was the last thirty years, but not what she'd done to get in the cane field? And what the hell *did* she learn . . . exactly?

Because she really pissed someone off this time.

The sound of a motor penetrated her thoughts, and she darted back into the field and crouched. A small aqua blue car bounced up the dirt road. When it got close enough—she wasn't that comfortable with her body to go parading down the road—she stepped out.

The car slammed to a stop and the man behind the wheel stared for a second before he got out. Alexa didn't think she could be more humiliated when she realized he was a priest.

I'm going to hell for this.

He walked toward her, removing his jacket, and when he reached her, bless him, he kept his eyes level with hers. She slipped the jacket on, the knife into the pocket, then climbed into the car with him. He didn't ask questions, didn't utter a word as he drove and parked near a tin building bearing a cross on the door. He came out moments later with pants, shirt, and shoes, and some water. After handing them over, he turned his back. Thanking him, Alexa drank, dressed, then climbed out of the car. Behind him, she swept up a dented gas can, closed her eyes briefly, begging forgiveness before she brought it down on the priest's head, and took his car.

He'd want to go with her, help her, and the less he was involved with her, the better. Zarek wasn't known for his Christian charity. The life of a priest would be meaningless. But Zarek was the least of her problems.

She was compromised.

Break cover and game over. Those were the rules.

She had to come in.

Two

West Cali, Colombia
Day 14
1100 hours, Zulu

When Killian was escorted into the grand room, Alejandro Carrión's lap was full of woman, a voluptuous Latin creature who was working her hands inside his trousers.

Killian paused, glanced at the guard, who merely shrugged, then cleared his throat.

Carrión looked up. "Dominic! You're in this country a week and now you come visit?" He kissed the woman behind the ear, whispering something that made her giggle before she hopped off his lap.

"And you were just all twisted up over it, I see." Killian's gaze followed the woman, and she cast him a long meaningful glance, provocatively licking her lips before she stepped out.

Carrión came around the side of a large teak desk, smiling. "The last time I saw you, you were bleeding and fighting for your life. I heard the Americans took you away in handcuffs."

It was a fact Killian wasn't proud of, but Alejandro

Carrión's people were the ones doing the shooting. With the cartels, it was a "cut your losses and duck for cover till the dust settled" mentality. Rescue was not an option, not that Killian expected it. To them, to everyone in this area, he was Dominic Cane, a mercenary, procuring weapons and drugs for clients in the States.

Killian shook hands with the cartel lord. "You believe what you hear?"

"Never. What can I do for you, my friend?" Carrión gestured to a chair, then leaned his hip on his desk.

Killian didn't sit and moved to the window, glancing over the grounds and picking out at least five men with machine guns watching the perimeter from the roof. "Assault rifles, gas powered, American military." The quickest way to finding an arms dealer was to become one.

"I should be asking you for such a weapon. How many?"

"Two hundred will do to start."

Carrión looked concerned. "This is my winter home, and, well, as arrogantly as I'd like to think I own this territory, too, I do not." Carrión gestured to the guard standing near the door and he fetched a box of cigars, offering them to Killian.

Carrión was a cigar aficionado, and in that alone he and Killian were matched. He clipped the tip and lit up. "Since when has territorial boundaries ever stopped you?" Killian said through the haze of smoke. "Isn't that why you're here, to begin a takeover?"

Carrión's territory was Venezuela. The whole damn country. Was he thinking of matching his forces against Zarek? It'd be a bloodbath.

"I'm vacationing," Carrión said innocently.

"Next time pick a place with no extradition."

Carrión laughed, amused by the American. He was a big man, and his military background showed in his stance. He was ruthless, efficient, and most important, he kept his word. Alejandro had tried several times to get him to join his operation, but Cane preferred to freelance. The money, he said, was always much better when you were in demand, and never obligated to any one organization. A wise move.

"As to the weapons, I know who could help you, but he is not available."

While Killian hadn't seen Zarek for days, his men were around. "Everyone is available for money; arrange a meeting with Zarek."

Carrión's dark eyes narrowed. "You knew he had them already?"

"I deal with the enemy I know, Alejandro."

Carrión laughed, the sound easy and rich. Killian had to admit he liked the man, even if he was on America's most wanted. He had a slick charm that made him seem less threatening. Yet like Zarek, he'd managed to slip past the authorities and come out smelling freshly clean. The man was untouchable, always with a backup plan to save his ass and his assets. Even after losing twenty men in a gun battle three years ago. At the time, Killian had been on the inside of Carrión's drug operation. And he'd failed, the whole transfer going sour because of some Intel leak.

"He has not been about, though for him, that is not so unusual. He has many enemies." Carrión frowned. "I don't like doing business with him. He'd slit his mother's throat if there was a price in it."

Killian met his gaze. "I need this, Alejandro."

"I will not promise anything, but I'll see what I can arrange for you."

"Excellent. When?"

Carrión frowned, his eyes turning a cool black.

"A usual, I'm on a timeline." Killian needed to draw Zarek out, and to lock on some of his men and tail them. By the time his jet landed in Colombia, he'd memorized a dossier on Lucien Zarek that would make a CIA analyst scream with joy. Surveillance recordings of his compound, his coffee business, friends, associates, his hired muscle, even his latest prostitute, all mostly courtesy of Gavlin. Killian had enough to recognize the right faces if he saw them. Gavlin was caught in a couple photos on the arm of Zarek, looking incredibly lovely, but they were shots taken over a month ago.

Neither had been seen since, and presumed together. Killian dealt in facts. Gavlin could be a rotting corpse for all anyone knew. Price didn't seem too concerned with that, and out of pure rage, he'd keep the cast-iron bitch out of the loop till the job was done. She'd fucked him over before, and now had left behind strong feelings there was more to Gavlin's disappearance than she was saying. Or rather, not saying.

"I will make some calls," Alejandro was saying. "Come have lunch. I pay a fortune for this chef, and rarely put him to good use."

Killian couldn't risk alienating the man, and followed him out onto a veranda. "I'm not sure I'd know good food, Alejandro, with what I've been eating." A servant was already setting another place for him.

"Then this you will enjoy."

An hour later, they sipped strong coffee and Killian admitted that was about the best meal he'd had in ages. Crime paid, apparently.

"You look distracted, Dominic. Is there something else you need?"

The man was being strangely accommodating, Killian thought, but then he was always pretty good-natured. Even about killing.

"I'm looking for a woman."

"I can offer you several." He started to call in the guard, but Killian stopped him.

"Christ, Alejandro, if I want to get laid, I can find my own."

Carrión smiled and shrugged.

"I'm looking for one woman in particular." He handed him a photo and Carrión studied it.

"She is very beautiful."

Killian admitted he'd looked at the photo of Gavlin enough times to be utterly fascinated with her face. It pissed him off. Considering he'd authorization to kill her, and what she might know, it was tough keeping an emotional distance. "Have you seen her recently?"

"No, but then I have not been social lately."

Killian let his features tighten, show his emotions. Though completely artificial, giving the drug lord a vulnerability was playing a card that could bring on big trouble. Wars began over women, but he'd had a week of hunting with no trace of the woman. He needed information.

"What do you want with this little bit of female?" He handed back the picture.

"That's my business." He pocketed it.

Carrión scowled. "I will not feed a delicate angelfish to a shark, Dominic."

Killian snickered. "She's no angel. She's my woman."

"Perhaps you should ask her if she knows this."

"I'm here to see that she does."

"Oh, my friend." Carrión's laughter annoyed Killian. "Women are not meant for this business, but for making love, to dress in pretty things, and make us look powerful."

"Damn medieval of you to say." Killian drained his coffee and stood, handing Carrión a card with his cell number. "I'll be waiting, but not long. You'll get a cut, and I'm running out of time."

"You need to enjoy life more, Dominic."

"I'm enjoying it just fine."

Killian shook hands and left, careful of where he went next, knowing well that Alejandro Carrión would put a tail on him just to cover his ass. They might have a strange friendship, but Carrión would just as soon eliminate you than deal with the trouble you brought him.

Killian was hoping to stir some up, and lure Zarek out into the open.

Find Zarek and he'd find Gavlin.

The relay patched through, the screen blinking up the bright Colombian sky before the camera lowered to the cane field. Casta was probably sweating from his perch in the hills, Lucien thought, pouring thick gold coins from hand to hand.

The canes rustled, as if a panther moved slowly inside, hiding. His man focused the zoom. The top of her dark head appeared, some movement again, and he smiled, knowing what she saw.

Wondering what she was feeling, thinking. Grief, anger, panic, and he knew, disorientation. Complete and absolute. Her life was in his palm. He'd twist it, abuse it. Then crush it.

He hated himself for letting her in, under his skin. He left his leather chair and poured himself a drink, his gaze still on the screen as he popped in a palm full of ice cubes.

She stood on shaky legs, naked and lovely. She'd never let him see her body like that, rarely touch it. His gaze raked the flesh exposed as she staggered through the field. He'd done more than see every bare inch of her. His heart punched his lungs at the memory, and he leaned in, his fingers slipping slowly over the screen.

I'm going to have such fun with you.

Day 14
1345 hours

Alexa flicked a bug off her arm, and adjusted her footing as she watched the CIA station house, surveying the area, the grounds. There was no one around, no sound coming from the estate that had once been home to a coffee planter. She'd never been inside. No reason. These people spied with diplomatic papers. NOCs were on the outside, alone. *On the far rim,* she thought. But rule was, anything goes wrong, get in fast. She figured today topped the scales.

Yet instincts told her to stick to the side of caution. She didn't come through the front door, but slipped around to the veranda, avoiding the cameras and sensors. She'd seen the plans once, and her memory was her best asset. At least it was till some of it went missing.

She inched to the glass doors, the hacienda filled with computer desks, maps, and a strand of phones. She recognized Whitmer leaning back in a chair and scanning the satellite surveillance photos on a computer screen. Another man walked in, armed and sweating. His gaze flicked to the exits, and she wondered what was so important. There was nothing outside but her and a few guards.

"Anything on her?" she heard.

Her. *She* was the only woman in country on assignment. Procedure had it that they didn't know anything about her, except that she was female. She pried the door open to hear better, flattening to the wall and watching for anyone's approach. She needed a secure line to Price and they had the only one. But she couldn't stand here all day waiting for them to clear the room.

"I hope she shows up so I can nail her ass." Wade; they'd been through the Farm together. Such a pansy.

"Everyone wants to nail her and not with bullets," Whitmer snickered.

She rolled her eyes. That was just so macho horny it was gross.

"Santiago got a knife in the chest, so I'm betting he'd have liked a bullet between the eyes."

They think I killed him.

Even if she got the chance, she couldn't plead her case because it was quite possible. If she killed Santiago, there was a damn good reason. Because he would have been her first.

She eased closer to the glass door, and peered, taking in the layout, exits, the armed men, the computer screens. One showed at least three cameras at Zarek's compound, another on her apartment. They'd already sanitized it, she figured, removing any trace of her that would lead anywhere.

"We should be out there, admit it."

"We have orders. Stay put till she surfaces."

Alexa couldn't hear the rest of the conversation. It didn't matter; she had to get out of here now. She moved back, retracing her steps around the cameras and sensors. She had a short stretch out in the open, and taking a breath, she started running.

A bullet chipped the ground at her feet. The report echoed. *This is gonna hurt,* she thought as she dove for cover in the trees, hitting the ground hard. Instantly she rolled to her feet, bolting across the manicured lawn, around fountains and parked cars. The jungle loomed ahead. A bullet hit a foot in front of her and she veered. Another picked off the corner of an urn. Somewhere Whitmer shouted orders and she heard footsteps in three directions.

They were ready for her! A fence blocked her way, and she jumped on the hood of a car, a bullet shattering a window as she threw herself at the iron bars. She dragged herself over the top, the sharp points tearing her pants and slicing her leg. She fell to the ground, eating dirt, then scrambled up and kept going. Her lungs burned, the heat and humidity cutting into her strength as she slipped over logs and down a ravine.

They were still coming as she popped out on the dirt road, the priest's car a few yards ahead. She bolted to it, jumped inside, turned over the engine and jammed on the gas. Tires spit gravel and dust and she glanced in the rearview mirror. Wade stepped onto the road, taking aim. She swerved and the shot took out the side view mirror. Well, that's not an option anymore, she thought, zipping in and out of traffic.

But it answered one question.

The Company was hunting her.

To retire her.

That was just so one-way of them.

The bar was two clicks shy of sleazy. Dark, relatively clean, and populated, it smelled of rotten fruit and Bavaria beer. Three years ago he'd been a frequent customer, and his return to Colombia brought old acquaintances out of the jungle, men who'd sooner kill you for a few pesos, and women, God, the women who'd fuck for a good meal.

That's not to say the clientele were all lowlives. Even a profitable drug lord had several *jeffe* to do his dirty work and they were well paid to take the fall. And from his position in the rear of the bar, proof stood out in enough gold to make Cortez quiver in his grave.

Killian tipped his chair back, his shoulders braced on the wall as he watched.

He'd been doing that for days now. And getting nowhere.

No one was talking. Loyalty like that came with

threats or a shitload of money. Killian had bought himself enough allegiance to make certain he heard the latest.

Zarek was deep underground somewhere.

Killian had a man at the compound, another at the airport. If Gavlin were smart she'd stay clear of either and from what he'd learned, she was one slick spook. He'd flashed her picture a few times, but the locals claimed ignorance. It was the way they did that alerted him. Too brief, too vague. Paid to lie.

Hell, he didn't think it'd be easy or Price wouldn't have blackmailed him into this. He'd spent a week searching her hangouts, traced her last movements, and worked backwards. Destroy her contacts, cut her off from escape or help, and squeeze till she came out into the open. That's *if* she was still alive and in the country. And Colombia was a big-ass country. Finding one woman who didn't want to be found, who was an expert at evasion, was a definite challenge.

He glanced to the right, mentally marking off the time that two men polished off their drinks, Aquadiante, a sweet anise liquor they'd been working on all afternoon. Killian was surprised they didn't stagger when they stood, and within a few minutes, they were greeted by two more. It was shift change. They were watching something or someone. But like all things in Colombia, the only thing that moved swiftly was bullets. Everything else tripped along, paused for siestas, a beer.

He tossed back the dregs of his beer and dropped the chair legs to the floor. Men glanced, then went back to their drinks, the chatter growing louder with the music.

"Cane?"

One of the men who'd just entered moved toward him.

"Casta. Life is treating you well?" Killian kicked out the chair near him, then waved for the bartender to bring a round. He'd been waiting for this moment, for someone familiar with a little knowledge to show up. He'd seen only troops, cannon fodder in the last couple days.

"I'm surprised to see you alive."

"Glad to be alive." The bartender placed the drinks down. Killian paid and saluted Casta.

The man drained half of it in one shot, and it gave Killian the chance to see how well armed he was, that he had a two-way radio clipped near his gun.

"Still with Martinez?"

Casta shook his head. "He is dead, you know. You were there. The Pole took his territory."

Zarek. Killian arched a brow and sanded his fingers together.

"*Sí,* much money. You should come with us."

"No, thanks." Prime opportunity for some Intel, but Killian would tip his hand. "I work for no one but me."

The man laughed and Killian's gaze slipped to the door. It brought their attention, a little shift of their chairs so no one could approach without their knowledge. They were jumpy, tossing back Bavaria beer as fast as Killian could buy it. Which suited him fine. Making them feel as if he weren't alone and waiting for someone had a point. When he left, it wouldn't look suspicious, since he had every intention of following Casta and his pals.

Then sound came through Killian's ceramic earpiece.

"Mustang, we have movement." It was Max, his post was outside the CIA station, in a tree probably.

Killian sipped his drink, clearing his throat since he couldn't respond in his present company.

"I don't see a prey, but I hear gunfire."

Killian's pulse accelerated slightly. Max couldn't get too close or CIA surveillance would pick him up and it would be all over. Killian trusted no one outside his team, especially with Price's agenda, and there was no way in hell he'd clue the agents in on his operation. Dealing with the CIA is what got him into deep kimshee in the first place.

Max's breathing came through as he ran to catch up with the agents and find out who they were chasing. Killian stood, excused himself, went to the men's room, and checked the stalls before he spoke.

"Max?"

"Yeah, I'm here. I see a car speeding away. Small, bright blue. Crap, it's over. Whoever it was, they've given up."

"Who was driving?" Christ, it smelled like piss and vomit in here.

"Didn't get a good look, Mustang, sorry, but I saw long hair."

That didn't mean much. Everyone here had a ponytail. "Outlaw, can you pick it up?" Sam Wyatt was in the chopper, risking restricted air space. The only thing keeping him in the sky was the false National Geological Society logo.

"I'm on the hunt, boss. Ooh-rah."

"Max, they get in a shot, blood trail?"

"Nope. And they had an unbelievably clear shot."

But the CIA officers didn't hit a moving target within range?

Killian signed off, repositioned the mike and went back to the table. If he was on the right track, the next shift change wasn't for a couple hours. He'd wait for Sam's report.

Alexa was on the edge of desperate. Not one of her assets would speak to her, half of them running in the other direction or threatening her if she didn't beat it. It wasn't the norm. She paid well for good information within Zarek's organization. Going to Zarek's compound for a look-see was out of the question and pointless. He was fanatic about altering alarm codes so nothing she remembered would be useful. She was out of options and it pushed her over the edge.

Standing in the tight apartment landing, she knocked. Consuelo opened the door, then immediately shut it in her face, but Alexa shoved her foot between the jamb and threw her weight into the wood. Consuelo stumbled back, looking for a weapon, but Alexa was on her, forcing her back against the dresser.

"Avoiding me, Connie? How rude."

"Get out, I have nothing to say to you." Consuelo struggled.

"Too bad." Alexa grabbed her by the hair, jerking her head back. "I've paid a lot of money into you, girlfriend. Time to earn it."

The prostitute pushed back, and Alexa brought her knife to her throat. Consuelo inhaled sharply, and knew Alexa meant business. The Latin beauty was her snitch, a resource, and she'd graced Zarek's bed a few times. She was just his type, curvy, with a doe-eyed innocence and a throaty voice. The silk dress she wore was probably from Lucien. It was his taste. Classy slut. That she was dressed like that already said she had an appointment.

"I've told you what you've wanted, always."

"Where is he?"

"I have not seen him in weeks. Nor you."

"Have you been to the compound?" Alexa would like to know what was going on in there.

"*Sí,* for Franco."

Franco. His image flickered in her mind. Thick bodied, square face, always armed and glued to Lucien's side. The doer, Alexa thought. Franco got his hands dirty so Lucien didn't. "When?"

"Two weeks ago, maybe."

"Nothing since?"

"No."

That was odd—Consuelo was a regular there. "Franco say anything useful?"

Consuelo smiled like a cat with a mouthful of bird. "He likes my blow jobs."

Alexa's eyes narrowed and she pressed the knife a little tighter. "I'm not in the mood for games."

"He talked on the phone to Lucien while I was giving it." She got a cat licking cream smile. It turned Alexa's stomach. "In Porta Buenaventura."

Ships. Zarek was a legitimate coffee grower. Alexa hadn't been on his ships, he hadn't allowed her that close yet, but she knew the dock, the slip. "What else did Lucien say, Consuelo?"

Consuelo weighed her options, and Alexa tightened her grip. "He warned me not to help you!"

"Excuse me?"

"He said he would kill anyone who did!"

Well, that explained a lot, Alexa thought. Lucien was trying to box her in. And then what, capture her? It didn't make sense. He'd had her captive once already, obviously.

"Are you going to cut my throat or not?" Consuelo arched a finely tweezed brow. "Do it quickly, *chica,* because you stink."

"It's a new fragrance I'm going for." Alexa drew back, slipping the knife into her waistband.

"It's appalling. You reek of the dead."

You have no idea.

"Take those off. I will have them burned." Consuelo waved a manicured hand, locked the door, then moved to the dresser, pulling out a bra and panties, then went to the closet for slacks and a blouse.

"No. More average, Connie."

Consuelo sniffed the air and put her selection back. "I do not *own* average."

Alexa nudged her aside, flipped through the clothes and pulled a dull beige shirt from the back of the closet.

"I was going to give that to the maid."

Alexa went into the bathroom, using the shower, and leaving the door open. Consuelo might be a source, but Alexa didn't trust her.

Trust no one, use everyone.

She'd lived by that for twelve years. Everyone was a potential asset; everyone could be used or bribed into helping her in her mission. She could think of about a dozen people she could use right now, but none of them were the same bra size as Consuelo. She peered out to see Connie lounging in a chair, reading *People* magazine. She was obsessed with America, saving her money for a new life. Alexa suspected she was a drug mule. God knew she had enough curves to hide a couple kilos.

She stepped out, dried enough to get into the clothes and run a comb through her hair. The cut on her leg was minor and had already stopped bleeding. She slid into the old shoes. Anything of Consuelo's was useless, the woman only wore stiletto heels.

"Tell me everything, Connie." She started braiding her hair.

Connie shrugged and tossed aside the magazine. "There has been talk of you two, he was in love with you, *sí*. Which cost me money, you know."

"I'm sure you'll make it up with stellar blow jobs."

Consuelo went to her computer, tapping keys with the tips of the curled nails. Alexa saw a stock market page come up. Good Lord.

"I already have," she squealed, clapping like a child, then turned off the screen and looked at Alexa's outfit. "You need makeup."

"No, thanks, I'll go natural."

Alexa never went anywhere not looking her very best. It was part of her cover. She was a face, a lure. The distraction. *A pair of tits and ass for the good of the country,* she thought bitterly. Get the men to feel comfortable, important enough to brag about their assets. Lucien was no different. He fell like a stone, and she didn't doubt that he'd left her in that cane field as payback.

Plain Jane suited her just fine right now.

Connie sucked her lip, then shrugged. "You will never catch a man like that."

"I don't want one." She had enough men after her.

Consuelo cocked her dark head. "I did not know you were queer, you should have said something."

Alexa laughed for the first time since waking in the field. "Oh, honey, I'm not. If I was, I'd have been on you already."

The whore pouted. "If he asks me about you?"

"He won't." Lucien didn't believe in mixing pleasures. He might have loved Alexa, but he screwed the daylights out of Consuelo. "But I'd advise you not to say anything if he does. He'd kill you just on principle." She planned to be far away before Zarek got wind of her movements.

Holding her braid, Alexa searched the dresser for a rubber band. She found one around a newspaper, and slipping it off, secured her hair and shoved the braid down the back of her shirt. The newspaper uncurled and she glanced at the front page.

Then she snatched it up, her breathing quickening as she read the date. Oh, God. "How old is this paper? Days?"

Consuelo edged a look. "Yesterday's. Take it."

Alexa closed her eyes. *I'm a dead woman.*

She was wrong. She hadn't been in that cane field for two days. She'd been somewhere else entirely . . . along with four weeks of her recent memory.

Three

"What's wrong?" Consuelo said. "You don't look so good."

Alexa's gaze snapped to the whore's. Consuelo stepped back, fear coloring her pretty features. "I need cash. Now."

Consuelo hurried to a box under the bed and gave her money. Alexa took a handbag for the simple fact that without one, she'd draw attention. Connie snatched it back and shoved in a lipstick and embroidered handkerchief, but Alexa didn't let her stuff in more. She needed to split, get to her stash, and get out of this country.

A month missing, no contact. And Zarek missing, too. Could it get any worse?

Then the downstairs buzzer rang and Alexa's gaze snapped to Consuelo's, her body sprung tight. "Expecting a customer?"

She scoffed. "Not *here*," she said as if Alexa were mad. "My manicurist." Consuelo opened a door in the rear of the second-floor apartment, then leaned against the frame and inclined her head. "Be careful, *chica*," she said softly as Alexa slipped into the corridor leading to the back stairs. If Consuelo wouldn't sell her out for a couple hundred pesos she would have been moved by that.

Alexa hurried down the steep stairs, leaving the building, then turned onto the side street, crossing through backyards filled with old tires before slipping into the alley a couple blocks down for the car. Leaving it here would get Consuelo killed, and she needed to get to her stash. She'd have passports and a way out of here before someone took a shot at her again.

Alexa made a series of turns and backtracks, but the going was slow, the streets congested for a festival tonight. She headed toward the east side, toward the jungle. Her skin grew hot, a sure sign of her fear.

A month gone. Wiped clean. Anything could have happened in that much time. And with no memory, God, she could be a sleeper, for all she knew. Without much strain she knew how: drugs, GHB, or something as lethal. She'd been trained to resist brainwashing; narcotics would be the only way.

The CIA believed she killed Santiago. Then how the hell did they know already? He was beside her in the cane field only this morning. Pictures, she decided. She wouldn't have hurt Santiago, he was her relay contact. Her friend. He'd get her what she needed: assignments, car, travel, surveillance gear, and turned over information for her when she was deep six in the enemy camp.

No, I didn't kill him, she thought but doubt badgered, and she drove till the engine suddenly choked toward empty. She cursed, needing to ditch this aqua blue eyesore, and get lost. Her instincts were usually on target and right now, they screamed surveillance.

* * *

Inside the small apartment, Consuelo waited till she was gone out the back, then turned to the door. She pulled it open. "*Buenos dias,* handsome."

He smiled and stepped inside. Cooing, she reached for him and never saw it coming.

He slashed the knife across her throat, nearly severing her head. She fell where she'd stood, blood gurgling, eyes already dead.

"Stupid bitch," he muttered, then headed toward the back door.

Alexa drove till the car chugged to a stop near a scattering of houses, cut the engine, then searched the car for anything useful. All she found was a few pesos and a tattered bible. Using her sleeve, she wiped down the car for prints, then left the keys on the seat and started walking. Children raced past, women calling to them, carrying baskets on their arms and scuffling along toward the market a couple miles uproad. Alexa walked in the opposite direction, toward the forest, stepping close enough to a clothesline to yank a dark scarf off and kept walking. A few yards later, she tied it over her hair.

Her mind sifted through scenarios and speculations, trying to assemble facts from assumptions. Getting out of the country was wise. Doing it would be next to impossible.

And then what? Hide? That made her grind her teeth. There were too many unanswered questions to just disappear somewhere. What happened in that missing month? Why did Lucien do this to her? Did he really, and where was he?

She glanced behind herself, her gaze moving rapidly over the terrain.

This land has eyes. And she was walking blind.

* * *

Radios crackled. Casta stood and moved away, speaking into the walkie-talkie, then cursing rudely. He inclined his head, and the others followed him out the door. Killian waited a moment, paid the bill, and stepped outside, catching a glimpse of them crowding into a car.

Turning toward his car, Killian raised Sam on the wire.

"I had to set down. Colombian regulars threatening to shoot me out of the sky."

"That's never stopped you before."

"Yeah, but they weren't armed with heat-seeking motherfucking missiles, either. Riley is on the road, it's a bright car, we can't miss it."

In his rental jeep, Killian contacted Riley Donovan. He sped toward Donovan's coordinates. "Start twisting arms, flash her picture around. If that was her in the car, then we need to close her in, ASAP." Before Casta did.

"She's a naked, penniless woman. How could you possibly lose her?" Lucien Zarek glared over the edge of the newspaper at the two men standing near the door looking as if awaiting execution. He kept his gaze on them, watching the men sweat, then like a father unwilling to punish his favored child, he let out a long-suffering breath. "Never mind the details."

He folded the paper neatly, laying it aside before picking up the small, delicate cup and saucer. He sipped cinnamon-laced coffee as if time stood still for him. "She's still in the city." He'd cut off enough of her avenues to know that.

The men didn't move.

"That means *find her*," he gritted out and his people quit the room.

Franco entered behind them and posted himself at the door. He wiped his hands over and over on a white cloth.

Lucien ignored the bloodstains and rose, then moved to the glass doors, stepping through and onto the balcony. His dog Degas hopped up and followed him. The salty air of Buenaventura pushed at his sandy hair and he inhaled the scent of flowers wafting up from the garden below. His accommodations were pleasant, though not enough to bring attention to himself. He had to remain hidden, and didn't doubt that her comrades were searching for him, as well as her.

Lives hung in the balance, he thought, sipping coffee. He wanted to be the one to tip the scales. He tried imagining where she would go, who she would run to, his little fox. His Jade. It wasn't her real name, he knew, and he didn't know which one she'd been born with, but it didn't matter. He would know soon enough. Just as she understood now that he was not a man to cross. His gaze thinned as he thought of her penniless, scrounging for answers. She'd betrayed more than his business. She'd betrayed his heart, his love for her.

And for that, she'd never sleep peacefully. Never know if he wasn't right behind her. Never. Until he was finished with her. He lifted the cup to his lips, smiling as he drank. A deservedly smug sensation rippled down his long body.

When she learns the truth, she'll wish I'd killed her.

Alexa was walking behind a family with a horse-drawn cart when she rounded a curve and saw a checkpoint up ahead littered with Colombian troops. She slipped off the road and ducked into the jungle, crouching low. Armed men barricaded the road, examining papers.

Great. She didn't have any and needed to avoid them at all cost. If she were caught, that'd be it. She'd rot in some jail. No one would come for her. No one would notice she was missing. When they realized that, she'd be better off dead. She'd have to go around, which would take a day, and when she stood and turned, she found a soldier about thirty yards away, answering the call of nature. Her movement caught his attention and before she could throw her knife, he grabbed his weapon propped against a tree, and aimed at her head. He gestured for her to move.

Alexa obeyed and walked closer, then closer still, holding his gaze. For a moment, she considered stripping to distract him. Instead, she stopped within inches of the barrel.

"Move, this way." He inclined his head, and out of the corner of her eye, she saw another soldier turn toward the tree line. Her pulse quickened. "My commander will want to know why you hide in the woods."

"Same reason as you." Her gaze dropped to his crotch, to his open fly and everything that was limply hanging out. His gaze followed hers and Alexa planted her foot right in his package. He groaned loudly, dropped to his knees, and before he could fire, she grabbed the rifle and brought the stock down on his head. He went down hard. She tossed aside the weapon, relieved him of his cash, side arm and ammo, then took off running.

Soldiers thrashed in the forest behind her as she raced back the way she'd come, thinking she wanted to be any other place than Cali right now—and she was trapped here.

* * *

Killian sighted through binoculars and knew something was up when Zarek's men didn't bother to search the tiny car that looked more like a skateboard with a growth. He wanted to dust it for prints, but going near it would tip his hand.

Then the opportunity arose. Zarek's men picked up a trail and followed footprints toward the jungle.

"It's got to be her," Riley said beside him on the rooftop. "Who else would run from the CIA?"

Killian scoffed. "Half the free world."

"Price said treason, with Zarek. My Intel says she's alone."

"Yeah, I got that, too. But alone for how long?" Were Zarek's people watching her, or someone else? And if she was teamed with Zarek, why was she doing the duck and hide?

Hunched low behind a cistern, Riley worked electronic equipment, trying to pick up their frequency. The sound whined and Killian glanced at the man. "Try not to give away our position, will you?"

"They're using antiques. With all that money they couldn't afford Sony?" Riley put up a finger, holding only the earpiece to his ear. "How's your Spanish?"

"Crappy."

"Got to be better than mine." He handed over the headset.

Killian listened. Between the static and rapid Spanish, he made out a few words. *Bugs, go left, spread out,* then something about the boss not paying them enough to chase his gringa bitch into the jungle. A woman. Ooh-rahh. But why go into the jungle? What was there to help her? Or who? There were drug factories and gunrunners galore hiding with their goods out there. Not exactly a safe house.

"Close up shop." Riley frowned at him. "She's smart, she won't be coming back this way." Killian scoped out the terrain east of the building, then climbed down the rusted ladder. Riley left in another direction and Killian waited in the trees till it was clear. No sense in alerting the locals, he thought, and saw Riley in the open, head to his vehicle.

Killian slipped into the crowd of people shopping and looking for a meal or a drink. Shopkeepers and café owners were more than ready to accommodate, outside hawking for customers or tacking up decorations for the night's festival. People bumped him, some already in costume and half-drunk. He'd covered several blocks when his gaze lit on a woman paused at the edge of an alley less than a block down. She glanced around, left, right, behind. That alone shouted suspicious. Her head was covered, her clothing baggy; it was hard to judge her age or get a good look at her face. But when she left the alley, she was moving fast, cutting behind the nightlife traffic that was quickly picking up speed. He lost sight of her and hurried down the street, skirting people and vendors.

"Mustang, you taking chasing woman literally?" Riley said through the earpiece.

"Chalk it up to desperation. Keep on their frequencies," Killian murmured, moving swiftly. "Get two streets over, west side." He didn't gesture, didn't say more, and kept moving. "Be on the watch for a woman, her hair's covered in a dark scarf, beige shirt, dark slacks, and she's walking like her shoes are too big."

"Roger that." Riley threw his gear in the car and got in.

Killian headed after the woman.

An awareness of being followed riddled her senses and Alexa moved faster. Her palms sweat, her muscles pulled tight. She tried shaking it off, but as she turned the corner, she flattened against the wall and looked back. People moved in throngs, salsa music spilling like spicy wine from the cafés and bars lining the streets. It wasn't exactly the best part of town, but then, the man who could help her was a first-class dirtbag. Not seeing anyone suspicious, she turned away, and her balance vanished. Her world tilted and she slapped her palm flat on the wall and waited for it to pass. Her stomach rolled loosely.

She couldn't remember the last time she ate.

Swallowing, she pushed off and quickened her pace, snitching a banana from a grocer's produce waiting to be displayed for sale. He shouted, threw a rock at her, but she kept moving, eating, shifting between buildings, people, and the filth in the alleys.

To think last month she'd been in a limousine on her way to a pedicure. She burst onto the street, heading toward the west. Then she saw him. Big and beautiful, dark chocolate hair, and so damn sexy women were trying to get his attention as he passed. But his attention was riveted on her.

Alexa spun and ran, not looking back and counting off the steps to Enrique's door. She went past it, turned sharply left, then came around to the rear. The door was locked, but the window wasn't. She opened it, climbed in, then flipped the back door lock before checking windows and hard exits. She moved to the front. Enrique sat at his work desk, looking at negatives through a magnifier. She glanced at the glass storefront, expecting to see sinister and sexy pass by.

"Enrique." The man flinched and jerked around.

For a second he stared, his brow knit tight, then his attention dropped to the gun in her hand. "*Señorita?* Where did you come from?"

"I need a passport, now," she said in Spanish.

"*Señorita,* I take pictures, portraits."

She was in his face in a heartbeat. "I know what you do, Enrique Valdez. You spent some jail time because of it. So let's not play this game. I need a passport and I need it now."

His gaze wandered over her and she knew what he was thinking; what did she do and who was she running from? Wisely, he didn't ask.

"Now."

Enrique stepped back, and she slapped money on the desk. He snorted. "That's not enough."

"Make it enough." She wasn't in the mood for negotiations, but when he stalled, she turned to the desk, opening drawers, flinging pictures and papers, then went to the storage closet filled with developing chemicals. She aimed the gun. One shot and it would go up in flames, and likely alert anyone near, but that was beside the point right now.

"No, no, please, please! I will do it."

Alexa motioned for him to get busy, and pulled off the scarf, and loosened her hair before she sat in the chair with a white board hanging behind it. She finger combed her hair and wiped her face, hoping she looked anything but ragged and afraid. He snapped the shot, then another, and then went to his computer. Alexa stood, moving toward the door, watching the street for the man. Enrique processed the picture, and she noticed his hands shook. Then he gave the shop front a covert glance.

She came up behind him, pressing the gun to his spine. "Who did you signal?"

He stiffened, looking over his shoulder. "Why would I? I do as you ask." He tried to nudge the desk drawer shut, but Alexa caught it, yanking it open. A cell phone, the line still open. *"Basta ya!"* she demanded. "Who did you call?"

"Me."

Alexa's head jerked up, her eyes going wide.

Big-and-gorgeous was in the shop, moving toward her in long, quick strides.

She bolted for the back through the long narrow building, slamming doors behind her. He was stronger, faster, shattering doors and leaving them dangling on the hinges behind him. Panicked and light-headed, Alexa threw open the back door and darted out. He was right after her, lunging, catching her by the shirt.

Alexa tried getting out of it, not caring who saw what, but he yanked her back against him, locking her arms to her sides. She threw her head back into his, but he jerked aside, catching only his cheek. She drew her knees up, jammed them back into his shins; he buckled but held on, and his grip grew punishing.

"Easy, wildcat, I don't want to break anything." Yet he squeezed so hard he cut off her breathing; any movement, and Alexa's brain would go fuzzy. Her strength vanished, and she sagged in his arms, royally pissed.

He loosened his hold and then his voice came again, like thick syrup near her ear. "Well, Alexa Gavlin, you're a hard woman to find."

Alexa twisted a look at him, hiding her shock. To the population of Colombia, Zarek included, she was Jade Everett, a dealer in fine art, sometimes stolen. Only Price knew her real name and it was on a secure list with about a thousand other NOCs.

Hope disintegrated. He was CIA sanctioned. She'd be dead before dawn.

His hands moved roughly over her body, searching for weapons. A keen awareness of him slithered over her, his scent, his unbelievably blue eyes—those big hands—and the powerhouse of muscle locking her to him. Why couldn't he be fat, slow, and ugly?

He pocketed her gun and the knife, his face emotionless. Yet in his dead-calm eyes, Alexa saw intense rage, and the inevitable flourished in her mind, tearing at her composure. He *wanted* to kill her. God, she really didn't want to die. Be nothing more than a nameless star on a wall. Or an unidentified body discovered rotting somewhere. She'd worked too hard to get this far and stay alive.

She had her job and nothing else. No family, few friends she trusted, and her reputation with the Company. Along with a month of her memory, it was wiped out. Her pity party abruptly ended when he pushed her forward, slipping handcuffs on her, then ushering her down the alley.

"No fight?" he said.

"You're bigger than me, armed, and I'm cuffed. Do the math." If she ran, he'd shoot her. In the back. *Not* how she wanted to go out.

Then he slipped out a cell phone and hit speed dial. "Ready the jet. I have her." He pocketed the phone.

Great. She was hoping for some chance to escape, but the airfield wasn't far from here. Unmarked, of course. He could have her out of the country in a couple hours and a deep-seated anger settled in her. After all she'd done for her country, she'd rather die first than go home accused of murder and treason. Too bad those were her options. Suddenly, he stopped, uncuffed one hand and slapped it on himself. His left hand to her right. He didn't want to draw attention to them, she thought, and keep his gun hand free. Then he gripped her hand like a lover. The warmth of it seeped into her till she remembered it was her killer's hand. Her gaze skipped around for something to pick the lock as they stepped out of the alley and into the busy avenue. He didn't look at her as he moved along, didn't speak. Music blasted from every café or bar they passed, competing with the band and people dancing in the road.

"Does my jailer have a name?" she asked as he guided her around a group.

"Not that you need to know." His voice snapped, something warring inside him. As if he wanted to say something but couldn't spare the time.

Alexa's gaze moved rapidly over the crowd, her senses jumping, and she glanced at the man beside her. His attention was far ahead. She followed it. Men were coming this way, ignoring the festivities, the people. They stood out because they were wearing jackets and it had to be ninety out today.

One man's hand moved inside the jacket, another signaled, and firecrackers went off, whistling into the afternoon sky. Partiers cheered, and big and handsome had her against the wall in a heartbeat, his body covering hers as he drew his weapon and turned. He fired just as the wall above his head splintered. They dropped, chips of stucco sprinkling over them. He didn't waste a moment, pulling her along with him past the storefronts and cafés, his sight-mounted pistol tucked to his stomach.

"Have some enemies you don't know about?" she said and flinched as another shot thumped into their path. Silencers.

"They're after you."

"Really? Then why are they aiming at *your* head?"

Killian scowled, dragging her with him. She was right. He slipped along a wall into the alley and put on a lip mike. "Riley, I'm taking gunfire, you see anything?"

Great, she thought, there were more of them near?

"No. Where the hell are you?"

"West, two streets down from the photo shop. I've got lots of company. Give me some cover fire from the north." He barely flinched when a bullet shattered the wood near his shoulder. He didn't return fire, too many civilians.

Alexa couldn't see the source. "I hope you're willing to carry me, because running is not an option."

Killian didn't look at her. "You'll run or I'll drag you."

"Now there's a real caveman image for you."

"Max? If I don't see a vehicle in the next thirty seconds I'm gonna beat the shit out of you just to work up an appetite!"

"I'm on my way. Jesus, don't these people have traffic laws!"

Killian pulled her with him, his steps so wide she was forced to run hard. They made it to the end of the alley. People were just figuring out that the noise wasn't firecrackers and running in all directions.

Then a man stepped out into the open, firing straight at them.

Killian dove to the ground, taking her with him. The impact nearly knocked her out and Killian rolled, his back against a wall. He aimed, pulling Alexa's arm across his stomach, and making her stretch. He was oblivious to her.

"Dammit, I really didn't want to kill anyone today." He leaned out to return fire and Alexa heard a scream, then the thump of a man down.

"Except me, of course."

He looked at her. Her face was nearly in his lap. "You're sure this isn't a rescue?"

She scoffed, yanking on the handcuff so she was at least at a dignified, upright position. "Why don't you just retire me now and go chase down those guys."

"You in a real hurry to die?"

"Hell, no. But you seem pretty intent on being a sweeper."

His eyes turned icy pale, and she knew she'd hit a

nerve. Then, in the top of her vision, over his head, she saw a shadow flicker. "Twelve o'clock!"

He swerved, firing off four fast rounds. Bullets shredded the edge of the roof and a body rolled over the rim. When it hit the ground, it bounced.

Alexa backed to the wall. "Oh, God. That's just gross."

Killian stared at the dead man's face, then hers. She was white as a sheet. "A friend?" He looked American.

"Never seen him."

Scowling, Killian pressed the earpiece, glaring at her. "Max? I'm getting really pissed now."

"I can't move. The streets are blocked for the festival. Be advised, police are on foot. Come around the west side."

"No deal, there are three of them. Two down. Somebody fire a fucking weapon, clear the streets!" They had no cover, nowhere to go but into the bullets. He heard three quick shots and screams. Good boys.

"*Avenida de la Porta,* west end."

Killian stood, Alexa followed.

"Mustang, I'm southeast," Riley said, "but it's jammed with cars and people. Sorry."

"Roger that. Elvis has left the building."

Alexa had to smile at that and moved behind him. Not that she had a choice. "How many of you are there?"

"Not enough today, Miss Gavlin."

"Alexa, please, since we're sharing handcuffs in a gun battle and all. If you know my name, then I know who sent you." Lania Price. She'd recruited Alexa, trained her, and thought she owned her. Would this guy understand that the deputy director considered Alexa a friend (if a viper like Lania *ever* had friends) and her personal operative? They'd had lunch together at Marco's, shopped in Georgetown. But whenever something was sensitive or that as Lania referred "needed the options only a woman could provide," she called Alexa. Lania had pushed the right buttons and applied the correct amount of pressure to her sense of duty to get Alexa to go after Lucien Zarek. A man apparently more dangerous than they all thought. So much for good Intel.

But twelve years of service, and with only one month missing, Price sent a pack of sweepers after her? Talk about lack of trust. What did Price know that she didn't? With a month gone, that could be a lot, she thought, but why was she so hot to take her out of the equation without debriefing? Lania had trusted her for years, why stop now?

"You're Company."

"Not a chance." Killian paused, tucked her behind him, and spared her a quick glance. She was more beautiful up close, even under the dirt. Movement near the street end and he moved out, prepared to fire. "Max!" he warned. "I'm here, where are you?"

"Police, everywhere. Can't force it, Mustang. Not with all this gear inside the van."

Shit. If the local cops got one look at their equipment, they'd be hauled in with no way out. "Bug out, regroup at the plane."

A shot plunked into the wood right between them. Air hissed between his teeth and he slammed his eyes shut for a second.

"Jeez, I felt the wind on that one." Alexa stared at it, then the blood dripping from his bicep. "You're hit."

He glanced, pulling up the ruined shirt. "Man, got my tattoo."

"Oh, honestly." Alexa hurriedly tore a sleeve off her shirt and wrapped his bicep. It wasn't easy, cuffed to him.

Killian met her gaze and something worked between them. "It's just a nick."

"I'm not impressed by your pain threshold. Later we can compare scars." His gaze rolled heavily over her, lighting something she thought had died years ago. Why now?

"Is that an invitation?"

"You wish."

He jiggled the cuffs, reminding her of her lack of choices.

Alexa sneered, yanked on the knot as Killian watched the area, only glancing at her. Those big green eyes turned him inside out, but why was she helping him when she knew he was sent to kill her?

Killian heard screams, and bodies dropped. "There are two different shooters. My people aren't close enough to get in a shot."

"You noticed that, huh? I think there are three." She gestured down the street.

It was Casta, aiming for Killian's head, and looking mean-ass pissed. Before Killian could fire, Casta's body flexed sharply, blood fountaining from his mouth and spilling down his chest. Choking on his own blood, he sank to his knees, gun falling. The bullet had gone through his throat, taking most of it on exit.

"That's Lucien Zarek's man."

"I know." Killian's gaze snapped to the left. He saw a sniper on the roof. It made him feel special.

"I don't get it."

"Neither do I." Killian inched out, gauging the sniper's range. "See that old jeep up there, we need to get to it."

"Are you nuts? I saw the rifle muzzle. He'll pick us off! And that thing's an antique!"

He nudged her, smiling for the first time. "Come on, wildcat, you can do it."

Before she could argue the point, he was moving fast and Alexa felt like a rag doll dragged behind him.

When she stumbled, he tossed her over his shoulder and booked. She couldn't breathe, her lungs shoved up to her throat. She just knew she'd puke them up any second.

At the jeep, he threw her in, and climbed behind the wheel, then gunned the engine. Bullets plunked into the door.

"Move it before they hit the gas tank!"

"No, you think?" He laid on the horn to scatter people and nearly drove into them.

Alexa was jerked all over the place as he drove, her hand still cuffed to his left. "Gimme a break, will you? I like this arm."

"In my right pocket, the key, free us."

She faced the rear and pressed to his side, wiggling her hand into his pocket, the warmth of his body penetrating the fabric.

"If you think rubbing your tits in my face is going to change anything, it won't."

She gave him a dirty look, pulling out the key. "I'm an NOC, not a slut." She uncuffed herself, leaving the bracelet on him just as he made a hard left, smashing crates and trash cans as he drove.

"Oh, you are *so* not getting your deposit back," she said, fastening the seat belt and slapping her hand on the dash.

"I wasn't expecting company." He drove fast, chiseling corners where there were none. Tires screeched, the car leaned, but he didn't seem the least bit fazed. "Who was the guy who landed at out feet?"

"How the hell am I supposed to—"

"Cut the crap," he bit out. "I saw your face, you knew him."

What was the point? "Dan Wade, he's CIA."

He cursed, then yanked off the lip mike. They were out of range anyway. Casta, a bullet in his throat. CIA shooting at them, and Zarek's men firing at CIA *and* him? Christ, what a mess.

"If CIA sent you, then why were officers aiming at you?"

Good question. "And you."

"Oh, that's a given, they'd already tried today."

She was far too calm for a woman in deep trouble. "What's in the jungle, Alexa?"

She said nothing, giving him a bland expression.

Carrión's place was on the edge of the jungle, Killian thought. Though several miles in the other direction. Would she go to the drug kingpin? It made sense if Price's theory were true, that she was the mole, considering it was Carrión who came out smelling good while Killian's life went to shit. Without a word, she turned her face to the rear, looking to see if they were being followed. Killian knew he wasn't getting anything more from her.

"You've won, we're almost at the airport; how about you tell me your name at least." He looked a little familiar.

"Killian Moore."

The name tumbled through her mind till it hit on the source. Dragon One. Outside private services? Price must be desperate, and Alexa planned to find out why. "What did Price do to get you into this?"

Killian's grip tightened on the steering wheel. He might not show emotion in his expression, but it radiated from his body. Everything in him locked, screaming with anger. Yet, he didn't say a word.

"Let me go, Killian. It's dangerous to be near me."

"After nearly two weeks of looking for you, hell, no."

Two weeks? That meant Price didn't wait long before she sicked the attack dogs after her. Two weeks out of contact was nothing. Four was. "Didn't the last hour prove anything? You're in danger." Santiago was already dead, Killian injured—she didn't want anyone else to die.

"So?"

"Don't you value your life?"

"Sure, but danger and death are two different things."

She sagged into the seat, unconvinced. "I'd rather not visit either." His gaze slid to her, glazing over her body with the power of touch.

"You're a package that needed retrieving." She meant nothing to him. It had to be that way.

She shifted, checking his wound, her face near his. "Then why did you protect me back there?"

He scoffed. "You have to be alive to interrogate."

"You can stare into my eyes and pull a trigger?"

Only his gaze shifted. Clear and razor sharp. "Yes. I can."

Alexa felt the chill of his words rip down her spine, freezing any doubt.

Killian Moore might be as handsome as the devil, but he was Price's dark angel.

"And here I thought Dragon One had a noble conscience."

Four

Killian's jaw flexed, but he didn't rise to the bait.

She inched closer, her voice low and damn sexy. "So what's stopping you, Moore? Information you think I have?" Boy, was that a joke. "I'll never talk, so you better do it now, because I have nothing left. Nothing."

And that made her dangerous, he thought.

"You have no resources. You're cut off."

Let him think that, Alexa thought. "I've always worked alone. And I have a job to finish."

"So do I. And I've never failed."

His gaze slid to hers, briefly, yet the intensity in those blues eyes tightened her muscles. Fury bounced off him in waves. He was a dangerous man to cross. She didn't have to know more about him to understand that. But Alexa had no choice.

Killian steered the car around a curve and saw the checkpoint a half a mile or so ahead. "Keep quiet and sit back," he said, slowing the car.

She looked. "They don't look happy."

"When do they ever?" Zarek owned the police in this area. She was messing with his bandage when Killian heard a distinct click. She eased back, and he realized he was cuffed to the steering wheel. "Fuck."

Alexa aimed his gun, and tossed the key out the window. "All that equipment in your backseat is really going to make for interesting conversation with the *Federales*." He swore again. "Turn the car around now."

"Forget it."

"How's your Spanish? Mine's fluent."

Shit. She could scream kidnapping, rape, anything and the regulars would come running after him. He had to hand it to her, she was clever. And he was screwed. He turned the car.

"Take that road, now." She reached inside his shirt, retrieving her gun, her knife, then searching the car for anything useful. She eyed the gear in the back again.

"I wouldn't."

"Sure you would." Alexa leaned, prying open a bag. A lot of surveillance gear, yet she bypassed it and stuffed her pockets with power bars, Chem-lites, and a compass, then left it at that. Too much to carry.

Killian noticed the food in her pockets, wondering when she ate last, or slept. Zarek was known for his generosity with women. So why wasn't she reaping it? For that matter, if Price's theory were true, why was she alone and not *with* Zarek?

"You're in the crosshairs, Alexa, a hunted prey in a small arena. What do you plan on doing?"

"I'm sorta winging it as I go." She checked the compass, then directed him another mile. "Stop the car."

Killian obeyed, humiliated beyond his imagination. "I'm coming after you, you know that."

Only her gaze shifted. "I'm looking forward to it." Then suddenly she leaned close to his handsome face, touched his jaw. It clenched beneath her palm. He was furious and she suddenly admired his control. "You should have put a bullet in me, Killian."

Killian was snagged, by that voice, those serious green eyes penetrating any wall he put between them.

She was damn righteous and determined for such a little thing, and the chips were stacked so high against her, he knew this wouldn't end pretty. He'd get her. He'd drag her back to American soil in a body bag or by the hair, but he'd get her. It almost hurt to know that.

"I won't waste a second chance."

"For what? It's over for you, wildcat."

The tenderness in his voice slayed her, had her reaching for something she could never have because true emotion was so absent from her life, her work; Alexa hungered for it. "Not today," she whispered softly, brushing her lips over his.

Killian opened his mouth on her, plunging deeply, taking her into him. To distract as he gripped the steering wheel, trying to break it. But she took control, eating him alive, her tongue thrusting between his lips and unhinging him in seconds.

Good God.

He was a prisoner, his dick going stone hard, his shoulders pulling tight as he tasted her. Savored her. The woman had more weapons than he thought. Then suddenly she was gone, leaving him breathing hard, blood rushing to his groin. Christ. He could kick his own ass from here to Bali for that.

Alexa swallowed, flames still licking wildly at her body as she stared at the man who put them there. She didn't trust it, didn't want it, even as her heart screamed for something beyond her NOC life.

He's the enemy now, she reminded, backing away and out of the car.

A response would give him an opportunity to dig deeper and work on her emotions. That would give him power, and she wanted control in her fist, to exploit her environment, the people in it. She hated losing that edge, even a shred of it. She was an expert at manipulation. It was her job. Select a contact, initiate friendship, lull them into betraying their country to get what she needed, then fade away. She'd been doing it all her adult life. It made her read people easily. Men were easy. Men responded to breasts, and sex, and allure. Sometimes the damsel in distress worked. Women responded to sympathy, kindness, and feminist viewpoints. Even though most never said it aloud.

Alexa responded to denial.

The world denying her the chance to do what was right. And right now, that was finding out what she'd learned to bring this hell to her door. She took several steps away.

"I don't know how Lania forced you to come retire me, but don't trust her."

"Why should I believe you?" he snarled. "You're a professional liar."

"True, but I know when the job stops and life begins. Price doesn't."

She shot out the tires, then the engine. Moore didn't even flinch, his glare grinding over her and speaking of deadly retribution.

"CIA were trying to kill both of us, Moore. Both." Alexa broke the gun down and tossed the components near the car, then turned, striding into the jungle. The pieces on the chessboard had changed. There were new players, she thought with a glance back at Moore. Her foes had shown themselves.

Bad move. Really bad.

Zarek backhanded the man so hard he fell against the table, spilling wine and breaking glass. Degas leaped to a corner, cowering.

"I told you to protect her!"

"We did."

"Then is she free to move?"

The man shook his head, swiping the back of his wrist across his bloody lip.

"Now this man has her captive. Who is he?"

"I think it was Cane."

Lucien moved away, thoughtful, running his thumb and forefinger down over his lip line. Degas heeled beside him. Dominic Cane was a rich man with many valuable connections. Lucien didn't want to cross swords with him right now. Carrión had suggested a deal. If Cane wanted to buy, it was wise to deliver. But what was he doing with his woman? Was he simply protecting a woman in trouble?

"We can't be sure, sir," a man said. "There were other shooters."

Lucien snapped his fingers for the phone, dialing with his thumb. "Hello, my friend. I have the merchandise, arrange a meeting. The coffeehouse." Lucien cut the line. If Cane had Jade, then Lucien needed to get close to him. Understand what the man was to her and the trouble he could become.

Jade had to roam free—so he could push her where *he* wanted her to go.

The dense jungle swallowed her, and for a second Killian felt a tinge of fear for her. Anger quickly smothered it and he jerked at the handcuffs, then gripped the steering wheel, taking his rage out on it till it cracked. He slipped the cuff free, then leaned over the seat, alert for unfriendlies. Her gunshots were going to bring the troops. His hand dove into a pack for a second set of cuffs and the key. The moment he was free, he got out his satellite phone and dialed his team.

"Where the hell are you, man?" Max said. "We thought the Feds got you."

"Lock in on my GPS. Get your asses here asap."

"The lady giving you trouble?"

Killian wasn't in the mood for jokes. "Oh, yeah," he said, looking toward the woods as he loaded a weapon. "My ride is DOA, and be advised, Colombian regulars are near my location."

"We're locked on you, Mustang. Carrión's been trying to reach you."

Killian loaded himself up with tactical gear and weapons. "Say again."

"Zarek's ready to deal. It's two clicks north of your six. His coffee plant. ATF is moving in now. Rendezvous at high noon tomorrow. Yee-haw."

"Excellent," Killian said, popping a magazine into the machine pistol. "I can kill two birds then." He fixed the sight, then moved forward, letting the jungle sweep closed behind him.

The wet vapor of the rain forest smothered down around her as the trees blocked the setting sun. Alexa hacked through vines, stepping over logs and forest debris. Her knife was getting dull fast, but it was this or out in the open and the chance of getting snagged again. Moore wouldn't give up; she could almost smell his anger. Almost taste him on her mouth still. God, the man could kiss. She couldn't remember the last time a man kissed her with such power. She couldn't remember the last time she slept with a man.

She'd done it once in the line of duty. Once. When she was young and stupid. It left her feeling so foul and cheap she'd thrown up for a week. She never let her targets get that close again. *Nobody else either, huh?* She shook the thought loose, straining to see. On the forest floor, it was pitch-black, the rustle of creatures telling her she wasn't alone. Every step was an effort, her body battered and screaming for rest. She opened a power bar, eating slowly because retching her guts out would just top this day.

She tried remembering something, even a scrap, but nothing was coming back. The blank slate scared her more than Dragon One, the CIA, and Zarek hunting after her. Them, she could avoid. But without some serious debriefing and a good psych probe, Alexa had to assume the worst. Someone—that it was Zarek was a given after seeing Casta in the streets—had erased or planted something in her mind. Or both. She told herself she was taking a logical course of action, that nothing she'd done was preordained. But she didn't know. She could be moving on a programmed cycle, and it was the not knowing that terrified the hell out of her.

Stuffing the wrapper in her pocket, she kept walking. Getting to her stash was paramount. The contents would widen her prospects, give her some advantage when everyone wanted her dead. She kept her eyes on the path to her far left. Barely passable by car, it was more of a horse trail. This area was pretty much uninhabited, a small village about a quarter mile north. A patch of jungle stretched before her, the setting sun turning the area bright orange-gold. She hurried across to a thick line of trees, paused long enough to locate her marker cuts in the trunks, then edged around one.

Her shoulders sagged, hope vanishing.

The spy gods are against me today.

The land where she'd buried her steel box had been plowed over.

"Mustang, she'll surface. We blow this meeting and it's curtains for the guys in the white hats," Max said.

It was the third hail from his team and Killian acknowledged the transmission, then stopped, dropped his head forward and sighed. Aborting the hunt left him more irritated than angry. If he ignored the rendezvous, his cover would be shit. It was his one advantage over Gavlin. He was on the inside. She wasn't.

He turned back, pissed that he'd been so taken with those green eyes that the little witch got the jump on him. Humiliation poured through him again, yet part of him ached to know a woman that fast on her feet. God, he'd never seen it coming.

Of course, you were lip-locked with her and not thinking about much else.

The sun was beating the edge of the horizon when he made it back to his jeep. He snarled at the flat tires and smoking engine. A cloud of dust kicked up, and drawing his weapon, Killian took cover till he saw the SUV slam to a halt, his men spilling out. Max hopped out of the vehicle, his hands on his hips as he inspected the damage.

"I can fix that."

"Don't bother, let's get out of here."

In record time, they transferred gear, and climbed into the SUV, taking off at a hard speed. Moore looked behind, his jaw aching from grinding his teeth. She'd surface. She had a deep-seated need to finish her assignment. And that would bring her into the open again.

Alexa refused to accept it was gone and quickly paced off the area, then stopped at the burial ground and knelt. The earth was tilled black, and she sifted her hands through it. It was loamy, and a little dry. Wet when she dug deeper. It'd been plowed in the last couple days, she realized and looked around for tracks and footprints. She found them, man size, and a smaller set. They led off to the road with clods of dirt.

She dug, ruining her nails, and kicking up dirt like a

dog after a bone. At a foot down, she found nothing. She sighed, leaned back on her haunches, swiped her wrist under her nose. The sound of gunfire burst in the silence, rapid and close. She jerked a look in the direction. Assault rifles. Colombian regular troops, or a drug deal gone bad?

A second later a skinny boy about ten burst out of the forest. He froze when he saw her, his gaze darting to her face to the hole she'd dug. Then, if he could look more frightened, he did. He bolted toward her.

"Come, come quickly," he shouted in Spanish, grabbing her shoulder. "Army, ELN. They come, hide. Hide!"

Oh, hell. Caught in a fight between rebels and regulars was just bad news all around. Alexa leapt to her feet and when the boy fell, she snatched him up, carrying him for a few yards till he squealed to be let down. They ran, the boy pulling on her hand.

Troops were all over the area. She sensed them, spreading out in the jungle, combing it like snakes covering Ireland. *I'll be snagged first,* she thought. A white woman in this mountain region raised too much suspicion. She had to separate from the boy.

She pulled free, and he stared at her. "Go home," she said in Spanish. "Quickly, hide."

"No, no, come with me, I can hide you."

"My God, no! Go!"

The boy wasn't changing his mind and jumped at her, dragging her down. "They will kill you, woman. Come with me! Please!"

The earth pounded with footsteps and gunfire. Alexa heard the blades of a chopper rev. Scrambling up, she ran with the child. Neither had a choice. She didn't get many of those lately and took it. She spied a house up ahead, a shack tilting a little on cinder blocks and a woman standing outside calling out for her son, Raul.

The family panicked at the sight of her, and the boy spoke rapidly, telling them the gunrunners and troops were headed this way. Instantly, the woman pulled her inside, shouting orders to her family and they moved a chair at the table, and flipped back a rug. Beneath was a hatch in the dirt floor.

"You go, now please, *señorita.*"

Alexa yanked it open and slid down into the small hole. "Thank you," she said and let them cover her from light. She heard the scrape of the chair moved back in place, and Alexa crouched, listening, her heart pounding. Rebels killed for no reason; the regulars were just as careless.

Less than two minutes later, masculine voices filtered to her, muffled, angry. National troops entered the house, heavy footsteps, then the crash of something fragile hitting the floor. The boy's mother pleaded with the soldiers not to ruin her home.

Please don't hurt them. Then she heard a definite crack of flesh to flesh. Someone dropped into the chair above her, dirt sifted through the wood slats.

Then silence. Not a sound, not the scuff of a shoe. Alexa's heart broke for the young family till she heard scrapes and hushed tones. The hatch opened. Alexa gasped for air, just realizing she'd held her breath, then climbed out and dropped to the floor.

"Thank you," she said in Spanish. Someone offered her water and she drank, then looked at the mother. Her cheek was red with the imprint of a hand. "I'm so sorry."

The mother scoffed. "If this is all they do, we are lucky, *señorita.*"

Yet before she could climb to her feet, the boy appeared. He held her box. Her world tilted right again. Alexa lifted her gaze to the child. He looked scared, poor thing.

"Did you find it?"

"*Sí.* I opened it, but I did not take anything. I swear." He crossed himself. His mother cuddled her son, but he shrugged it off as if facing his punishment like a man.

"It's all right, Raul. Thank you for saving it." Her stash was her salvation.

She withdrew her knife and pried it open, then motioned the boy down. His family peered. She understood why the child liked it. The contents looked like a child's treasure box, filled with a bag of marbles, balls of string, old keys that unlocked nothing, some smooth crystalline rocks, a bird egg, and some bottle caps. Raul was rather interested in it all, bringing a smile to her lips. She scooped it out and dumped the treasures in his lap.

"Thank you for helping me," she said, and he beamed at her.

Then she pried up the false bottom. They all tried to get a look, but she couldn't allow that and carefully slipped out some Colombian currency and closed the box. She stood, handing it to the mother. She wouldn't take it, but Alexa insisted. She'd be dead if not for her brave son. Alexa clutched the box, wondering how she was going to get it out of here and herself into the city without drawing attention. Especially Moore's. Mama understood and hurried to a small cabinet, offering a shoulder bag made of grass from the river. She'd empty the contents into it when she was alone. When the woman opened the door, motioning that the way was clear, Alexa shook her head and climbed out the window, waving thanks before melting into the forest.

She covered her tracks, then turned and started running.

CIA Headquarters
Langley, VA

To the first-time observer, the deputy director of operations, Clandestine Service, looked average. Average height, average figure, average hair color. But David Lorimer knew better. He prided himself in being one step ahead of her, which was a hell of a thing to do since the woman was the most closedmouth, cool-under-pressure person he'd ever known.

From his desk in the outer offices, Lorimer tipped his head into the office. The deputy director had been acting odd in the last week or so. He knew it was some touchy operation, but wasn't privy to the details. He acknowledged that a long time ago. At the CIA, there were men and women who had been here twenty years who didn't know what went on in this office.

Suddenly she left her sanctuary, and David hopped up and followed.

She stopped, turned. "Did I invite you?"

"No, ma'am."

"Then don't assume." She took a few steps away, then stopped. "Come along, David."

He was used to her swift mood changes, and followed her down corridor after corridor. People perked up, watched, then went back to work. The DD slipped into the SatCom room. Techs sat up a little straighter, focused a little harder. She enjoyed that power, wearing it like a cloak. Her position afforded her a "no questions asked" priority.

"Key up Cali," she said softly as she slipped into a padded chair inside a soundproof dome. David stood outside like a guard. Like he knew why she was in there? He didn't.

The technician obeyed and he saw the secure satellite pinpoint Colombia, then Cali, then wedge open

screen after screen as the probe went deeper. He tried
not to watch, but she dialed a SatCom phone, then put
on a headset. She didn't want anyone to hear the conversation, he realized. She tapped the keyboard. The
satellite linked a connection. Price glanced at him,
glared, and he turned his back.

She spoke briefly if at all, and in less than a minute,
she burst out of the room with quick angry steps.
David rushed to catch up. She went straight into her office, pacing for a moment, pushing her fingers through
her neatly styled hair.

That alerted him. Price was, if anything, a perfec-
tionist.

"Ma'am? Is there something I can do for you?"

She scoffed. "Like you could?" He frowned deeper.
"I don't want to be disturbed," she said, crossing the office to shut the door in his face.

David blinked at the wood door, then returned to his
desk in the outer office, frowning to himself. Price
never showed emotion, never. Even when things were
going well for her operations she'd maybe opted for a
celebration drink, and that, always alone.

Whatever news she got from that SAT call wasn't
good.

And that usually meant one thing.

Someone was dead.

Or about to be.

five

Alexa woke in a disoriented panic, her gaze shooting around the hotel room, honing in on the door. The booby trap was still in place, a lightbulb balanced over the doorknob.

She flopped back onto the bed and stared at the cracked plaster ceiling. She'd found this place at dawn, hid her box, kicked off the dirty sandals, and fell face first onto the bed. She still felt bone tired. All that running for your life, she thought, and forced herself up, then went into the vilest bathroom in the free world to shower. She came out, toweling her hair and removing the box from the air vent, then sat on the bed. Opening it, she lifted out the false bottom, then overturned the box onto the bed.

The money was enough to make her smile, though there was more here than she remembered. A lot more. Her first thoughts were, had she done something stupid or sold something of her own? Her things in her apartment in Cali would have to stay there. Going back was too dangerous. She groaned, suddenly remembering the hot little outfits hanging in the closet with the tags still on them. She didn't own furniture, an apartment in the States, nothing.

"That's really pathetic," she murmured. "I'm only a Swiss bank account."

Yet sometimes targets gave her little bits of jewelry and while she liked wearing the gems, she didn't want to keep them and be accused of taking bribes. The targets wouldn't take it back, so most of the time, she pawned it or gave it away. Maybe that's where this cash came from, she thought, counted the cash, then sifted through the other items. A couple sets of contact lenses, her Glock, photos of her mark, Lucien Zarek, and his associates. The details of his background and suspected crimes she had memorized before she'd stepped on Colombian soil for this Op.

An uneasy feeling slipped over her, the same one that she'd had since learning she'd lost a month of time. She'd shoved it aside for survival, but now the fear spirited through her. She covered her face and sighed, a million scenarios flying through her brain. Mind programming was the worst of them. Used in a porno flick ran a close second. Suddenly she stood, dropped the towel and in the dresser mirror, checked her body for marks. The last twenty-four hours had rewarded her with a few bruises, and a cut on her leg that was no more than a deep scratch now. If there were any needle marks, they'd have healed by now.

Wrapping the towel around her, she sat again, shuffling through her passports. She kissed them, smiling. But it faded fast. There was a thin blue silk box in the bottom and she opened it. A piece of paper was folded on top and she started to open it, when she saw there was more.

What the hell is this? Was she suddenly collecting rocks? Two stones, one white one black. She tipped them into her palm, rolling them. No bigger than a dime and a little flat, they looked like onyx and maybe quartz. And there was writing on them, Kanji, possibly Chinese, she suspected. It looked faded, almost worn off, yet gold sparkled in the grooves. She clutched them, concentrating, forcing her mind to produce something about them. Blank. Nada. Zip.

No news flash there, she thought. But if they were in this stash, they were important. She wasn't going to try to decipher the writing. It was too faded to be clear and her ability to read Chinese or Japanese was poor, though she could speak enough to get by.

She opened the paper. Nothing unusual, a torn corner of a larger sheet.

Zhu King Conquers was printed near the bottom.

The rest, if there'd been any, was missing. She moved to the lamp, flipping it on and tipping the paper to the light. No watermark. She sanded it between her fingers. Average copy paper, she decided. Evenly printed so it must be a computer printout. She squinted at the edge; it was torn as if pulled, right to left, the tear on the underside, not the top. As if yanked in a hurry.

Then she noticed a dark spot. Ink. A thin layer of it and only a shadow of what had been there. She brought it closer to the light and saw the "at" sign. An e-mail address? She wet the tip of her finger and dotted it, hoping to bring it up. Then she recognized the dot com. Remailers. People could send e-mails and the company would send them out, cloaking the original sender. It was giving analysts fits because they were hard to trace, and a convenient way for stalkers, criminals and whoever to send threats or info to anyone, and remain untraceable.

She looked at the bed, the money, passports. And the stones. Were they Zarek's stones? And what would he be doing with Chinese anything. She looked back at the words.

Zhu King Conquers.

Break it down. Work backward with what you know.

Okay, Zhu could be a Chinese name. Male, she figured. Or a province. Nothing untoward there. *King.* Chinese didn't have kings, but emperors. Conquers what? Land, people, another clan? And what the hell did it have to do with her mission. And was she even interpreting this correctly? It was a code, obviously, and without her resources, she was screwed. But logic said this paper wouldn't be here if she hadn't discovered it sometime during her investigation into Zarek's arms deals. Though the meaning of the stones escaped her completely. No time now, she thought, gathering her things, stuffing them in the grass sack before getting dressed.

She needed clothes, a wig, a better pack, and some girl stuff. She wasn't ready to be out in the open unprotected. Not with Dragon One and Zarek after her. Armed with her Glock, she stowed the soldier's weapon with the intent of ditching it in the trash as soon as she could, then stepped out the door, glancing back to see if she'd left anything behind. Then it hit her.

King. Emperor.

Zarek had a cargo ship called *Red Emperor.*

Killian had to hand it to the man. Lucien Zarek was a brash son of a bitch. The meeting was inside his coffee warehouse, a vulnerable position yet one of power. He had to know that ATF watched him. Like DEA kept a finger on Carrión. Eternally suspicious by nature, Killian's senses were hiked up a notch since this deal came about way too fast for his liking. Gavlin's reports gave a decent inventory of Zarek's arsenal, including

AK-47s, Galeals, Uzis, Centex, and some crates that were too well guarded to get near.

Killian wondered if he was looking at them now or if it was something else.

His awareness sizzled as he inspected the weapon, throwing the bolt, checking the sight. Yeah, these were the ones stolen from the docks before being loaded onto a troop carrier bound for the Middle East. He hadn't expected Zarek to have them; the ATF had found no connection to him specifically, but to four small-time smugglers. Killian had thrown it out there simply for the purpose of the buy. He'd bet his best K-Bar knife that the smugglers were in a shallow grave somewhere—erasing all traces.

"Ammo?"

Zarek lifted a brow in a practiced motion. "You did not request it."

"Don't patronize me, Zarek. I'm not in the mood." Killian tossed the weapon in the crate. "No test fire, no deal."

Zarek's eyes narrowed. His men inched forward like trained dogs. Just what he needed, a couple of trigger-happy puppies with enough firepower to knock off Fort Knox. It'd be a bloodbath he'd no intention of taking.

A few feet away, Carrión, leaning against a stack of coffee crates, smoked a cigar with the patience of a man who didn't have a stake in this. "He's right and you should provide a target."

Killian waited a moment, meeting Zarek's pale gray gaze, and when the man said nothing, stroking that damned dog, he turned toward his car. Sam Wyatt trailed behind him, the cowboy looking his mean-assed best, and fascinating the Colombian guards. Sam might look like he couldn't care less, but he was edgy when he wasn't at least five hundred feet in the air. Ground level made him nervous.

"Cane."

He stopped, glancing over his shoulder with a look that said he'd get his weapons somewhere else. Zarek flicked a hand and Franco, a mother-huge man with Cro-Magnon features, moved to a storage closet and produced the ammo.

Killian was on Zarek in an instant, gripping him by the throat with one hand, and squeezing. Zarek choked and clawed at his hand. Sam Wyatt drew his weapon on Franco before the man could move toward his boss.

"Didn't I warn you not to fuck with me?" His rage was false. He'd expected Zarek to make a show of power. But Dominic Cane had a short, nasty temper.

Zarek's face turned a darker shade as he grappled at Killian's hand. His legs softened. The dog bared his teeth.

"Dom," Sam said tiredly, his weapon to Franco's temple. "Wait till this is over if you want to kill him. He's no use to us dead."

After a moment longer, Killian let him go. Alejandro hadn't moved, his reaction no more than lifting an eyebrow. Lucien swore in Polish, rubbing his throat and coughing. He'd have the imprint of Killian's fingers to remind him not to be so stupid.

He righted his clothing, smoothed his thumb and forefinger over his upper lip line, then cleared his throat. "Forgive me, Cane," Zarek said easily. "It was just a bit of fun."

Killian glared as he turned back to load the weapon. Sam blocked Franco from getting closer as Zarek led them out into the service yard. A target dummy was already set up. Bastard. Killian didn't waste a moment and opened fire. The others flinched and lurched back, cursing.

He inspected his target. "The sight's off."

Zarek looked at the dummy. The head was gone. He turned his gaze on Killian.

"Don't fuck with me again." Killian tossed the weapon at him, forcing him to catch it. "Load them up."

Killian whipped out a cell phone and made a call. Within a minute, two trucks rolled onto the acreage. Undercover ATF hopped out.

"Payment?" Killian asked.

Zarek put his hand on the crate, meeting his gaze head-on. "Cash. Now."

Killian inspected him from head to toe. Zarek's jaw had enough whiskers to look rough, but his tailored clothing said otherwise. Ferragamo shoes, raw silk jacket, and loose slacks. GQ with illegal weapons. And not a single agency had managed to get a thing on him that wouldn't garner more than a slap on the wrist or be easily bribed away with local authorities. Getting a few hundred assault rifles off the black market was just a drop in the shitter to stopping the transfer of more dangerous weapons into the United States. But these weapons had cost four MPs their lives and Killian wanted their deaths to mean something by getting them back. It would never be enough.

"The future's in computers, go electronic, difficult to trace." Killian waved. ATF agents hustled forward with Moore's payment. Zarek laid the case on the crates, opened it carefully, then flipped through a stack of the bills before shutting it and handing it over to Franco without a glance. It would take a currency expert to figure out it was all counterfeit.

"Tell me, Cane. Why were you with Jade Everett yesterday?"

He knew this was coming. "What's it to you?" Killian was checking the crates as they were loaded. He wouldn't put it past Zarek to fill the rest with rocks.

"She's . . . my lady."

Killian glanced at Carrión, who merely shrugged and looked amused, then he pinned Zarek with a hard stare.

"She was mine before you got near her."

"I lost a few men trying to protect her."

"Funny, that's what I was doing."

"In handcuffs?"

Killian gave the man a smug look that was sinister and real. "She likes 'em, or don't you know that?" Experiencing one kiss with the woman was enough to tell him she'd be raw and scorching between the sheets.

Zarek's expression didn't change as he smoothed the contours of his lip again. A nervous habit, Killian thought. He wanted her. But she was running from him. Curious. And dangerous. Since neither of them knew where the little spook was right now. The longer he was here, the faster Price's theory blew apart. Not that he ever believed half of what she said. The CIA always had their own agenda, and he wondered if Alexa had made it out of the jungle. In a dark spot in the back of his mind, thoughts of her bit by a scorpion, or shot by some eager-to-get-promoted troops sparked concern. He didn't want to, but he had to admire the woman; she was quick, smart, and damned daring.

He lifted one of the crates onto the truck, his gaze moving to the armed guards on the top of the buildings, in perches that were made for surveillance. The hills were to the right, the sea to the left and a few blocks down. The place reeked of scorched coffee beans and the steady thump of paddles in the vats pushing the beans back and forth marked slow time.

An uneasy feeling made the hair stand on the back of his neck, and his attention slid covertly to the hills, the sunburned grasses.

* * *

In the lens of the binoculars, Moore's gaze pinned her and Alexa lurched back, gasping for air. *He didn't see me. He didn't,* she thought, then inched up on her stomach again, slipping out on a cantilever formation, and bringing the compact binoculars to her eyes again. Buying weapons, huh, Killian? Was he working for the CIA or the ATF? Or both? Was he a freaking Boy Scout or something? He was sent to get her, but why was he . . . oh, hell. She knew. Bring Zarek out, and bring her close.

Clever boy.

Her attention slipped to Zarek. He was rubbing his throat again. A small part of her adored Killian just for exploding on him like that. A bullet between the eyes would have been better, but she couldn't be choosy. She'd take having his throat ripped out by a pissed off ex-Marine any day.

She scanned the participants, recognizing Franco, and Alejandro Carrión from his dossier. She'd never met him up close and personal. Carrión was Latin gorgeous and had a way of looking at people that said if you assumed you knew what he was thinking, you were dead wrong. She'd stayed clear of him. Drug lords weren't her territory, and Carrión was a dangerous man with a lethal touch. She knew a half dozen damn good DEA officers who'd died because of him. But since he wasn't in Venezuela raking in the big bucks with drugs, she suspected he was up to no good with Zarek. They weren't friends, that's for sure. Lucien didn't trust anyone enough to have friends.

She slithered back, stowing her binoculars, then moving down the hill enough not to be seen, she retraced her steps around the guards' line of vision. She knew the systems, the posts of the warehouse; she'd been here dozens of times and inside. What she couldn't understand was why Zarek was dealing weapons here and not in the jungle somewhere. Which was his usual. That he was so confident he wouldn't be tapped by the ATF or Colombians meant he had someone in his back pocket.

The local government wasn't all that hot and ready to catch them anyway unless the United States pressured. Money that men like Lucien and Carrión poured into the local economy was about eighty percent of the economy. Who'd want to kill the cash cow?

She slipped onto the motorcycle, stuffing her hair in the helmet, then took off at a sedate pace. She had places to go, a little B&E to commit. And she hoped something triggered her lost memory before Moore pulled the trigger on her.

Zarek watched Cane leave. He could have had him killed instantly, but as long as Cane believed Zarek needed this sale, he was satisfied. Though he'd return the favor, he thought, rubbing his throat.

Lucien wanted the weapons gone. A few of his people behaved stupidly and had attempted to steal them for themselves. Killing the military policemen would only bring more Americans sniffing closer, and Lucien had already expended a fortune to bribe his way out of the mess and throw suspicion elsewhere. He turned toward his office in the warehouse, ignoring Carrión and ordering the secretary to bring him tea. Degas trotted at his heels and inside the office curled up on his bedding. Now the American authorities would turn their attention to Cane. Lucien already had the bodies of the killers delivered to the American authorities.

His secretary hurried in with hot tea. He took it,

shooing her, then cleared his throat before sipping. The heat soothed the bruised muscles. *I should have had Franco kill the bastard,* he thought. But Dominic Cane had Carrión in his corner. He looked out the window to see Carrión get into his Town Car and leave. The Latin might not say it, but that he'd joined him today spoke loudly of their alliance.

Understanding how Cane knew Jade was a matter he'd learn soon enough. She never spoke of him, though she didn't speak much of herself, he'd come to realize. Perhaps Cane's claim was a ruse and he had simply protected the woman but didn't want anyone to know he'd been that soft. Lucien leaned back in the plush leather chair. If Cane searched for Jade, he was going to be a problem.

He called for Franco. "Where is he?"

"The trucks are heading toward Los Comas airfield."

In the jungle, Lucien thought. "His plane?"

"No, a smaller one."

Lucien had been alerted the instant Cane's black aircraft had landed. It was as big as a dinosaur, and he wondered how the man used it for quick escapes.

His gaze flashed up as a thought occurred to him. "Cane is with the trucks?"

"He got into a car about five miles from here."

"Why didn't you tell me! Going where?"

"Into the city. I have a man on him."

Lucien scowled. Franco was a little too patronizing today, but Lucien could count on him with his most delicate details. "He doesn't have her."

Franco's expression shaped with doubt. "Neither do we."

Lucien glared. He didn't want to possess her. He wanted to watch her struggle to find her memory. To find what was no longer there. To do what he wanted.

"You still believe she will go to the docks."

"She has no choice but to investigate there," Lucien said cryptically. "She is cut off from anyone, alone, and without a peso to her name. She'll want to get out of the country and the only way to do it without a passport is to stow away or walk."

"Of course."

Annoyed, Lucien dismissed him, then went to the mirror. Cane's fingerprints glared red on his skin and he vowed before he was finished with Jade, he'd kill the man himself.

The ship had sailed. Two days ago.

Alexa didn't waste time learning where the ship would call next. The sailors and shore men on the dock were more than eager to tell her. Hong Kong. Fragrant Harbor.

Now things were starting to make a little sense.

But gave her a whole new set of problems. Her gut told her there was more on that ship than coffee, but the paper, *Zhu King Conquers* could mean anything. If it wasn't for the stones. Still not enough, she thought, and feared she was chasing shadows. She couldn't go to Zarek's compound for a deeper look-see and turning back was out of the question. CIA shooters and Moore were in the city somewhere still looking for her.

Adjusting the leather backpack, she hopped on the motorcycle, leaving the docks, her mind tripping over her next moves. If she had any. She headed toward the airport. She could buy a ticket and fly to Hong Kong. It was just too weak a lead, dammit. She needed more to go on. Experience told her the sellers of weapons didn't often accompany the cache to the destination. Money transferred hands, mostly electronically, and the buyer picked it up. Alexa's job was to follow the weapons and stop the sale. And on occasion, blow them up. But Zarek wasn't like most. He enjoyed his riches—his annoying habit of toying with ancient Mayan coins said as much.

The bike hummed between her legs and she ducked low, speeding over the roads. Alexa's brain latched onto the gun battle, playing it in her mind in slow motion. Fact one: the CIA sniper on the roof firing at both of them. Lousy aim, too. Fact two: Casta shooting at Killian. But not her. Casta's men probably intervened on orders from Zarek. They were Pavlov's pets when it came to doing as he said. Santiago was her man, her aide. And somehow, Zarek found out. Santiago was trustworthy, or she wouldn't have worked with him. If she'd learned something about big weapons, then why ensure her freedom now when he'd left her in the cane field. Why send Casta to make sure of it? He didn't know she had the stones, and if they were valuable, then he'd do everything to find her.

She'd had better odds before he stole her memory, that was for sure. She'd been in deep enough that he'd invited her into his world, specifically, his weapons arsenal. Her reputation as an art dealer with lucrative and less-than-reputable ties had found its way to him. He saw her as a new way to transport his goods with her art shipments. She had no reservations about him using her, since she was doing the same to him. Filtering weapons off the black market was her job. Yet she had problems with paying for them with U.S. funds. U.S. intelligence could only transfer computer-generated dollars once before the jig was up. So cash had to come into play. Lucien was slick, and the authorities—Interpol, Scotland Yard, Mossad, MI-5, ATF—had collectively arrested Zarek seven times with no convictions and ended up being sued and paying damages through the nose for busts gone sour. She'd had pictures, solid evidence of his arsenal, only the man moved it before she could do anything. As it was now, she was the only one who knew something big was in the works. Unfortunately, if her instincts were on target, what it was exactly had been erased from her memory.

She slowed and paused for a stoplight, straddling the small bike. Traffic moved in front of her, and she barely noticed it till a dark four-wheeler rolled past, then pulled over and made a U-turn.

Alexa sped off to the right, zipping in and out of traffic. The four-wheeler was three cars back, and gaining.

An intersection up ahead; the light was red. Alexa couldn't stop. She cut to the right, horns blew, tires screeched as she hopped the curb, flying down the sidewalk, scattering people, then darted back onto the road.

She didn't know who it was behind her, but she didn't want to meet them.

Killian swerved around a family trying to cross the street. They lurched back and he glanced in the mirror, cursing Alexa. "Outlaw, you up there?"

"Right over your head, Mustang."

"Get ahead of me."

"The bike is already at the airport. She's got at least ten to fifteen minutes on us, dammit. We're not going to stop her."

"The hell we aren't." Killian slammed his foot down on the gas, breaking speed limits, then minutes later, drove through the barrier of the private airport.

Colombian regulars opened fire.

Alexa strode into the small airport terminal and up to the desk. The attendant didn't look up. Too much makeup and big earrings, she thought. She'd get kicked off the U.S. airlines for that.

"I need a flight to Hong Kong."

The ticket agent looked up, her gaze moving over Alexa before she spoke. "We don't have any. Only the private jets."

She glanced to her right. The white Gulfstream jet gleamed on the flight line, its fuselage tucked to the boarding corridor. Luggage handlers were filling its belly. "I need a seat on it."

The woman gave her a pious look. "I'm sorry, it's a *private* jet," she repeated. "The owner specified the manifest." She dangled stapled sheets of paper like a tease.

It was enough for Alexa to shift her arms on the counter and knock over the luggage tags and pen cup. The woman cursed under her breath, hurrying to gather them up. Alexa leaned over, glancing at the screen, then the paper print of flights. There were three private charters out of here. One was Zarek's.

"Do you mind?" The ticket agent pushed her back. "No flight to Asia until the morning and that's to Peking."

But Alexa was already turning away, her head down, and her gaze darting around for watchers. She was walking past the wide glass windows when she saw the luggage handlers with Zarek's dog. The Afghan hound was so antsy, it was hard to miss. Zarek didn't go anywhere without the thin, sleek animal. Alexa swore he slept with it. Two jets, both to Hong Kong? That was like a call to "come and get me."

She had to get on that plane, right now. She slipped into the ladies' room, pacing, and thinking. A toilet flushed and a woman left a stall, a full flight bag on her shoulder. She threw Alexa a practiced smile, then washed her hands. Alexa went into a stall, waiting, and when the woman left, she did, too, following. The dark-haired woman walked toward the boarding area. The doors opened and a handler took her small flight bag. Alexa heard Spanish, laughter over having an easy flight and a big tip, then the stewardess went into a "staff only" room. Alexa took a deep breath, slipping in behind her. She didn't waste time—she didn't have it. The engines were already revving, the cargo handlers moving away from the craft.

The woman was scribbling on papers, and she turned, frowning. "You cannot be in here."

"Yeah, and I'm really sorry about this." The woman looked confused and Alexa put her whole body into a quick, powerful punch to her nose. The woman chirped in pain, eyes rolling as she folded and Alexa shot forward and eased her to the floor.

Alexa shook her hand, knuckles stinging. "How do guys do that all the time?"

She hurriedly stripped off the woman's uniform. She was dark-haired, so she could pass for her till the plane took off. Dressing quickly, she pinned on her ID, fluffed her hair and with her backpack, slipped out, then directly onto the boarding corridor. The boarding agent said good-bye and Alexa replied, masking her tone to match the other woman's as she hurried into the jet. She was the only flight attendant. *Well, I always wanted to make believe I was a stewardess,* she thought, plastering on a sweet smile and stowing her gear. She stuck her head in the cockpit, smiling and introducing herself.

The pilot frowned. "Where is MarieAnna?"

"Ill, very sudden, terrible cramps and bloating," she said, and the men flushed and turned toward the panel. That always did it with guys. She stepped back into the cabin, and grabbed the flight prep card. A quick glance and it was in her memory, though she'd flown enough to know it by heart. The engines whined, the aircraft shifted away from the corridor like a limb cut from a body. She stood in the door frame as the hydraulics lifted to close it.

Then she saw Moore running toward the jet. He slammed to a stop, shouting something, but the authorities grabbed him, hauling him back. Alexa smiled and waved a moment before the hatch sealed. Not a happy camper, she thought, securing the hatch and turning to walk the aisle. The cabin was elegant and equipped with all Gulfstream had to offer: sofalike seats, personal computers, phones, and movie screens. First-class.

Laughing inside, she asked the passengers to put the trays and seats in their upright position, and helped an elderly Asian man stow his flight bag. It wasn't until she was in the middle of the aircraft that she recognized a few faces.

And one of them was Alejandro Carrión.

Killian gave up the fight when the jet started its taxi. He shrugged off his captors, cursing and walking away from the jet's path. Riley rushed up to the police, making up a bullshit story about how his woman was on the plane and he couldn't bear to lose her. The white-helmeted troops looked at him pityingly and let him go.

Riley caught up with Killian. "I saved your ass from jail, you know."

"I'll show my appreciation in your paycheck."

"Wow. I'm all warm and fuzzy now."

Killian slid the Irishman a glance, and his lips curved a bit. "Tell Sam to get the chopper loaded. We fly as soon as we can."

"Where?"

"Wherever she's going; use the glib tongue and find out."

Riley stopped and did an about-face, heading for the terminal. The Latin women would never see it coming, Killian thought, angry at himself that Alexa slipped through his fingers again.

A few minutes later, Killian was leaning against the SUV when Riley walked toward him, smiling. "Want a phone number?"

"Jesus, Donovan."

"The jet is headed to China."

"Why'd it have to be Communists?"

"Due to land in Chai Wan Airport in nine hours or so."

"Hong Kong? Zarek has a coffee export business, and a trade deal with China."

"Guess it doesn't matter who gives you your morning coffee as long as you get the caffeine, huh?" Riley shrugged and slid behind the wheel of the SUV, turning over the engine.

"She was coming from the docks when we spotted her."

Riley drove, Killian didn't watch. The man learned to drive on the left side of the road with his foot permanently on the pedal. He turned the SUV into the jungle to the abandoned airstrip dealers and gunrunners used. Landing there had made it convenient to get into the cartel again and to get the hell out of here fast. Riley skidded to a jackrabbit stop at the deserted airstrip, kicking up a cloud of dust.

Killian met his gaze patiently. "Giving away our position again, Riley?"

Riley looked chagrined. "We're here, aren't we?"

Killian left the car and headed to the shiny black aircraft. It was already refueled and had been about two hours after they'd first landed here. Dragon Six wasn't pretty, wasn't a sleek javelin like the jet Alexa was in now. And she sure as hell didn't hit Mach One on take-off. He'd bought the cargo plane before it was salvaged for scrap, outdated and disabled. But between Sam, Riley, and Max, the thing flew like it just rolled off the factory floor and was a flying command center equipped with satellite links, Logan's computers and medical equipment, and Max and Riley's electronics. Not to mention Sam's chopper. The hydraulics were pulling the chopper into the cargo bay and he hopped on the lift, moving to secure a cable, then moved farther into the aircraft. The rear was for gear, and the smaller armed chopper fit neatly, its blades folded down. It was Sam's baby, souped up and hypercharged with a half dozen weapons and state-of-the-art tracking and radar. Riley had designed it and most was illegal as hell.

Logan secured his medical gear as he glanced, frowning. "You look ready to kill."

"Yeah, well, she's a slick little thing. She got on that plane so easily."

"And she looked damn cute in that uniform," Riley said, clearing the vehicle of gear and fingerprints.

Killian made a growling sound, glaring back at the man, then said to Logan, "I need Zarek's location. And open up all contacts in Hong Kong; I want her followed the minute she steps off that aircraft. Let them know she might look different. She had a backpack and she's got the skill to change her looks. Tap anyone you can." Aside from being a field surgeon, Logan was a computer expert, with skills that rivaled MIT grads and the best hackers. There wasn't much that could stop him. And those that did, hell, give him a couple hours.

"Roger that. What's she after that she's risking getting double-tapped in the head?"

"You read her dossier, her reports. She was a weapons specialist. Not rifles, grenades, but the big blasters:

JPams, stingers, heat-seeking SAMs, nukes, weapons of mass destruction. It was what she and the agency suspected Zarek of dealing."

"Then she knows something we don't," Logan added.

That was moot. "She's finishing what she started and going after the weapons."

"God love the little patriot," Sam put in, without stopping his prep of the chopper.

Killian ground his back teeth. "For who? Us or them? This doesn't figure. We need to know where the hell she's been for a month, if not with Zarek. He was concerned that she was with me, but didn't ask if she still was. He had to know we left together. There were enough witnesses."

"Maybe he already knew the lady had handcuffed you to the car and took off."

Killian's gaze narrowed, irritated with that still. That burning kiss was imprinted on his mind—forever. Damn it. "He knew she'd surface for some other reason." People all around her were trying to stop her, capture her, and she still kept going. Killian admired that kind of determination. "And I don't think he gave a damn. He was too confident about her."

"I got that, too," Sam said. "The man was jealous of Dominic Cane, but he didn't take it further. He had a tail on us the whole way, and to the airport." Sam grinned. "Poor guy's probably still pulling himself out of the ditch and wondering how he got two bullets in his tires."

"Price was lying, you know that," Logan said, securing the cases in the lockers anchored inside the aircraft.

"Oh, you think?" Killian said, moving forward toward the cockpit.

"It's possible Gavlin's not the Intel leak," Logan called out. "She's weapons, not drugs."

Killian looked back. "Let's not all sing her praises so fast. She can do what she wants or needs, she's an NOC. No control, no ethics. And I never believed Price, she's a trained liar. But don't forget, so is Gavlin." He walked into the cockpit, sat in the hot seat, and did the preflight check.

"Safe to come in?" Riley said after several minutes.

Killian smiled. "Yeah. It's her throat I want to wring."

"You didn't think this would be easy, did you, boss?"

Hell, no, but nothing was adding up. "Stop calling me that." Killian flipped switches and checked readouts.

"Yes, sir."

Killian glared.

"You've been running us like your company again, so I figured . . ." Riley shrugged, his Irish accent barely detectable.

"Sit, ass bag."

He did, saying, "We need to work on your people skills, Moore."

Killian put on the headset, adjusted the mike.

"Secure and ready to rock, Mustang," Sam said over the speaker. "All's clear out there, no Zarek in sight."

Killian powered up the engines.

"Oh, by the way," Riley said. "I got a look at the passenger list."

"And?"

"Carrión was on the jet."

"Well, shit."

"Yeah, I thought you'd like that."

Sipping a fine Riesling, Lucien stood on the balcony watching the white aircraft pass overhead. He'd paid well to have someone on the inside and be informed.

He smiled, then turned back into the hotel room, re-filled his glass, ready for the flight right behind his little fox.

Franco entered the room.

"Good, you're back." He'd send him to the compound, into his safe. "Bring the box to me." Lucien tossed him a single key.

Franco obeyed, his loyalty unquestionable. Lucien had saved his life a couple years ago when a gun dealer had wanted to cut off Franco's balls for some petty offense. Lucien had killed the entire group except the young man, taking him and the territory for himself. Behind him he heard the door open, Franco's heavy tread.

"Lucien," Franco said and he whipped around. Franco never dared call him by his first name. Unless he forgot himself.

The man moved forward, his expression sad. "The box, it's gone."

"No."

"*Sí*, the case is in there, but not the box."

Lucien stared at him, the ramifications hitting him and the goblet snapped in his fingers, splinters of glass dusting the floor.

The bitch had the stones. His plans depended on them.

"We leave, now. Now!"

"But what of the stones?"

"She has them, but she doesn't know what she has, Franco." The only person to get within feet of the stones was Jade and it didn't matter where or when, only that she had them. Lucien recognized his vulnerability where she was concerned. He'd allowed himself to trust her, even a little. He should have just killed her.

Lucien dusted the glass from his fingers, sucking a small cut. "We have to find her before she understands that." Lucien was already moving toward the door.

Yes, he thought. Or they were all dead.

Six

Day 18
Hong Kong, China

Carrión flirted through the entire trip. No subject was taboo and he was merciless, making no bones about wanting to sleep with her. To give her "hours of erotic pleasure," he claimed. For reasons she didn't want to examine, Killian's face popped into her mind. It ticked her off and made it easier to fend off Carrión. He wouldn't say why he was in Hong Kong other than business. He dealt in drugs, that pretty much said it all.

As the passengers stepped off the plane, he paused, his gaze devouring her from head to toe. "There is a gathering this evening, formal. Boring business, but you there with me would ease the pain of it."

"I'm a little tired from jet lag, Señor Carrión." Though that's not why she turned him down. She needed to see if *Red Emperor* had docked and what was on it. She prayed this wasn't the dumbest goose chase of her life. Since it was on the line.

"Please call me Alejandro."

"Jade." She figured she'd stick with what she knew.

"I can beg quite nicely, *mi dulce*."

"I'm sure you can. Please step off the craft, sir, the pilots have to pee."

He laughed and moved down the gangway. Alexa grabbed her things and left. Carrión was standing near a limo, smiling at her, and she didn't have to remind herself he might be charming and sexy, but he was also a killer. The deaths of DEA agents were firmly planted in her mind, forever. But what was he doing here, when he was last with Moore and Zarek? The tie was just too uncommon to ignore and she expected Zarek to show his face soon.

Alexa breezed through customs, the advantage of being on a private plane and skilled at evading authorities. The Hong Kong police were, if anything, thorough, but the flight attendant had a penchant for sexy underwear. Man bait. It was nasty enough for the police to avoid digging deeper in the bags. But it amused the heck out of Carrión.

She hailed a cab. It was time to shop for some equipment.

Hong Kong was ten times the size of Washington, D.C., but housed nearly seven million people. To say it was crowded was an understatement. But it was a beautiful city, tranquil despite the congestion. Alexa leaned up in the tub of luxurious bubbles and sighted through the binoculars. Her view of the harbor was excellent, the reason she'd chosen this hotel and the twenty-seventh floor. Not good for escape, but a terrific view. The accommodations were a hundred times better than her last hotel, for certain, and this time she was followed. She didn't recognize who it was, looked like some guy in the military, a pal of Moore's likely, but she'd evaded him easily enough by checking into one hotel, then slipping out the back, and going to another. Pay cash, false name, and be ready to move at a moment's notice.

She squinted at the harbor again. The ship hadn't docked, but it was out there, beyond the bay. Launches left the ship but only with men aboard. What were they waiting for? She'd paid a couple of shore men to keep watch, old resources of a friend. Behind her, the TV buzzed with CNN's third report in a half hour of the secretary of state making the rounds for world peace.

She shut it off, loving the quick silence, then eased back into the hot water, laying the field glasses beside her weapon. Hong Kong was gadget central. Anything could be had and she'd spent a small fortune in an hour equipping herself. She closed her eyes, the scented water soothing her battered body as she ticked off her next moves. Get some dinner, some rest, then get on the ship. She cracked one eye open, spied the silk box. The stones really were secondary right now. Her first order was to search the ship for weapons. Gut instinct said they were there. Evidence said Zarek wasn't that stupid. And then there was Moore, who was mad enough to be right behind her, and she wasn't looking forward to another encounter.

He had something that weakened her. Not so much his looks; she'd been around hundreds of handsome dangerous men. It could be that kiss, she thought, melting a little at the memory of it. He could touch her in places she didn't want any man to. The vulnerability warned her that connections had no place in her life. She'd avoided emotions like that, yet the only one she kept handy was her sense of commitment to duty. If she didn't feel the need to work in secrecy for her government, she wouldn't be here. No one else got hurt that way. No one to upset, worry . . . or to care.

She soaked till the water grew cold, then left the tub,

wrapping herself in the terry robe. She popped a soda from the bar and was going over her belongings, inserting batteries and checking sound when a knock startled her. She threw the spread over it and grabbed her Glock before answering the door.

A bellman with his arms full of packages startled her and discreetly, she tucked the gun in her robe pocket. "I didn't order anything."

He said nothing and handed her a small cell phone. It rang instantly. She hit send. "Hello."

"My ego would not let me believe you would not join me tonight."

"Alejandro?"

"You were expecting another man? You wound me."

Yeah, sure. "I wasn't expecting this." This meant switching hotels had failed.

"Good. I've surprised you, then."

Oh, yeah. "How did you find me?"

He chuckled, the sneaky bastard. If he could find her that easily, then so could Moore and Zarek. "What do you want?"

"For you to join me tonight, of course."

"It's formal, I don't have anything to wear." Sounded good enough.

"I have seen to that. Take the boxes from the bellman, *mi dulce*."

She did, setting them on the sideboard and when she went to tip the man, he refused and left.

"Keep the phone, I will pick you up at eight."

"Alejandro, I can't go to a party tonight. I'm busy." *Playing spy,* she thought.

"Eight."

The line went dead.

"God, I hate arrogant men," she muttered and threw the phone on the bed, then opened the first box. Oh, good Lord. When the man pushed, he *pushed*.

* * *

Killian glanced around the room. Several ounces of strategically placed C-4 and half the world's crime bosses would be history. That wouldn't stop the trade, but it had a nice ring to it.

He strolled, uncomfortable in the tuxedo, and listened to conversations, picking up details. Russian Mafia and Chechens were eyeing each other like a timer on explosives ready to ignite. It was nuts to be in the same room with some of these people. Apparently wanting to deal had them shelving their differences for the exchange of narcotics with the Triad. The purpose behind the dinner was secret, the clientele was not. There were enough DEA and the Ministry of State Security outside this room—he'd bet they looked like monkeys hanging around for a fresh banana. Intel officers and police couldn't get past the front door, though corruption was merely glanced at as long as communism stayed firmly in place.

Killian was wired, the camera undetectable in the jacket button of his tux. A ceramic mike in his ear was so small it would have to come out with tweezers. Logan and Riley were at the command post, a house in the hills. Max was on the outside, rounding up sources. He gave his empty glass to a waiter who never raised his eyes above his throat, and he was about to go out on the balcony for a cigar when the noise level dropped measurably. He glanced, then followed the attention of everyone's gaze.

"You guys see what I see."

"Now there's a fine-looking lass," Riley said, the words too loud in Killian's ear mike.

Yet like most of the men in the room with blood in their veins, it rushed to his groin. He stepped back out of her line of sight. Reddish brown hair, not the dark, nearly black she'd had before, spilled down her back, barely caught in some jewel at her crown. But it was her in the dress that had every man's attention.

It was her alone that had his. Gone was the scruffy woman with desperation in her eyes, her hair in knots and more dirt on her than the roads. The gown was no more than a plunging drape of something silky and pearl gray, showing off her tan, her muscles, and a tight ass that made him groan.

"Down, Killian, down."

"Jesus," he muttered. Then she smiled and it hit him between the eyes, dammit. He liked the grubby female better. She was easier to ignore.

Men moved near, wanting a closer look and she greeted them with poise and the grace of a woman used to this kind of attention but didn't think it her due. With every move, the fabric clung to her curves, her nipples, showing him the lushness of her body. The dip between her thighs.

Killian rubbed his mouth, grappling with his body's sudden need as his gaze rose past the rope of diamonds circling her throat and riding on the swell of her breasts, then to her face. He was in trouble. Catlike eyes, a pixie nose, she looked so delicate and fragile. Nothing like the woman who bravely stepped into the darkened jungle alone. He glanced around. The men stared, the women sent her dirty looks.

Carrión looked damn proud of himself.

The only thing unexpected about her on Carrión's arm was her transformation. Killian knew where she was staying the minute he stepped off his jet. Royal Pacific, twenty-seventh floor, harbor view. He had a room right next door, but he didn't expect her to stay there. Now Carrión knew. Or perhaps she was using the man, just as he was using her for arm candy. "Dress them in beautiful things and we look powerful." Well Carrión was armed and dangerous tonight.

Damn. He was hard. Just what he needed, a woman who could turn him on like a heat-seeking missile. Carrión left her to get her a cocktail and more men moved in. The twinge of jealousy sparking through him brought anger, and he paid attention to duty. She'd been accused of treason, had made no move to declare her innocence, nor tell him where she'd been for the past month. Or with whom.

He glanced to his right as another man entered a private well-guarded room. That had been going on all evening. Some left pleased, some royally pissed. Apparently the price of dealing with the Chinese Tong was too high for some and the weakest of the kingpins were shut out.

Killian made his move when Carrión disappeared into the room.

"Hello, wildcat."

She turned slowly, lifting her gaze as if she knew he was there. Probably did.

Alexa felt something clutch through her, seizing her heartbeat, her muscles. He shouldn't have this much affect on her, but those blue eyes and dark hair were a force to be reckoned with. She just had to remind herself that he was sanctioned to kill her and she could easily control her feelings.

"Moore." She looked around. "Alone? What a shame."

"Who says I am?"

"Your team doesn't count. Why are you here?" she asked.

"Following you."

"I'm touched you traveled about six thousand miles to do that."

"I told you I'd come after you."

"A man of his word, I like that. It's rare."

His gaze lowered to her breasts, the fabric barely holding them in. "That's some dress."

"This is Carrión's work, not mine. I'd have chosen something a little more conservative."

"So you can be bought for a gown and diamonds?"

Her eyes took on a feral gleam. "Is that what you think? That I can be had for gifts?"

He arched a brow. "How can you be had?"

Her lips tightened. "I should hit you."

"Go ahead."

"I'm above it."

"But not decking a flight attendant and stealing her clothes."

"Necessary." He knew too much. "A minor factor, and if you keep antagonizing me I'll make a nasty scene."

"And I'll cart your sweet ass out of here over my shoulder."

She tipped her head, looking more lovely. "You really have a caveman complex, don't you?"

Not before meeting her, he thought, annoyed with it. "Will you come peacefully?"

"Of course not. So are you going to kill me here?"

"You're so sure about me, aren't you?"

"I know the kind that Price hires."

"Like you."

She stepped closer, her voice low and her perfume stirring everything in him to a boil. "I've never taken an assignment to assassinate anyone. But you have."

The rage in her tone was subtle, viperous and stinging over him. Killian couldn't deny it, he had. The information he'd been given had no bearing on the truth. If he'd had clear evidence of her betrayal, he'd have killed her.

"The truth bites, doesn't it?" She shifted away, and he lightly caught her arm.

"You aren't getting away that easily."

Her gaze moved to Carrión coming toward them. "Wanna bet?"

His gaze flicked to the kingpin and he let go. "What are you looking for, Alexa?" he said before Carrión reached them.

My memory. "I lost something and I mean to get it back."

Killian understood that too well. "By finishing the assignment?"

"God, she gave you the file?" She glanced away and anger simmered in her eyes. "That's desperation." He knew about the weapons, her reports, her Intel! God, Lania, what have you done? Her gaze flashed to his, hard and so different Killian frowned. "They tried to kill us both. You agree?"

"I have a wound to prove it."

"Then look to Price or Zarek or somewhere else."

"I need to know where you've been for the last month."

"Sorry, no can do." Carrión was coming closer.

"Alexa." Killian moved closer, hemming her in, and forcing her to look him in the eye. "We can figure this out."

We. There never was a *we* anything in her life, not since her parents were killed. That weakness attacked her again, the need to share, to not be so alone. But she couldn't. Alexa knew her job well and everyone was not as they seemed. Even her. She couldn't remember the last time she was just herself and not putting on someone else's personality or clothes for the job. Like now.

"Ahh, Dominic," Carrión said, coming up beside

them and slipping his arm around Alexa. He handed her a flute of champagne.

Dominic? Alexa's brow knit for a second, then smoothed as she took a quick sip. She didn't blow his cover. It was to her advantage to keep it.

"Alejandro." Killian rocked back on his heels, his hands clasped at his back. But his eyes were locked on her.

"You know each other?"

"Look closely, Carrión."

He did, his gaze bouncing between them. Then he chuckled. "Then I was right, she wasn't aware she was your woman."

Alexa's eyes flared, then her lips curved in a delicious smile. "He assumes quite a bit." She shifted closer to Carrión and gave him a splendid view of her breasts.

But Killian wasn't so easily played. "We need to talk, darling," he said, snatching the flute from her and passing it off to Carrión. He swept Alexa in his arms, into a dance. "You'll give me a fighting chance, won't you, Carrión?"

Carrión's eyes narrowed with his tone. "Only because I do not want to have to kill you, Cane."

Killian knew he meant it.

Over his shoulder, Alexa threw Carrión her best "save me from this soon" look, and yet let Moore pull her farther onto the dance floor. He moved with surprising ease and grace as if he'd danced with her all his life, and she was instantly bombarded with sensations. His height, how he made her feel small and delicate, the scent of him, and his eyes boring into her. She inhaled deeply, trying for logic, yet feeling her hand on his broad shoulder, his around her waist. The warmth of his broad palm made her want to peel the gown off and feel it against her skin.

Slowly, she lifted her gaze. "Very clever, telling him we were acquainted."

"I do what's necessary."

She didn't have to say she would, too. Then he urged her closer, his words a whisper in her ear. "What were you doing at the docks in Colombia?"

"Catching fish."

"Why come here?"

"The food, the nightlife. Then there is the incredible shopping."

His features tightened. What a hard case. "You can trust me."

"You're packing a bullet with my name on it."

"If I did, you'd be dead."

She stopped, stared. "Price won't stand for failure."

"I can handle Price." He pulled her back into the dance.

Alexa scoffed. Let him think that. "Leave it alone, Moore."

His lips grazed her ear, sending a delicious chill down her throat as he said, "It's Cane, Dominic."

"Pleased to meet you. I'm Jade Everett."

"You're in deep trouble."

She met his gaze, plastering on a fake smile. "Look, Cane, I don't trust you. I never will. Deal with it. You don't want to go all gallant and try to protect me. You'll get killed. So do yourself a favor and back off."

She pushed out of his arms and walked to Alejandro, pretending anger, with her body still warm from his, her heart hopping all over Hong Kong and back, damn it. She smiled at Carrión, lacing her arm with his and brushing a kiss to his cheek.

"Everything fine or I dare hope, not fine?"

She didn't commit to a thing. "He's persistent, that's all." She offered a bright smile for him alone.

Alejandro reached, the back of his fingers grazing

her jaw and sliding down to the pulse in her throat. "You are so lovely."

"I won't sleep with you, Alejandro." She wasn't accomplishing anything here except complications. She unclasped the diamond collar, dropping it into his hand, then added the earrings.

His expression turned moody and sexy. "And if I ask for the dress back?"

"It's not your color." She turned away and felt both men watching her cross the room.

Killian's gaze traced her, the sexy walk a treat for the eyes. She smiled at the men ogling her, acknowledging the compliment with a nod. He wouldn't have noticed more except for an elderly Korean fur trader's expression. As if wondering who she was and why she was here.

Carrión moved up beside him. "Apparently we both lost, Cane."

"Not yet," he said, and spared Carrión a glance. The man grinned. Jesus. Happy little fucker.

"I understand why you want her, though. She's beautiful, witty and has a—"

"A body that'll haunt your dreams."

"Yes, there is that." Carrión spilled the diamond necklace from hand to hand.

"Don't interfere. You know how I can be."

Carrión's gaze thinned sharply. "You would fight me?"

"You'd lose." Then Killian went for the whole ball of wax. "You have others, this one has my heart."

"Oh, my friend, so little ruins your objectivity like a woman, especially one like that. Do not let your heart be involved. Only the appearance of it. You should kill her, then."

Killian hid his shock. "And the reasoning behind that is?"

"Take away the threat and keep the power in your palm."

Carrión pocketed the necklace, giving her a longing glance as she left. Then he sighed and turned, searched the crowd of women, spied his preference, then started walking.

Killian turned away, and said softly, "You guys on her?"

The reply came through the ear mike. "Like white on rice."

From his suite of rooms Lucien watched her, the cameras scanned well enough, and he leaned forward, touching the screen. He could almost feel her skin beneath his. She looked better in green. Gray was a poor choice. She definitely didn't have the stones on her in that gown.

Franco slipped into the room.

"Where is she staying?"

"We followed Carrión from the Royal Pacific."

Kowloon. "Did you search her rooms?"

"There was nothing in them."

Lucien looked up from the screen.

"Except a soda can and dirty towels. She'd cleared out."

Lucien cursed. She knew she was being watched. He should have taken her tonight. But Carrión assured him he'd keep tabs on her; the man didn't care which authorities saw him. Lucien turned the screen toward him, connected the cable and logged on.

He typed. *Zhu King awaits. The royal seal has arrived.*

Then hit send. He watched the screen, taking a sip of aged whiskey. The soft ping announced new mail, and he opened it.

An audience is requested. Celebration in his honor.

Translated, they wanted a meet.

Lucien replied, *The moon rises on the blue water.* On his ship.

Confirmation came in a blank e-mail.

It didn't make him smile as he logged off, cleared the history and trail. He didn't know who he was speaking with. That was the beauty of this. No trail. No names. The only connection was the stones.

He turned back to the screen, searching for her, then lurched forward, spinning the camera. "She's gone!" He was out of the chair and moving to the windows. "Radio the guards." Lucien saw her hail a cab. "She's leaving, stop her! Now!"

Then it was too late. The cab was speeding away.

He cursed. He couldn't follow, he had a meeting to make that was more vital.

Franco returned, huffing out of breath. He shook his head.

"Keep looking, Franco. Don't stop till you locate her."

The darkness folded around her as the small junk meandered through Star Harbor, steered by an old Mandarin woman who sold food to the sailors and shore men from the junk like a floating diner. Alexa nibbled on fried dim sum as the boat drew closer to the large ship. The old lady didn't ask questions. Money talked enough for her. She never spoke, took the cash and steered the vessel. Alexa would have swam if it were in the harbor but it was on the edge of the bay. The threat of sharks nipped that idea. Movement aboard was the norm for a ship at port. Launches left for the city full of crew ready for a night of drinking and women.

The junk neared, sweeping quietly alongside.

"Near the anchor," she said softly in Chinese.

The woman nodded and maneuvered. Alexa stood on the bow and as the woman slowed the vessel, she leaped at the thick anchor chain, wrapping her arms and legs around it. The junk slid away as if it had never stopped. She got the feeling the old lady had done that before.

Alexa gained footholds in the fat links, and hoisted herself up, her muscles screaming with a burn. She used to be in better shape, and attributed that to the month of missing memory. She strained, her body perspiring under the black cat suit, the small pack adding to her workload. She reached the top, under the aft line, and was small enough to slip through the anchor line collar, but didn't want to risk it. Her hips might not be as slim as she thought. She peered through the opening. Men moved in and out of cabins, some just chatting quietly and drinking. The ship lacked luxury, dirty, rusty and even from here the scent of coffee overpowered the salty air. Shipboard lights were no more than bare bulbs strung along the gangway. Half were burned out.

She dangled on the rail, swinging her foot up and trying to catch the lip. *Wish I was a ninja,* she thought, then caught the rim. In moments, she was crouching on the deck, and scanning her surroundings. She spied the forward hatch and moved low around the keels of rope, equipment, and a forklift. She heard voices, and slipped to the edge of the pilothouse, flattening against the wall. She peered, and got a view of the corridor along the housing to the aft deck.

Lucien. Of all the luck.

She shifted back and closed her eyes briefly, then took another peek.

Two more figures moved into view. Two dark-haired men. Carrión? She couldn't tell; he had his back to her.

There was another man, short, skinny and Chinese. He didn't look happy. He wasn't shouting, the Chinese were too poised for that. Just stiff and reined in. Lucien looked as if he were trying to persuade the man. Zarek usually demanded.

Alexa turned in the opposite direction, ducking through the hatch. Inside, she followed her nose down into the belly of the ship. She was almost hoping the gut feeling she'd had since finding the stones and note was wrong. If she was right, there were missiles aboard. She'd take care of those, somehow, but her real fear was, who was buying them? And what country would be the unfortunate target.

Her quick steps were soundless in felt-bottom boots, cushioned as she overtook the steel stairs. The area above was strung with catwalks, a loading hatch open in amidships. A crane would hoist the crates out and onto the deck, then off the ship. Antiquated, she thought and skipped the last flight of stairs and shimmied down a bracing pole. She dropped to the deck on the balls of her feet, then moved to the pallets stacked about six feet high. She went to the largest of the long wood boxes.

She unhooked the cable line, careful to lay it aside without a sound. With her knife, she cut the ropes, then glanced around for a crowbar, and grabbed one from the floor. Voices filtered down to her, men laughing and getting drunker, and she waited impatiently till the noise level rose a notch and pried open the box. Coffee—in thick burlap sacks.

She cracked another crate, then another. Coffee. Then she spied a stack that wasn't as high as the rest, only two levels. She crawled to it and it took all her strength to pry it open. The wood cracked loudly. Should have bought a reverse drill to take out the screws. She stuck her hand inside. More coff—

A hand closed over her mouth, one around her waist, and yanked.

Alexa threw her head back into the assailant's face, drove her elbow into his solar plexus, then slammed her fist into his groin. He grunted and buckled as she pulled her knife from the leg sheath as she twisted and clipped him behind the knee. He dropped to the deck on his back, and she was on him, straddling his chest and pinning his arms with her knees as she swept the knife under his throat.

Within a black mask, blue eyes stared back. Shock bolted through her.

"Moore?" She yanked off the mask.

"Now this is an interesting position, wildcat."

Alexa looked down. Her crotch was nearly in his face.

"But I have a better one."

Before it registered, he bucked, knocking her knees off his arms as he lunged forward. The force drove her down onto the deck with a breath-jarring smack, and Killian landed snugly between her thighs.

Then, the idiot smiled.

It dissolved as Alexa put the point of her blade under his chin and said, "I like being on top."

Seven

"I'll have to remember that."

"Don't bother, it'll never happen." Who was she fooling? She wanted this man from the moment she laid eyes on him. And now he was lying between her legs, availing her with every detail that was between his. God, he was so . . . warm—and *there*.

"You planning on using that?" His gaze flicked to the knife.

She let her arms drop. "Why do you keep at this?" she whispered.

"You're stubborn and stupid to be in here." His eyes darkened. "You're looking for weapons."

No sense in denying it. He had her Intel file. "Well, it's a lost lead, there aren't any. Do you mind? You weigh a ton. And I think I have steel shavings in my butt."

"Want me to check?"

She scoffed, shoved at his chest. It was like trying to move a tree. Killian eased back. Alexa rolled and crouched behind the crates.

"You couldn't have searched them all." Killian had his back to a crate, occasionally peering around the edge for unfriendlies.

"No, but I have to," she whispered.

"You know he's up there."

"Yeah, with several armed men, so?"

Killian shook his head. "You're supposed to arrive when *their* defenses are low, not yours. Why risk your life?"

"It's my job, and you risked a lot more dealing rifles with Zarek."

His brows shot up. It was uncanny that he'd sensed her and kept that to himself, yet told her about the assault rifles.

"I'm surprised you didn't just kill him for those MPs."

"You seemed to need him alive for the moment."

She looked up sharply. *Does he really believe me,* she wondered, yet knew he was doing everything he could to lull her into trusting him. "So are you going to just bitch at me or give me a hand?"

Killian thought something happened just then, resolution, concession, he didn't know. It paid not to examine his feelings around her. She had a way of digging them up and spreading them around. "You go left, I'll go right."

It didn't slip past Alexa that going right was in the line of fire and out in the open. Men were so macho sometimes. She crawled to the next crate, cracking the lip. She dug her hand in and found nothing but bags of coffee beans. Damn.

How can I be so wrong, she thought, then reminded herself she was here on nothing but a hunch.

The catwalk rattled and Moore ducked, glancing at her. She was flat between two crates, her body blending into the decking. Above them men walked and Killian prayed they didn't look down too hard or they'd see her sweet round butt.

Alexa was perfectly still, a shadow. Killian listened,

judging when they were far enough toward the other side of the hull to move. He turned, watching the guards. One looked down, scanning the area, following it with his rifle barrel. Shit. One movement and they'd open fire, ask questions later.

Across the deck, Alexa breathed shallowly. She couldn't tell where the sound was or who it was from her position between the pallets. Everything echoed off the sides of the hull. *Stay down, Moore,* she thought, *don't be a hero.*

But she knew he was smarter than that. Than her. Hell, she'd hotel-hopped across Hong Kong and Kowloon, and he still found her. But then, he had other men watching. The odds were just not in her favor.

Well, there was Zarek's ship, you ass. Anyone could find it. And he knew she wanted inside. She almost laughed, the air moving slow into her lungs. Then she smelled it. Oil. Chemicals. Something bitter. Not gear grease from the pulleys or the heavy equipment in here; it was familiar. Yet she couldn't pinpoint it, not with the scent of coffee.

Something touched her foot and she went rigid.

"It's clear."

She eased back.

"Let's get out of here. We can come back."

"Like hell. It'll be too late, everything could be off-loaded into the port, and we'll never have access like this. And I smelled oil." She gestured. "Open this one." Killian met her gaze in the dim light, realizing he'd never get out of here till she was satisfied. He went for the crowbar, prying the lid, easing the screws out. He didn't have to open it all the way for the impact to hit them.

"Mother of God."

Killian's features went taut. "We're in some big trouble." He looked down the length of the missile.

Russian. Medium range ballistic. It could travel fifteen hundred miles before hitting a target.

"Where's the rest of it?"

Killian frowned.

"It's in pieces. Look." She pointed. "The nose cone is missing, but the guidance is here. Unassembled they are just junk. And these aren't new."

"No, but laser guided."

"They look like SSN-2s."

"Then where are the launchers?"

"Out there." She gestured to the length of the ship. It was the size of a football field and this was the first half dozen crates.

"We can't search the entire ship."

"I know." She eased the lid quietly aside, then instantly pulled off her pack, and slipped out a case of tools.

"Leave it," Killian said.

"I have to . . ."

"Get killed?"

She put on a pair of magnifying glasses. "Danger and death are two different things, right?"

"Now that's just plain mean."

"So are these. This is no different than you buying rifles off Zarek."

She had him there.

"Check some crates, see if there are more guidance housings."

"And do what? It would take days to search all this, and you can't blow them up."

"Not with me in here, no, thank you. But I can take out the guidance chips to figure out what the yield is, till I can blow them." That would give her some extra information.

He moved away for a few minutes, then slid back

beside her. "I found some parts, under the coffee crates. Looks like the fuel ignitions."

"The coffee will discourage any scents the customs dogs would pick up. I'm betting there are drugs in here, too."

Killian kept watch, glancing as she laid the plate cover carefully on the body of the missiles before going deeper. "You know what you're doing, right?"

"Of course. But I feel the need to warn you that if there is enriched uranium in here, one touch on the wrong circuit and they could detonate."

"Jesus H. Be careful."

She flashed him a bright grin. "Trust me."

Killian thought *he* had nerves of steel. Alexa probed, lifting out wires and computer components. Killian kept watch, his weapon out, his back to her. His gaze moved to the entrances, the stairs and catwalks. He glanced at his watch. Security watches would be making shift changes soon.

"Someone's going to spot my Zodiak."

She met his gaze, paling. "Well, that was stupid."

"I was assuming you'd make the right decision and leave with me."

"Well, we see how well that turned out, huh?" She lifted out the guidance chip like tweezing out a splinter, and dropped it in his hand.

"Keep working." Killian thought she looked like a bug there for a second with the magnifying glasses. He moved boxes, and uncrated another housing. She got busy, doing her thing. "Any idea who he's selling them to?" he whispered, loosening screws with his knife instead of cracking the wood lids with a crowbar.

She shrugged, setting the cover aside and straining to reach inside the housing. "Kazakstan, Uzbekistan . . . Whogivesafuckistan. In anyone's hands, it's a terrorist weapon."

"Got that right." He restacked the coffee crates.

"I have to watch this ship. If they off-load, I'll follow."

"Oh, hell no. This is proof enough. Let the Chinese Intel take it from here."

She looked up briefly. "Would you? Who's to say they aren't in on this? No customs seals? No Chinese inspectors, yet this ship has been here for a few days? And I *want* them to be off-loaded and transported." She focused on getting the chip out. "My mission isn't done till I find out who the buyers are. The buyers are someone with enough greed, hate, and money to get more than this batch. I sure as hell don't want Russian SSNs floating around on the black market. Besides, they could get more guidance chips."

Killian held up the one, and broke it.

"Not good enough. Zarek has money and the connections. He could have them Fed-Exed in a day."

The catwalk rattled. Killian whipped around. Men spotted movement and opened fire. A hail of bullets plinked into the surrounding crates. "Time to split!"

"I have to get the chip out."

"Christ, woman!" He flipped the bolt of the machine pistol and fired back three times, then three more. It barely made a sound and without looking Alexa knew there was a custom-made silencer on the thing. She heard two successive thunks to the ground, and swallowed.

Overhead, men spilled onto the catwalk, a barrage of gunfire taking out chunks of the crates and cooking coffee beans. "Jesus, don't they know what's down here! Hurry up!"

Alexa struggled to get the chip out. "Don't rush me." Her hands shook and she took a deep breath, let it out and plucked the chip free.

"Wildcat, we have to go. No time for cleanup."

"Those guys don't know what's really up. Zarek never tells anyone anything except Franco. They'll think we were caught stealing and had to flee." A bullet sank into the crate near her shoulder. "Would you just shoot something, please."

Killian fired, taking out a man, and when he glanced and saw her put the last screw in the missile, he grabbed her, pulling her behind him. "Outta time, baby."

"Okay, okay." They masked up and she drew her gun, aiming at the doors, and picked wood near a man who entered without looking first. She couldn't kill a man who was just guarding.

Killian rushed to the stairs, Alexa behind him. "The odds are piss-poor, stay back there."

"Oh, jeez. Don't go all hero on me, will you?" He didn't respond, moving quickly forward, and Alexa covered him. He didn't need it. Killian disarmed a man so quickly she heard grunts and bones crack. He didn't leave it at that, and with the man's head at his chest, he gave it a quick snap to the side, laid him down and went for the next. As if eager for the tangle. He let them think he was unarmed, arms up, then whipped out a blade from under his collar behind his neck, driving it in and out of a guy's chest with such force, he couldn't scream. Killian looked back, sheathing the bloody blade, then motioned to her.

Alexa stepped over bodies, keeping her gaze on him. Jeez, and she'd pulled a knife on this man?

She followed him through the hatch, up a nearly vertical staircase onto amidships. Killian didn't speak, motioning to the windward side, aft. Great, they were at the wrong side of the ship. She nodded, moving with him, her Glock out. Killian eased backwards, scanning the level with his machine pistol.

It was too quiet, she thought, too easy. The place was deserted. They were halfway to the leeward side when gunshots came from two directions. Rapid fire from the deck. Alexa dove for cover and a shot whizzed past her. Killian didn't give her time to think on it, grabbed her arm and shoved her toward the rail.

"Jump!" He laid down cover fire as he ran low and fast, grabbing her around the waist and bailing over the side of the ship.

The impact of the fifty-foot drop was like landing on wet concrete, tearing her from his arms. Killian popped through the surface, looking first at the ship, then for her. She was already grabbing the lines and crawling onto the Zodiak. Then she moved to the engine. For a second, he thought she'd leave him behind when she turned the craft in a fan of foaming water. She rode the curve alongside him, throwing out the towline and Killian grabbed on, rolling into the boat as it sped across the water.

He crawled to her, taking over.

Shots fired, disappearing into the water too damn close. Alexa looked toward the shore; the crowd of smaller boats floated aimlessly in the harbor.

"We can get lost in there." She pointed, holding on as he pushed the throttle forward. "Toward the ferry." Water sprayed them as the boat thumped on the waves.

Killian suddenly twisted, searching the night sky near the ship. "Oh, hell. Jump."

Her gaze followed his. Rockets? "I'm jumping, I'm jumping." She dove.

The mortar round hit the dead center of the Zodiak.

"Czy nie palic sie! Do not fire!" Zarek lunged to stop the launch, then watched in horror as the rocket arched toward the rubber boat. The explosion was instant and fatal, blasting the darkness with yellow-white

light. Debris soared into the air. Yet his gaze was on the black water as he demanded the searchlights.

Then nothing. No sign of life. Only the white churn of the remains of the boat sliding into the sea. He gripped the rail. This ruined it all. Fury swamped him and he whipped around, and drew his weapon. The crew stepped back. He aimed at the man still holding the launcher, and fired. His skull exploded.

"Anyone else want to fail me?" He threw the gun aside and walked off.

Carrión walked to the rail and looked at the water, frowning as he flicked at skull fragments on his jacket, then stripped it off and tossed it over the side of the ship.

This was too messy for his tastes. Something had to be done.

He hadn't seen a face, but the body of a woman was unmistakable.

Killian dove under water as black as ink, searching for her by feel. He caught a piece of the boat, some rubber, and he surfaced, his gaze snapping around for her.

Alexa. Jesus. Then he caught sight of the slick wet reflection on her suit, the shoulder torn to the skin. She was facedown. He swam hard, grabbing her and turning her over. She didn't move, and she wasn't breathing.

Aw, hell. He was just starting to like her. He treaded water long enough to try his com link. "Mustang to base, Mustang to base!"

Nothing. He swam for shore, water and debris hampering. He held her above, praying he was wrong. Blood filled his eyes as he fought the current. Small boats littered the shoreline, junks and high-priced speedboats. Killian swam toward one idling. A man was staring at the explosion, a woman holding a wineglass in her hand. Killian latched onto the side, rocking the craft, and they looked at him.

"Drive for shore," he ordered. When the man glanced between him and the ship, he shouted, "Now!"

Some rapid Chinese went on between the couple and the young man obeyed, trying to help them in. "No! Drive this damn thing!"

He couldn't waste time. Alexa had been out or dead too long. The man gunned the boat toward shore and the drag on his strength tested his muscles. The boat curled toward shore and when Killian felt his feet touch down, he let go and put her over his shoulder, hoping to push water out of her lungs. On solid ground, he laid her on her back and performed CPR.

He could use Logan right now, he thought, breathing into her mouth. "Jesus, Alexa, you keep being a pain in my ass."

He pushed on her chest. One, two, three, breathe, one, two, three. He checked her pulse. Crap. He tried his radio.

"Dammit, you guys, get here, she's dying."

No, he thought, she was dead.

People walked near, watching, speculating. A drunk stumbled close but Killian unhooked the machine pistol bandoleered across his chest and kept working, forcing air into her lungs and keeping her brain alive. The screech of tires, the slam of doors.

"Jesus, Killian." He looked up, Max and Logan pushed through the crowd, then Logan knelt and opened his case.

"Keep working, Kill." He cleared the defibrillator pads, watching the gauge as it charged. "Open her clothes."

Killian flipped out his knife and slit the catsuit open, spreading it as Logan slapped the paddles to her chest.

"Clear." The jolt made her arch.

Max crouched, checking her pulse and shaking his head. Killian pushed them back, continuing CPR, while the paddles charged.

"Come on, Alexa, fight! You're too damn stubborn to let this take you." Over his head, Max and Logan exchanged a look.

"Get back," Logan said and hit her with another jolt.

Max checked her pulse. "Something. Very faint."

Logan used his stethoscope. "Come on, little gal, show us your strength," he whispered, putting the oxygen mask over her mouth and Killian squeezed the bulb. Logan readied the defibrillator again, about to hit her when she flinched and coughed.

Logan turned her on her side. Water spilled and she choked, a gurgling sound that made Killian let out a long breath and sit back on his rear.

He rubbed his hand over his mouth, then leaned forward. "Alexa, look at me. Look at me!" He gathered her close. Her lids fluttered but didn't open. Her lips moved, and he bent to hear her.

"Bad first date," she mumbled. He groaned, kissed her forehead, then stood with her in his arms.

Max pushed people back, Logan gathered his equipment, and Killian cradled her in his arms and carried her to the SUV. Alexa was unconscious, limp in his arms.

Inside the truck, he looked out the window at the crowd of shore men and drunks, gang members and the filth. Police were driving down the street toward them as Max and Logan climbed in.

"Let's move, Max. Now! Now!" If the cops questioned them, it would be all over.

They were speeding away as the Hong Kong harbor

patrol pulled onto shore. The HK police were coming toward the docks.

"We have to hide, right now. Pick a place." Killian held her close, his lips pressed to her temple as the car sped through the wharf to parts unknown.

Day 19

Alexa stirred in sleep and wished she hadn't. One hell of a ride, she thought, shifting.

"Careful, darlin', you took some heat from that blast."

It wasn't Killian's voice and she opened her eyes. A brown-haired man's face swam in her vision. She blinked. Whoa. Cute. "Who are you?"

"Logan Chambliss, ma'am."

She detected the Carolina accent instantly. "Where from?" she said, letting hers slide back into her voice.

He smiled, but not quite to his eyes. "Low country," was all he said, then moved away.

So much for pleasant conversation, she thought as he gathered up gauze and syringes. Her gaze moved to the far side of the red-walled room. It was gaudy, with lots of gold tassels, and three men leaning against a wall like an ad for tight T-shirts and worn Levi's. The door opened and Killian stepped inside. He had a small cut on his forehead near his hairline but other than that, he looked fine.

She inched up, then slapped her hand to the sheets, covering her chest. "I'm naked."

"We noticed that, lass."

She looked at Killian. "You recruited the Irish?"

"Riley was a runner for the IRA till his mother caught him and shipped him to the U.S."

"She feared for my immortal soul, you know. I'm an American citizen, love. Former Marine, and damned

pleased to meet you. Finally." He winked and Alexa thought he was darling, boyishly handsome, and filling out those jeans quite nicely.

"The brooding bull is Sam Wyatt." Sam only nodded, staring too hard. "I'm Max Renfield," the third man said. The crinkles around his eyes said he smiled a lot.

She inclined her head to the door. "Are there any more out there?"

"Not in the country."

Alexa fell back into the pillows, scanning the room. "This has got to be the ugliest hotel in Hong Kong."

"That's because it's the House of Seven Immortals."

"A whorehouse?" She slid a glance at Moore. "Me. Alone with four men, I hope you're not implying something by that."

Killian let a smile work loose. "We're in Tong territory."

Her eyes rounded. "Oh, bad choice, Moore, really bad." She started to get up.

"We're okay for now. Just customers. And paying well."

"For what, exactly—no, don't answer that." She pointed at Riley, who was grinning. God, what a hottie.

Killian threw Riley a dark look. "Out, all of you."

"Hmm. Possessive. Remember, Killian, she's a trained liar," Riley said.

Alexa's brows rose.

"So are you, Donovan."

"Yes, but I don't have a badge that says so."

"Neither do I," she snapped, irritated that they were talking around her.

Killian closed the door, his back to her for a moment before he faced her. With her staring up at him like that, wrapped in lavender silk sheets, she looked frail and small. Nothing like the ball-busting woman on the ship.

"I was dead."

He nodded, not liking the feelings racing through him. CPR on the docks with a half dozen drunks stumbling around was not the way anyone in her profession wanted to go out.

"Why did you save me? You could have let me drown and be done with the whole mess. Price would have been satisfied."

"I wouldn't have."

There was an edge to his voice. She didn't care. He got into her business and the consequences were his problem. "I want my clothing."

"It's shredded."

"This is a house of women, find me some. Where's my gear?" He gestured to the chair. "I assume you went through it."

"Thoroughly."

Alexa was glad now that she didn't have the stones with her. Clutching the sheet, she grabbed the bag, sifting through her equipment. She wasn't shocked to find it all soaking wet, but she was when her fingers closed over the Glock. He didn't take it? She pulled it out, checked the load, then stuffed it back in. "Clothes, please."

"You don't like being naked?"

"Not without good reason," she snapped, tossing the backpack back in the chair. "Get a long look, did you?"

His lips quirked as his gaze moved over her bare spine. "Logan wouldn't let me. And quit bitching, he's the doc, not me. He didn't know what else happened to you."

It shouldn't bother her, but it did. Not that all of them got a good look at her, but that it was like waking in the field again. Disoriented and isolated. No barricades. The only difference now was Killian staring at her like he wanted to jump into her head and peel it open. She clasped her hands. "You have questions, ask them."

Killian moved to the window, peered, then faced her. He folded his arms like a man throwing up his own defenses. "I need honesty, Alexa."

She nodded, willing to reveal only so much. "What about?"

"Three years ago the DEA had an undercover operation in Colombia."

Her brows shot up. That wasn't what she expected to hear. "Yes, to get Carrión. It failed." Badly.

"Were you involved?"

"In part, yes."

His features tightened, his voice taut. "Elaborate please."

"That mission is classified."

"Don't push me . . . Looker."

Her eyes flared wide. Oh, no. Looker was her NOC code. The one word linked with her real identity and only one person had access. That bitch. *Lania's thrown me to the wolves.*

"Alexa!"

She flinched. "All right! I was to pass information I learned to undercover DEA agents in the jungle with Carrión's cartels."

"Did you?"

"Yes. My part was to get in, deliver, and get out, nothing more. At the time, I was developing my own assets. Some were drug runners. And for reference, I'd never met Carrión till seeing him on the jet to here, and I didn't want to. I've seen his calling cards." The image of her first asset gutted from neck to nuts flashed in her mind and made her shiver.

"You vanished in the middle of the operation." That was the key to it. She'd passed info and left a dead trail, showing up months later, according to Price.

"It was a little hard to move around when I was tied to a stake in the ground." He scowled, impatient for the rest. "I was to meet with a DEA agent. I was at the rendezvous point, waiting. Rebels came and I took off but I wasn't fast enough. I was captured by ELN rebels and stuffed in a box."

"For how long?"

"Eighteen days and seven hours. They demanded ransom, but no one paid, of course. I don't exist."

He lowered his arms. "Then how'd you get out?"

"The DEA bust turned into a bloodbath all around the encampment. Some escaped, ran, who knows . . . I couldn't see much, but there was no one left to antagonize me and no one knew I was there." She looked away, staring at nothing and having no trouble remembering the details. "There was gunfire for hours, I could see only slivers of the battle through the slats." She flipped the sheet back, showing him a long thin scar on her upper thigh. "A shot went into the hut, then it got really quiet. About a half hour passed before I heard helicopters, but couldn't see who manned them. Didn't matter. I couldn't be seen or *my* Op and cover would be blown to hell. Too many questions. They left without even searching the area. I was staked close to the ground at the neck and foot."

She scooped her hair off her shoulders and twisted. Faint rope burns drew a line halfway around her throat. She let it drop and met his gaze. "The floor was dirt, I'd already started digging, but it took me two more days to dig my way out. By then the bodies were in rapid decay in the heat. There wasn't one undercover agent among them." His expression hadn't changed one iota since she started talking. "You don't believe me."

"I have good reason not to."

"How so?" She threw her legs off the bed, wrapping the sheets like a toga. He went to a black case she hadn't noticed before, next to the doctor's pack. He removed a file, and handed it to her. *Eyes Only.* She stared at it, trying to wrap her mind around the fact that he had Price's files with him.

"There was an Intel leak, Alexa. A big one." She lifted her gaze to his. "Carrión knew about the DEA agents. His men picked them off like buzzards on a fence."

She opened the file, reading, flipping pages, and reading again. Shock ripped through her, settling hard in her bones. This is wrong, all wrong, she thought. "No wonder you came after me." And let her live so he could interrogate her.

He'd paid for it with his career, his reputation. He'd been on the inside of Carrión's operation. Undercover. There was no other intelligence, nothing that said she was a relay. "This is incomplete."

Killian took the report and returned it to the case.

"You have to believe me."

"No, I don't. I was accused of being the leak and had nothing to back it up, no way to confirm that I didn't give up the agents to Carrión!"

"But Price knew what I was doing for the operation. She knew!"

He said nothing, staring at her, obviously weighing his information against her confession. If she were in his shoes, she wouldn't believe her either. "I was setting up Zarek."

He scoffed. "For three years?"

She gave him a sarcastic glare. "No, not only him. I was working on other assignments, one in Morocco, but he was all over the place, talking to the wrong people then and I had to make him come to me. Spent that year on an operation in Morocco, then cultivating assets in Colombia. I was in and out of the country. I'd run an antiques shop in three countries, high prices, wealthy clients, connections. Killian—" He met her gaze. "I wouldn't do this to you, to anyone. I have no reason to, you have to know that by now."

"How could I? Your dossier is on weapons and retrieval, nothing about you. Or where you've been for the last month."

"I can't discuss that." If he knew she'd lost a month of her memory along with all the intelligence Zarek could have gathered, he'd shoot her now. Fresh fear riddled her skin with heat and she closed her eyes. He had every reason to want to kill her. She'd nothing except her word to back herself up. The report was sketchy, leaving her out of the final draft. Which was typical. Reports found their way all around the agency and she had a cover to maintain.

"Alexa."

There was a plea in his tone. He wanted to believe her. But the paper trails said don't. "Price used your ties to Carrión to get you to come after me."

"No, my ties to Carrión just made it easier." His hands at his side, he clenched his fists.

"You're looking for someone to blame."

"*I* wasn't the mole."

She looked him over, wondering if he was a better player than she was and if she could trust that answer. "So that leaves me? How many more were there who survived the operation?"

Killian's brows knit. "Several."

"Why blame you, then all of a sudden—why point at me? I wasn't a big player in that Op."

"That doesn't make a damn bit of difference!"

"Of course it does! *You* were friends with Carrión and still are. I was nothing, a messenger, a relay." Her thoughts rolled back to Price, the attack by the CIA officers and Zarek's in the streets. This wasn't washing, none of it was. Why all this *now*? Then a thought occurred to her and she snapped a look at him. "How long did she give you to find me?"

"Twenty-eight days."

"And you've used up, what? Two weeks?"

"Nineteen days."

"So why the timeline?"

"Impatience. According to Price you were a threat to national security and anything you know is void."

"Oh, for pity's sake, what could I possibly know? I can't even—" She clamped her lips shut. The missing month, what was locked in those days. Did Price already suspect and that's what made her send him? God, she hated this uncertainty, and went back to the common thread. Zarek, and Santiago. "Price does everything for a reason, even put a time limit on an assignment. Something will happen at the end of those twenty-eight days. I'd bet my life on it."

"You probably have."

She went still, tipping her head back. This stinks. She didn't have choices, all avenues were gone, including Killian. Everyone involved wanted her dead because she knew something she couldn't remember.

Then the realization bloomed.

Zarek didn't want her dead. He wanted *her*. Whatever she knew—or what she had in her possession— was to his benefit.

I have to get out of here. She started searching the room for what clothes she could find. Everything was whips and black leather, or shirts with nipple holes. "If you think I won't walk out of here in nothing but a sheet, you're wrong." She looked at Killian, clutching the fabric to her breasts.

"There are four men on the other side of that door. You won't get far."

Can't be any worse than the priest, she thought, grabbing the knob.

"Alexa," he warned. "Don't."

"Screw you, Moore."

Killian lurched, grabbed a handful of sheet and yanked. The silky fabric slid from her body and the momentum tumbled her into his arms.

Outraged, she slapped her hands on his chest and lifted her gaze, blowing hair out of her face. Her anger softened at the look in his eyes. Like he wanted to eat her alive.

"Is this what you wanted all along, Killian?"

"A sexy, naked woman in my arms?" He bent, his attention on her mouth. "Oh, yeah."

Eight

For the first time in his life, Killian was breathless. The anticipation of kissing her riddled through his blood like a burning fuse on its way to detonation.

"I don't trust you one bit," she said and her words breezed across his lips.

"Who said trust had anything to do with this?"

"Like danger and death, two different things?"

Oh, yeah, he thought. A double-edged sword, sharp and dangerous—and poised between them. One of them would get cut. Killian had a feeling it'd be him. So he lived in the moment, breathing her in, absorbing every nuance. The heated fragrance of her bare skin beneath his palms, her lush naked contours pressing to him and making him so hard he thought he'd come right now. Jesus.

"Killian."

"Huh?"

"Kiss me before I die."

He did; like an animal devouring its prey, he took her mouth like he owned it. Like she was there for him alone. And the fire between them instantly raged.

There were no games, no sweet, tender desire. Only irrepressible power. Seething with hunger, boiling over with passion. He'd never known any woman who could do this to him. Make him lose control. Lose everything. Even his ethical boundaries.

He didn't give a damn either, and pushed his tongue between her lips. His own deep groan shocked him. Inflamed her. And she took back, battling like they had since first contact. The same struggle he'd felt in her before she unleashed the first blow.

His hands slid around her, molding the curves of her spine. The simplicity of the move heightened everything inside him, and his erection throbbed and flexed. Eager to be free, to be pushing inside her. God, the thought made him tremble. She wasn't being still, either—or quiet. Her eager whimpers drove into his bones with the power of a mallet, each little begging sound he had to hear. Needed.

His hand swept lower to cup her smooth behind, pull her tighter, and she moaned and thrust, then latched onto his belt, throwing it open.

"Alexa." He couldn't believe the question in his own voice. *Shut up and take,* his body screamed.

Then she said it. "Come on, Moore, this is what you wanted, right? To fuck me."

Hearing that from her was just too damn ugly. "No, not exactly." Another shock.

She stilled, looked up, frowning. "Make love? Oh, you've got to be kidding. No one does that anymore." No one cares that much.

"I do."

Her eyes went thin and she pushed back. "I don't want that. It's a complication I can't afford. Not now, not ever." She snatched the sheet, wrapping herself, then started rummaging through the drawers for clothes.

Killian felt like a man tottering on the brink of insanity and scowled. "So you want to be screwed like a whore?"

"No, well . . . oh, forget it." She snapped a skirt out of the drawer. "You've lost the moment."

He reached, gripped her arms, dragged her back against him. "We can get it back." Slowly, as if waiting for a blow, she met his gaze, and he saw something he never expected.

Fear.

Of him, and whatever was going on between them. In a flash, he got a rare bit of insight. Exposing herself—the real woman, not the operative—terrified her. He didn't know why that excited the hell out of him, but it did. Nothing seemed to faze this woman. Running for her life, missiles, knowing she was on a hit list from hell. But a couple kisses left her this shaken?

He passed his hand over her hair, tipping her head back. "Let me try."

"Are you always this confident?" Her voice trembled, and she caught her lip under her teeth.

"In some things."

Before she could say anything more, deny herself this, he kissed her. Like mad. Hot and passionate and blowing any control he had right out of the water.

He overcame her, slaughtered her with sensations and Alexa's legs softened like warm putty as he trapped her against him with one hand, the other exploring her body with ruthless intent. She groaned as he enfolded her breast, and wildly thumbed her nipple, sending a pulse of heat through her veins, stirring every cell and making it scream.

Oh, God, oh, *God.* It had been so long since any man had touched her. Her. Not Jade, or whatever persona she'd had to wear, but Alexa. Part of her wondered if he was just horny and she was available, yet her body had other plans. Dark, lonely spots ached to be handled, touched, smothered by a powerful, sexy man, to make her feel like she existed, and not floating between identities and missions.

"I'm losing you," he murmured as his hand slid heavily over her hip.

Between heated kisses, she met his gaze. "You started this. Try harder."

He ducked and closed his lips around her nipple, flicking and tugging and there was no time to think, no thoughts allowed to manifest. His hand was heavy as it rode over her hip, pausing to squeeze, then slide between her thighs.

Suddenly her world sparkled. Her legs gave out. He parted her and pushed deep inside, stroking her toward a climax.

"That better?"

"Oh, yes."

She breathed his name over and over and he watched her writhe in his arms, his gaze glancing down to watch her hips following his moves. "Christ, you're hot."

"What gave you a clue?" She peeled his T-shirt off over his head. The ropy muscle and wide chest were a playground for her mouth and hands and she licked and teased, kissed.

"I want you on fire."

"Then get these off!" She yanked his jeans open.

His fingers plunged into her softness, then retreated, over and over, never giving her a chance to catch her breath. Alexa gave in, and leaned back over his arms, spreading wider, then hooked her leg around his calf and unbalanced him. They fell to the bed in a tangle of arms and legs, and she went crazy on his clothes, pushing his jeans down and diving her hand inside.

Killian flinched when she enfolded him and he flexed in her palm. "Jesus, wildcat."

For a moment, he closed his eyes, savoring her touch, and Alexa felt the power of being a woman, sliding her fingers over the slick tip of him, feeling him lengthen in her hand. She wanted him on the edge, as helpless as she was, and showed him no mercy. She spread her thighs, urging him between, and guided him a little into her.

He trembled, pushing without control. "Condoms," he moaned as if it were a personal offense.

"This place is littered with them, oh, Killian, hurry."

He reached, slapping the end table and bringing back a handful. Alexa grabbed one, tore it open, rolled it down and made it worth the wait.

He quaked down to his heels. "Oh, God, woman."

"I want this." She guided him. "Inside me," she whispered in his ear. "Deeply." The soft erotic words pushed him over the edge and he thrust.

Alexa gasped and arched on the bed, gripping his shoulders, then fell onto the thin mattress. He held himself above her, plunging into her slowly. She was small and tight and he felt the velvet vise trap him. It was heaven, a thick pulsing that punctured him to the core, yet he watched her face. Her body rippled beneath him with pleasure, and he called her name.

She looked at him, smiling softly. And he saw the barrier she'd erected slowly fracture. Her features softened, her green eyes glowed with open desire, and Killian didn't know what he wanted from her, if she gave a damn, but his body inside hers was more than two people satisfying a need.

Oh, yeah, it was more, and he pushed her legs around his waist, then rolled so she straddled his hips. She blinked down at him.

His brow shot up. "You said you liked being on top."

She laughed, a devious feline purr, and he knew he was in for a wild ride. Her hips moved, and he cupped them, helping her motion, driving up into her. But Alexa took control, sapping the life from him with her deep, licking kisses, her hands leaving no part of him untouched. She was untamed and exotic; chestnut hair spilling over her shoulders, moving with her as she quickened.

Faster and faster, then she pulled him up to her, her hands cupping his face, her gaze locked with his. It was sexy and personal, watching her features, the flare of her eyes as he thrust back. She was coming, he could see it, feel it, and he wanted to tell her what she made him feel, but knew she didn't want to hear it.

"Killian."

He pushed her to her back, his hips pistoning, and her nails dug into his shoulders.

She moaned and whimpered, as if suddenly fighting her body.

"Look at me." She did and for a second he slowed, leaving her completely, then thrusting deep. She arched to greet him, cradling his face, and her eyes went glossy.

"Alexa?"

"This hurts," she said. "I didn't think it would."

He didn't stop, knowing she didn't mean him inside her, but her heart. "Don't fight it." He kissed her, his thrusts quick and smooth as he whispered in her ear, "Let go, Alexa, I'll catch you." She made a sound he'd never forget, between ultimate pleasure and surrender. Her muscles clawed him, sent him beyond the boundaries. In one hard thrust, he erupted and warmed her slick flesh, fusing to her.

Alexa felt the rush of pleasure, so unfamiliar she almost didn't recognize it, and as if Killian understood, he held her tightly and watched. Her breath hitched, her body jerked and she flexed, melting into him, pulling him tighter. He closed his arms around her as she rode the throbbing sensations with him. It went on and on, her body clamping and flexing around his and she didn't want to stop, or leave his arms. Or face the world.

Why was he the only solid thing in her life right now? Why did he have to be the one?

They collapsed, breathing in each other, and Killian's hand smoothed her spine as he watched her world come into focus. He fell to his side with her, nestling her in the curve of his body.

Alexa felt shielded from the world, but it wouldn't last. It never did. "You still have your boots on."

"You didn't give me a chance."

"And your jeans on."

"I didn't hear you complaining a few minutes ago."

"Few was right," she said, her eyes dancing.

He just chuckled. That was the most exciting sex he'd ever had. Well, there was the time when he was seventeen. But he'd learned control since. He looked down at her. Apparently, it was shot to hell around her.

Man. The ethical boundaries he'd just crossed were too many to count. What an idiot. But he didn't regret it.

Alexa rose up on one elbow, meeting his gaze. His moved over her, as if searching for something he couldn't see before. It made her uncomfortable. She'd had sex with the man sent to kill her.

When you go into stupid mode, Gavlin, you don't leave anything to chance.

She moved away from him, but he pulled her back. "Been a while."

She scoffed. "I don't sleep with targets if that's what you're asking."

"Good to know, but no I wasn't." He knew that in the middle of making love with her.

"Then, yes, a long while."

Killian stared into her green eyes, and knew he was losing her, almost seeing the barriers closing around her. The emotions she'd showed him faded, hidden, yet in his mind was that moment when she was peaking, tears in her eyes, her heart in her expression. It would stay with him for a long time, he thought, and it changed his perspective. Not a good thing. When she eased away, he let her go, watching as she went into the bathroom that was no bigger than a locker.

Alexa stared at her reflection in the bleary mirror. Her mouth and body were rosy from his kisses, between her thighs still throbbing a little. She closed her eyes and dropped her head forward. She could walk away. Run from him. She had to.

Because she'd just made the biggest mistake by getting emotionally involved with him. He wanted to stop her, or help her, and she couldn't trust him, either. She had a job to complete and if he was anywhere near her, he'd end up dead. She couldn't bear that because the only decent thing in her life right now was Killian Moore.

He was honest and strong and God, the sexiest thing on the face of the earth. But that made her vulnerable, and if it came down to it, he'd protect her, and that would get him killed.

She washed and ran a brush through her hair, then left the bathroom. When she came out, he was pulling on his T-shirt. Alexa went to the chair, grabbing her panties—the only thing left after the explosion—then found a skirt. She rooted for a top. Everything was trashy and small. She dug deeper, and found a bra and a V-neck T-shirt that didn't show her boobs too much and slipped it on, then went for her boots near the pack.

"I can get better clothes for you."

"My, aren't you accommodating after sex."

He sat on the bed. "I try. Helps when the next time arrives."

She looked at him and arched a brow. "Keep dreaming." She grabbed the pack.

"Gee, I feel so used."

She paused, glancing back. "We used each other, Killian."

His eyes were so blue, so deep with concern, and she tried so hard to be cool and unemotional, but the instant she met his gaze, something inside her just collapsed. She went to him, touching the side of his face. She didn't have to urge him, and his arms slid around her, riding her body, stirring her again as she kissed him. The power of it rocketed through them and he pulled her down onto him, his hands under the skirt. She held on, kissed his neck, breathed him in one last time.

"Christ, you're an addiction." Hunger had nothing to do with this, he thought. But it was something neither would forget. Though he knew she'd try her damndest.

"And I'm sorry to say, you're a prisoner."

He heard the familiar click. She backed off him, shouldered the pack. He was cuffed to the cheap bed frame. "Fuck!"

"Yeah, sucks when I get you twice, huh?"

"God dammit, Alexa, I'm not going to hurt you!"

"But you'd try to stop me."

He grabbed her hand, tugging her close. "I have the resources, the men, you won't accept help?"

"I'd have to trust you for that." She twisted out of his reach and went to the window, peering. "Damn." They were two floors up.

"I can't let you leave."

"I know you'd like a love slave in a whorehouse, Moore, but I'm busy."

Moore. Not Killian. He hated her bitter tone. "Running from yourself?"

She whipped around, his words hitting with deadly accuracy. "Don't push me. I found two sets of cuffs and a whip."

The hurt in her features made him regret the dig, and he swung his legs over the side of the bed, sitting up with his wrist still latched. "You know, for a woman who just begged me to fuck her and came like a storm, you're in a shitty mood."

Her face reddened. "I wish this hadn't happened here, now." She opened the door. The hall was empty, telltale noises coming from the other rooms. God, they must have sounded just like a whore and her John. It made her ill.

But she couldn't leave it like this. Her job said make him hate her, not want anything to do with her, yet her very soul rebelled at the thought.

"I'll make a deal with you, Killian." After a moment, she met his gaze. Her heart did a little spin, her body remembering moments ago and how much she craved more. But they'd connected so fast, so deeply, it scared her. Even more than being alone with nothing. She was used to nothing.

"And that would be?"

"When this is over and provided I'm alive, I'll find the leak in the Carrión operation."

"I couldn't and I had three years to look."

"Trust me," she said.

"That works both ways."

"I've already trusted you with my life, what's your ante?"

"Give me an option here." She said nothing. "Dammit, Alexa, they'll kill you!"

She left. Killian sat there, staring at the empty doorway, then bent to get a look at the cuff. Porn toys. Looked real but wasn't, and he popped the release, then stood.

A knock rattled the door. "In."

Logan opened the door, his expression emotionless. "The marker's working."

Killian pushed off the bed, glanced back once, and remembered every second.

It wasn't enough. Alexa Gavlin was a complicated woman and even in bed, she'd shared only a brief glimpse of who she was. Outside she was strong and confident.

Inside she was lost. Like him.

His only good fortune right now was that she didn't blow the missiles.

"Stop here, Franco," Lucien ordered, and Franco slammed on the brakes, sending Lucien forward. "Could you make any more of a scene?" he said tiredly, then he thrust out of the car, pushing his way through the onlookers. He didn't give a damn about the police swarming over the wharf, the explosion, or the dead men littering his cargo hull. He needed her with him. Now.

He approached a man. "Did anyone come on shore?"

The man frowned. He didn't understand English. Lucien asked again in three languages. The man offered nothing useful beyond babbling about flashes and explosions.

A meticulously dressed Asian in a long jacket moved closer. "What is your interest, sir?"

Lucien knew Third Bureau Ministry of State Security when he saw them. "I saw the explosion, I had a friend who was in a boat on the water tonight," he half-lied. "A woman."

"What is your name, sir?" he said, pen poised.

Lucien knew better than to give that, and offered an alias.

"Witnesses say that something was fired from that

ship." The man pointed to the *Red Emperor*, watching him carefully.

"I wouldn't know about that."

"Then how did you know there was an explosion?"

"People talk and I came to see for myself."

"You were just passing by? It is not on the radio yet."

The grilling grated on Lucien's impatience. "I saw it from the Royal Pacific Hotel across the bay," he lied.

The man wrote it down. "Witnesses saw gunfire."

Lucien didn't give a damn what anyone saw. "The woman? What of the woman!"

"No one came ashore."

Lucien eyed the man. That was a lie, a body had to wash up at least. Perhaps she survived and was picked up by a junk, or tourists.

Beyond them, the Hong Kong police forced the crowd to disperse, and as Lucien was turning away, he glimpsed workers in jumpsuits gathering debris and putting it into a van. The rubber boat, he thought, turning back to the car. Franco was nowhere in sight and Lucien glanced around, pissed and impatient. He didn't want to be anywhere near Chinese Intel.

He located Franco near a warehouse speaking to a thin Chinese woman with long stringy pink hair. Even at this distance, Lucien could see she was an addict, her skin muted, her hands shaking. She dragged on a cigarette as if it was her lifeline, put it out, and lit another, constantly glancing at the cops. Franco slipped something from his pocket, a small white packet, and held it aloft between two fingers long enough for her to salivate. She spoke rapidly, grabbing it, then stuffed it between her breasts. Franco said something and the woman hurried away. He returned to the car, smirking as he climbed in and drove.

"Well?"

"She's dead."

Lucien's heart seized for a moment. "How reliable is that source?"

"Barely, she's in withdrawal. But she did say that men took a woman away in a black truck, and she wasn't moving."

Lucien refused to believe that. "Hire more men, Franco, I need her now."

"That's supposing she's alive. When I find her, do you want me to take what we need and dispose of her?"

"No, bring her to me. Quickly. I don't care how." Lucien watched the scenery pass. "What I do with her will be *my* pleasure."

She knew too much. He'd been stunned that she was on the ship, that she'd seen the hardware. Jade Everett was more than nosy, she was an operative of some sort, MI-6, CIA, Moussad, he didn't care. He only needed her body in his possession. It truly didn't matter if she was alive or not.

"They won't be pleased about this."

Lucien glared at the back of Franco's head. "Shut up and drive."

Alexa took a quick cab ride out of Tong territory. Not that *everywhere* in Hong Kong wasn't, but she didn't want to encounter a gang right now. Moore would have someone following her; then again, he got what he wanted from her. Alexa smirked to herself. Information. *She'd* wanted the sex.

The streets were thick with people either walking fast, riding bicycles or scooters. She maneuvered around, the scents of food and gas fumes creating a haze in the air, but her mind was on Killian, making love to a stranger, a woman she hadn't been acquainted with in a long time. She smiled. No roles, no lies, or disguises. She felt . . . *released*. Her only regret was having a mission to complete and not being able to explore more of him and herself. She didn't want to examine why he affected her so much and just accepted that he did and it was mutual.

Alexa inhaled deeply, then let it out, shaking off the night as she quickened her steps. That sharp prickle worked up her spine and she slowed, using the glass fronts of shops to get a look behind herself. Suddenly, she stopped and turned, her gaze ripping over Victoria Circle. The hub of car and people traffic rolled past, yet in the frantic rush to get to work, there was stillness. A woman swept off her front stoop. A slim man near the newsstand kiosk paid for a magazine. A shoemaker set up his shop between two high-rise buildings, content to arrange leather on a steel pipe for customers to select. No one looked at her but everyone seemed to be in a hurry.

She turned away and hustled to a side street between skyscrapers, passing through and out the other side a street over. She halted outside a small modest door, the traditional doorway looking ancient sandwiched between the contemporary surroundings. She knocked, then glanced down at the pillars of salt on the stoop. Mi Ling was superstitious, a witch of sorts. The salt meant someone had been here and either carried a lot of hate and evil or argued with the older woman. The salt cleansed her home and kept evil out.

The door opened, and she wasn't surprised to find the older woman dressed and looking lovely this morning. Mi Ling smiled, the beauty of her youth still vibrant in her aging face.

"Ah, little tiger," she said, and ushered her inside, inspected the street, then closed the door. Mi Ling stared at her, brushing her hair off her face. Then suddenly she hugged her tightly and Alexa closed her arms around the old woman, feeling like she was ten with a skinned knee.

"It is good to see you safe."

Alexa stepped back. "You can be righteous since you warned me."

"Gloating is very un-Chinese," Mi Ling said. Alexa laughed.

Mi Ling wasn't an asset, but a friend, trusted. Her home was a safe haven, and when she needed help or comfort, or just a break, Mi Ling was there for her. Alexa was desperate for someone to trust or she'd never have come here.

The woman poured her some tea, then patted the chair near her.

"I can't stay."

"Tea and some food, you are too skinny." Her tone was no-nonsense and Alexa knew when not to argue. "You did not come to me first, why?"

"And give you my bad karma, no way."

Mi Ling stared back, her black eyes penetrating. "Child." She pushed a plate of sweet pastries closer. Alexa bit into one.

Mi Ling had been married to a well-loved diplomat, and that gained her permanent care from her government. The locals loved and revered her, and the cures she made. But Alexa's connection was more personal. Mi Ling and her husband had been friends of her parents. She hadn't seen her since she was fifteen, until five years ago when she was bleeding in the streets, and a young man who'd found her brought her here. The man was Mi Ling's son.

"It was too dangerous, Mi Ling. I don't know enough to be safe." Alexa was halfway through the pastry when she noticed she was calmer, less tense. She looked at the woman. "What's in this?"

"Flour, eggs, sugar, chamomile, and some other

things. Harmless." She sat, folding her hands. "You were with him."

Alexa paused, mid-sip. "Who?"

"The big American."

"God, that's uncanny," she said, setting down the cup. "What do you have, radar?"

Mi Ling tsked softly as she tipped Alexa's head back, eyeing her throat, the swells of her breasts. "He's marked you and I can smell him on you."

Alexa touched her skin. "Okay, I need a shower, then."

"It is not a bad scent, this man's."

Alexa didn't want to get into this with her. She'd have her crying and pouring her heart out. Examining her feelings for Killian Moore was not in her best interest. "I need the package."

Without question, Mi Ling rose and went to an ancient medicine chest fashioned into the shelving. Fifty little drawers housed herbs and spices, roots and whatever she needed for healing. She opened one, and handed Alexa the small zipper-lock bag.

"Did you figure out what they are?"

"You should go to Nguyen's store. They are very old." Before Alexa could push the matter, she put up a finger, and said, "Nguyen can tell you more."

"Mi Ling." She'd like to know before she left here.

"Hush, child, drink your tea. You will feel better."

"I feel fine."

Mi Ling made a sound of disbelief. "If you are so *fine*, then why are you dressed like that, walking the streets at this hour?" Mi Ling went to a set of drawers stacked with sheets and blankets, pulling out clothing. She shoved them at Alexa, then inclined her head to the bathroom. "Use the red oil, it will soothe the trouble in your soul."

Alexa blinked.

Mi Ling gave her a tender smile, touching her face, her hair. "Your mother shows in your eyes." Alexa felt tears form. "She would tell you not to think beyond this thing you must do now."

She was right and kissed her cheek. "You know Mi, I love you like a mother"—the woman beamed—"but that Chinese Confucious stuff is just creepy."

Mi Ling laughed delicately, her smile in place. Alexa went into the bathroom, trying not to imagine Killian, and how she'd much rather be in his arms than preparing to hunt down renegade missiles.

Killian was in a command post high in the mountains, accessible by a long winding road, and a chopper. The location offered unobstructed communications over Hong Kong. They could hear everything from Ministry of State Security to the Hong Kong cops. Logan would filter it, pick out what was useful.

The satellite link was up and running. The bio marker Logan injected under Alexa's skin would degrade after seventy-two hours. But at least he knew where she was. Victoria Circle, **stationary and alive.** He glanced to the right as Max walked in and handed him a cup of coffee. He returned his gaze to the screen.

"Price is burning up the SatCom phone."

"I'll just bet she is." The deputy director of intelligence had called twice a day. He never answered.

"The ship is still in the bay. Lots of Chinese police on shore. Maybe Zarek decided not to sell?"

"Fat chance, he's too greedy."

"At least we're not chasing the lass all over kingdom come," Riley said, strolling in eating a sandwich.

"Zarek?" Killian said.

"It's not even past nine yet, Killian, he's probably sleeping. In the Regent on Canton Street."

"You said Carrión was on the ship."

"That, I wasn't expecting. He could be a buyer. But I didn't see anyone else. His location?"

"Hotel, too," Max said. "Looks like they are all recovering from last night."

Killian yawned, sipped coffee.

"Like you."

Killian glanced to the right. "I'm fine." His gaze shifted between Max and Riley. "Why shouldn't I be?"

The men smirked at each other. "We have ears, man."

"Thin walls," Max put in.

"And she was . . . vocal."

"Shut the fuck up."

"You've compromised us, Killian."

Killian stared at the coffee in his mug. "No, I've compromised me. Price sent me, blackmailed *me* and tried to kill me. I'll deal with Gavlin and the DD." He fished in his pocket and dumped a guidance chip in Max's palm. "Check that out for me."

Max examined it. "Simple microprocessor, detonation trigger on range and altitude." He handed it to Riley.

"She'll get wise, you know," Logan said.

"I never doubted it."

Alexa would realize soon that he'd tagged her. Or just that he wasn't close when he'd been on her tail for weeks now. It would make her nervous, scared.

And maybe a little cautious.

Alexa took the subway under the city. Mostly because it was easy to spot anyone coming with all the mirrors and glass, and reflecting chrome. The crowds jostled her, and when she took the stairs to the surface, she was glad to be out of the underground tunnels. It reminded her too much of the shack in the jungle. She walked as briskly as she could toward Nguyen's shop. She'd done some business with him in the past, all legit, thank God. He had some of the oldest antiques in Hong Kong. If anyone could tell her what the stones were, he could. She passed tea parlors and jewelry shops, gaming stores that would make an American video game lover whimper over the geek ware. Nuygen's shop was three blocks away and she focused ahead.

Suddenly pain shot through her skull, radiating in waves. She stopped, her hand on the building wall as pain punctured her senses, and her stomach rolled loosely. She fell back against the stone wall, trying not to throw up, and rubbed her temples.

The knifing in her head just increased, making her eyes water.

A humming sound in her ears, from inside her head, grew louder and more agonizing.

Images blinked in her mind, quick and harsh, each one making her wince. A long flat silver table. The hum turned to a static tapping, then to a hum again. Voices, too muffled to understand. A light blared in her face, and she squinted even now, seeing a plastic oxygen mask come down to cover her mouth.

She couldn't move. Couldn't breathe.

No faces, only cold air.

And the humming.

Nine

Whatever plan she had in the works was rapidly falling apart.

It was subtle things at first. More coffee than normal. Defying regulations and smoking in the building. Digging through files till all hours.

Twice today, she used the secure SatCom link. The techs were starting to bitch about it. This morning she'd resorted to calling operatives. NOCs who didn't have names. Or identities. Waking up the deadliest the CIA had to offer.

That it was in Hong Kong made David Lorimer more than curious. There was nothing on the books for Hong Kong, but surveillance. Although he was accustomed to not asking questions about her procedures—which were way off target lately—he could ask them of himself.

He figured that her last order was to retire *whoever* went over the wall. Because she called in the Professor. No one knew who this person was: male, female, light or dark, nationality, nothing. A ghost in the truest sense.

But what if Price were wrong and the agent didn't go over. Her behavior was a bit too covert for this to be official and leaning toward something more personal going on.

David turned back to his desk, the picture of his latest girlfriend tilted so he could see into Price's offices in the glass's reflections.

Her secure phone rang on her desk. She snatched it, turning toward the windows. He heard little, her voice too low. But she wasn't getting any argument on the assignment, but then, from the Professor, no one did.

"It's imperative that I know the instant it's . . ." he heard. "No, me alone."

David wondered about that again. *No other contact with the other heads of operations?* She usually brought in a staff, had surveillance and SAT contact linked up so she was informed as if she were on site. Not this time. It was too unorganized, too many loose ends. He had a feeling that none of this was sanctioned.

And David knew his lower-echelon head would be the first to roll. He stood, moving to file cabinets, and pulling dossiers. He didn't want to know what was going on, but self-preservation said to get some cards in his pocket. Short of getting into her personal files, he went on instinct.

She was off the phone, moving to her coffee service.

"Ma'am, do you have the file Delta 9-4-1?"

Her features went tight for a split second before she took a sip. "Why do you need it?"

"You have it slated for the burn bag."

"Not for a few days. Perhaps Roister has it, I'll ask. Don't concern yourself with it now."

"Yes ma'am."

"And David?"

He looked at her.

"If you want to keep your job, turn that picture away. I'm not stupid."

David's features pulled taut. A dead giveaway. One reason he wasn't in the field. Too expressive, the instructors at the Farm had said.

He flipped the picture to the right. Jesus.

Nothing got past her, he thought, nothing.

Alexa rolled into an alley, gasping for air. Moisture in her mouth evaporated, behind her eyes burning. She sank to the ground, her head between her knees and breathed slowly. After a few minutes, the pain eased to a dull throb and she looked up to the small strip of morning sky between the buildings.

Well, that was interesting.

Something triggered the memory she didn't know she had. It was part of the missing month, too foreign not to be, and she tried calling up more of it, searching the mental pictures for details. A steel table like in a morgue. Gross. Oxygen mask. That meant drugs. He wouldn't have gotten anything from her if she had full control of her faculties. God knows what they pumped into her. The humming had been something surgical, almost a static tapping sound. Cutting? Whatever Zarek had done, was it to take something away, or implant something? She'd need a full MRI to see if there was something inside her and a good deprogrammer if there wasn't. She hadn't gone through a metal detector at the airport, and other than this episode, she didn't feel different. *Where does that leave you?*

She gripped her skull, hopelessness setting in. She should have stuck with Killian, at least he could help her. She wanted to unload everything, share the burden, but like in Colombia, she couldn't. She climbed to her feet, her legs rubbery for a few minutes, then she left the alley, checking her surroundings.

Jesus. She was a time bomb ready to go off.

Killian paced, the phone to his ear. "Cut the dancing around, Byrd, this line is scrambled. Was she or was she not your relay?"

"That was three years ago, what does it matter?"

"Men died, I got blamed, it matters." Byrd was the DEA commander, an asshole, but a good agent.

"The mole was your problem."

"Fuck you, and I can bring this back to your door. You were in charge of this operation. Was she?"

Byrd stalled for another moment, then said, "Yeah, Everett or whoever she was, gathered some good Intel from the locals, mostly the girlfriends of dealers. I don't know how and I didn't ask. Even she didn't know specifics. She gathered, gave it up, and we ascertained what was valuable. We got some crap, but most good."

Killian closed his eyes, letting the truth sweep through him. "What happened to her?"

"Hell if I know, she was undercover. She was gone. If she resurfaced, I don't know."

She was in the shack, tied to a stake, Killian thought. *We left her there. The U.S.A. and CIA just left her there.*

"To protect her clandestine identity we were all ordered not to mention her in the reports."

"But you couldn't have told me?"

"You were arrested, Moore, you had no rights. Besides, none of us actually laid eyes on her. That was the bargain to use her. Only one of my people saw her face-to-face and he's dead." Byrd's voice lowered. "It was Gordon."

Killian ground his teeth. Gordon Psalt had been a former Marine, wounded right along with Killian in

Somalia. In the DEA Op, he and Noah Morgan had been blown into so many pieces they couldn't identify either of them "Someone had to give her orders; who was the liaison to your offices?"

"Liaison? Yeah, sure. More like begging for info, and we got crumbs. I swear those God damn Company people—" Byrd stopped cold. "It came through the senior analyst at the time."

"Let me guess, Price."

"You said that. I didn't."

The line went dead, and Killian tossed the SAT phone on the sofa, then scraped his palms across his skull.

"Well," Max asked softly, then sipped his beer. "Was she telling the truth?"

"As far as I can tell. She was in an ELN prison when it went down. She couldn't have ratted anyone out. She didn't know what the information was being used for till after it was over." Her cover and his was intact because Gordon and Morgan were dead. But now Zarek threatened it, and Killian was certain the man knew she was an operative. He slipped on his jacket.

"Where the hell are you going?"

"This isn't good enough." Killian gestured to the screens, the tracking marker showing Alexa was on the move.

"Wait a sec. We all agreed that if it got too comfortable, we could follow easily."

"And how long would it take to get to her if she were in danger? This city has a million and a half in it."

"Killian," Max said patiently. "She's trained to evade. She's eluded everyone but you this far, hasn't she?"

"Yes, and I don't want to be wrong when her luck runs out. She told me the truth. But she's hiding something else, and it's not the mission. She laid that on the table to me. Everything but where she's been for that month. Whatever it is, scared her out of the safe house and our protection."

"Maybe it was you."

Killian stared back.

"I know this is difficult for you to fathom, but women get a hard time from a man like you."

"You think this has to do with sex? Jesus, get the big picture." He glared at the team, stuffing ammo in his pockets. "She's tracking missiles, alone. With no backup and people trying to kill her. Does that sound like a woman who's out to betray her country?"

They didn't answer, looking at each other. "What if she was brainwashed or something? What if she is feeding you nothing but lies and that gorgeous body is taking you in."

"I've thought of that, but you didn't—" He clamped his lips shut. They didn't see her break apart for him, didn't see the tears and emotion so vibrantly poignant even he felt it. "CIA tried to kill us, and nothing Price said is panning out. Don't forget that." Max sent him a "gimme a break" look and Killian read beneath it. They could have been just bad shots. He doubted it, but stranger things had happened. "And there *were* missiles on that ship."

"In pieces."

"You can assemble a Tow missile without help."

"But they haven't gone anywhere."

"Only because the ship hasn't docked. We keep watching." They had surveillance going since they arrived. Killian would be out of chips to call in, he had so many buddies doing double duty for him.

"Seeing as there is no talking you out of this, you need backup."

"No. She'll run if she sees all of you. Logan, find me

something. There's got to be Intel out there to make sense of this."

Logan nodded. "I'm waiting for the satellites to pass overhead so I can link up."

Killian didn't hang around and was out the door.

The team looked at each other. "He's going to get her killed," Max said.

"How do you figure?" Riley popped open a beer.

"Too many enemies. Zarek wants her dead, and then there is Carrión, he's got a thing for Alexa and he won't let up."

"Then maybe you should locate Carrión and stop his Latin ass." This from Sam Wyatt, who sat on the window ledge, eating a sandwich.

They all turned.

Sam shrugged. "Carrión is easy to find, just go to the drug lords."

"Then maybe you should get your Texas ass in gear," Logan said, then turned back to the computer screens, three of them linked to networks, one to a bird in orbit over Eastern Europe that had yet to come into alignment.

Sam finished off the sandwich, dusted his fingertips and stood. "Yeah, sure."

"On foot or by car."

Sam shivered, then mumbled, "Sea level is too damn crowded," as he walked out.

The computer pinged and Logan turned to it, tapping keys. Satellite link engaged. He typed the location and frowned at the screen as it focused crosshairs, then split, peeling open a closer rendition. He'd created the software himself, for personal use, because something like this was illegal and would get him shot for breaking national security in about a dozen countries.

He was about to turn away, let the program work for

him, when something caught his attention. He paused the run, frowning, then slid into the chair, and went to town.

Behind him, Max inclined his head to Riley and the pair slipped out.

Alexa dished out money to the street vendor, taking the wrapped dim sum and a hunk of duck. She ate, walking, looking in the shop windows to see behind herself. No one paid her any mind and she kept going. The antiques shop was a few blocks away. The dim sum dropped like lead in her stomach, but she kept eating. She usually lost weight on a mission, but this was getting ridiculous. Leaning against a corner wall, she finished off her food. People greeted her, one old woman advising her to sit down to eat.

Her headache started to ease, and she watched her surroundings, the crush of people in a hurry to be somewhere. She was thankful that she got even a sliver of memory and while she never expected it to be all happy thoughts, she hated the feeling that she couldn't drag up more, no matter how hard she tried.

Nearby two older men came out of an herbalist's shop, propping open the doors and setting up a card table with two chairs. Familiar pals, she thought as they brought out a chessboard and cups of hot tea. It's a ritual, the pair chattering away and moving like clockwork. They opened the board that looked like graph paper burned into wood, then pulled out two silk bags.

Alexa's heart instantly picked up pace, then started to pound as one man poured black stones into a small, low bowl. She walked closer, buying a drink from a vendor and sipping as the second man emptied his bag into a bowl.

The stones were white.

They manned the board with stones, their moves fast and familiar to them both. That looks like Othello, she thought. Alexa kept a comfortable distance till one man glanced up, noticed her and smiled. She took the opening and moved near, asking in Chinese, "What is this game?"

The man replied in Mandarin so rapid she couldn't keep up. At her confused look, he called out, and a young man in his twenties came out of the shop, wiping his hands on a rag. The old men spoke to the younger.

He looked at her, smiling, holding out his hand. "I am Wy Fong, these are my uncles." She introduced herself as Jade. "They are always glad when their game draws attention. They feel it is their duty to spread the word to Westerners."

"Spread away, what is it?"

"Wei Qi. A game of battle strategy. Very, very old. You say Whey Chi, yes?"

The old man spoke fast, yet kept moving the pieces. It was a little like chess, she thought, but could see that with each move, the black stones were set to surround the white. The man with the white struggled to do the same, taking "prisoners" and dropping them into the bowl.

"How old is this game?" she asked.

The young man shrugged. "Nine hundred B.C."

Oh, good Lord.

"I've seen stones with markings on them."

The old man looked up. "Those are expensive, sometimes with the name of the owner engraved in them," Wy translated.

"Does Zhu King Conquers mean anything to them?"

The youth translated and the old men sat back, exchanging a smile.

"Some of the high Dan players name their moves in

a great match, national games. Dan Zhu was the greatest in history." Wy didn't seem to think much of it and seemed eager to get back to his herb shop. "The games are played in Korea, Japan, Okinawa, Taiwan, called Go."

"I get it. Popular. Thank you for letting me watch," she said, then walked away.

Wei Qi. She glanced back at the men, waving, then hurried along. The stones were key. Hell, she'd come here chasing missiles and it was dumb luck that she found them. Or was it?

Alexa entered Nguyen's shop. She hadn't been in here in years, and though it was empty of customers, she heard movement from the rear of the shop. The storefront was overcrowded with items, forcing her to be careful as she went deeper. Her gaze caught on a beautiful rosewood carving of Buddha, enamel inlaid screens glittering with gemstones. The rare and most colorful stood out, and while she didn't deal much in Chinese art—too much red tape from the government to get it out of the country—she knew a couple "customers" who'd be interested in some of Nguyen's latest finds. She dealt in glass and pottery. The large odd sizes made it easier to transport—or rather, made as *if* she was transporting items for her less than legal dealings for the CIA. It was hard to hide weapons in a flat canvas crate.

She paused at the rear door, spying Nguyen on a stool hovering over a tall table. He reminded her of a mouse, small, compact. In one hand, he held a small statue, in the other, a paintbrush. Between that and his face was a magnifying glass on a metal arm. She waited till he'd finished applying gold paint to a worn spot, and set down the brush and statue.

"Shame on you."

His head snapped up, his eyes thinning. "I am only bringing up the quality."

She walked in, eyed the statue. "It's about three hundred years old, that's quality enough."

"Not for the Westerners, the Germans mostly. They are buying a lot and want things"—he gestured to the horse statue carved in cinnabar—"as if they had not been handled in centuries."

"Excuses for tampering with a relic, I see."

"What do you want, woman?" He hopped off the chair and came to her, scowling.

She smiled. His somber face burst into a grin. "Jade! You have something to sell?"

"No, I need your expertise."

"You flatter me. What can I do for you?"

"Tell me about Wei Qi."

"Ahh, ancient game. Many tournaments."

"A little more please, that much I got already. Do you have any sets here? I saw some in a game store, but they were just cheap plastic and glass."

"Yes, I have some old ones. The older games are in the Forbidden City. In pieces, I'm afraid. Mine are completes."

"I'm not buying, so cut the sales pitch."

He sighed and went to a large chest, throwing open the doors and brought out an enameled box inlaid with golden topaz.

"Oh, my God, this is beautiful."

"I sell to you very cheap."

She laughed. "That Peking University education goes right out the door when you want a sale, huh?"

He blinked, then laughed, bringing the box to the table, handing it to her before he spread a cloth over the smooth surface to protect it from scratches. He opened the top.

Alexa inhaled. The contents were even more breath-taking. The board was aged ivory, the grids of the game inlaid with onyx. He opened one bag and removed a stone. It was onyx, the white was abalone, glittering with fine swatches of blue and lavender.

"How old is this one?"

"Maybe seven hundred."

Alexa asked if she could touch it and when he agreed, she slipped her fingers over the smooth ivory, marveling at being able to touch something that was created seven centuries before now. She drew her hand back, shaking herself loose of the moment. It was the reason she'd chosen to be an art dealer for her cover, the history of things fascinated her. Perhaps because her own personal history stopped when her parents were killed.

"Zhu King Conquers. Ring a bell?"

He smiled patiently, then put the box away. "Dan Zhu was the son of Emperor Yao Di." He went to the rear again, pouring water into two handleless cups. "Also it could be a move on the board." He added spoonsful of tea and stirred, then on a tray brought them to her. She sat on a work stool, listened to the stories, trying to pick out what could possibly be connected to her stones.

"Yao Di was a great emperor, very generous. He gave his throne to Shun who made all the Tangs dukes. But there are always wars, and after Xia, Shan, and Zhou conquered Tang provinces, that's when the followers took the name Tang. Very common in China."

Alexa was almost zoning out over all these names she couldn't pronounce when Nguyen said, "Our history says, Yao invented the game of Wei Qi to enlighten his son Dan Zhu. He was a little slow." He tapped his temple and grinned. But Alexa's body locked up as she waited for the rest. "Unfortunately, Dan Zhu mastered it and had no interest in anything but playing the game. When Yao was advanced in age he needed to elect a Tiandi official."

"Like a prime minister, right?"

"Yes. His followers recommended Dan Zhu but Yao disagreed, stating that Dan Zhu was no good at anything other than Wei Qi, that he could only conquer and rule in the game."

Alexa sat back, absorbing this. There was a message locked inside the phrase. She worked backwards. Zarek liked codes. He changed the codes for his compound alarm systems daily. That was mostly paranoia, but he thrived on solving puzzles. She recalled the cluster of twisted metal on his desk, the clear blocks with a bead inside one block. One correct move would free the tangle or would release the bead.

He'd got his hands on Wei Qi stones and was using them for something. Bargain, barter?

Zhu King Conquers.

"Dan Zhu was a Tang emperor?" she said aloud.

Nguyen looked up from his tea. "No, he was *son* of an emperor, but never king. Too stupid."

She smiled quickly. Dan Zhu King Conquers, she repeated in her mind.

Dan Zhu was an expert at Wei Qi. He was a Tang . . . a Tang emperor conquers. Tang King wins? Man, might as well be Chung King or Who Flung Dung. She was grasping at straws.

The dealer reached for a plate of small cookies, offering her some. Alexa shook her head, and from under her shirt, slipped out the bag.

"Nguyen, I have some Wei Qi stones. Can you tell me what they are worth?"

He wiped his mouth and hands, and waited. She spilled them into her palm and held them out.

He stared and stared, his breathing increasing. "Where did you get those?"

"I can't say."

His gaze flashed up. "Leave."

"What?" She closed her hand, scowling.

"Leave now. Do not come back."

"Nguyen?"

"Hush, leave my store!" He pulled her off the stool and pushed her out the back door. "Mention that to no one, woman." He slammed the door and she heard him throw the lock.

She banged on the door, glancing up and down the alley. "You'd better open up and tell me what's going on!" He didn't. "I have a gun, Nguyen, I will shoot the locks."

The shades dropped and the lights went out. She hit the door with the side of her fist, calling his name. He was forced to open it, but only a small crack. All she saw was one eye and some skin.

"What is the problem?"

He scowled. "Go away! You'll get us both killed."

"Why?"

"The stones . . . from an old game."

"Yeah, I figured that."

"No, Jade, *first* game."

Her breath stopped and a tingling raced over her skin.

"Two pieces missing for a thousand years. Said that Dan Zhu gifted a Tang woman with them."

"Jesus." How the hell did Zarek get them? "The rest of the set, where is it? Who has it?"

He shook his head, started to close the door, but she stuck the barrel of her Glock between. He wasn't even fazed.

"Who owns the rest of the game?"

He hesitated and she saw terror in his eyes. "The Tong." He shoved her gun out, and slammed the door.

Alexa looked down at the stones. "Jeez, why did it have to be them." Hurriedly, she put them back between her breasts, concealed her weapon, then left the alley.

Oh man, oh man.

Zarek she could handle, even Price, but the Triads?

She was a dead woman. Again.

And if she wasn't, she'd definitely be losing some valuable body parts along the way.

Now, she shook her head, and she said the truth. They . . . she couldn't handle it. So what . . . Damn why the hell have I started this? she thought to herself back on the subject . . . her face drawn . . . and the situation that . . . of the night.

"Oh dear, oh dear."

Yeah, she could handle Peter Price, but the driver . . . She was asking a most . . . trip.

And it was a matter . . . of falsely behaving, some of it . . . that you'd, see too clearly.

Ten

"She should be coming toward you in five, four, three . . ."

"I have visual. Excellent. Thanks." From inside a car, Killian cut the cell phone call before Logan could respond as Alexa appeared between two buildings.

What was down that alley?

She moved fast, her hands shoved into the pockets of the Mandarin Chinese shirt. Her hair was braided and down her back and if no one looked too close, she could almost pass for a local in those clothes. She wore a small leather backpack. But it was her face that caught his attention, tight, pale. He glanced at the shop. A few moments ago, the owner had shut the doors, locked up, and rolled down the bamboo shades.

When she hailed a cab, he pulled into traffic, following the little red car.

He'd give her some breathing room, watch her back. But he wasn't letting her out of his reach.

This couldn't be all of it. A couple antique rocks? Her missing memory spanned a month, give or take a couple days. In that missing month was when she took the stones and hid them in the jungle. Zarek had to have more reason to eliminate that piece of memory. A lot of trouble for some rocks that weren't even diamonds. These were highly traceable. One of a kind. Not something you'd fence without bringing notice.

Except with the Triads, jeez. That covered a lot of ground, and what family, what gang? In the mountains, or here in the south? Panic electrified up her spine with each new thought. They wouldn't care who they killed to get the stones back.

She inhaled, letting it out. *They don't know I have them.* No one does. Her mind instantly shifted off the danger and onto logic. Why did he have them and why did she take them? Dan *Zhu King Conquers. Boy, did you take a leap of faith,* she thought.

Zarek was obviously using them to get something he needed. Part of a weapons bargain? Hard to believe since the Triads got their own easily. And what the hell would they do with missiles? The one thing the Triads wanted, was to keep commerce in China. Pissing off MSS wasn't in their best interests. Was it simply to make port with that big damn ship, or traveling rights in the country? The Triads had a lock on just about anything that generated money. And Zarek had all the goods.

Well, the Tong *thought* he had them. She smiled to herself when she realized he was probably in big trouble, too. Double-crossing the Tong was suicidal.

She hailed a cab, feeling safer inside the locked car. She couldn't fix this one so easily and hoped Zarek kept his mouth shut and didn't tell anyone he didn't have the stones. If he did, they'd both be out of luck.

She asked the driver to stop a block from her destination. She hurried down the street, glancing at the addresses and moving into the doorway as if it were familiar. Been a while, she thought, pushing through the front doors of the building and taking the stairs up three floors. At the top landing, she rapped on the door, all the while checking for exits, windows, and chances for escape.

The door flew open. "Good, you're home."

His dark brows shot up, his smile wide. "Well, well. Look what the Cold War dragged in."

His Aussie accent made her puddle inside. Along with that bare, muscled chest. "I need help."

He checked behind her, then stepped back, sweeping his arm wide. "At your service."

She noticed his gun hand tucked behind his back as she entered and turned to face a shirtless Cal Pritchard. He set the electronic locks, then put the weapon in a nearby drawer.

"Shave much," she said, touching his lean, whiskered jaw.

"Been recovering from a party." He strolled back to the living room, barefoot.

"Yeah, the wrinkled clothes are a giveaway. And it's two in the afternoon, Cal."

"Time is irrelevant and I could say the same about you. That outfit isn't your stellar best."

Alexa smoothed the linen shirt and cropped slacks Mi Ling had given her that was starting to look like a wrinkled rag. "I know, not a priority either."

He frowned, the look changing his entire face, and for a second, she compared the almost diabolical expression with Killian's. Moore won, hands down.

"If we're done flinging fashion insults, can I get you something? Coffee?"

"Oh, God, yes," she said with feeling, and moved behind him into the small kitchen.

He prepared the small pot, and she was fascinated with the way he moved, quiet and graceful, his tall lanky body a treat to look at. His sandy brown hair was mussed from sleep, his black slacks riding low and showing her the turn of muscle and hip.

"Put a shirt on, will you?"

He turned, folded his arms over his bare chest and grinned. "Nope. I want you to remember every time I've tried to seduce you and what you missed."

"You always had somewhere to go. I like to wake up with my men." God, what a lie, she thought. The only man she's woken up with in recent years was Killian.

"So what kind of help do you need?" Behind him, the coffeemaker sputtered, and Alexa was salivating for a cup by the time it finished.

"I need to use your room."

"I was hoping you said my bed, but—" He leaped on the coffee, pouring two cups and inclining his head to the balcony.

"I'd rather not and I'm short on time."

He arched a brow. "That says a lot." He strolled across the apartment, and shifted a vase on the sideboard, then flipped a switch. A false wall moved back on a soft *shoosh*.

"God, you're so James Bond."

"Bond was on the move all the time. No place like home," he said, and she entered the habitat. The walls were padded black and soundproof, a bank of computer screens occupying the curved gray desk. A transparent LCD mapping screen was suspended from the ceiling, enabling him to see it from both sides and use the touch pad to focus on a location. *I bet Killian would love this,* she thought, then leaned close as encrypted messages trotted across a screen, deciphered by a program.

"Street Intel mostly," he said, tapping keys to give her access.

"Who's been talking?"

"Everyone. I haven't listened in a couple days." She looked at him. "It backs itself up, don't worry. Who are you looking for?" He gestured for her to sit in the next chair. Behind them against the wall were chrome shelves filled with gear.

"No one in particular. Just the interesting noise."

He didn't believe that, but let it go. "Well, Third Bureau is chatting."

MSS. "About?"

"Traitors, suspected traitors, which, according to their standard is most of the free world, the last Intel on the Koreans, Taiwan, Philippines, etcetera."

"Etcetera," she said and tapped the keys, reading over traffic transcripts from the day she arrived. The bugs didn't have to be monitored twenty-four hours a day. With this technology, the data was turned into computer synthesized voice patterns and tones, and would ping a warning when certain words came up. And the list was long, starting with Al Queda and ending somewhere simple like packages and load. The pings were constant and she turned down the volume, and read, her memory locking on facts that had nothing to do with her mission but might be useful someday.

She had one of these systems in Colombia; the CIA likely had it now, though hers was less elaborate and more portable. A way to talk and listen in without risk. Even local police traffic came through. However, the Chinese had the best eavesdropping agencies in the world. Hundreds of stations and operatives gathering Intel. They could be tracking them right now.

Cal sipped his coffee, reading over her shoulder till it irritated her. Sitting at a terminal, he opened another window, this time in Chinese Ministry of Trade.

"How many bugs do you have?"

"Not all mine, the really good ones are in the bedrooms." He wiggled his brows. "I'm piggybacking others, a couple Russian and two British."

She looked at him, stunned. "You surprise me, Cal."

He winked. "See, I'm not just a pretty face."

She laughed. "Well, then, get to using everything else."

"We're not in bed, we can't."

"At the risk of opening a door I won't enter, that statement lacks a certain amount of creativity."

He leaned over, cupped the back of her head and before she knew it, he was kissing her crazy. Alexa felt her insides twist, and when he drew back, he was smiling, all cocky and darling Aussie. "Ahh, love, come to bed with me, I could make your blood sing."

"Does that line really work on women?" He looked a little disappointed in her response, then smiled. "And if I was looking, which I am not, I'd want more than one night."

He jerked back as if burned. "Okay, that just made me go all limp."

Alexa laughed deeply, then focused on the screen.

"MSS is looking for a pole?" Cal scowled at the screen. "That's got to be a bad translation."

"No, Pole, Polish. I bet that's Zarek."

"He's here?"

"All week. My Lord, you really were recovering. When did this party start?"

"Four days ago. It was pretty much a sex fest."

"Spare me."

"Jealous?"

"You wish."

"Yes, I do every night." He leaned close. "And when I'm sliding into some other beauty, I think it's you."

Chills danced down her throat and she rubbed it.

"Did I ever mention that I loathe men who just want me just for sex."

"And don't want your brain as well?"

She thought of Killian, who wanted both. Too bad her brain was short a month of Intel. "Keep that up, sweetie, and I'll act all needy and clingy. Make you give up your black book and demand you're home for supper."

"As if you'd cook."

She snickered and struck keys, peeling open windows of computer synthesized voice Intel. "There is a lot going on." Unstable in Sudan, UN and secretary of state in negotiations with North Korea, suspected terrorist cells in Taiwan. They couldn't get too close to Okinawa or American Intel or the military bases would blow covers trying to learn if it was us or them. Nothing close to Hong Kong except the explosion of Killian's Zodiak. The police didn't have anything except the remains of the craft. Nothing on Dragon One. Good.

"Tell me what you're really looking for, I can help maybe." He typed one-handed, refusing to give up his coffee.

"Too dangerous." He gave her an impatient look. "Okay, who's in the market for guided missiles and in the area?"

"Whoa. Zarek went big league, huh?" He set the cup down and beside her, worked the board. "We have Chechens in the Baltic. Got NSA there, let's see . . . surveillance on the Chinese embassy by the Russians. See, nobody trusts anyone anymore. Third Bureau being vigilant on South Korea, nothing new there."

"Russia and China have enough of their own weapons. Come on Cal, remember it's the man who wants one missile that's more dangerous."

"Ship in the bay? No, outside the bay."

"That's it."

"So that was you? The explosion. There was speculation that a man brought a dead woman on shore." She gave him a deadpan look. "And the man?"

She wouldn't mention Dragon One and risk blowing Killian's cover to Carrión. Not that Cal didn't know better than to talk.

"You're breaking my heart, love," he said even as he tapped the keys. He read quietly for a moment, then glanced at her, and tipped the screen. "Trucks standing by to unload the ship."

"How many?"

He read off the screen. "Four. Big ones. The ship hasn't docked." He glanced at her. "As I'm sure you knew already." She didn't blink. "They've been waiting for a couple days, it's just walkie-talkie traffic, disgruntled drivers." He leaned and read. "*My ass hurts and I'm sick of food in a box. Shut up and keep off the radio.* It's dead for about an hour, then picks back up. Same shit. Chinese Intel is listening, too." He pointed to the threads listed in the upper right of the screen.

"Trucks . . . that means they're transporting them over land. Do they mention direction, or anything?"

He read back a few hours, then a day. "No. Could be anywhere. The target?"

"No idea. I need to stop this buy, Cal, so there is no target."

He took up his cup and leaned back. "I could think of a few places that need a cleansing."

She sent him a bitter look. For an accomplished flirt, he lacked certain emotions. Which was why she couldn't take any of his never-ending seduction for real. "I'm done. Thanks." She stood as he did. He was close, gazing down at her with the bone-melting smile.

"I could demand payment."

"You could," she said, her eyes narrow and full of warning.

He let out a long-suffering sigh, and they left the habitat. He sealed the door as she carried her mug to the sofa, but not before pulling a lacy bra from the cushions. "How could she miss leaving without this?"

"Rushing to get home before her husband, I guess." He took it, tossed it, and flopped into a chair and propped his bare feet on an ottoman. He had a laid-back attitude that put people at ease. Alexa knew it was a front.

"So why don't you tell me why you're so accommodating. You never wanted to help much before."

"That was before I got interrupted with this." He waved to the empty bottles of wine, the cheese turning transparent, the strawberries going soft.

He had a mark. If it was in Hong Kong, he'd never say. But then, it rarely was since this was where he lived. He did his work elsewhere. Hong Kong was his haven where he was an opal miner with a thirst for lots of women. Alexa had no problem recognizing that his skills were necessary. Hers had been her face and body, his were sanctioned eliminations. Sometimes nasty people needed to be taken out so democracy could reign for everyone else. They weren't supposed to discuss anything, not targets, assignments. They were both NOCs and the only reason they knew that much about each other was because she'd rescued him from a Niki-Khita prison in the mountainous Kurchaloi region of Chechnya and spent two weeks dragging his ass back to civilization.

He'd been trying to get into her panties ever since.

"So when do you leave?" She slipped the leather pack off her shoulder.

He smiled and pulled a silencer loaded Walther PPK from between the seat cushions. "I don't."

Then he aimed it at her.

* * *

Exacting revenge had been a mistake.

Lucien had allowed his emotions to rule his plans, to involve her as a vital piece, and now she was missing, perhaps dead. He'd be held accountable for it, the consequences deadly, he thought, pouring gold coins from hand to hand when he heard a thump, something hitting the floor.

He turned, feeling every muscle go limp with shock. He nearly lost the coins.

Three members of the Tong stood inside the doorway of his suite. Franco was out cold on the floor, blood spilling from his mouth.

"Was that really necessary?"

The tallest of the three moved silently forward and stopped within inches of him. His almond eyes were slitted, his face lacking any emotion beyond lethal determination.

Fear gnawed at his spine, and he fought for composure.

The man pushed him into a chair, the others surrounding him, one posted a few feet away, watching the exits. He made no move to disguise the automatic weapon in his hands.

"You were to deliver them today, why have you not?"

"I'll get them, you have to be patient."

"He no longer trusts your word." He made a motion and the largest man grabbed Lucien's hand, placing it flat on the table.

Gripping the coins, Lucien was confused till the tallest drew a knife. "I will get them, I swear!" He dropped the coins, struggling. "My God, no. Please."

Casually, the tallest inspected the knife edge. "You swore before and have broken your bond." He poised

the blade over Lucien's little finger. "For your betrayal."
He sliced off the first digit of Lucien's little finger.

Zarek's breath locked, and he stared in horror as blood
spurted from the tip, the pain not even registering.
Then it did and he howled, yanking his shirttail to stop
the blood, then fell back into the chair.

Images and sounds muddled, his heart beat in his
ears, pumping blood from his finger.

The larger man collected the fingertip and wrapped
it in a white cloth.

The leader, slender, with long fingers and his hair in
a knot tied high on his head, struck him three times
with such speed that Zarek couldn't anticipate a single
blow. Yet he felt his nose shift, his shoulder dislocate,
and his kneecap pop to the side of the joint.

He slithered to the floor in agony, landing on his
coins.

The man straightened his clothing, wiped his hands.
"Your time is over. Where are they?"

"A woman, she calls herself Jade Everett. Small,
dark-haired. She took them from me!"

Over his cringing body, the man glanced at his comrades. "We will find her."

Lucien cursed his own arrogance for allowing her to
leave his side for a moment. "I've tried, I have fifteen
men out there looking."

The lieutenant scoffed and turned away. The three-
some left as silently as they had come.

Lucien lay motionless on the carpeted floor, pain
clawing through his body, fogging his vision. His dog
yelped and rushed in to lick his face, and he caught
sight of his own blood dripping down the wall.

Then the agony was too much.

* * *

"Eagle Eye to Mustang."

Killian frowned at Riley's call sign, and picked up the hand radio. "Mustang. Where the hell are you?" He should be used to them showing up. Hell, he hadn't asked them to join him on this retrieval, but they came without a second thought.

"About two hundred feet above you."

Above? "I don't recall asking for backup."

"You said she'd run *if* she spotted us. I'll bet twenty even you can't see me."

Killian looked around high on the rooftops, examining windows for shadows, moving curtains, then down the street at spots that had a good viewing angle.

"Good thing we disobeyed, you've got a black eye."

Black eye, a tail. Casually Killian glanced in the rearview and saw the small black BMW pull into a spot behind him and across the street. No one got out. "Introduce us." It was loose code chatter from now on—if he had a tail, then they could be listening in. Dragon One didn't want to give them anything to go on.

"The stakes in the ground. HALO is too high." Stake, pole, Polish. *Zarek.* HALO . . . High Altitude, Low Opening. *Not from up here.*

"Who's in the dirt?" On the ground.

"Dracula." He heard a second later.

"Roger Thornhill's on the move." It referred to the film *North by North West.*

Satisfied anyone who listened was confused, Killian left the car, locked it and walked north. Several minutes later the black van passed him and turned right. Killian strolled at an easy pace to the end of the street and turned. The van door was open a little and he climbed in. Max drove off, handing Killian the headset. He climbed in the back with the surveillance gear and spoke to Logan on a more secure frequency.

"Talk, pal." She'd been in there a while, the sun was going down.

"The building is owned by a large corporation. There are forty apartments, one penthouse rented under Down Under Gems. Opal dealers. No connection at all to our players, Mustang, sorry."

Killian's brows knit. Price did warn him; *she has contacts all over the world. She has people who will help her.* Maybe this was it.

"LZ's location?"

"In his suite at the Regency. Hasn't been seen all day. His giant rushed out, then came back asap with a bag, though I don't know what he couldn't have gotten from the 'my job is to suck up' concierge there."

"Then he's hiding something from public notice."

"Outlaw is on the Latin. He's dining with some cocktail cookers."

Drug cartels. "Notify the white hats, the noise might be sweet." DEA needed some good Intel right now. Carrión was a master at covering his ass.

There was a long pause before Logan said, "She's not going to come to you for help. Face it. She's got some personal vendetta going."

Killian could feel Max's sympathetic gaze on him.

"It's more than that. She was missing for a month. And the Wicked Witch sent monkeys after her *before* she surfaced. She knows more, a lot more." Killian rubbed his mouth. "Finn, you got a view to a kill?"

"I can see inside, but just getting movement. Setting sun is glaring."

Killian lowered the headset. "Drive around the back, see if there is a loading zone for the apartment."

Max turned in traffic, heading south.

"I'm trying to get out of the sun," came over the frequency.

Killian shifted between the van seats to sit in the

front. Max drove beneath an overhang into an underground parking garage. "Finn, you see anything," Killian said as Max made a quick pass around the garage, then drove toward the elevators.

"Must—I see he—" Riley said. "A man—"

"Finn, you're breaking up," Killian said into the radio. "I say again, you are breaking up, come back."

No response.

He dove in the rear of the van to try another frequency. He got static. "Finn, do you read? Come back."

Killian lifted his gaze to Max's and dread washed over him.

Eleven

Alexa stared down the long slender barrel for a second before the shock settled. "God dammit, Cal!" She started to stand, but he raised the weapon and she dropped back down.

"Sorry, love. Boss lady called before dawn. I was trying to figure out how to locate you and there you were on my doorstep."

"How convenient."

"This hurts me, truly."

"I'll bet." Alexa couldn't reach her gun in time. Cal was too fast, an expert.

"Put the Glock on the table." She arched a brow. "It's your weapon of choice, I recall."

She obeyed. He hooked the table with his foot and pulled it closer to himself, taking it out of her reach. Then he continued to sip his coffee as if he had all the time in the world. Like she'd just sit there and let him put a bullet between her eyes? Not hardly. Yet she didn't know a way out of this. Unarmed and at this distance, she had few options.

"Why did you let me use the habitat?"

He propped bare feet on the low table. "Curiosity. None of the information would leave this apartment anyway." He tilted his head. "You must have really pissed off the big Shelia this time."

She still couldn't believe he'd taken a contract on her and tried for reason. "Price is part of this, up to her eyeballs. She's sent someone to find me, then tried to kill us both."

Cal frowned. He understood. A sweeper.

"I'm being framed and used."

"That's a damn shame, but I have orders." He raised the pistol, flicking the barrel. "Move."

She didn't. "I'm begging you, there is more at stake than my life. Missiles are being transported; if I don't stop it, then will you?"

"No."

"Then innocent people will die! It could start a war!" He just stared back. "Jesus, why the hell do you even do this job?"

"The pay, the women. The perks." He shrugged, then stood, motioning her to do the same. "Over there," he said and she just noticed the drop cloth on the floor behind the dining table. "I've never eliminated anyone in my own place."

Her stomach coiled and she tried stalling till something brilliant came to mind. "What did Price say?"

"It won't make any difference now, but she ordered you retired and a confirm call."

Jesus, it's like she was an item to be checked off a to-do list. "Don't you question the reasons behind this?"

"It keeps the mind clear when I don't."

"God forbid you grow a conscience, huh? Cal, I saved your life, you owe me."

"Yes, I know, it's why it hurts me to do this." He raised the pistol to her head, and Alexa saw the determination in his eyes, the lethal killer come forth. "It won't hurt for long, love."

"She'll send someone after you, too. Another sweeper like you."

"I don't think so."

"The Triads are involved, Zarek has weapons of mass destruction he's marketing here . . . now. Within days."

"Like I said, not my problem."

Oh, Jesus. He's really going to shoot. "It will be when you kill the only one who knows they exist!" His finger flexed on the trigger.

Time slowed.

She heard a hissing sound, instantly followed by a loud snap as the door burst open, banging against the wall.

Cal twisted, firing into the haze of white smoke. Alexa dove for cover. A split second later, the soft thump of silencer gunfire popped the air. The crunching impact was sickening. Blood splattered, then nothing. Cal stumbled back, squeezing off a round into the sofa.

Alexa remained tucked against the kitchen cabinet as he fell, his body smacking on the plastic cloth. There was a clean hole in his forehead, blood pooling fast beneath his skull.

Oh, God, oh, God. Alexa peered. Killian stood in the foyer like a phantom in the pale mist, his arm still extended for aim.

"Alexa?" He didn't lower the weapon as Max moved further in behind him, checking the perimeter. "Alexa!"

She shifted from behind the kitchen counter. "I'm over here."

His gaze locked on her. He got an "all clear" from Max, then rushed to her, sliding to the floor and gathering her in his arms. She buried her face in his chest, breathing hard and letting his strength wrap her.

"Oh, God, I am so glad you don't give up. Thank you."

Above her Killian closed his eyes, rubbing her spine. He almost didn't make it through the door, and thanked God for Max's skills with electric locks.

She tipped her head back and met his gaze. In a breath, he was on her, his mouth rolling heavily over hers, his hands riding up her back to lodge in her hair. She wanted it, wanted more, to hide away with him and forget this mess.

"Quit scaring me . . . dammit."

"Big bad commando scared? Bet that's a first." Yet his words warmed her right up.

"Not with you around." He kissed her again, then pulled her off the floor. "Who is he?"

She told him, picking up her gun and stashing it behind her back. "Price ordered this." She had blood splatters on her clothes.

"We have to get out of here."

"Not yet."

He let out an anguished sigh and pinched the bridge of his nose. "Jesus, why does that not surprise me."

She snatched her pack off the sofa, moved to the sideboard, pushed the vase aside, then flipped the switch.

"Cool," Max said, and they entered behind her. She went to the chrome shelves and started loading herself up with Cal's gear.

"You knew him well?"

She met his gaze, eyeing him for a second. "Yes, I got him out of prison in Chechnya. The Company had written him off as dead and made no claims he existed, of course."

"Why did you go after him?"

She looked back over her shoulder. "Because it should have been me."

"Ungrateful bastard."

"See why I don't trust anyone?"

"Hell, yes."

"Help yourself, Killian." Alexa had a free-for-all with the gear, stuffing mini binoculars, cameras and weapons into the black bag.

"Where is Logan when I need him." Max was at the terminals, trying to access.

Alexa reached over and typed the code in. "He didn't think I was watching," she said, then asked Killian, "What should we do with the body?"

"Leave it, let Price worry about it."

"She's waiting for a confirmed kill." Just the words sent a chill up her spine.

"Then she can stew. When she doesn't get a confirm, she'll look for another shooter."

"That's comforting."

"This stuff any use?" Killian said to Max.

"Well, he's got some good Intel going, what he did with it is another issue."

"Nothing," she said, shouldering the bag, and they looked at her. "I'll explain later. E-mail it to your accounts for all I care."

They left the habitat, but not before Killian put a magazine's worth of bullets into the hard drives. "Max, wipe down for prints, then get out." He stopped her from closing the false door and she frowned up at him. "Let the Chinese find it," he said.

"And give them a reason to accuse the U.S. of spying?"

"Like that's news?"

"No, but we close it for diplomatic measures. The U.S. has enough assholes to contend with right now. We need friends in bad places."

"God, I hate it when you're right."

"When am I wrong?"

Max was busy obliterating prints, and before they made it to the door, Riley was there.

His gaze moved to Alexa, then past to the body. "Man, this is getting messy."

A phone rang somewhere in the apartment. Killian crossed the room, listening, then opened a wood box on the coffee table and retrieved a cell phone.

He read the number, then showed it to Alexa.

"That's Price's code."

Killian hit send.

"Well, did you find her, is it done?"

"You mean the cold-blooded murder of Alexa Gavlin?"

There was a stunned pause then, "Who the hell is this?"

"You've fucked with the wrong man, Price, and when I'm done here, I'm coming after you."

Alexa grabbed the phone. "No, he's not, Lania. *I am.*"

She cut the line, then dropped the phone to the floor and smashed it. Without a look at anyone, she left.

Killian caught up with her in the stairwell. "Wildcat, stop." She didn't and he latched onto her arm, pulling her into him.

"I have to leave."

"Not like this, you're not." He held tighter.

"Damn her, damn her. Damn *her.*" She thumped his back.

What was he supposed to say to this? Killian pressed her head to his shoulder, trying to soothe and being pretty much useless. It was an ugly feeling when you knew someone wanted you dead.

"I've done everything she's asked of me. Why would she fold up stakes now?" Her fingers dug into his back. Her small body trembled with rage she wouldn't vent.

"She turned her back on you when she ordered me to kill you."

"But I haven't done anything to warrant this." At least she couldn't remember if she had. "As strange as it is, that's easier to take, but that she ordered a friend to do it, a man who owed me his life was just really . . . shitty."

He pushed her back to look her in the eye. "She knew you'd let him get close enough."

"I liked him." Her eyes teared. "We'd helped each other out before. I had no reason not to trust him." She looked down for a second, blinking, then met his gaze.

A lone tear rolled and the sight of it sliced through him.

"She won't let this stop her. There are more hitters in Asia. You need to just get away from me." Alexa wanted to dump the stones in the trash and forget this. The Triads. Lucien. She'd be lucky if she lived till morning. "Far away."

"No deal. So you might as well clue me in on the whole story."

She turned on him like a wild creature. "You fool! I'm not being evasive, I'm trying to keep you alive!"

Panic rolled through her, radiating off her in waves.

"*I'll* keep you alive, dammit." She stared up at him for a long moment, then finally nodded. "We need to split." He took her hand, pulling her into the express elevator. The door swooshed closed and Killian immediately unscrewed the silencer, then put it in his back jean pocket. As he checked his gun, his gaze flicked to hers, and he frowned. "You okay?"

"Wonderful." She rubbed her face, shaking off the last few minutes. The elevator hit the lobby floor and he ushered her out of the building and across the street to his car. The black BMW was gone, but he stopped short when a deep green sedan pulled up before the building. He radioed his men to get out—now.

Alexa got in the car, watching the Chinese man enter the building. Killian started the engine and pulled into traffic.

"I've seen that man before, but can't recall where," Alexa said, twisting to get a last glimpse of him, then faced forward. She didn't get a good look at the man on the ship to be certain, or was it something in her missing memory? She needed it back, yet was afraid of what she might find. *Price knows,* she thought. *Whatever it is, it's lethal.*

She sat up straighter. "I need to get to the docks."

"No."

"Don't go all caveman now, Killian. Stop the car now and let me out." He didn't and she drew her gun, aiming.

He glanced, barely. "Or what? You'll shoot me? I just killed for you, woman."

Alexa stared at him for a long moment, something strange hitting her. Not that he shot Cal to save her, but that he was there; no matter how many times she pushed him away, he was still watching her back. She lowered the weapon. "I did say thank you for saving my life, didn't I? I'd hate to be rude."

He smiled tightly. "Put that thing away. I have surveillance on the ship and Zarek. Neither has moved, Sam is watching Carrión."

"Alejandro isn't working for Zarek, that would be beneath him. Whatever he's doing here, it's for himself." She stowed the gun and sagged into the seat, then suddenly rooted through the car, which was quick work. It was a rental.

"What are you looking for?"

"A cigarette and no, I don't smoke anymore, but it's either that or knock over a liquor store and get drunk."

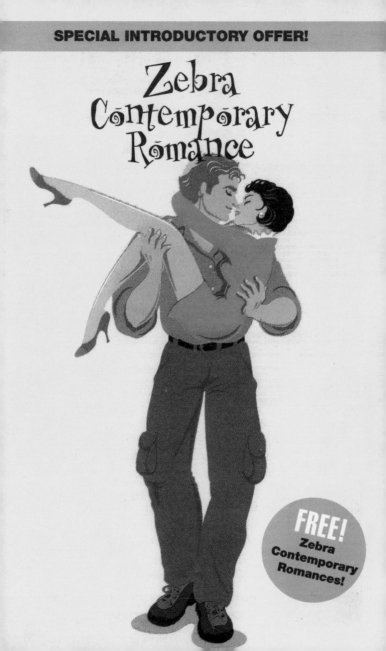

Zebra Contemporary

Whatever your taste in contemporary romance – Romantic Suspense... Character-Driven... Light & Whimsical... Heartwarming... Humorous – we have it at Zebra!

And now Zebra has created a Book Club for readers like yourself who enjoy fine Contemporary Romance written by today's best-selling authors.

Authors like Fern Michaels... Lori Foster... Janet Dailey... Lisa Jackson...Janelle Taylor... Kasey Michaels... Shannon Drake... Kat Martin... to name but a few!

These are the finest contemporary romances available anywhere today!

But don't take our word for it! Accept our gift of FREE Zebra Contemporary Romances – and see for yourself. You only pay $1.99 for shipping and handling.

Once you've read them, we're sure you'll want to continue receiving the newest Zebra Contemporaries as soon as they're published each month! And you can by becoming a member of the Zebra Contemporary Romance Book Club!

As a member of Zebra Contemporary Romance Book Club,

- You'll receive four books every month. Each book will be by one of Zebra's best-selling authors.

- You'll have variety – you'll never receive two of the same kind of story in one month.

- You'll get your books hot off the press, usually before they appear in bookstores.

- You'll ALWAYS save up to 30% off the cover price.

SEND FOR YOUR FREE BOOKS TODAY!

To start your membership, simply complete and return the Free Book Certificate. You'll receive your Introductory Shipment of FREE Zebra Contemporary Romances, you only pay $1.99 for shipping and handling. Then, each month you will receive the 4 newest Zebra Contemporary Romances. Each shipment will be yours to examine FREE for 10 days. If you decide to keep the books, you'll pay the preferred subscriber price (a savings of up to 30% off the cover price), plus shipping and handling. If you want us to stop sending books, just say the word... it's that simple.

FREE BOOK CERTIFICATE

Yes! Please send me FREE Zebra Contemporary romance novels. I only pay $1.99 for shipping and handling. I understand that each month thereafter I will be able to preview 4 brand-new Contemporary Romances FREE for 10 days. Then, if I should decide to keep them, I will pay the money-saving preferred subscriber's price (that's a savings of up to 30% off the retail price), plus shipping and handling. I understand I am under no obligation to purchase any books, as explained on this card.

NAME _____

ADDRESS _____ APT. _____

CITY _____ STATE _____ ZIP _____

TELEPHONE (_____) _____

E-MAIL _____

SIGNATURE _____

(If under 18, parent or guardian must sign)

Offer limited to one per household and not to current subscribers. Terms, offer and prices subject to change. Orders subject to acceptance by Zebra Contemporary Book Club. Offer Valid in the U.S. only.

Thank You!

CN026A

THE BENEFITS OF BOOK CLUB MEMBERSHIP

• You'll get your books hot off the press, usually before they appear in bookstores.

• You'll ALWAYS save up to 30% off the cover price.

• You'll get our FREE monthly newsletter filled with author interviews, book previews, special offers and MORE!

• There's no obligation – you can cancel at any time and you have no minimum number of books to buy.

• And – if you decide you don't like the books you receive, you can return them. (You always have ten days to decide.)

Be sure to visit our website at www.kensingtonbooks.com.

ll..l..lll...ll.l.l..l.l..l.l..l.l.l..ll..l..l.l..ll.l..ll.l...lll...l

Zebra Contemporary Romance Book Club
Zebra Home Subscription Service, Inc.
P.O. Box 5214
Clifton NJ 07015-5214

PLACE
STAMP
HERE

He offered her a thin cigar. She snatched it, bit the tip and lit up. She coughed twice, then took a soothing drag. After the second puff, she said, "My head is spinning."

He took it back.

"Hey, it felt good." A drunken oblivion would be better.

"It won't in the morning." He clenched the cigar between his teeth as he sped through the city and away from killers.

David didn't know what sent her out the door so fast but didn't care. He typed fast, searching data files, tapping into records. He had about three minutes before someone in Tech would notice, and trace him. He opened her private records, mortgage, water bill. Then he found the phone records. She had two of them. Personal and a private. He tapped the private. Alarms would be sounding somewhere in the building where a bored technician was reading *PC World* and eating a danish. David's fingers flew over the keyboard, and he sent the file to his AOL account, then logged off and cleared the history. He was a techy, a geek of the first water, he admitted. He removed the secondary trace and sent that to another account.

She entered the office and he glanced up and smiled. She didn't even look at him, her steps quick and silent on the carpet. Her face was flushed, her eyes a little red. She paced the office for a moment, then got some coffee. Even from this distance, David could hear the cup and saucer chink nervously.

If he didn't know better, he'd swear she was scared.

* * *

On the wood deck, Alexa wrapped her arms around her waist and stared out over the landscape. The sea breeze rolled up the hillside, whipped at her blood-stained clothes before pulling through the house. She knew why he'd chosen it: windows on three sides, and the surrounding lot could be surveyed from any corner, the steep drive exposed to see anyone coming. Killian had been outside, canvassing the perimeter. Setting traps, she supposed.

Her shoulders relaxed a little. She was safe for the moment.

Then suddenly he was near, a strong presence when she felt her weakest. She lifted her gaze to his.

Killian saw defeat in her eyes and it tore at him, pissed him off. He liked it better when she was ready to chew him up and spit him out. "There's your ship," he said, handing her a pair of binoculars. "Customs inspectors were on and off too fast for it to be anything more than for show."

Alexa sighted in. The *Red Emperor* sat on the edge of the bay, a launch anchored near. She swung her attention to the shore. Trucks lined the wharf, a couple men leaning against one, smoking. Just as Cal had said. The thought of him made her heart sink. *This is going to get worse before it'll get better.* She handed over the field glasses and turned away. "Thank you."

Killian stared at her back. "There are some clothes in the closet."

She glanced. "She won't mind?"

He arched a brow.

"The décor is feminine and there was nothing but women's products in the bathroom."

"This"—he gestured to the house—"belongs to my sister's best friend."

"Really? Interesting." Especially that he had a sister.

"Get that smirk off your face. She's like a sister, too."

She let out a breath, smiling. "And here I was, prepared to be jealous and make you suffer."

"Wait till you see the clothes. She's an artist." He made a face.

"Don't knock it, that was half of my cover." She looked at the paintings, liking them, wondering how much they'd be worth on the open market. It was a distraction she welcomed. She laid her gun on the table, and unbraided her hair.

Then his SAT phone rang. "Yeah, we got out fine," Riley said.

"Excellent. Any activity after?"

"Men in black going in but we couldn't risk seeing where they went. Doubt it was the penthouse. I didn't find any cameras, except in the bedroom." Riley snickered.

"Keep the twenty-four seven watch on that ship. It moves, I want to know about it." With the customs inspectors in and out, Killian figured something would happen soon.

"Roger that. Logan called, he's got something you need to see."

"What?"

"Hell if I know, he's being weird about it."

"Tomorrow."

"Going to do a little night maneuvers, sir?"

"If you were still a Marine, I'd bust your ass for that."

"And if you were, too, we'd both be in the brig."

Shaking his head, Killian cut the call.

Alexa sat slowly on a wicker love seat, cradling her head in her hands. Her long hair fell forward, shielding her eyes.

"Talk to me."

She let out a tired breath and sat back, staring at nothing. Everyone wanted a piece of her, in a grave or with them. Even her own country. She lifted her gaze to Killian.

Except him.

The words just spilled. "I've played a lot of roles. A call girl, an exiled princess, a tycoon's trophy wife, a cat burglar . . . always someone else and never on a hit list from my own boss."

"And now you're not any of those things."

"Nope, just an NOC on the run. Abandoned to the sharks."

"Is this an exclusive pity party or can anyone join in?"

Her gaze flashed to his, angry, hurt, then it melted, and she smiled slightly. "Yeah, you're right. I'm whining. That part of my life is over, you know. I'll never get back credibility, or trust. Which makes me pretty much out of a job."

"Don't count yourself out." He walked near, handing her a glass with two fingers of Japanese Sun Tory whiskey.

"I don't plan on it." She tossed back half, and melted a little more. "There was a time that I thought Lania Price was my friend."

"This I gotta hear." Killian lowered to the love seat that was far too delicate for his size.

"She trained me herself. We took a spring cruise together, Cayman islands. We had a blast. It was a lot of eat, drink, be merry, and tease the men. She looks great in a bikini, believe it or not."

Killian smiled. "Not."

"Then we got to the island and I learned it was all for a mission, producing a cover of two women ready to get wild on vacation." She sipped the drink, her limbs going soft, and she kicked off her shoes and curled her legs to the side. "It got us into the darker areas. There was a slave ring of sorts going." She shrugged and drained the glass. "That's when I knew that Lania Price couldn't separate the job from her life."

She closed her eyes, laying her head on the back of the sofa.

"Tell me what's going on, Alexa, I can help." She looked as if she'd melt into the furniture any second.

"I can't fix this. You can't." It hit her again—what she possessed, what the Tong would do to get it back, and she rubbed her forehead. Killian noticed her hands shaking.

He took one. "We can sort it out."

She inhaled, then exhaled slowly. "I have something the Triad wants."

He lurched back a little, his brows shooting up. "Could you make any more of a mess of this?"

"It was getting dull around town. I thought we needed a little more excitement."

She left the sofa and went to her backpack, then handed him the plastic pack of stones. When she spoke, it was a flood of words and before she finished Killian realized that she trusted him. It might be just desperation, but she was giving him precious trust.

"We have to return them to the owner."

"Yeah sure, fine . . . and who would that be?" she bit out. "Triad is a big world, you know. And which family, which gang? Just asking questions will start trouble, and what if I give them to the wrong ones and they'd go missing forever. Or were used to start a gang war. I don't have much to go on, and how the hell did Zarek get them?"

"That doesn't matter. He knows you have them?"

"Oh, yeah."

"Why did you take them?"

She couldn't remember that so she gave him what she could. "They were with a torn e-mail, the words Zhu King Conquers. The source was a remailer," she said before he could ask. "So tracing it wasn't an option."

Only his gaze shifted. "That's it?"

She turned away. "Yeah, that's it."

"How did you get this far being such a crummy liar?"

She didn't turn, didn't face him.

"I can see right through you, Alexa." He crossed the room, stopping behind her. "What led you to Hong Kong, these stones?"

"Not just those, add the e-mail, the ship sailing unscheduled. Then there was his jet being fueled and loaded. I wouldn't have had much reason to follow though, if the dog hadn't been on the jet. He never goes anywhere without Degas."

"That's a little weak."

"I don't usually have that much, just bits and pieces and some instinct."

"They were right."

Despite his words, Alexa felt his distrust as if he were dancing around her. Then he laid the first bomb.

"Where were you for that month?"

She didn't answer. He turned her to face him.

"I can't talk about it."

"It's what got you marked, so you might as well tell me. I can help you."

"No, you can't. No one can. Not even me."

"Jesus, woman, what could be so horrible?"

"Don't you get it? I don't know! He wiped out my memory. Over a month of it." His eyes flared and she talked fast. "I woke up in a sugarcane field twenty miles from Cali, naked, penniless, and worse, the body of my relay decaying beside me."

Killian backed up.

"Don't leave, it gets better. He had my knife in his chest. I knew I'd been compromised, so I took the next required step. By the book. I trustingly tried to come in at the CIA station, and I was greeted with a hail of bullets. They had a picture of Santiago with my knife in him, apparently." At the bar, she poured another drink, wishing for some sunny beach in Pago Pago. "I went to my sources, but Zarek locked down the town, no one would speak to me. I went to Consuelo, she's a hooker, and I forced her to give me clothes and money. That's when I realized I'd been out of touch with my own mind for a month." She took another gulp of whiskey.

"She's dead."

She whipped around. "What?"

"I found her with her throat cut. I wasn't far behind the killer, either."

"That's Franco's style, God dammit!" She stormed outside to the balcony, gripping the rail.

"I'm sorry about her."

"She wasn't a threat, for pity's sake! She died because of me." She brought the drink to her lips. He snatched it before she could drain it, and she scowled at him.

"We may have to leave fast; don't you want to be in control?" He pulled her back inside.

"I haven't been in control for over a month, Killian."

He pushed her into a chair. "Back up and regroup, start from the beginning."

"There is no place to go. The last thing I remember before the cane field was being in Zarek's compound. In his bedroom."

"Doing what?"

"Trying to get an invitation to tour his shipyards."

"I bet that was the last thing on his mind."

"You don't know Zarek. He'd screw a whore out of need, but he treated me like I was the Holy Grail."

"Did you?"

She shot him a thin look. "We covered this subject before."

"You don't have a memory of it."

Oh, hell. He was right. "If we did, it was rape. Somehow I think I'd remember that."

"You don't recall anything?"

"Not until yesterday. I felt more than heard a strange sound." She tried to bring it up from under the cloud of her memory. "It's like a cross between a hum and tapping. It's familiar, too. Like one little nudge would give me the answers. I got the image of a steel slab table and then an oxygen mask coming down."

"Surgery?"

She shrugged.

"Where were you, and what were you doing at the time?"

She scowled at him.

"Something triggered that, Alexa. God knows what you learned, or what he planted. Brainwashing doesn't take cutting you open. Besides, in a month, a small cut will have healed."

"Why do you think I didn't tell anyone? I could be a mole, an assassin, anything he wanted. He had enough time to implant whatever he needed!"

He gripped her hands. "Don't panic, we need to piece it together."

We. She'd never get used to hearing that. "I've been trying, don't you think I have? Sometimes I think he just did whatever to torture me with not knowing."

"Not Zarek. He's clever."

"I took his stones and he wants them for something other than their value. He isn't an antiques connoisseur, he collects people, not things."

"They're for bargaining with the Tong, it's obvious."

"I'm not stupid, I know that," she snapped.

He looked her over. "When was the last time you slept or ate?"

Inside, she went soft. It was just strange having someone be concerned over her. "In the House of Seven Immortals."

He pushed her back inside. "Go take a shower, change. I'll scrounge for something to eat."

Her brows rose.

"What?"

"Why are you being like this, why do you care so much?"

He looked uncomfortable for a second. "Hell if I know. Noble conscience." He went to the kitchen. "Since you've been nothing but a pain in my ass from day one."

"Killian."

He looked up from the fridge, then shut the door and came to her. Alexa felt the pound of her heart in her throat as he gripped her arms. Then he kissed her, not with the hot fire and passion of before, but slow and infinitely more cherishing. It was seeking, a soft probe, and Alexa moaned, gripping his waist. His mouth was supple and slow-moving, drawing everything inside her like a ribbon pulling at her soul. He framed her face in his big hands, his attention only on the kiss, on telling her what he couldn't say.

Then he pulled back, breathing hard as if stunned by that, too. He pressed his forehead to hers.

"If that was the noble conscious speaking, I heard."

He didn't respond, simply urging her toward the bathroom, then turned back to the kitchen. He heard the door close and Killian walked outside. His body was telling him to forget food and go join her in the shower, but thoughts encroached, one after another.

A month missing. Everything she'd said till now could be a plant. Orchestrated by Zarek. *Man, this blows.* He didn't want to believe it, but he had no choice. Being an NOC, she possessed a great deal of sensitive classified information. Zarek could have extracted it and replaced it with what he wanted.

Killian was back to square one. Alexa posed a threat to America's national security.

Price wanted her dead. Now he understood why.

Alive, she was like a timer waiting for the perfect trigger.

Twelve

Killian stopped short when steam rolled out of the bedroom. He moved in, waving at the mist. Alexa lay sprawled across the bed, facedown and naked. The gods were torturing him, he thought, then shut off the shower. He stared as any red-blooded man would. Her hand dangled off the mattress, her hair covering her face. He pushed it back, his gaze traveling over her long slim body. He grew hard, instantly, painfully, and yet his instinct told him to search for marks on her skin, for a sign that she might have been implanted with something or tortured. There was nothing different from the last time he'd seen her bare, or from her stat sheet in her file.

He threw a blanket over her and ignored the gear she'd taken from Pritchard's. He'd seen her stow it and it'd been untouched since. Killian left, checked the locks and traps, then grabbed a beer from the fridge and sat in a chair. He propped his feet on an ottoman, and laid his gun on the table beside the SatCom phone. He should call his team. They had a right to know what was up. He tipped the beer to his lips.

Fuck it. He just couldn't bring himself to betray her tonight.

Day 20

Killian flinched, slapped his hand over his gun, instantly awake. The drapes leading to the deck blew inward and he slid to the floor, tracking shadows and moonlight. The remaining door was still locked, traps in place, and he rose slowly, moving to the open door, then relaxed when he saw her. She stood at the low rail, the east China breeze pushing her hair back with the folds of the silk robe.

Hell of a sight, he thought, like a fantasy played out: hair flying, the thin fabric whipping and molding her body in the moonlight.

"Alexa." She didn't open her eyes, knew he was there.

"I didn't mean to wake you."

"Are you nuts to be out here?"

"Maybe."

He came to her, leaving the gun close. "How'd you get past the traps?"

She smiled softly. "I have my talents," she said, staring out at the port.

There was something different about her, her expression was more relaxed than before, almost serene.

"Isn't it beautiful out here?"

He glanced; the city and harbor lights sparkled on a sea of black. "I guess."

Alexa smiled. "Spoken like a true warrior," she said.

Killian was still, tempted to reach for her, but if he put a single finger on her, it was a mark he could never erase. Alexa could be programmed, a traitor, even if she didn't know it or had no control. That he hadn't updated his men said he was bending the wrong way in this battle, yet she'd proved to be his ultimate temptation. Everything he desired in a woman. He'd faced that somewhere around the witching hour, yet knew it long before, probably from that first kiss in the jungle. Halfway through his third shot of whiskey, he went macho, telling himself she was the best fuck on the planet and that's all it was. But he wasn't into lying, even to himself.

He didn't want just her body, he wanted her soul.

He took a step, crossing a line, and moved behind her, sliding his arms around her waist.

"Oh, I was hoping for that." She sighed back into him, closing her hand over his.

Just to feel her soft length against him was enough to make him rock-hard. The sleek curve of her throat beckoned him and he pressed his mouth there, feeling her pulse beneath his lips. It nurtured something in him, this need to close the distance between them, and when she twisted enough to kiss him, pushing his hands where she wanted, Killian wanted her more than ever. He pulled at the sash, exposed her warm flesh to the moonlight, circling her nipple with his thumb, his free hand sliding down to lay flat on her belly. She wiggled in his arms, pushing his hand, deepening his touch. He slid lower, his finger diving between her warm folds, coating with her liquid. She moaned beautifully, a delicious purr as she pushed back into his erection. She turned, sliding her hands under his shirt and pushing it off over his head. Then her mouth was on his nipple, lips tugging.

"No clothes this time," she whispered.

"I thought you said there wouldn't be a next time."

"I lied." She slicked his nipple and Killian felt his world shudder. "Aren't you glad?" She opened his jeans.

"You have no idea."

She hooked her fingers in the waistband, riding them down. He worked them off, staring down at her, watching as her tongue snaked out to lick the tip of him. He wanted to slam his eyes shut, but he had to watch. He had to. She wrapped her hand around his erection, stroked him his full length, then closed her mouth over the tip.

"Alexa. God." She took him greedily, tightly, till Killian thought he'd come in her mouth. But he wanted to feel her wet flesh on him, her body suck him in, and he grasped her under the arms, dragging her up the length of him.

His mouth came down on hers hot and heavy, making her head spin, electrifying her nerves. The power of it drove her back over the rail, and his mouth left hers, storming a path down her throat to her breasts. He enfolded one, massaging, sucking at her nipple as if starved, taking it deep, then pulling.

Alexa squirmed, between her thighs throbbing to be filled with the hard thrust of him. She held onto the rail, offering him a feast of her body, and his mouth wet a path to her center. She flinched, laughed, and he pushed her thighs wider, and bent.

Her scent aroused him, and he peeled her open, flicked his tongue over her tight little bead. She gasped for air as he tortured her, each stroke deepening with pressure, probing and thrusting. He felt her climax coming.

"Killian stop, please, I want to feel you inside me, please."

He rose, enjoying her struggle for air, smiling as he wrapped his fingers under her knee and lifted it to his hip. They didn't say a word, didn't need to.

He plunged, penetrating her deeply, his thrust making her flex like a pagan offering as she leaned back in the breeze, moonlight slipping over her body. He withdrew and thrust again, and again, her flesh gripping him, combing his erection like strong wet fingers. He smoothed his hand down her body, thumbing her nipples, teasing her sensitive bead.

She leaned up, and he cupped her behind, pulling her legs around him, then he sat on the chaise and like before, she took control, straddling, her hands on his shoulders. A slender wisp of woman undulating in the dark. He'd never forget seeing her like this, the sun breaking the horizon, painting the sky purple; her ripe body ribboned with passion. He looked down to see himself disappear into her, wondering why it felt so amazing with her, and then didn't care. He kissed her, gripping her hips, and pulled her harder and harder. She cradled his face, her gaze locked on him as she came, pulsing with him, shuddering and flexing as the eruption ripped through her like a creature of madness and hunger.

He groaned, his kiss all-devouring, his hips pistoning in a wild ride till he caught up with her—and burned. Killian's mind went blank, sensations hammering him, and he fell back with her, cupping her ass and trembling for long delicious minutes.

She lifted her head and smiled. "That was almost volcanic."

He chuckled, cradled her face, laying a sweet kiss over her mouth that made her heart turn over. "You never cease to surprise me, Alexa."

She swallowed. "Same here." He did things to her, erased old pain and loneliness. She knew it couldn't last, but discovering that she wasn't dried up inside was the only good thing she'd had in a while.

He rose up, scooting off the chaise, and carrying her still intimately locked with him, into the house. In the bedroom, he lowered to the bed with a groan. Forget about moving, he thought. He was helpless.

"Hell, I need to check security. We're too exposed."

Her gaze rode down his fabulous body, stacked with muscle, ropy and twisted. "I think this is as exposed as it gets."

Killian couldn't allow security to lapse because of some great sex. He leaned, left her with a kiss. Really amazing sex, he thought.

"I'm going to take a shower. Unless you want to join me?"

"Jesus. Give me a minute."

"Wuss."

He laughed, grabbed a towel and wrapped it around his waist.

"By the way," she said, and he looked up; she was half in the bathroom, naked and well loved. "When I had the memory flash, I was on TiaPan Street, west end."

"I'll have to look at a map to see what's there."

"Several shops and two restaurants. One's a British pub. There is a church and a Catholic school bisects the street at the end."

"How do you know so much? Was this your operation theater?"

"I went to grade school here, Killian. My parents were State Department attachés. They were killed in a car crash." The way she said it made him believe it wasn't an accident. A family of spies, he thought as she rolled into the bathroom and closed the door.

Killian mulled that over as he went back for their clothes before removing the traps in the house. Sunrise was already here, and though he'd like to join her, in a couple hours they'd have to leave. After he dressed, he fixed some coffee, found some frozen bread for toast. He was buttering bread when it hit him.

He was lying to her. He'd have to bring her to Logan for an exam, to see if she was programmed, or implanted. The thought of putting her in handcuffs made him grind his teeth, but Alexa couldn't be trusted right now. It wasn't her fault.

Killian waited till he heard the shower, then reached for the SatCom phone. Half the night, he'd warred with his conscience and his duty. To himself, his country, and mostly, his team. They'd joined him on this mission because they believed in him, that his judgment was right, and he'd been innocent of the charges.

His emotions weren't in the game then. Alexa Gavlin was a picture and some blacked out pages in a file. Not a living, breathing woman who'd just exploded on him. He stared at the phone for a moment, then punched the number.

He got Riley complaining about the early hour. "I need to speak with Logan." When Logan got on the line, Killian said, "Don't talk, just listen." Then he told him, all of it.

"Holy Hannah. Do you think Price knew about this?"

"No, I don't. Price, odd as it is, was in the right. She was compromised more than anyone thought. But that doesn't negate that she tried to kill me, too."

"Maybe the hitters thought you were in on it with her since you were protecting her."

"It's possible, but right now, I'm not sure of a damn thing other than this is the major fuckup in history."

"What do you need from me?"

"Be the judge, because I can't right now." He rubbed his forehead, agonizing over how to handle this. She was going to hate him. "I've just gained her trust and using it against her feels like betrayal."

"She doesn't deserve to die for this."

"Jesus, I know that! But we can't let her go on. She might be the trigger for those weapons for all we know. She knew exactly how to take out those chips, Logan. Christ, she could be being led along to get her to set them off."

There was a strained silence, then, "Bring her in, Killian, I can try to figure out what's in her head." Logan had the training and enough medical equipment on the jet to give her the works.

"She won't go easily. She's still all hot to follow those missiles."

"And if that's programmed in her? And she gets to them?"

He could barely bring himself to say it, but did. "We'd have to retire her before that. It's possible she's given Zarek what he needs to move those weapons. And with her out of the loop, she can't contact authorities and let them know what's up."

"But we can."

"No, we can't, we're unofficial, too. Save that for a last ditch. We have to take this threat out ourselves." Killian pinched the bridge of his nose. "Man, this sucks."

"I was thinking the same thing."

His head jerked up and his gaze locked on the gun pointed at him, then rose to her face. "What are you doing?"

"Saving my own skin."

She was dressed, her hair damp—and she was prepared to run, wearing her backpack and Pritchard's gear bag.

"Put the gun down, Alexa. Let's talk this out."

"Was this your real plan? Gain her trust, fuck the spy, then put a bullet in her head?"

"What are you talking about?"

"I heard all of it."

His features pulled taut. "Then you misunderstood."

"I've been at this a long time. It's my job to decipher Intel."

"You're wrong."

"You said you'd have to retire me."

The hurt in her eyes devastated him. "Logan has the training to deprogram—"

Her expression went cool, lacking any emotion. "That's not what I asked! Answer the question!" She breathed, calmed, then said, "Would you do it, Killian?"

He met her gaze, his shoulders slumping. "If I had no choice, yes."

Something broke in her. Hope? Her faith in him that had grown overnight? Whatever it was, he'd just destroyed it.

"Put the phone down." He tossed it at the sofa. Alexa moved to cut the connection.

"Don't do this. I can help you."

"I've listened to that bullshit. I trusted you!"

"This is more serious than just running from the CIA and Zarek."

"Gee, you think?"

"He could have put anything in your brain, or you could have told him secrets."

"I didn't tell him anything!"

"There are drugs that—"

"I know that! Don't you think I've gone through this scenario? I told you to back off. I told you to stay away from me. I knew it would come to this."

Killian moved near.

"Don't," she warned.

"Put the gun down, baby."

Alex shored up her heart. Don't listen, she thought, don't remember the last hours, the feel of their bodies molding and moving together. That hour of love and hope. *Damn him.*

"Logan thinks he can get to the bottom of this, find a trigger, help you learn it."

"And if I committed treason? Then you'll kill me."

Killian moved another step. "I can't let you go out

there again, Alexa. I can't, you know too much that's sensitive and you're vulnerable." He moved nearer.

"Please don't come any closer." She took a step back, tears in her eyes. "I'll never forgive you for this, Killian."

"I'm your only option. Let me help you—"

He took another step and she fired. Killian blinked, stunned, then sank to his knees. He was conscious long enough to see Alexa turn her back on him and leave.

Logan threw down the Sat phone, already moving. "We have a big problem."

Max stumbled out, buttoning his jeans. "Hell, man, I was up all night watching that ship do nothing."

"I think she shot him."

The team went into action, Riley rousing Sam. Logan threw gear into his medical kit and was already headed out the door to the helipad. "What did you hear?" Max asked.

"She had a gun on him and she was pissed. She asked him if he had to, would he retire her."

"And the honest son of a bitch told the truth, didn't he?" Sam said, adjusting the headset and grabbing the stick. Everyone secure, the chopper lifted off.

Alexa took Killian's car and drove on automation, blocking out the last few hours, few minutes. She'd been betrayed before. She should be used to it. But not from him.

She smacked the steering wheel and knew her heart was breaking. A little faith, she thought, just a little. That's all she wanted. A day or two. She wasn't a hair-brained idiot, for pity's sake. She would have let him join her, watch her if he wanted. As much as she didn't want to, she understood his position. But she figured after all this time, he could have given her the benefit of the doubt.

Now everyone was turning on her. *God, I hate this job.*

It wasn't until she pulled over to ditch the car that she realized she was crying. *I shot him. Oh, God help me, I shot him.*

Logan put a hand out, tossed a rock to check for traps; the others surrounded the place and came in from the deck. "I see him, he's on the floor. Christ."

Max had the locks open and they pushed through the deck door. Logan rushed in, sliding to his knees and rolling him over. Killian didn't move. Logan checked for a pulse. "Barely there, and slowing. Killian?" Then he frowned at Killian's chest. "He's not bleeding like he should be."

"But look at this place," Riley said. "It's small, she had to have been in close range. It should have gone right through him."

Logan ripped open Killian's shirt. The bullet was visible, and with forceps, he tugged it. It made a sucking sound and he held it up. It had a needle point. He sniffed it, then leaned into Killian's face, calling his name. He roused slowly, and blinked up at them, then down at his chest.

"Shit. That little bitch."

"Tranquilizer dart."

"She must have gotten it from Pritchard's gear," Max said and collectively, they relaxed.

Killian pushed up, groaning as pain stabbed through his chest. He crawled into the nearest chair and slumped, closing his eyes and despite the pain, all he could remember was the hurt on her beautiful face, the utter desolation. Damn. He blew it and she was out there, alone again. He examined the wound before Logan swabbed it and did his doctor thing.

"The bullet fires like the real thing, but penetration wasn't that deep," Logan said.

"God damn hurt like it did!"

"It injects a narcotic strong enough to knock a man out in a second or two." Logan injected him. "It will revive you faster."

"So you want to tell us what happened?" Max asked.

He did, leaving out the fantastic sex before dawn, and finishing when she overheard him. "She was just mad and hurt."

"She shot you!"

"She knew they were tranquilizers, Riley."

"And that matters why?"

"She didn't want to kill me or she would have used her gun. She's going to finish what she started without us."

"At least we still have the marker on her," Sam said, standing guard at the exits.

Logan checked his watch. "Not for long."

"Shit," Killian said. "If that thing deactivates, we'll never find her. Logan, get on that computer and see if you can still track her. Sam and I will be in the air."

"How long do we have?"

The doc was putting away his gear. "About sixteen hours. Then it's dead."

And she could be, too. Killian stood, his equilibrium off for a second. He started for the door. "Give me your shirt." Max looked down, sighed, then stripped off the shirt. In the chopper, Killian checked his weapon, stuffing it behind his back.

"You planning on using that on her?" Sam asked, popping in a stick of gum.

"Anything is possible."

"Killian, she's told you everything."

"And?"

"You said yourself she doesn't trust a soul."

"If you have a point to make, Sam, make it."

"She gave you her trust and you broke it. In her eyes," he added at Killian's look. "Do you honestly think she'll do anything but shoot when she sees you?"

"Just fly, God dammit."

"Yes, sir." Sam steered the chopper skyward in a fast sweep toward the harbor.

If she went anywhere, Killian thought, it would be to watch the ship, or the trucks.

Alexa turned down the narrow street toward the docks, brushing at her tears and getting madder by the moment. She quickened her pace, knowing damn well the Tong were out there, somewhere. With Zarek. *Please don't let the ship be off-loaded.* She slowed as a creepy feeling slipped over her spine, and she ducked into a doorway, looking back. Early hours had the streets filled like last time. Hop the subway, she thought, keep moving. She continued, head down, glancing left and right, then decided on a cab, and lifted her arm to hail one.

The noise level around her increased and she frowned, wondering why the subway was so loud. Out of the corner of her eye, she saw a taxi coming closer to the curb, then slowing as she stepped onto the street. Then the noise suddenly registered and she looked up. A black helicopter dove between the buildings, the *whop* of blades beating the air, lowering rapidly to a soft hum. Jeez. Whisper mode. Her gaze focused on the cockpit. Killian.

Immediately, she turned in the other direction. A car slammed to a stop, nearly hitting her, and as she side-stepped to run, three dark-haired men climbed out, reaching for her.

Alexa reacted instantly, drawing her gun. "Back off!" Alexa's aim was tight and locked. From the far side of the car, a man stood, turning toward her.

Alejandro Carrión.

"Don't you think you're taking this sore loser thing a little too far?"

Carrión glanced at the hovering chopper. "I told Cane he should take away the threat you brought."

Kill her? "Well, aren't you just the sappy, romantic fool," Alexa said, and didn't take her eyes or her weapon off Carrión.

"Women are a dangerous vice." He aimed a pistol at Alexa's head.

"I'll cut you to ribbons, Carrión," came over a speaker from the chopper.

In the chopper, Killian watched, his heart pounding violently. "Get ready to open fire, Sam."

"My guns aren't sniper rifles, Killian. I can't be that precise, they're too close."

"Shit." He popped the window open. Killian knew he could take out two men before Carrión got off a shot. But he didn't want to risk the Latino's aim.

Alejandro's men turned their weapons on the chopper. "One well-placed bullet and the aircraft crashes. Come with me, Jade, and he lives."

Alexa stared Carrión down.

"Think about it, my dove," he said. "Because I do not need him alive." The men prepared to fire.

"Okay, okay!" Alexa let her gun dangle from her fingertips and the men took it.

"Forgive me, *mi dulce.*" His expression was sad. "Sometimes we make bad choices and must do what we can to repair them."

A man pushed her into the backseat, then crowded

in beside her. The car sped away. Alexa turned to look out the back window at the chopper. Hong Kong police were barreling down the road, but the chopper was already climbing. "He won't give up. He'll follow."

"It will be over soon."

That was not comforting. "You want to give me a clue here?"

Alejandro was in front on the left side, the driver speeding toward Kowloon City. He finally turned to look at her, then inclined his head. The two men pawed her, searching her thoroughly, and Alexa sat for it till one squeezed her breast. She shoved his hand away and it went right back. She drove the heel of her hand into his nose so hard it broke.

He howled, clutching his nose and made to backhand her. Carrión caught it mid-strike. He glared and threw it back.

"She doesn't have them."

"In English!"

"He said I don't have them," she translated.

Carrión arched a brow. "Oh, another skill I wasn't aware of."

"I have lots, like ten ways to kill. Want to try them out?" He smiled, the arrogant sucker, and Alexa wanted to slap him.

"You won't have time, and perhaps you can compare death threats with them."

So, they weren't his people. "Where are you taking me?"

Alejandro faced front, silent. Oh, my God, he's nervous, she realized. That scared her. Carrión was a killer in his own right. Who could he possibly fear? They rode for a couple miles, crossing the harbor through the underwater tunnel and emerging in Kowloon. As they pulled off onto Canton Street, and took a couple turns, Alexa didn't recognize the area. They cornered into a driveway before a large warehouse, the wide door riding up as they approached. The driver continued without stopping till they were inside.

We're expected.

The door shut, the lights came on and Alexa felt like a mouse snagged in a trap. Alejandro said nothing as he got out and pulled her from the car, his hand on her arm, guiding her to a staircase. The three men with him disappeared into the darkness of the warehouse. At the top, a Chinese man met them, saying nothing as he stripped Alejandro of his weapons. That Carrión didn't bat a lash gave her the willies. She knew.

No one had to say it. Even as they were led into a beautifully styled office, the walls rich green with ornate Chinese trim work. Tong. Several Chinese men stood almost in assembly, looking up as they stepped in. All attention was on her. She wished she was dressed better, then mentally laughed at that.

One man went to the door, knocking softly. The wait was interminable, everyone staring. "Alejandro?"

"Be silent, woman, and we may get out of this alive."

"Jesus, what have you done?"

"Not me. You."

An elderly man walked between the crowd of suits. Carrión paid him respect with a slight nod. This man was the head of the family. A Tong leader.

"You have something of mine, Miss Everett."

His English was perfect. "And what would that be?"

The man stepped closer, his hands folded in front of him, his posture warm and almost fatherly. Her heart seized at the first words.

"Dan Zhu had a Wei Qi game he cherished above all else. He did nothing but play the game, challenge anyone who would sit with him. Then a woman did, and she did not beat him, but matched him. He lost his heart to her. Unfortunately, he was an old man then and while he loved her, he died soon after."

"And what does this history lesson mean?" Idle talk, she thought.

He put up a finger, silencing her interruption. "He gave her two stones from his prize game. She kept them close to her heart in a bag tied around her neck. When she passed away, another possessed them. They'd stayed in the family for several centuries." He walked nearer to her, meeting her gaze, making her feel the blood in her veins, the beat of her heart in her throat. "Till recently. They were stolen."

"I'm sorry."

"And then stolen from another," he said without missing a beat. He was inches from her, his gaze like an arrow to a target. "I want them back."

"Who *are* you?"

"I am Xia Lin Tang, direct descendant to Yao Di and Dan Zhu of Tang Dynasty."

He must have seen it in her expression, the realization that this man was the rightful owner. "You have the stones."

"Yes."

He let out a breath. "Please hand them over."

"I can't."

Carrión tensed beside her. "Woman, give them up!"

"Butt out, Carrión. This is between Mr. Tang and me now." She met Tang's gaze. "I will give you the stones, but I need privacy first." Embarrassment burned in her face.

He glanced down her body, but didn't question and pointed to a door. Alexa went into it, sealing herself in. She stripped to remove the stones. This had been such a clever idea till now, she thought, then discarded the small plastic sack and stepped out again. She walked to Mr. Tang.

"The stones, sir." She held out her hand, palm up. Mr. Tang smiled and he was reaching for them when her gaze moved to the right. She snatched them back.

Lucien Zarek stood near.

"Give me the stones," Tang demanded, his voice still soft and controlled.

"Why is he here?" Lucien's hand was bandaged, his shoulder in a sling.

"Because they are mine!" Zarek took a step forward, limping. "I paid three million for those."

She looked at Tang. "And what did you pay?"

"That is not your concern, give me the stones."

"Carrión?"

"Do it or we do not leave here alive!"

Alexa poured the stones into Tang's palm, then stepped back near her only ally, Carrión.

"You promised me her," Zarek shouted, hobbling forward.

Carrión stepped between her and Lucien. "Do not test me, Zarek. She is under my protection."

Alexa's brow shot up. Interesting.

"By God, I will kill you for this!" Zarek hissed.

Carrión's look was condescending. "You seem to have bigger problems than me."

Tang waved his hand, holding the stones close, entranced by them as his lieutenants moved forward. Alexa anticipated the Tong doing as they pleased, bargains be dammed. But Carrión faced her, put his hand on her arm and urged her out under an escort.

"We are not done, Jade," Zarek shouted. "This is not over!"

Alexa turned to say something but Carrión pulled her along. His weapons returned to him, they were in the car, driving out of the warehouse in moments.

* * *

Lucien watched her leave, seething with anger. He turned to Tang. "Our deal is done. Let my ship dock."

Tang looked up, almost surprised to still find him there. "You have brought far too much attention to yourself. You have four hours."

Lucien started to protest till Tang waved. Two men stepped in front of Lucien, gesturing politely toward the exit. Lucien ground his teeth and limped to the door.

Damn Chinese. Always about saving face.

In the car, Alexa's hands hadn't stopped shaking. "How did you know I had them?"

"Simple logic. Mr. Tang and I are . . . acquainted. He expressed concern over the payment due him from Zarek. Zarek was hunting you. I assumed the stones were the reason."

"Why get involved at all?"

"It is wiser to fight the enemies you can kill. The Triads are far too powerful for even me to cross, my sweet."

"Cut the adoring Latin lover crap. You've just opened a can of worms bigger than you know."

"And you, woman, owe me your life."

"How you figure?"

"They were coming for you, any way they could. I agreed to bring the stones and you to them with the promise that you not be harmed."

"How gallant, I'm just all a-quiver." She paused and then, "What did Zarek get in the bargain?"

"Docking privileges."

She'd thought as much. "In Star Harbor, now?"

"All I know is that the stones would allow him to dock."

"Where, dammit!"

A dark van crossed in front of them and Carrión slammed on the brakes, swerving.

Alexa took one look at the driver and shouted, "Drive through it!"

"Are you mad?" Men in black masks spilled out, aiming with automatic weapons.

"Madre de dios."

She jammed her foot on top of his, and the car plowed into the van, shoving it sideways into parked cars and taking one man down. Metal scraped, and she was nearly in Alejandro's lap, reaching across him for his gun. "Move! Move!"

Alejandro shoved her aside and swerved around the edge of the van. "Duck." Bullets sprayed the back of the car, shattering the rear window.

Alexa returned fire till his gun was empty, then lunged over the backseat for her gear and found her own. "Don't stop, head west." She popped in a magazine.

"Why?"

"Do it, Carrión. Unless you'd like to stop and say hello?"

"Sarcasm does not become you." Bullets chunked into the rear of the car as he tried dodging people and cars, blasting the horn.

"Really? I thought I was good at it." She aimed at the back, firing two rounds into the van's engine. The men were trying to get in and start it. She saw one man, big as a bull and standing in the center of the street. He cricked his neck before he sighted down the barrel of a rifle. Alexa recognized the move and fired. The shot hit the van window near his head, shattering it. Damn. "Faster! Go faster!"

"I am, this isn't a highway." Carrión glanced in the rearview. "Who are they? It can't be the Tangs."

"It's Franco."

"How can you tell?"

"Trust me, I've seen his work." She heard a chopper, and leaned to look. It was following them. Killian. "Turn here." He didn't, and she put the barrel of the gun in his crotch. He obeyed and cursed rudely.

"Slow down and take the next right."

"You know this area very well."

Her look was deadpan. "I looked it up on Map Quest."

"You lie, but then I think everything you are is a lie." She glared at him. "Stop."

Alejandro looked around as he slowed the car, frowning at the large Catholic church on the corner bisecting two streets.

"Here, stop here. If you're smart, you'll go home. Lucien has been a very bad boy and you do not want to be caught in it."

"I have business here and a nuisance like Zarek will not interfere."

"Don't be an ass." Alexa grabbed her packs and left the car. Carrión climbed out. She turned the gun on him. "Follow me and I'll shoot you."

"*Mi dulce,* it's too dangerous. I cannot let you go like this."

The church bells started ringing. "I'm so touched, Alejandro. Perhaps you're right." She gave him her "save me big strong man" expression, and he smiled with triumph as she moved toward him. Behind her back, she aimed the gun and fired twice at the car. The sound was only partially muffled by the church bells.

Alejandro lurched back, cursing rudely.

"I wouldn't start the car, I smell gas."

When he looked around for her, he caught a glimpse before she melted into the sea of people.

Thirteen

Sam flew the chopper over the city like he was heading into battle, the skyscrapers' antennae and satellite dishes threatening to slice through the underbelly of the craft. Killian spared him a "cut the dramatics" look, but Sam just grinned.

Killian turned his attention back to the LCD screen with the transmitter receptor beeping a pulse and fading in and out. Alexa was going to be untraceable by nightfall. He'd already lost track of her once.

"She's on side streets, walking, I think." He sighted through field glasses. "Too high up to get a good look. Land this thing, I'll go on foot."

"That's not wise, man," Sam said. "Moving on the ground is damn slow."

"Just do it."

Tight-lipped, Sam searched for a place to land.

Killian clenched his fist on his thigh and admitted he was worried. He had to assume whatever transpired in the Tang warehouse had to do with the stones. He prayed she gave them up, and was damn thrilled to see her—with all her fingers—in Carrión's car when it left the premises.

The radio crackled with Logan's voice. "We got some MSS Intel going, Mustang, come back."

Killian hit the switch, pressing on the headset. "Go ahead."

"They know about her. I'm hearing talk about an American woman and her suspicious behavior. They mentioned someone named Pong."

He had to reach her first. "Can you tune up that responder?"

"Sorry, it's wilting fast."

Sam swooped low and set the chopper on a corporate building helipad. Before they touched down, the security cops were waving wildly and shouted not to land. Killian got out and Sam immediately lifted off.

The guards were coming toward him. *Looks like I'll have to negotiate my way down to the ground.* He threw the first punch.

The sky split, letting loose torrential rains. Alexa was grateful for the cover it offered, and ran till she got a stitch in her side, hurrying back the way she'd come, toward Mi Ling's. She slopped through muddy streets between skyscrapers, dodging children and people on bicycles, then ducked under a vendor's awning and bought a sampan hat. She tucked her hair into her shirt, but blending in wasn't an option; her hair and eyes gave her away. She checked behind her, then dashed between buildings sandwiched too close, and stopped at Mi Ling's door. She knocked, watching the street.

Nothing.

Then she noticed the scuffed pillars of salt on the threshold. *Someone's been here.* She tried the door, her body tensing when she found it unlocked. She drew her gun and pushed gently, swinging it wide. She entered, scanning the room before she checked behind the door, then closed it. Alexa moved slowly, quietly looking in closets and under tables. Then she saw the kettle steaming on the stove.

"Mi Ling?" She called twice more, louder, then heard, "Little tiger."

Alexa moved quickly into the next room. "Oh, God," she muttered, checked the windows and exits of the sewing room before she went to Mi Ling. She stuffed her weapon in the back of her slacks and helped her off the floor and into a chair. She brushed the hair back off Mi Ling's face. Her lip was swollen. "What happened?" Alexa grabbed a scrap of fabric, but Mi Ling took it, blotting her own mouth.

"They were looking for you."

"Who? Here?"

She expected her to say the Tangs, or Zarek, anyone, but . . . "MSS."

Ministry of State Security. "Great. You're certain?"

Mi Ling sent her an impatient look. "I am the widow of a diplomat, I know who I spoke with."

"Of course." That meant they'd seen her coming this way yesterday. "Do you think they know how we know each other?"

"No, that I know for certain. They followed you."

The Chinese man on the corner, she thought, at the magazine stand. "What did they say?"

"They know you were on a ship." She said it like a question.

"Damn."

"That was stupid, girl."

"I had a purpose," she said as she went into the kitchen area, and took the teapot off the burner. Mi Ling followed her in, and Alexa rushed to pull out a chair for her, but Mi Ling snatched it from her, setting it down with a thump and giving her a "do not treat me like I'm feeble" glare. Alexa dropped her packs on the floor, then went to spoon in tea and set the kettle on a trivet to steep.

"The man, very tall, he wanted to know what you were doing in China."

Alexa looked up.

"I told them nothing."

And they struck her for it. Mi Ling's savior was her dead husband's reputation. Hurting her would have brought scandal and stirred the People's Republic into an uproar.

"You knew what those stones were, didn't you?" She strained the tea into a cup.

She scoffed. "I am Chinese, of course I knew. I suspected they were old."

"Very old. They belonged to the Tang family." She glanced to catch her reaction, but Mi Ling's face was impassive. So typical. She sighed and went on. "I had the opportunity to give them to their owner."

Mi Ling inhaled, her eyes widening. "You will tell me everything."

Alexa spoke as she brought her the tea, and remained standing.

"You are lucky to be alive."

"Don't I know it. Now I have Chinese intelligence this close." She gestured to Mi Ling's swollen lip. Alexa gave in and sat, cradling her head. "I'm so sorry you were hurt."

Mi Ling scoffed and clutched Alexa's hand. She gripped back. "Look at me, Alexa." She lifted her head, and Mi Ling stroked her hair off her brow, then swept her fingers under Alexa's chin. "You are such a brave girl."

Alexa smiled, tears blurring her image. She'd lost her girlhood the day she was recruited.

"Perhaps you should let this go?"

"I wish I could. I really do. But I'm too much a part

of it. It's not like before, Mi Ling. I used to be on the outside looking in, manipulating the players. This time, I'm being manipulated." The cane field, Santiago with her knife in his chest, the cryptic e-mail she shouldn't have been able to get near, the ship sailing ahead of schedule, Zarek's dog being seen loaded on the aircraft, Carrión, the buyers at the party. She had to give Zarek credit, it was like a well-paced dance leading to a big finish. And she was terrified that finish would be hers, too.

The older woman's expression questioned, and Alexa debated telling her the truth. Telling Killian got her another target on her back. She shook her head. "It's too dangerous for you to know."

Mi Ling leaned even closer, her eyes intense. "Then you must leave the country. The MSS, they're suspicious and what they do not know, they will stop at nothing to learn." Mi Ling swallowed. "And keep you from telling anyone."

Alexa had to take the risk or she'd never get her memory back. "I promise to be smart and careful." It was the only reassurance she could offer as she slid off the chair, and hugged her mother's friend. "Good-bye."

Mi Ling said nothing as Alexa grabbed her packs and walked out the door, never looking back.

Lucien hobbled to the window, cursing Tang and his people. His body ached, the dull throb in his finger as if the digit were still there. He bent, peering through the telescope. Rain misted his view. The rented apartment wasn't the best accommodations or location. He couldn't see the port side of the ship, but he could see the line of trucks as they were loaded. But his prime interest was the appearance of one woman. She would come. She'd been on the ship, she knew what was in there.

His patience wasn't infinite. He was already exhausted with pain, and his own mistakes had cost him too dearly. Yet the pieces on the chess board were in full motion. Third Bureau of MSS had just enough anonymous information to hunt her. It would push her closer to the source, the ship. He no longer needed her alive. The thought didn't please him as he'd hoped. Then without fail, her image came to him, that night in his bedroom, the sexy way she'd looked at him before he'd kissed her. His body hardened and he shifted position, his knee threatening to collapse under him. Beside him on the floor Degas slept, flinching at any little sound. It infuriated him. Given the opportunity, he'd kill that man who'd struck his precious beast.

He straightened and let out a long breath, calling for assistance. He lowered into a chair as Franco repositioned the telescope so he could sit and watch.

Franco stood by.

"You've disappointed me, Franco."

"Carrión assisted the woman."

Lucien twisted in the padded chair to look at him. "Is that an excuse?"

"No, sir."

"I'll deal with Carrión. Shouldn't you be out looking for her?"

"She'll surface, sir. She's been predictable."

"If she was, then we'd have her by now and be done with this!" Lucien waved and Franco glared down at him, then left the room.

Lucien leaned forward and sighed.

Day 21
Late afternoon

Alexa sipped Blue Mountain coffee in a sidewalk café near the harbor, watching the trucks being loaded.

She could almost feel the surveillance breathing down her neck, making her skin prickle, yet she couldn't see anyone suspicious. At least Moore didn't have another chopper in the sky. That was pretty daring, flying below the skyline, and it warned her that Moore would do anything to take her in. It hurt. Even if she understood his position, even if nothing had gone on between them, it still hurt that he'd hunt her instead of help her like he'd promised.

Her gaze zeroed in on the trucks, the workers moving fast after being stuck there for three days waiting. Lucien should be nearby, but she didn't see his men anywhere. Franco ought to be overseeing this, she thought, but then, since Lucien was badly injured, he was probably schlepping trays and puffing pillows. Lucien didn't take pain well. Her lips curved at that.

When the last crate was loaded, she paid her bill and started walking. It was good to be in her own clothes and looking halfway decent for a change. It wasn't a risk going to her hotel. It was intentional. She had a tail and she wanted to make certain where her trailing puppies were. She'd had to be seen to do it, and had led them around, having her nails done, buying walking boots, then an early lunch and a night's rest interrupted by one call from her shore man watching the ship. She'd cleared out the hotel room, leaving the flight attendant's suitcases behind and ditched some of Pritchard's gear in the trash, keeping only the essentials. She'd done a bob and weave to find them, then to lose them. She wasn't sure if she had.

Time to find out, she thought, pushing through the glass doors of a boutique. The hooker she'd bargained with was waiting. The woman was the same height and build and wore a dark auburn wig. "Move fast and don't leave the city." Alexa handed her the key to her hotel room, which was rented for another day. "Stay in the room for a couple hours, ditch the wig, change into the clothes I left, then split."

"The rest of my money?" The half-Chinese woman sanded her fingers together.

"In the room, under the TV." Alexa didn't trust her to take the first payment and not stiff her for the job. She needed her for some cover, a diversion.

The woman primped in the mirror, their clothes almost an exact match. For good measure, Alexa gave up her jacket. "Go, now."

Tossing her a sharp look, the hooker left the shop and Alexa stood back from the windows, the congestion of people making it hard to see her. She was beginning to think her plan didn't work until the hooker was a couple blocks down. A car slowed behind her, tying up street traffic for a bit. The hooker got into a car Alexa had rented, then drove toward the hotel. The sedan followed.

Alexa glanced around the shop, needing something to hide her pistol, and selected a brown leather jacket from the rack, paid cash, then moved through the back of the shop, out the rear. In the alley, she stopped short when she saw the dirty, dented Land Rover that looked on its last leg. Glancing around, she got in and started hot-wiring the engine. She peered over the dash a couple times and when the engine turned over, she shifted behind the wheel and headed after the trucks.

David leaned over the counter at the SatCom entrance and smiled at the young woman. She wasn't half bad, if she'd change her hair and had a lesson in makeup. Hers made her look like a fifties mom, and she had to be about twenty-four.

"My boss in there?"

She blinked up at him. "No, sir."

"Call me David."

"No, David, she was in earlier, I understand."

David glanced at his watch. "How long have you been here?"

Her features tightened and she looked at the log sheets, then said, "I see your point, sorry."

"No problem, Director Price does what she wants. I spend half the day trying to catch up with her and I'd really like to be on top of things for a change."

The girl, Maggie, her ID tag said, rose and went to the secure door, opening it with a key code. David memorized it. Not that he could get past this security on his own. He walked in behind her. She investigated the room, waving at the tech, and looked at him suspiciously a couple times. David just smiled and admired her ass. Which was small and tight. *Bet she has great legs, too,* he thought. But who could tell under those baggy pants? He stayed a step or two behind to give her the feel of authority.

Surrounded in soundproofing materials and glass with giant screens against a sea of black, the section was state-of-the-art. But it was the "Throne" he salivated over. A padded chair he'd seen Price in several times, most of those, recently.

She caught him staring at it. "You want to sit in it?"

"I can't."

"Says who?" She winked at him and David moved into the hot seat, keying it up. "Oh, you can't do that." She rushed forward, glancing at the others. "You've been in it before."

She looked damn cute pouting like that. "No, I've seen her call up stuff. Learning is seeing, seeing is learning."

"Oh, my gosh, my dad used to say that."

He looked at her. "So did mine." For a second, he was captivated, then remembered that if they were caught, he'd be fired, or worse, charged. He glanced down at the screen, the numbers rolling. Several were the same, a jumble of numbers ticking off that he didn't understand. But needed to. If Price had been calling, why not just use a secure phone? Why come in here?

"What's up there?" he said, and hadn't meant to speak aloud.

"Birds. Satellites," she explained. "Listening to intelligence traffic." She gestured to the analysts. "Every country has some and we watch them, they watch us," she said and tugged him from the chair. He kept reciting one number over and over to remember it. Later he'd find out what it meant.

She frowned at him and he realized he wasn't holding up his end of the conversation. Outside he smiled and leaned on her counter again. "Want to go for some coffee later?"

"The coffee here stinks."

"I meant after work. Away from here."

"Well, I don't know."

"Come on, Maggie. Let your hair down with me. It's just coffee." She smiled and pushed up her glasses. "You should wear contacts, you have beautiful eyes." He wasn't lying.

"Okay. But I'll meet you somewhere."

"A cautious woman, I like that."

He took a piece of paper and jotted the numbers down he'd memorized, before his own cell number, distracting her with knocking over her pencils. He slipped the first into his pocket, then handed her the other. "I'll be waiting."

As he turned away, he was surprised that he really wanted to see her again.

Not a field man, my ass.

* * *

Max was on the ground with Killian as he radioed Sam in the sky. "You're wrong, Sam, I'm looking right at her." He kept his distance and slowed the SUV.

"Not unless she changed bodies. She's north and moving fast."

Scowling, Killian's gaze followed the woman as she pulled the car into the hotel's underground lot and got out, then headed to the elevators. "He's right, it's not her."

"Looks like her, walks like her," Max said.

Killian left the SUV and ran to the elevator, and when the woman stepped inside and turned, he raised his gun. Her dark almond eyes went round and she stumbled back. He tipped the weapon to the ceiling as the door shut. He should have known. Alexa didn't sway like that when she walked. No use questioning the Asian woman, either.

Killian ran to his SUV, and they tore out of the underground lot. They got snagged in a traffic jam a half mile down the street. He smacked the steering wheel.

"She'll have an hour on us."

Max was listening to the team on the radio. "The marker is fading so fast Logan keeps losing it."

"If we lose her, we'll find her dead."

"Anyone ever tell you you're a pessimist?"

Killian yanked the wheel to the right, driving up on the curb and laying on the horn.

"I stand corrected," Max said and held on.

Alexa kept far behind the trucks, the hilly terrain in the north making it hard to keep up and not be seen. She crested a steep hill; a checkpoint lay ahead. She instantly veered off the road. Okay, this is damn unusual. Checkpoints were only near restricted areas, even in China. So why here? Northward, Guangzhou was bursting at the seams with military bases, but not here in Fujian.

She eased the car to the far left under a banyan tree and cut the engine. The region was rocky hills and thick brush that reminded her of Chechnya. Except for the rice paddies. She'd passed a village a few miles back, but other than that, she hadn't seen a soul. She pulled out her map, sketching possible locations for the drop. There was a small port northwest, but Shanghai was just as far.

Coming this way didn't make any sense. If they were taking weapons north, why not just make port there? Maybe the Tang clan wouldn't allow them to port anywhere but Star Harbor. She still didn't know who was buying the cargo, or if the transaction was complete. It could have been done electronically, though Lucien liked dealing in cash. The Mayan coins he toyed with constantly was enough to tell her he enjoyed the feel of money in his palms.

Alexa left the car, stripping it, then slipped on the shoulder harness and checked her weapon before holstering it. It felt heavier under her arm, but she'd be walking fast to catch up. She pulled on the backpack over the jacket, and took off into the forest, moving to higher ground to get a good look at the checkpoint. She needed to see inside the trucks, search at least one.

She hiked for a half mile, then positioned herself on a ledge of rock, and between the branches of the bush, sighted through field glasses. Four large trucks. A single truck could easily accommodate at least half the pieces. Unless they were assembled already. The drivers were outside, having a smoke and stretching their legs while local police checked papers. Children watched from the road and she swung the glasses, spying a village in the northwest.

They're going to be a while, she thought, sitting

back on her butt and taking out an energy bar. What she wouldn't give for a good meal and time to eat it right now, she thought, finishing off the last of the dry bar. She was storing the wrapper when a hand covered her mouth.

She struggled violently till she felt the hard barrel of a pistol against her temple.

A second later the electrical charge of a tazer lit up her insides like firecrackers.

"Cutter to Mustang, get on the wire, asap."

Killian fished for the radio. "Mustang, go ahead."

"The marker stopped. It's dead."

Killian checked his watch. "Should it be?"

"Only if she is."

Killian's heart seized. "Give me her last known location."

"She was south of Fujian when it stopped."

Killian glanced at the GPS as Max pointed it out.

"Nearly a hundred miles? She must have been booking."

"There's more . . . I thought this could wait but—"

Killian braced himself. "Go ahead."

"I'm getting low voltage signals, like someone's trying to come under the wire."

"Cell traffic, police radios?"

"No, more distant. It's not reaching here in anything but a scramble of ones and zeros."

His brows knit. "Can you find the origin?"

"Been trying, I think I need to call in an expert."

Killian didn't know anyone who was better than Logan. "We're going north, I'll keep radio contact only if necessary. Get Sam to refuel and on standby."

"He lives for that," Logan said and cut the connection.

Killian tossed the hand radio aside and barreled out of Kowloon City toward the north.

David Lorimer was alone in the offices.

Price was somewhere in the building probably biting off heads and spitting them out, he thought as he slipped behind her desk. He pulled up her computer files, typing fast and watching the door. A fresh coffee service was set and if need be he could dash to it. She liked that, a man cleaning up after her.

He opened any file within the Colombian theater of operation, reading fast, then closing. That Evelyn Wood course was suddenly worth the money. He kept it up yet didn't find anything untoward, then searched the files she'd worked last to find out exactly what she was doing. Or had done. Where was that Delta 941 file?

He didn't get the chance to find out. The door handle rattled. He signed out, cleared his path, then shot out of the chair and to the service as she entered the office.

"What are you doing in here?" Her gaze went to her desk. More importantly, to the safe behind it.

With as bland a look as he could muster, he turned, holding out a china cup and saucer. "I was replacing the service."

"The cleaning staff does that."

"Yes, ma'am, but they didn't this morning, so I did."

She eyed him, then took the cup. David didn't wait and walked back to his office, sinking into his chair. His hands shook as he laid them on the keyboard.

Christ. What was he thinking? He could go to jail for this.

David weighed his options. Gavlin, he knew, was a small part of this. A pawn. He knew that because she wasn't consulting any of her aids or department heads.

Price didn't normally keep files in her safe. She couldn't take anything out of here. Well, *he* couldn't. The security didn't search her so thoroughly. He needed something concrete before he alerted someone who could question her openly.

He had to retrace her steps, and fast.

Killian approached the Land Rover cautiously, Max watching his six. He moved behind the wheel, noticing first the pulled wires, and that the car was clean. He searched it anyway, finding Chinese registration. Stolen. He left the car, looking into the mountains.

"Any idea what's in the area?"

"A village farther north, a port in the west." Max shrugged.

"You take the road for a bit, I'll track this way." He followed her footprints from the car up the hill. He kept a steady pace, his heart lurching every time he found a piece of her trail. A bent branch, a skidmark. He could tell where she paused and he was a quarter mile from the car when he found where she'd stopped.

Killian knelt, lifting the energy bar wrapper. *She wouldn't have left this*. He scanned the ground, seeing the grasses mashed a few feet behind. A blind approach. He could still see her body print, the crushed grass shell of her shoe and knee. He fitted himself in the same position, then looked around. He spied Max on lower ground, walking back and forth. He hit the walkie-talkie.

"What is it?"

"Tire tracks. Lots of them, and footprints, they stopped here. Tons of White Horse cigarette butts."

Chinese brand. Nothing new about that. "Come up here."

Max turned back and jogged to him. Killian stood when he met up with him. "She was right here looking down at the trucks. Why were they stopped?"

"Grass crushed on the shoulders of the road. Maybe a checkpoint or a breakdown. Other than that, nothing I could see. No oil or antifreeze. But then, it could have just been a coffee break."

"The way Zarek was chasing her down for those stones, no. He's anxious and the trucks wouldn't have stopped without reason."

"Then where is she?"

Killian looked back at the angle Max had come, then took a couple steps west. Several yards back from her position, the tall grasses were smashed as if someone had been lying in them. Waiting.

His head jerked up. "She was here."

"What? You smell her perfume?"

"Someone was waiting for her. They knew she'd watch the trucks."

"A checkpoint?"

"If it was, it was fake as hell."

"This is pretty elaborate for Zarek. Even if the missiles were off-loaded."

Killian followed the track through the shifting grass, his boots sinking into waterlogged rice fields. They couldn't have gone this way. He changed direction, walking north and faster.

"A helicopter?" Max asked.

"I'm thinking, yeah, Third Bureau and they're close." Killian's gaze moved over the landscape. In the quickening darkness, he could barely make out the rice paddies blending up to mountains that cut through the black sky. Mist rolled in slowly, blurring everything beyond a few yards of visibility.

Where are you, Alexa? Where would they take you?
He didn't have an answer.

National Military Communications Center (NMCC)
Current Action Center (CAC), The Pentagon
Day 22

Air Force Staff Sergeant Walter Scoggins moved from desk to desk collecting sheets of information from his techs. The men and women of his unit were information gatherers, spending endless hours hacking into files of foreign nationals. In the U.S. and abroad. His job was to gather the information and form it into a value-listed report for the Joint Chiefs. He paused, glanced over the paperwork and looked up toward the glass gallery that offered a view to the command center. A couple three-stars stared down, chatting between themselves.

CAC was a hub of activity. Always. The fight for freedom never rests.

He slid behind his desk and organized his material, paused to get a fresh cup of coffee, then sat to decipher. His job was to see beneath the normal. To learn if the black hats were where the U.S. thought they were, and behaving. He was an expert at it. He smiled when he thought of his wife and how she had said "his anal retentive side finally found a home."

As good as he was, it would be another four days before he realized what he had.

And its significance.

Fourteen

Small homes surrounded one larger building, all paths leading to the flat wood structure that was aged by the wind. Max Renfield sat on the hill, watching. No one paid him much attention. A few stopping to stare, wave, then go back to work. He'd grabbed a backpack of gear and a ball cap of Killian's. His hair was long enough that it stuck out and made him look like a youth hostel student walking across the country. Children gathered, giggling and waving as if waving to a dragon. One got brave and climbed the slope.

His Chinese was awful, but he and the boy about seven managed. His English was far better anyway. It was when he heard the word coffee that his ears perked up. The kid pulled his hand and he moved down the hill with him toward the building. The closer he got the more it reeked of roasting beans. Familiar, and making his mouth water.

The Chinese elite and restaurants that dealt with tourists needed coffee while the rest drank tea. He stopped at the edge, trying to get the kid to understand that he didn't want him in trouble for bringing him there. Then a man came out, short, more Japanese-looking than Chinese and wiping his hands on a stained apron.

Max played the role of the curious foreigner, trying his language skills and sucking so badly, it got a rise out of the workers. As he moved inside, he noticed the trucks were backed up to the warehouse door. But the crates were inside, broad as a car and tall. The workers already had them cracked open, cutting the bags and pouring the beans into a hopper for roasting. A couple of young men were breaking up some of the crates for wood for the fires.

The older man handed him a cup of coffee and Max savored it, staring at the crates. He watched impatiently as the last were broken open. He thanked them, said good-bye, and before he left, he gave the kid his last Butterfinger candy bar.

Killian hunted like a wolf after a fresh scent, for anything to lead him to her. It was like searching for dirt in the sky. At dark, he finally accepted it and radioed Max.

"The village has one source of income other than farming," Max said. "It's got a processing plant."

"Come back?"

"It's a coffee processing plant, Mustang. We've been had. I can account for every crate that was loaded on the trucks. All coffee."

They must have deliberately switched the crates and that meant they knew they were looking. "A decoy, damn."

Then Max said it. Words he never wanted to hear.

"Yeah, we lost the missiles."

Day 23
Fujian

Alexa flinched, wet stone scraping her skin. Like leftover static, energy reverberated down her body. She lay perfectly still for several moments, waiting for it to pass, and wanting to sink back into the oblivion where nothing mattered. She forced her eyes open and got a mouse's view of a long narrow cell that looked medieval. At one end was a small rough wood table beyond the cell bars. Other than that, nothing else, not even a bucket.

Gingerly, she inched back on her hands and knees, then sat on the floor, her back against the stone wall. She felt drained and chills wracked her, her limbs quivering violently, and she occupied herself with watching it till it passed. Her heartbeat felt erratic, yet the feeling was coming back into her mouth again. Her fillings felt cooked to her teeth.

She pushed her hands into her hair and held her throbbing skull. "I so hate tazers."

She remembered nothing beyond watching the trucks, then a hand over her mouth before the electric charge. *They were waiting for me. Makes you a really lousy spy this week, doesn't it?* She looked around. There were two other cells, far apart and empty. More like animal pens, yet the bloodstained hay on the floor told her the last occupants didn't fare so well. A gray cat sat on a fresh pile, cleaning itself till it spied something moving near the wall and dove for it. There was one high window on the opposite wall, two doors: one small and severely padlocked, the other, a pair of tall steel-enforced wood doors wide enough to drive a tank through.

She leaned back, relaxing her arms, wishing she was with Killian, wishing she'd hung around long enough to let him explain. "But no," she mocked. "You had to jump the gun and run."

She didn't know how long she was there having a nice little pity party before the tall outer doors scraped open, shadows breaking behind the figures moving past the entrance. She wasn't all that surprised to see the man in the long coat moving toward her. He really had a whole *Matrix* thing going on.

He stopped outside the cell, staring at her through coal black eyes. Cantonese, she figured. He was tall, slender, and aside from the telling scar across his throat, he was attractive. A uniformed troop moved up beside him and opened the cell door.

"Stand up," he said in English.

She did.

He entered. "What is your name?"

She said nothing.

"We know you have been watching the *Red Emperor,* why?"

She stared straight ahead.

"You are an American spy."

Alexa focused on his chin, a centimeter below his lips. He removed his gloves, then his jacket, tucking the gloves in his waistband, fingers down, then dressing the chair with the coat. On the table, the contents of her backpack was displayed like a museum. The gig was definitely up.

He kept asking questions over and over. Alexa heard all of them. They were watching Zarek and that meant her, too. Possibly Killian. *These are the people who hurt Mi Ling,* she thought and that gave her a little more willpower. Besides, admitting what she knew would be treason. Even to save her own life.

"What was in the cargo of the ship?"

Man, the Tangs must have some power in these parts if they couldn't get on it.

"The People's Republic do not like Americans spying on them. But I am certain you know this."

I wasn't spying on you, sir, but the ship.

He took satisfaction in saying, "The *Red Emperor* has left Hong Kong."

Oh, crap. Was it headed back to Colombia already?

He moved near, looking her up and down. Sweat pooled at the base of her spine, at her temples. The clamminess of her skin reeked of fear. She had nothing in her favor. Without preamble, he backhanded her so hard she fell across the chair to the floor.

For a moment, she simply lay there, absorbing the pain exploding in her face.

"You will talk to me."

She worked her jaw and glared, arching a brow. *Not after that crack, pal.*

It was the wrong thing to do. He motioned to the troop, who dragged her off the floor and shoved her into the chair. Then dark and thin grabbed her hand and placed it on the table. "We will see how you like it after I am done."

He withdrew a blade and held it primed over her hand.

Alexa lifted her gaze to his. He wanted fear, terror. He wouldn't get it.

See me, she thought. *I'm Alexa Gavlin. This is who I am.*

He brought the knife down.

She didn't even scream.

The Pentagon

An Air Force colonel stepped into the staff conference room, and moved to the general's side, bending low to whisper, "Sir, you have a call from Pryznovich."

The general frowned and nodded, keeping his face impassive as he stood and left the Joint Chiefs of Staff lining the long maple conference table. In a secure room on a scrambled line, he nodded to the colonel and he put through the call from the Russian Secretary of Defense.

"Andre, it's good to hear from you, perhaps I can call you back and we can—"

"There is no time, General. I call in the gravest of moments."

He remembered the school full of people blown up only a year ago. "What can the U.S. do to help?"

"We have recently learned that we have lost some missiles."

Oh, Christ. "Be a bit more specific, please."

There was a heavy sigh on the other end of the line and the general knew what it took to alert the U.S. government of this trouble.

"We were to decommission and dismantle hundreds for destruction. They'd been deemed too inaccurate for use and were already in pieces and loaded onto trucks to be transported to the harbor." He said that as if he still could not fathom the crime. "The pieces were destroyed, yet during the final count, the components for three were missing. All personnel guarding the weapons were killed."

"I'm afraid to ask, but what type of weapons?"

"MRBMs."

Medium range ballistic missiles. They had a range of one thousand to three thousand kilometers. A good thousand miles.

"They were our first versions of laser guided SSN."

The general jotted it down and handed it to the colonel. The message read, *Get me an expert on Russian weapons.* "Why didn't you come to us before?"

"Come now, Richard," Andre said, his Georgian accent lighter than his colleagues. "Would you have without first searching? Pieces were stolen. No complete operational missiles. The rest were to be sunk with other salvage. Useless."

"Obviously not to everyone. What do you want the U.S. to do about it?"

"Nothing." He sounded affronted at the mere implication that they'd need U.S. assistance. "I am merely warning you."

General McGill pinched the bridge of his nose. "Those missiles in the hands of terrorists would be aimed at the U.S. and her allies."

"I will leave it to you to warn them."

"What about the launchers?"

"Need I remind the general that those are not as closely guarded and are easily adaptable?"

"No, you don't." God dammit. A launcher could be constructed with an MIT grad and a flatbed trailer.

"I will be in contact."

McGill hung up and read his notes, then walked quickly into the action center, putting everyone on alert. Damn Russians refusing to ask for help till it was a major screwup no one could fix. Jesus, laser-guided. Painting a target could be done by anyone. Even a child. What the hell was the U.S. going to do about it?

He stopped at a captain's desk. The young man snapped to attention. "Sir."

"We have information on Russian missile trash being hijacked?"

The captain frowned. "Yes, sir."

"Why wasn't I informed?"

"I did, sir, it's in the report on your desk."

McGill strode into his office, leafing through his in box till he found it, then read it. It was four days old. "Christ. I need locales, names, association, buzz, anything."

"We have, sir. Staff Sergeant Walker is on it."

The captain trailed him as the general went directly to the staff sergeant's desk.

The man jumped to his feet so fast he overturned his pen cup. "Sir?"

"At ease, Staff Sergeant. Russian missile salvage, where is it?"

His gaze shifted to the captain's. "It's actually Chechen, and it was just a theory, sir. The Russians haven't voiced what they did with it. It could still be in the bunker, recycled, or—"

"It's not a theory," the general interrupted. "It's been stolen. I want to know by whom and where the hell it is now."

"I can try."

"You do that, Staff Sergeant. Anything you need, you do. Captain, priority one. Your ball game."

Someone assembling the missiles was scary enough, launching them would start a war—somewhere. General McGill headed back to the far end of the quadrant. He braced himself before he stepped back into the Tank and addressed the Joint Chiefs.

Going to be one hell of a morning, he thought.

Lucien slammed the phone down, then winced as pain spiked through his hand.

"You're a failure, Franco. Do you know how far she could be by now?"

"I followed her to the hotel, and Dominic Cane was right there. In a helicopter. It was as if he knew her next move. But she's vanished again."

"No, she has not." He refused to believe that. "Pray that Cane finds her. Find him."

"We don't know—"

"*We?* You have someone working for you?"

"Of course."

"No, they all are mine, my people." He wanted to pass his coins but his wrist hurt, so he fingered them in his pants pocket. "Put a man on Cane, and his friends. I'll be on the ship."

"Doing what?"

"Waiting for you to do your job!"

"As if you'd work a day," Franco muttered and walked away before Zarek could shoot him in the back.

Alexa looked down at her hand. *No blood* first registered. Then, no pain.

He'd missed completely. Intentional and he wouldn't the next time. He looked at the troop, smirking, then said something too soft for her to hear. The troop left them alone.

He leaned down, tucking her under her chin till she met his gaze. "You are very lovely."

"Thank you."

"Ah, you do have a voice, what is your name?"

"Betty Crocker."

He frowned for a second, then when it registered he scowled. "Who do you work for?"

"Pillsbury Dough Boy, he's a slave driver."

He hit her dead-center in the solar plexus and she buckled over, gasping for air and fighting the pain swelling out to her limbs. "We can go on all night."

"I don't have plans." *Shut up*, she thought. *Just shut the hell up*.

The troop returned with another man carrying a large barrel full of water. She knew what would come: sleep depravation, near death experiences. Drowning seemed top of the list today. Alexa told herself not to be afraid. Not to give him an inch. He wanted information. He thought she had it. No matter what, an American telling a Chinese officer that she knew WMDs were in their country was just plain dangerous.

He forced her to stand and tied her hands, then shoved her to the ground. She rolled to her side and he moved around to the front of the barrel and motioned. The troop lifted her off the dirt floor and grasped her by the hair.

"Who do you work for?"

She didn't answer; sarcasm was just not appreciated here.

The troop shoved her head under water. Water flowed up her nose and she forced out precious air to clear it. He held her down hard, the edge of the barrel cutting into her stomach. After a minute, her brain felt as if it would come through her skull at the back of her neck any second. After thirty more seconds, her heartbeat resonated in her ears. It was all she could hear beyond the strain to hold her breath. Her lungs grew tighter by the millisecond and she desperately wanted to exhale.

She let out more air through her nose, she had to, and when she didn't have any more, couldn't hold it in, she faced her death. Just when she started to relax, she was yanked back. Alexa drew in a long harsh pull of air, coughing and vomiting. She'd barely cleared a lungful when the troop pushed her back under again. He repeated the torture, just long enough to fill her lungs less and less each time. The questions were no more than words scattered in the air, random and angry.

Then dark and thin took over, holding her down longer. Alexa felt her energy slipping with each plunge. No blood to her brain. She'd be a vegomatic before this was over.

If she lived.

* * *

Killian watched as Sam landed the chopper. He didn't wait, ducked and ran, then flung open the door. Max climbed in behind him. "Back to the CP, asap."

"Y'all got some big trouble, huh?"

"Yeah, big."

Killian watched the land shoot past, putting his thoughts in order. He didn't want to leave Fujian, but Max convinced him they needed more to go on before hunting. Killian faced the fact that he wasn't firing on all cylinders where Alexa was concerned. They'd lost the missiles. Zarek had won. He'd transported them somewhere without anyone being the wiser.

It was another fifteen minutes before they landed at the command post; a luxurious house with carefully landscaped gardens that did nothing for his mood. Alexa was lost, a prisoner somewhere. Nabbed by MSS or another bureau of intelligence. Christ, the Chinese were Intel thieves, stealing technology and anything they could from other countries. Mostly the U.S. They used anyone: students on visas and businesses based in the U.S. That always frosted his ass. The U.S. of A. was sometimes too damn easy with educating foreign nationals. How many terrorists did they let go through Ivy League colleges, he groused, then shit-canned the train of thought and focused.

The Chinese had listening posts and spies. More than the United States, more than the Russians, and they didn't share, not even with their allies. With 1.29 billion people, there were plenty who were willing to do what the government demanded of them.

He strode into the living room, every available space housing equipment, weapons, and Logan's computer systems.

"What about that message coming under the wire?"

"Comes and goes. I still can't unscramble it. Might just be interference."

"You think so?"

Logan's expression fell. "No. The program is taking forever to decipher it and that makes me nervous. I have something newsworthy." He turned to the screens. "I saw this when we first arrived. North Korean troops have been moving to the southern border all week."

"That was reported to be for the ceremonies, a show of force for the Secretary of State and the U.N. All pomp. Besides, they're always staring across the wall at each other." Like in Cuba.

"I agree, lots of troops, but no rocket launchers, tanks or APCs." Riley pointed to the TV newscast. "More armored personnel carriers and artillery would mean a new division on the borders."

"Let Central Command watch, not our problem. We have a bigger one."

Logan swung the chair around and pulled off his glasses.

"We lost the missiles."

Curses and groans, and Killian wanted to smash something.

"I don't get this, we had surveillance on the ship. We all saw it unload. The crates were sequentially numbered, just like you and Alexa saw."

"He switched the contents and played us all like saps. We should have done a lot of things and Alexa's way." Like checking the cargo on the trucks. "Get over it."

"Oh, hell, that means they're still on the ship."

"If he hasn't docked somewhere else, yes, we have to assume."

"Killian, the ship sailed this morning," Logan said gravely.

He looked over Logan's shoulder at the screen. "All right, all right. Damn. Riley, pull your equipment in. Max, we'll need some thermal imaging. The least bit of warmth, I want to see it. Around here." He pointed to the screen, Logan's illegal program that humped satellite links showing where Alexa was last.

"Roger that."

"What are you planning?" Riley asked.

"I have to go back for her. I can't leave her."

"But we don't know where she is."

"Then we find out. I want ideas, assumptions, shots in the dark, but we need to find her."

"Killian," Max said. "You saw the tracks. She's probably a prisoner of the Chinese intelligence. If they don't kill her right off, they will torture her to death, you know that."

"Then we'd better hurry, huh?" His insides wanted to lock up but he refused to let it happen. Alexa needed him and he'd be damned if he'd let her down. When the team just stared at him, he said, "Look. I can't abandon her. Can you? After all this, just let her die alone?"

They exchanged glances.

"I won't ask you to stick around. This is messier than we all thought."

"Not to mention she didn't clear you."

"That was Price's carrot. She dangled it. I bit and ran. Even if we don't find Alexa, we have to find those missiles. It's not over." He looked at the map, following his finger as he tracked her last location north and any access roads.

Behind him, his teammates exchanged looks, each echoing the last with a nod.

"I'm in," Riley said and the others chimed in.

Killian looked back. "You could get killed."

"It's one of those save the world things I wouldn't miss," Riley said.

Killian let out a breath, grateful. "Thanks. Logan, did you find out anything on this Pong guy?"

"MSS Third Bureau." Logan turned to the second

screen and tapped keys. A picture came up. "Qain Pong, lieutenant commander in Guangzhou province. Under the provisional leadership of the Political Commissar, General Yang Deqing. Mean-ass sucker. Expert in information gathering."

Torture. Killian cursed and rubbed his mouth. "Alexa said there was a Chinese man on the ship with Carrión and Zarek." Killian leaned closer, staring at the man's face.

"Looks like someone tried to take the meanness out of him." Max pointed to the cut on his neck barely discernable above the collar of his uniform.

"Riley, check your film, see if Pong turned up on the docks or the ship. That'll at least confirm a direction." If Pong was involved, then he had the government's authority to take Alexa. Killian turned to Sam. "When Riley gets it working, load up the thermal imaging. You'll have to do a flyover, quick and fast to pinpoint anything, and with the People's police watching us after that stunt in Kowloon, it will have to be covert and speedy."

Sam hooked his thumbs in his belt loops. "I can be in and out, no more than forty minutes tops."

"I'll hold you to that." Killian headed toward the other room.

"What are you doing?"

He stopped, looked back. "We go packed and ready for anything."

Max's brows shot up. "We kill Chinese nationals and we'll never leave this country either."

"I don't plan on killing anyone unless it's necessary. Strictly black ops and we have"—he looked at his watch—"five hours before sunrise or we have to wait another day."

They all knew that Alexa could be dead by then.

* * *

Alexa stared at the space between her feet, watching water drip off her hanks of hair and puddle between her bare feet. The soles of her feet were raw from being forced to walk the length of the cell for half the day. If Colonel Qain Pong—he took great pleasure in telling her—wasn't dunking her head under water, a soldier was prodding her through the bars with a tire iron to walk and keep moving. Her body hurt from all the jabs and once she'd grabbed the iron and yanked hard, smacking the troop's face against the bars. The kid now had a broken nose.

That got her no food or water, and she was running out of stamina to fight back. Which is what Pong wanted. She hadn't slept in at least forty hours. Or was it thirty? Time meant nothing except a string of minutes stretched with pain. Her clothing was soaked, and she sucked at the fabric, trying to quench her thirst. The rank creek water would make her ill, but with every cell in her body aching already, she didn't think it mattered. Nothing mattered right now. She barely found the strength to tip her head back. It thumped to the wall.

I don't want to do this anymore. I'm tired of keeping secrets and being someone else. Tired of having nothing to prove she existed.

Jeez, could you whine some more, Gavlin?

Her brain was fuzzy, time and day disoriented, and her stomach rolled loosely. No light came into the barn except from the thatched roof, but it didn't reach the stone floor. Idly, she inspected her sleeve, torn at the shoulder. She tried wiping off the dirt and even in the back of her mind where sanity still existed, she knew she was in a state of delirium.

He'd taken everything. Her shoes, her bag, passport, money. Most was on a table several yards beyond the cell door like a tease. Her equipment was obvious. Spy stuff. More evidence for Pong to use to hurt her, or send her to Jilin prison labor camps. Alexa understood why an animal would gnaw off its paw to be free. She wanted out. And she was ready to use anything to get that.

The tall doors opened and she rejoiced that it was daylight. For the little beam of warmth. Soldiers milled about beyond the door, trying to get a look inside. Pong walked up to the cell door, unlocked it, then gestured for the troop to set down the cloth-covered tray. Food, she prayed, climbing to her feet. When she moved, Pong aimed the gun at her and Alexa realized that in some way, he was afraid of her. Then he flipped back the cloth. The tray was neatly arranged with implements like a dentist used. Her gaze flashed to Pong's.

And for the first time, he smiled.

Fear gripped her spine. Holstering his gun, he picked up a syringe, held it aloft. It was filled with a pale yellow liquid that could be anything from drain cleaner to sodium pentothal. If it was the latter, she was trained to resist. Beside, SP would make one lose inhibitions, but not cough up the truth if you didn't want to like the movies portrayed. She prayed it wasn't drain cleaner.

"Hold her down."

The soldier approached her and Alexa drew on her threads of strength and punched him in the face. His already broken nose shifted again, bleeding faster this time, and he stumbled back into Pong. Pong laid down the syringe and pushed the troop toward the door and told him to send in another. Moments later a bigger man came in. He grabbed her by the hair and the shoulder, digging his thumb into her collarbone and forcing her into the chair.

He didn't let up. "You're such a pansy, Pong. You haven't been alone with me once. Do I scare you?" The soldier dug his thumb in harder and she gasped, curling away from the pain.

Pong's eyes narrowed. "Do you wish to die, woman?"

Get real, her look said.

The troop held her still, securing her arms behind the chair. Pong took up the syringe and she looked down as he brought the needle close. Seconds before he injected her, her vision blinked rapidly, like frames of a flickering movie. Pong inserted the needle into her arm with careless regard, yet she saw a smaller pair of hands, a smaller needle sliding beneath her skin. The hands drew away and her vision blurred. She tipped her head back, let it loll on her shoulders.

Zarek's image swam before her, a small man beside him. He grinned and faded, replaced with Pong's face. She wanted to stop it, grab the memory back.

"Now you will tell me what I want."

"Go to hell." Alexa started singing. Pong's face grew molten with rage as her off-key rendition of "God Bless America" rang through the cell.

Fifteen

Day 24

The five-hour deadline came and went—without a location, not even a whisper of her in the jumble of intelligence traffic.

It put Killian in the mood to kick some ass.

The first on his list was lying in a king-size bed with a petite woman sprawled across his thick chest. Killian screwed on the silencer and kicked the bed.

Franco stirred enough to look around, then settled back to sleep. Killian kept himself in the shadows and flipped on the light. Franco lurched up, and reached for the gun on the bedside table. His hand touched air. He shouted for his men. And since they were kissing the carpet in the outer room, no one came to his rescue.

"Now that we've got that settled," Killian said, then rotated his gun to the startled woman clutching the sheet to her bare breasts. "Get out."

The girl darted from the bed to the bathroom, taking the sheet and leaving Franco naked and vulnerable. "Get up, big man, and I use the term loosely."

"Shut the fuck up and give me a damn robe."

Killian went to reach for the robe, hesitating for a

second as something grippingly familiar registered, and behind thoughts of finding Alexa, the jigsaw of his past started forming. He grabbed the robe off the arm of the chair and threw it at him.

Leaving the bed, Franco pulled it on and faced him as he yanked on the sash. "Who the hell are you?"

"Sit."

The man folded his arms over his big chest and stared back, refusing.

Killian fired at his kneecap. The thunk was crunchy wet as Franco flexed with a scream and crumbled to the floor.

Killian rose and moved to Franco. "I should mention that I'm out of time and patience."

Franco was breathing hard, clutching his knee, calling him every name in the book and then some. Killian grabbed his jaw, digging his fingers into the hinge of bone. Franco howled and Killian shoved the barrel into his mouth. "Where is she?"

"I don't know."

Killian threatened to put the gun back in place.

"I don't, I swear. I've been looking for two days!"

Alexa had been miles away from the ship when it sailed, but that didn't mean Zarek didn't have her with him now. Choppers could land on the ship.

"Seems to me you're wasting time fucking the local female population."

"And you're wasting your time, Cane. He doesn't tell me a thing."

"But you see everything. Where is he headed?" Killian knew exactly where the ship was now; idle in the water, fifty miles west. East China Sea. Doing nothing.

"To a rendezvous point that'll be relayed when the package is needed." Franco held the edge of the robe around his wound. "Get me something for this, you asshole."

Killian didn't. He could bleed out for all he cared. "Why does he need her?"

"She holds information, but I don't know what," he said in a rush when Killian pressed the barrel against his other knee.

"One shot and the tendon is severed, Franco."

The blood loss was steady and Franco seemed to weigh his options before he said, "She's part of the sale."

Good God. "How?"

"Hell if I know."

Killian pulled the slide, assuring Franco there was a bullet in the chamber.

Franco looked back with determination. "Wise up, Cane, he kept her for a month and he put something in her that he needs to get out."

Christ. That could be any number of things. "Why not just keep whatever it was on himself?"

"Are you kidding? Interpol, CIA, Moussad, MSS— they are watching him constantly. He's searched all the time. He always stands back and lets it happen because he's good at hiding it. And the only reason he got the coffee off the ship was that Tang promised the inspectors would inspect just the coffee."

"Weak, try again."

"It's true, God dammit! Zarek had to get those crates off to—"

"—make room for reconstructing the missiles," Killian murmured. And the launchers. They're on the ship, just as Alexa insisted, and now Zarek and a couple hundred kiloton of weapons were mobile on the high seas off the coast of China. If the Chinese knew, he'd be blown out of the water.

"You have what you want, get out."

"We aren't done."

Franco's eyes narrowed questioningly. "What are you talking about? I told you what I know."

"Not everything. A few years ago, you were working for Carrión."

"I did no such thing. Ah, Jesus." His knee wouldn't stop bleeding.

Killian went on as if he hadn't spoken. "You could have gotten away with it for an eternity, Franco." Killian moved close, making him cower a little. "Until I saw your back." The same wounds in the same place as another man had once suffered. "And this." He tugged on his hair, pulling his head back. "Fine scars, and hidden by your hair. Bet all that plastic surgery cost you a bundle. But it was the voice. Funny that I'd never heard you speak till now." He moved back, taking a seat. "Because you knew I'd recognize your voice."

Franco paled, his bushy eyebrows flattening.

"Carrión had to know. Why he hasn't given you up, I don't get. Oh, wait a second," Killian said calmly. Inside, he was boiling with rage. "You betrayed your people *for* Carrión. You made a deal. What was it? Get close to Zarek, ace him out of his operation and take over for Carrión." The blood drained from Franco's face. "Carrión has you by the balls because he knows the DEA think you're dead. Isn't that right, *Gordon*?"

Franco's gaze darted, then he lurched out of the chair and charged at Killian. Killian didn't fire. In fact, he dropped the gun and laid the first punch. Franco folded at the waist, choking for air. Blood gushed from his leg.

"You bastard. You let eight men die." Franco's nose shifted under his fist. "Your buddies." His ribs cracked as Killian hammered. "Your friends . . . Americans!"

Franco got in a shot to his jaw, snapping his head to

the side, but Killian was relentless, his rage not for himself, but for the men who had battled drug dealers only to return home in flag-draped coffins.

Franco swung widely and staggered. "Fuck you, Moore. Yeah." Blood dribbled from his mouth and he swayed on his feet. "I know who you are. I've always known. I kept your cover for you, asshole. It was sweet to know I could bring you down with one word." He spat blood at Killian's feet. "You were so 'play by the book,' honor-some-fucking-code Boy Scout, and look at you now. Dishonored, and chasing a woman! You can't touch me." He held up his hands. "No prints, no identifying marks. I am who I say I am and I have enough money to buy my way out and buy you ten times over. I'm rich, fucking rich! What are you?"

"Still alive." Killian executed one sharp upward motion, driving Franco's shattered nose into his brain.

Franco dropped, face first. Dead.

"For the brotherhood," Killian said, then picked up his gun and walked out.

Her singing got her a sharp blow to her stomach that shoved the air out so fast she was still trying to get a lungful. She was on her knees on the stone floor, her hands tied behind her back. It wouldn't be so bad if there wasn't a noose around her neck and secured to her ankles. Any movement and she'd choke herself to death. Where did they learn this shit, she wondered, her ears ringing. He left her there for hours and it took every bit of energy to keep perfectly upright. If she so much as squatted, she'd be dead.

An hour passed, then another. Pong returned to ask her the same questions from outside the cell doors. Alexa just stared back. He wanted a confession that she was CIA. He was Third Bureau, he knew better.

There were enough of her brethren in this country already, just like the Chinese were in the U.S. Doing the same thing. She'd admit to nothing. If she'd betrayed her country with Zarek and that was what was locked in her memory, then so be it. But she wasn't doing that now.

Pong started to unlock the door, then changed his mind, spun around and left her. Alexa arched her back, trying to reach the nylon cord securing her ankles. If she could just loosen it. Her fingers touched it, and she shifted her hands a little at a time, stretching the cord and trying to move her fingers enough. The rope cut off her circulation. She could feel her palms swelling. She arched a bit more, heard her vertebrae pop as she shaped the knots, finding the end and tracing it, imaging it in her mind.

She worked at the ties slowly to pull against the cords. Nylon was strong, but it had give. She kept the door in her line of vision. If Pong caught her, he'd just push her head down and watch as she strangled herself to death.

Killian's list was a short one. He found Carrión in his hotel room, packing to leave.

"You knew Franco was playing both sides."

"Of course, and I played him."

"He's dead."

Carrión glanced, lifted a dark brow. "I have you to thank?"

Killian didn't respond. His vindication was with a dead man. His name was still soiled and ugly. But the pieces fit. Franco had sights on Zarek's operation and he learned how to take over from Carrión. "Once Franco got his claws in you were going to take the Colombian operation." It wasn't really a question.

"I still might."

Killian let out a breath. He couldn't change things now. His top priority was Alexa and the missiles. "You knew what was on that ship."

"The missiles, *sí*, I did."

"Jesus, you're a cold bastard, Carrión."

"*Sí*, my mother said as much, God rest her soul. But Zarek is far smarter than we give him credit for. He took them, transported them, made a deal and is probably waiting to deliver on it. And all it cost him was three million in stones and a woman."

Killian's features tightened. "He needs her."

Carrión looked at him for a long moment. "Perhaps, if you believe his lap dog. I never understood why Zarek was so obsessed with Jade. She is lovely, yet has too much independence for my tastes."

Carrión was intentionally missing the point. Still, Killian pressed him, "Have you seen her, heard anything?"

Carrión's look was sympathetic. "Sorry, Cane, I have not."

With some answers, Carrión could be trusted with the truth, as long as it didn't interfere with his agenda. Killian's cell phone vibrated in his pocket. He said good-bye, then left answering it. Logan was on the line.

"Pong was on the docks after the explosion. Looks like he was just asking questions, investigating."

"Third Bureau looking into a boating accident?"

"Yeah, I picked up on that, too. Has to be personal." A pause and then, "We have thermal."

"How'd you manage that?" He checked his watch. "Sam couldn't be in the air yet."

"He's not, I piggybacked off the GOES."

The Geostationary Operational Environmental Satellites, a constant vigil over atmospheric "triggers" for severe weather conditions like tornadoes, flash floods, hailstorms, and hurricanes. Damn clever. "Remind me to give you a raise."

She was almost free when the guard unlocked the cell door and stepped inside. Alexa kept herself upright, feeling the nylon ropes slide through her fingers, the slack around her wrists and ankles. She'd been at it for five hours. She could feel the warmth of blood pooling beneath her knees.

He set a tray on the floor a distance away and she realized he was afraid of her.

"You eat," he said.

Bread and water to keep her alive for more of this? "No, thanks."

"Eat," he insisted and she wondered if that was the only English he knew.

"The commissar doesn't know I'm here, does he?"

She didn't know if her Chinese was good enough till he paled. Interesting. So what was Pong up to under the guise of investigating? "If he's caught," she said, "you will be tried with him."

He hushed her, kneeling to undo her bonds. Alexa seized the moment and fell to her side, and with both feet, kicked out at him. The ropes jerked on her throat, blunting off her air supply, but the impact to his chest sent him smashing back against the bars. She scrambled to loosen the ties further and they slipped off her hands as the troop tried to sit up. She reached for his gun.

A shot rang out, chipping the floor, and they both froze.

Pong moved casually toward the cell and ordered the troop out. The young man scurried, ashamed. Her antagonizer stepped into the cell and took the ropes, tossing them beyond the bars. He looked around at the spilled water and crushed bread. He pointedly stepped on the crust of bread, smiled, then left.

Alexa hurried to the bread, brushing off dirt and eating. Three days without food and she was ready to eat her shoes. If she still had them.

David Lorimer sat at his home computer, tuning up his dish and hacking his way into secure lines. He'd been doing this for days now with no response. He knew the risks, and the price would be his career and his freedom, but he worked fast. He could stay linked only for short moments or Homeland Security computer geeks would tap in and trace him. But he had to warn them.

Dragon One, Killian Moore and five other highly trained Marines were being used and abused. He'd bet they knew that already, but now others did, too. That meant cleanup and sweeper if they weren't careful.

A noise startled him and David whipped around, his gaze shooting around his apartment for the source. He started to get up to investigate when his cat hopped down off a bookshelf.

He sighed and turned back to the screen. The signal was weak, connecting with the satellite communications phone, the number that Price kept calling with no answer. These guys were smart. How smart would be determined when and if they could decipher the encryption.

Day 24

Somewhere in the distant past of her training Alexa knew she'd reached the end of the line. She was inspecting herself for bugs. She'd even eaten two or three. What kind of good cell didn't have enough bugs, she thought, pulling strands of hair in front of her face and plucking out stones and straw. Her vision blurred and she flipped hair aside and tipped her head back, drew her knees up. A rat crawled near her foot. She didn't care. She'd eat it if she had the strength to catch the sucker.

The dirty bread had just made her hunger worse, leaving her nauseated. Pong kept her awake since he'd captured her to the point that she couldn't close her eyes even if she wanted to. Punch drunk, her mom used to call it. All she could do was sit when she could and pray someone would drop a bomb on this place. She'd tried taking apart the table for some weapon; he'd removed it and the chair. Just her and the rats and bugs now, but Pong was watching, waiting for the moment to pounce on her again.

She knew because he'd brought in battery-operated lamps, low voltage, enough for him to see in, yet she couldn't see beyond. She could think of a couple things to do with those lamps if she could reach them.

She went from trying to finger comb her matted hair to picking at her wet grimy pant leg. Her skin was raw with bug bites, her instep bruised where Pong had stepped on it, her ankle bones scraped from being knocked to the floor. Her ankle tattoo looked like a black blob in the dim light. She smoothed the lines of the tattoo no larger than a quarter and somehow, it gave her comfort. It had been a memorial for her parents' death when she was sixteen. A pair of winged angels so close they looked like double vision. But the CIA demanded it either be removed or periodically altered. Beneath the alterations was a butterfly, a bird. Now, ironically, it was a raging dragon. She pulled her leg to the side, trying to focus on it, blinking when the claws seemed to grow. It made her head hurt, and images flashed. Images she knew weren't really there.

The steel table, the mask, then the face of a small man. She remembered pleading with him before Zarek stuck a gun to his temple. The old man obeyed and the tapping/humming came again. Louder and louder. It made her eyes hurt.

"What did you do to me? What did you do?" She gripped her hair as if she could pull the memory out. *Show me!*

The door opened suddenly and Pong strode in. He moved close, staring down at her with that cynical smirk. At least he wasn't carrying a tray of drugs.

"So sorry, I'm not accepting visitors today."

"I can keep you here for a very long time."

"Nothing will change. You hurt Mi Ling Tsu."

"I would not dare."

She made a buzzer sound. "Wrong answer. Get your rocks off with beating the wife of a national hero?" Her speech was slurred.

His features paled.

"I'm sure the commissar will hear about it. Does he know what you're doing here?"

His stare narrowed. "No one will save you from your fate."

"Got that right." She knew the moment that hand had closed over her mouth, seconds before the tazer zapped her. She would die here.

"You are useless to me. We have nothing more to discuss." He raised the weapon, aiming at her head.

Alexa stared back, unblinking.

Killian. I am so sorry.

Day 24
Fujian
South Guangzhou Province
2300 hours

Dragon One couldn't assault till he knew for certain Alexa was inside. Or her location. Nor did they have any information to go on. Talk about walking in blind as a freakin' bat. Killian wasn't even certain she was in there except that thermal imaging singled out this area, this barn. Warm bodies and being close enough to her last location was enough for him to be here.

It was off the main road, far off, at the base of the mountains, and northern surveillance told them only four vehicles had traversed the isolated road. Two were accounted for as farm trucks. He was looking at the other two, a troop carrier and a black BMW sedan, tinted windows. Both had been sitting in the same spot for hours. The sedan, he recognized.

Dressed in black Ops gear and using throat mikes, Killian and his team approached the barn, wind blowing across the rice fields and disguising their movements. The walls were stone, two windows that were at least six feet above the ground. He signaled to Max to circle to the rear.

"One exit, north side, Mustang."

"Roger that."

"Six personnel standing guard," Max said. "AKs locked and loaded."

"Copy that, Drac, same here." Killian glanced left. "Finn, set the charge on the vehicles. Cutter, you're with me."

Killian motioned for Logan to cover his six, and when the troops' attention shifted, he ran to the corner of the building. He had about thirty seconds before someone noticed him. Damn the moonlight. Black on black, he moved forward, hearing chatter from the troops as he placed the small charge against the wall, sliding dead grass over it, then moved southwest to set the second charge. A little diversionary Centex and a remote detonator. He hoped the structure didn't crumble when he set it off.

Riley was near the only truck. He approached, rolled beneath, set the charge and rolled back out into the rice grasses in record time. Then they moved farther back into the field, their faces and clothing black and non-reflective. He wished he had more Intel. They were going on instinct, and nothing solid. He needed some luck here. She'd been missing for nearly three days, evaporating into the air till thermal imaging showed warm bodies, inside and out. No electronics, no satellite gear, and little landscape near the stone barn except tall rice grass and lots of mud. In daylight, they'd be spotted in seconds. Hell, they'd walked a couple miles out in the open, checking for sensors and traps. The lack said that either the MSS was confident, or it wasn't really an official prisoner detention house.

A few miles back, Sam was ready to move. They couldn't use the chopper. Hong Kong police were all over them since that stunt in the streets chasing after Carrión and Alexa. The last thing he needed was the Chinese grounding them permanently. Their National Geological Society front took them only so far.

Using infrared goggles, he canvassed the area again and again. No movement and they couldn't see in till someone came out. Or they made them come out.

"Mustang, I hear voices."

Max. Posted behind the structure, north side. "Male?"

"Negative. Sounds like they're hurting too, God dammit."

"Get in as close as you can. We need a little diversion smaller than the C-4."

"I'm on it," Riley said and took off to the right, bent low and moving fast.

Killian and Logan spread out and moved in, then Killian knelt, removing the cylinder from his Load Bearing Vest, then glanced briefly back at the troops. "When it blows, stay clear of foot traffic."

"See, he's talking to us like we're rookies again."

"Kiss my ass, Finn, and blow the party favors."

The fluorescent charges went off, a short pop, then a red rocket of light. Killian let loose a second charge and tossed it to his right. He and Logan maintained cover, low crawling toward the building. No one came out. The troops shouted, racing toward the explosions, yet a handful remained back and blocked the way.

"Guess they're smarter than we thought, Mustang."

"We'll see. Fire in the hole." Killian blew the charge on the south front.

The C-4 explosion tossed rocks up into the air, raining them down on the troops. Rapid gunfire ripped in streaks through the darkness. *They're firing blind.* Dragon One was less wasteful, picking off only the most threatening troops one at a time, double tapped and down. Killian raced to the north side to the small door and ran Primacord across the hinges, then backed up enough to hit the dead-man switch. The blast was fast and sharp, the old wood fell inward.

Qain Pong was framed in the door.

Killian opened fire.

So did Pong.

Alexa thanked God for the blast. Whoever it was. It stopped Pong from aerating her skull. He was slow to react, as if he'd expected it, and he went to the front doors, looked out. Whatever was out there didn't affect him and he came back to her, intent on finishing his task. He aimed.

A second explosion at the rear stopped him. An instant later the wood door sailed back a few feet, yet Pong was out of the cell, firing into the doorway six times without stopping.

A careless move. A bad one. Now he had to reload.

A figure slipped around the door jamb, remained in the darkened corner.

Alexa saw the opportunity and moved to the open cell door, but Pong glanced at her, popped the ammo in and swerved his arm in her direction.

"They are too late to help you."

The next shot went through Pong's chest and out his back, taking half his spine with it. As he fell, her gaze shifted to the figure, and he came closer. Alexa darted out of the cell, her weakness making her slow and frantic.

The intruder came toward her. She moved faster and stumbled.

"Wildcat."

Alexa stilled, swaying, and frowned at the black face. "Killian?"

"I thought you could use a lift outta here."

"Oh, God." Her legs folded and she staggered, reaching for anything to keep herself upright and hoping it was him.

Killian rushed forward, wrapping his arm around her. God, it was so good to find her alive. "Come on. We have to move. Can you walk?"

"Yes." She looked at him, smiling weakly. "Sorry I shot you."

He pressed his mouth to her temple, then urged her to hurry to the door. They stepped over Pong, but not before Killian searched him. The man had a cell phone and nothing else on him. Not even ID. Very unusual.

"Drac, radio Outlaw, I have the package."

At the door, Killian pushed a weapon into her hand, keeping her behind him. "We're coming out."

"Negative, enemy to your left."

Killian rotated and when the troop rushed forward, he fired, taking him out. But more came, bullets chipping the doorway. Then he heard a chopper. He touched the throat mike. "Outlaw, are you crazy?"

"Low and hot, sir. ETA one minute."

"God dammit. MSS will shoot you out of the sky!"

Farther out, Logan popped a smoke can.

"Outlaw to Cutter, I have visual, coming in."

"Finn, make a hole," Killian ordered and Riley set off the machine pistols on the west side; three mounted on tripods, they'd fire in a forty-five degree spread until the ammo was spent.

The PLA troops ducked and sprayed gunfire at the unmanned machine pistols as Killian pushed Alexa ahead, covering her as they ran into the rice field. Riley met up with them, moving backwards. Some of the PLA troops got wise and were rushing toward them, and Riley went down on one knee, returning fire.

Sam swooped low, the doors open, and Killian ran with Alexa, practically carrying her. Max climbed in first, then turned to provide cover. Sam didn't even set down, only hovering, the blades blowing the grasses flat.

Alexa threw herself in, curling from the entrance as Killian hopped on the edge, and sighted in on the ground below. "Finn, get moving."

Riley waited till the last possible moment, expending his ammo before he dove into the chopper.

"Go, go, go!"

Sam lifted the aircraft, banking right and flying it over the mountaintops.

"I guess my orders not to use the chopper didn't penetrate that thick skull."

"Yes, sir, it did. But I flew in below radar and the scrambler works." Sam pointed to the dash. "It sends out a sonic wave that distorts location. I look like a flock of birds to anyone who's watching."

"Yeah, moving at eighty miles an hour," Killian snarled, but had to admire his team. If they needed it, they didn't wait for technology to come to them: they made it.

He looked at Alexa, who was just staring at him.

"You okay?" Killian motioned to Logan, who started checking her out.

Alexa was oblivious. "I can't believe you found me." She looked at each man. "I can't believe you *looked!*"

That just about broke Killian's heart right there. She still didn't believe anyone cared enough about her. God, what a number Price and her job had done on her.

"We couldn't let you die, ma'am," Max said. "Besides, we want to see how this ends."

She smiled at Max, then turned her attention to Killian. Alexa was more than a little moved that he'd risked his life and his team to come for her.

Killian couldn't stop himself and gravitated toward her, shaking inside with the joy of finding her alive. He brushed his mouth over hers, oblivious to his team.

"You put it all on the line for me," she said, awed.

"Trust me now?"

Alexa latched onto him, kissing him hungrily, and Killian was just feeling the excitement course through him when she suddenly melted in his arms. It took a second before he realized she'd passed out. He laid her on the deck of the chopper.

Logan had his stethoscope out, checking vitals. "Some nasty cuts and a lot of bruises, dehydration, slight malnutrition . . . aw, hell, she's been injected." He leaned, sniffing her skin. "Smells like garlic . . . sodium pentothal."

"Well, hell, there went that cheery moment of freedom," Sam said as they flew to the command post.

Sixteen

Lucien knew the worst kinds of killers.

Men and even women who'd pull a trigger for money. His buyers. He contacted several, offering a juicy half a million to mercenaries who'd contact him immediately and arrive within twenty-four hours in Taiwan.

He strolled to his stateroom, feeling the ship cut through the sea and head toward the northern island. He poured the Mayan coins from hand to hand, the sound soothing him.

Franco had failed to locate her, and his death was only an inconvenience, yet while Franco had been distant and protecting himself, the hired killers would use any means to get back his prize. Impatient for progress, he spilled the coins into his pocket and left the stateroom, traveling the long corridor toward amidships, then stepping out on deck. The hard wind buffeted his face as he moved to the cargo bay.

People stepped clear. He liked that. He liked it a lot. Fear and respect sent the crew back against the walls. He was on the catwalk, looking down into the massive hull.

The area was buzzing with activity. At least thirty

men and women snapping to the orders of one skinny man, hired by the buyers. Two missiles, each fifty-three feet long, were being reassembled. The launchers were retrofitted to work with French-made MRBM launchers he'd bought from Iran.

The man in charge was on a short metal ladder, refitting God knew what. Lucien didn't care, as long as it brought this deal closer to the end. He turned away, and was stepping on the metal staircase when he heard a curse echo up to him, and he turned back. The man below picked up the ship's phone. Lucien reached for the handset on the steel wall.

"A problem?"

"Guidance chips are missing."

He was prepared for this, he'd already had a man in here checking to see if Jade had tampered with them. She had, of course, as he'd suspected. It simply confirmed to him that she was a spy. "Yes, I know, if you will come to my stateroom, I will offer you another."

"How much will this cost us?"

"Oh, really, no charge," he said and hung up.

The missiles had been in pieces, just waiting for someone rich enough and smart enough to see the potential. A few hundred thousand for fresh chips was spare change compared to the millions he was being paid for the completed weapons. What they did with them was not his concern.

Newly promoted Staff Sergeant Scoggins approached Captain Hammit's desk, standing at attention.

"At ease, Sergeant." The captain kept initialing papers for a moment longer, then looked up.

Scoggins thrust out the papers. "Sir, the general wanted to know when we had something—anything."

"And?" Captain Hammit took the papers. Scoggins

waited for him to read them. "You're the expert, Staff Sergeant. Give me the short version."

"The Russian salvage, that was decommissioning weapons, it was purchased."

"Good God."

"Well, that's what it would look like, someone put the pieces into a salvage pile that was purchased by the Cali Salvage Group. It's a small company with a couple ships that basically treasure hunt and when they can't, they purchase old vessels, lots of junkyard stuff, scrap, melt it down to make new."

"I understand your point, but who owns it?"

"I traced it to Campo Del Azúcar Coffee Company in Colombia. It means Sweet Fields."

"The owner is legit?"

"Yes, sir, the books are good."

"Drop the bomb, Staff Sergeant, and get out of the way."

"It's Lucien Zarek, sir. He owns both."

Hammit rubbed his mouth. "Where is he?"

"That's just it, we don't know. He was last in Hong Kong delivering coffee."

"Did he?"

"Yes, sir. NSA is due to report on his location soon, sir."

"Find out who we have on the ground and see if they can get a visual."

"I'll check on the harbor roster in Hong Kong." The sergeant started to leave, looked at the last page in his hand, then turned back. "By the way, sir—"

Only the captain's gaze shifted as he waited for more firepower to ruin his day.

"We've found a signal coming from the U.S. to China, to a SatCom phone."

"Lots of people have SatCom phones, especially with international businessmen."

"Yes, sir, but not this high frequency, and it's scrambled."

"Where is the signal coming from?"

"Langley, sir."

"Find out who's sending it."

"That's a problem. It came from inside a secure room."

"Then it's CIA business, you know that. Let it go." Whatever the communiqué was, it was highly classified.

"I know, sir, but I found a second signal. Whoever is sending it knows encryption and it's not constant either. It's from outside Langley. But to the same phone."

"Has it linked?"

"No, sir."

His people brought him pages of information and mostly it was pre-sifted. Lately, he was getting a lot of suspicion and chatter, but not much that was solid. If he had it, he might know where bin Laden was sleeping. "Why are we concerned about this?" he said with a touch of annoyance.

"The SatCom phone belongs to Killian Moore, sir."

The captain's features tightened, and he took the sheet from the sergeant. CIA trying to contact Moore?

"Thank you, Staff Sergeant. Dismissed."

The young man frowned, did an about-face, and left.

The captain looked at the memo sheet, and let his emotions rise. Moore. Scoggins didn't know they were acquainted. Moore had been his team leader and he'd kicked him off his Force Recon team for "blatant insubordination in combat." The charges got him stuck here pushing paper in a think tank between Intel and the decision makers. He was nothing more than a conduit here when he could be more useful in the field.

Hammit still believed Moore didn't want to share

the limelight. And now it was Moore who was on the outside, a black sheep and a disgrace.

As if it belonged to someone else, he watched his own hand crumple the paper.

Then he pitched it in the trash.

He didn't know that within forty-eight hours, that would be the most vital piece of Intel they had.

The cold blast of water hit her face and she blinked, spitting.

Killian held her tightly, fully clothed with her under the shower. "I embarrassed myself, didn't I?"

"Did they feed you?"

She scoffed. "I was lucky to be breathing. Pong was about to put one between my eyes when you showed up."

Oh, she loved his timing, his courage, she thought, holding onto him, letting the cool water drench away the odor of the cell. She snuggled against his chest, wanting to stay right there for just about forever. "Thank you, thank you so much for coming for me."

Killian squeezed his eyes shut; the tone of her voice, so pitiful and lonely, sawed through him and made him ache. When this was over he was going to make it his mission in life to see that she didn't feel that way again. He rubbed her back, the fall of water chilling and he warmed it up a bit.

"You okay?" he said, his lips pressed to her temple.

She eased back, meeting his gaze. "I am now. You make it really hard not to positively adore you, you know that?"

"Gosh, ma'am. Is that emotion I hear?"

Her smile widened as she started peeling off her shirt, and what was left of her slacks. The shoes were probably on some farmer right about now. Alexa was naked in moments and Killian would be interested in making love with her if he hadn't seen the bruises.

"Jesus, now I'm really glad he's dead. What did he do to you?"

She reached for the shampoo, her hands shaking, and she began, telling him all of it, her concentration on washing away the feel of Pong's hands on her, the filth of the cell. She gave him details, insight, every question Pong asked, the tone of it. When she tipped her head back to rinse, she swayed on her feet and Killian steadied her. He hurried her out of the shower and into a robe.

"I could get used to this," she said as he dried her hair, rubbed her scalp.

"So could I. Helluva lot easier than walking into the jungle with an MP5."

She laughed and nudged him, and he didn't want to lose the connection as he helped her to the bed. She sat, then flopped back.

"Don't go to sleep yet. You need to eat something." He called for Logan. Killian dripped on the carpet as he pulled off his boots, the muddied black Ops paint on his face making him look like a coal miner. He went into the bathroom to change and wash off the paint, and when he came back, Logan was checking her out.

"The wounds aren't that bad, are they?" She glanced at Killian.

"Nah." Her wrists and ankles were raw, her throat scratched, but under the robe she was bruised up pretty bad.

She gave him a sour look. "It's women who like scars on men, not the reverse."

"They'll fade," Logan said and prepared a syringe.

Panic shot through her. "No. No more drugs."

"It's an antibiotic. You said he tried to drown you. Water out there has a lot of bacteria."

She looked at Killian as if her ability to make a snap decision had stayed behind in the cell.

"Its okay, Logan's the best."

When Logan was done, she wrapped the large robe around her legs and drew her knees up. Her instep was purple. "I didn't tell him anything. He kept injecting more and more drugs, but I kept singing. I know sodium pentothal doesn't have power over your will. I didn't tell him anything I didn't want. For all Pong knew my name was Betty Crocker."

Killian snickered and she lifted her gaze. "Do you believe me?"

"Yes," came without hesitation and Alexa felt buoyed.

Logan didn't respond and collected his things.

"I remembered something, when it got really bad. A small man. With the surgery and the mask. He didn't want to do whatever it was Zarek wanted and the sound started."

"Franco said they put something in you that Zarek needs to get out."

Alexa paled and looked at Logan. "Can you find out what?"

"Maybe. It will take some time, my X-ray machine on the jet only does a quadrant at a time and, well, you need to recoup a bit."

"I'll be fine by morning, then we can start."

"Alexa, you need to rest," Logan said.

"We don't have time and I'll be fine," she snapped, then sighed, pushing her fingers through her hair and gripping her skull. She spoke to her knees. "Sorry. You don't understand what this has been like. I've been used and manipulated for weapons that could kill millions." She looked up, lowering her hands. "Can you give me something to make me remember?"

"You've had enough lethal drugs injected, I think," Logan said. He looked at Killian, that bleeding heart part of him telling him no more, even for the U.S. of A.

"Do it anyway, Logan," she said. "We have to know."

"Someone hungry?" came from the doorway. Max held a tray, smiling brightly.

"You're going to make someone a really nice wife someday, Renfield," Killian said.

The dig slid right off him and he brought the tray to Alexa, and set it on the bed beside her. "Go slow, okay."

Tea and toast. How motherly, she thought, touched by his kindness, then felt a little self-conscious when Riley and Sam appeared at the door.

"Thank you for coming after me," she said to the men. God, a girl could get to love being surrounded by so many good-looking men. "I'm grateful. You're my heroes forever."

While Riley seemed bashful at the praise, Sam just mimicked tipping a cowboy hat that wasn't there.

"That just raised the standards around here," Logan said. "And you're welcome."

She picked up a slice of toast, her gaze turning to Killian.

"Okay, clear the room, guys, the lady needs to rest," he said and the men departed. "You're the local attraction, sorry."

"They're sweet."

"Sweet? I'll save you by not telling them that."

She sipped tea, saying nothing and loving that she was being seen at all. "You tell them everything?"

His gaze jerked up, and he read her expression, the full throttle memory of making love in the little artist's retreat. "No, not everything." He sat beside her, a towel around his neck.

Alexa chewed, reaching to push her fingers through

his damp hair, her gaze ripping over his face as her fingers trailed down the side of his face. He grasped her fingers, kissing them, then pressing her palm to his cheek. The gesture was so tender and real, she felt her throat tighten.

He's amazing, she thought, *just amazing.* She'd never met a man so relentless to gain her trust, to make things right. He was a good man, a really good one. Tough, determined, and it didn't hurt his case that she melted into a puddle when he was near.

He leaned in, brushing his mouth over hers. "Were you afraid?"

"Oh, yeah. It was just so stupid to let someone come up behind me like that."

"They were waiting for you." They'd been airlifted out, Killian figured, since he couldn't find any tracks to follow.

"I figured the roadblock was a setup, just too late. I'd accepted that I was on my own. I've been in that situation once or twice." She finished off the tea and toast. "When I was in that cell, I thought, I don't want to do this anymore."

"Regrets are the first thing you feel when you're captive." Killian moved the tray to a table, then sat with her.

Alexa was crawling under the sheets. "Yeah, well, I didn't join the Company for anything patriotic, Killian. I joined for revenge."

His brows shot up.

"My parents' death was a car bomb in Tel Aviv that ignited during an accident. A little fender bender and my childhood, my life, was gone with seven other people who were too close to the explosion." She yawned and plumped a pillow, then patted the space beside her.

Killian shifted to his side, braced on his elbow.

"I was in jail when Price came to bail me out."

"You're kidding."

She flashed a quick smile. "I didn't know who she was, but I'd heard my mom talk about her. She must have been a contact or something." She shrugged and wiggled into the covers.

"What did you do to end up in jail?"

"I'd scaled a building. My plan was to jump off."

"Oh, hell, Alexa."

She glanced, embarrassed. "I wasn't in very good shape at the time. Two years after their death, passed around to foster homes, and I was pretty much wishing I was in that car with them. But I wasn't arrested for what I'd planned on doing, but for scaling the ten-story building without being noticed. Till someone in the penthouse happened to need a drink of water in the middle of the night and looked out the window."

Killian smiled. "Bet that was a shock, and Price saw potential."

"She gave me the opportunity to get my revenge. I had to wait two more years before I could train, and then, well, after I got the revenge I'd worked for, I was just used to the life. Besides, I didn't have any more family; my grandmother is in her eighties and barely recalls who I am."

"Must have been tough."

"It was easy to play someone else, Killian." She shifted toward him. "If I was doing that, I didn't have to think about myself and how alone I was."

"That's a lousy way to live."

"Yeah, I know, sorta hit me between the eyes when I was eating a cockroach in that cell."

"They're crunchy, taste like chicken."

Alexa chuckled sleepily, melting into the bedding. She felt safe. For the first time in years, someone was watching her back for her. She reached, sliding her hand behind his neck and urging him closer. Her mouth slid over his and Killian groaned, slipping his arms around her and holding her to his length. The kiss went on, slow and bone jarring. He drew back and her eyes were still closed. "Mmm, we will take this up later."

"You betcha."

Her eyelids fluttered open. "Stay with me for a while?"

Killian eased to the pillows, pulling her against his chest. On his stomach, her hand clutched his, as if still seeking an anchor in the storm threatening around them. He watched her face, her beautiful features go slack, her clenched fist unfurl.

He lay beside her for a long moment, sliding his fingers through a lock of hair and watching it curl on his finger. He'd never met anyone, man or woman, who was so valiant. She might talk about hating her life, but she was born to it, clever, resourceful. A survivor. He leaned, kissed her mouth, something inside his heart touching off when her lips shaped his, and she whispered his name.

He'd already killed for her.

What she didn't know was—he'd die for her.

Logan Chambliss knew this wasn't going to end well, there were too many people manipulating the information from the start. They couldn't rely on the government. They were cut off, and to him that meant they were being set up. Price would never admit to hiring them until a last resort. Hell, not unless she had to answer to the Joint Chiefs or something.

He needed backup, for someone to know they were on the trail. Killian agreed with him. At three in the morning, he loaded in the pictures from the party Killian had crashed the first night in Hong Kong. A couple known drug dealers were obvious, but it was the un-recognizable faces that would tell him more.

He attached them to an e-mail, encrypted it, then sent it to a pal, asking for a search to put names to faces. He was playing a hunch that might not produce, but it couldn't hurt.

His last line was, *If the shit hits the fan, make sure it's evenly distributed.*

NMCC

Walker wanted a day off, just to think about this piece of Intel. His brain was smoking and the higher-ups were breathing down his neck for results. There were enough satellites up there passing over the region that they could focus to see people walking on the streets. Yet in the spreads, there'd been nothing un-usual. No movement in the Far East that they weren't already aware of, regardless. So how was he supposed to find pieces of missiles that were obviously well hid-den? He faced the fact that after two revolutions of the satellite, which had been recorded so he could study the pictures, he had little that proved a clear path. Intel was all maybes till they had evidence from operatives on the ground.

He tossed the pen down, removed his glasses and rubbed his eyes before he headed to the general's of-fice. He knocked, entering the office.

The general eased back in the seat and took up his cup of coffee.

"Got something for me, Sergeant?"

"Lucien Zarek's ship is in the middle of the East China Sea traveling a course toward Taiwan. We have thermal graphics on the ship, but nothing more than the people aboard and engine heat. He could be sailing back to Colombia. However, he's been making some phone calls all over the world to Germany, Morocco, and Libya mostly, men suspected to have bought weapons off him."

"Sounds like he's either offering up goods for sale or gathering men for an army."

"I concur, sir."

"I'm laying odds that it's a sale since he's stuck on a ship."

"I would, too, except the men are mostly mercenaries, and they aren't meeting him. Near as I can tell, sir, they're headed to Hong Kong."

"What's there that's left?"

"Triads, drug dealers. International business."

McGill shook his head. "There's got to be some other reason. If Zarek has Russian weapons and they are on the ship, then why send men to Hong Kong?"

"I can't honestly say, sir."

"Then speculate, Sergeant. You interpret this Intel all day, you must have some analysis."

"A sweep, sir. Possibly covering his tracks by killing the players? The thing is, sir, Zarek couldn't have moved a thing without some of our people knowing about it. ATF at least. We've got people imbedded with all sorts of organized crime families. Someone has to know what's up. We might have stumbled into a covert Ops. Permission to access ATF?"

The general was quiet for a moment, then said, "Get to digging, Sergeant Walker. That will be all. Please close the door on your way out."

The sergeant frowned, then left the report and the general's office. A moment later General McGill picked up the phone. The sergeant was right. Someone had to know what was going on over there. And he sure as hell didn't want loose Intel coming back to bite him in the ass. He started to dial the Deputy Director of Intelligence, Clandestine Service, then changed his mind. He'd make more headway with someone lower in the food chain.

Down the hall and a floor below, Captain Hammit stared at the crumpled piece of paper in the trash can as if it were a snake about to strike. What the hell was Moore doing in Hong Kong? He should be in a hole somewhere, wearing his disgrace and drinking himself into a stupor. He'd no idea what Moore did for a living, he'd just vanished—kind of hard to find a job when you've been forced out of the Marines with your tail between your legs. Even as the thought whipped through his mind, he knew the last thing Killian Moore would do was duck for cover and hide.

His gaze on the trash, Hammit knew the Intel traffic could be significant.

Yet he didn't retrieve it.

Day 25

There was no one in sight when Alexa stepped out of the bedroom for the second time today. She'd done no more than sleep, bathe, and eat everything she could find since the team rescued her. It was pathetic that she'd needed more rest after Logan had taken numerous X-rays. She supposed he was developing them now. She glanced around and though she couldn't see anyone, she wasn't alone. A team member was somewhere guarding her. It made her feel so incredibly safe and just after a few hours around these guys, she felt the anxiety she'd carried slip away. Tons of it.

She looked to the bank of windows, the sun setting

over Star Harbor, and she crossed the vast living room filled with cream leather furniture and ornately sculpted tables. There was a dais near a bank of windows, benches for admiring the view, and a beautifully carved dining table. Instead of an elegant table setting, it bore a thick cloth and collection of weapons and surveillance gear. She moved near, casting a glance at Logan's computer systems and wanted to use it—three screens and hard drives with a satellite dish on the roof, Killian had told her. But she didn't think Logan would appreciate that. Men were picky about sharing their toys.

She inspected the equipment, recognizing some pieces, and could do no more than stare at the others. Nothing like she'd ever seen, she thought, picking up a pair of regular-looking sunglasses and slipping them on. Thermal imaging. *Cool,* she thought, removing them. She heard a noise, a door open, and footsteps. Alexa immediately switched the glasses for a pistol, popped in a magazine and aimed.

"You shot me once, I might not be so forgiving with real bullets."

Killian. Her heart did a hot little jump just seeing him. "Sorry. Habit." She lowered the weapon, removed the clip, and laid it back on the table. Then noticed he was laden with bags. "You've been shopping?"

"Well, you could parade that gorgeous body in front of me, but I'd take exception to the team seeing it." He came near, dumping the packages on the sofa.

"Oh, my, my, Killian, you actually went into a lingerie shop?" She pulled out bras and panties, and held them up, eyeing the garments, then him. "And you had fun, I see." They were sheer and sexy, more for a corner of his bedroom floor than for good foundation support.

He reddened. "Hell."

She laughed lightly and went to him, her arms sliding

around his waist. "Thank you. Your sacrifice will be rewarded."

"I was hoping for a fashion show." He wiggled his brows, then kissed her, softly at first, then there was no stopping it. "God, I missed you," he murmured and Alexa felt the significance of his words like a warm cloak sweeping over her.

Someone missed her, someone cared. She was thrilled it was this man, and deepened the kiss, pawed his stacked muscles. He opened the robe, sliding his hands over her warm flesh, and Alexa dissolved as his big hands rode her spine, cupped her buttocks. He pulled her to him, letting her feel the delicious hardness thrusting against his jeans, and she shaped him, sent the zipper down, and drove her hand inside.

"Are you trying to tell me something?"

"And here I thought you were so smart." He grew hard in her palm and she stroked him heavily as his mouth tore over hers, then down her throat, his breathing hot and fast in her ear.

"Come to bed with me," she whispered and pushed out of his arms, heading back to the room.

"They'll know what we're up to."

"Like I give a damn," she said and didn't pause, letting the robe slide off her shoulders and to the floor. She tossed him a sleek smile.

"Just the way I like you," he said, and scooped up the robe, following. In the room, he closed the door and leaned back.

She faced him, easing back on the bed. "Come on, Mustang. Get naked."

"Yes, ma'am." As he did she lay back on the mound of pillows, her own hands roaming her body. Seeing it made him harder, and he cursed when his boots were stubborn.

"Killian."

He looked up.

"We have all night."

Something in him settled, and he watched her twist on the bed. "Touch yourself," he said.

Her eyes flared and he watched like a greedy miser as her hands slid down between her legs. She spread a little, and fingered herself for a moment, feeling sexy and decadent. His reaction was worth it. He went still as glass.

"You, too."

Killian stood at the foot of the bed, all muscle and naked, his hand on his erection, stroking himself, watching her dip her fingers to come back slick and wet. The sight aroused him to madness and he knelt on the bed. "That seems such a waste of fun," he growled and draped her legs over his thighs. "Watch me."

He dragged his finger down her divide, rasping over her plump little bead, then with two fingers pushed into her. She arched hard. "You're so hot and wet."

"Then do something about it."

"I'll make you scream." Touching her was an erotic pleasure all its own.

"You'll make me come if you keep that up." Her breath hissed out as he withdrew and circled her clit. She flexed with each stroke, offering a view of every secret she possessed, and he wanted to explore her again and again. It would take weeks to discover her body, a century to know her mind. Killian leaned forward, kissing her mouth briefly before cupping her buttocks, and brought her closer. The heat of her sex pushed to his erection, making him want to drive into her like a madman.

Her thighs over his lap and around his hips, she was spread like a fine dessert, and he bent, taking her nipple deep into the heat of his mouth. He sucked and laved, his finger occasionally dipping between her thighs. She writhed, reaching between them to fondle him.

"You're playing with me."

"Oh, hell yeah."

"Keep going."

"My main objective, ma'am."

She laughed, and his mouth moved down her belly, nibbled at her hip, then in one motion he scooped her up and laid his mouth heavily over her center.

"Oh, Killian, oh, God!"

She came apart in seconds, her body rippling with pleasure. And he kept giving it, pushing two fingers deep inside her to feel her delicate muscles clamp him. Her lush moans caught him in the chest, her panting made him long to hear more, and it was a long breathless moment before he lowered her to the bed.

"All that tension gone," he said, grinning.

"Oh, yeah, I feel so noodley," she said, laughing at herself.

"Mission accomplished."

She met his gaze, pulling him to her. "Yes, but that was teasing." He lay down with her and she reached between them, her fingers closing over him. She rode up and down, her grip gentle and measured, and his eyes flared and he was kissing her, drowning in her, pushing his tongue between her lips and sweeping wildly.

"Let's see what you like, Killian Moore, my rescuer."

"Oh, no, hero worship, *again*."

She sent him a feline smile. "I've never had a real hero in my bed." His hands were warm and tender on her wounds as they swept her body, shaped her. "What shall I do with you?"

She shifted and took him into her mouth, diving

deeply, and it made him dig his fingers into her shoulders. She tortured him, making him groan, grit his teeth, and when he was moving against her, she rose, inclined her head. He obeyed and she put her hands on the headboard, then over her shoulder, met his gaze. The look on his face was indefinable.

Killian recognized a small moment of trust and behind her, he nudged her thighs apart and slid into her in one long push.

She gasped at the thick, solid feel of him. "Oh, yeah, this I like."

God, what a fantasy, he thought, and behind her Killian slammed his eyes shut. There was a mirror a few feet away on the wall, subtly positioned for this. He nudged her. She looked, her pleasure rising at the view of them, his grip on her hips, the strain of desire on his face and rippling down his muscled body. His hips thrust forward, hers pushed back.

They pumped and pumped, his erection thick and near bursting with blood, her folds slick and gripping him like claws. Suddenly he stopped, and turned her around, entering her again, laying her flat and hovering over her.

"I gotta see your face." Slowly he moved.

Sliding and pushing, scarred tanned skin met delicate softness, thick muscles bending for her when he wanted to slam, and become oblivious to anything but the sensations of being deep inside her. But it was his soul that kept him with her in this moment, and as he stared down into her soft green eyes, he knew he'd never felt anything so intimate, so crushing to all he thought he'd been, and could be. He was suddenly humbled. "Alexa."

"Oh, Killian." There were tears in her eyes. "You do this to me so well."

"We do," he said on a kiss. He was in tune with her.

This way, he knew her and he quickened, taking her with him as he sat back on his haunches, his strong hands guiding her hips, her feet planted on the mattress.

Their gazes locked, their bodies undulating.

The climax didn't come like the unleashed beast as before, but in a steady spine-tingling pulse, the climb unmeasured, but together. She cupped his face and slid on his erection, the base of him rubbing her clitoris, the head of him touching her womb.

"I can't get close enough to you." She heard the frustration and passion in her own voice, a hidden plea for more than his loving.

"I know, I know baby." He cupped her face, understanding and wanting the same thing.

But Alexa needed the link, the bond she'd lived without for so long. Her heart cried for it. "Mark me, Killian."

"Yes," he whispered against her lips, thrust upward once and hard. Everything in him ruptured, breaking apart for her, taking her inside himself. And Killian knew, as he did from the first kiss, he never had a fighting chance. And didn't want one.

Alexa trapped him to her, her heart tripping over itself as she leaned back, fusing with him, pleasure erupting in a fast slide to a wicked stop. Her nerves were raw and open, and she felt her body grip him, the full weight of him on her as they collapsed in a wild tangle of limbs.

Alexa was barely breathing as she swept her hands over his damp spine and realized she was very close to loving this man.

Seventeen

David Lorimer stood outside Mike Cooperton's office in Archives. They'd been mild acquaintances. David didn't like him.

Mike was the CIA's worst enemy. A backstabbing climber. He was the kind of guy that if he knew something that you needed, he'd demand you jump through hoops for it, acting all supreme that he had what you wanted so he looked good in front of his rivals. People saw through it. Mike didn't have a clue that they did. He was good at misdirection, dumping blame, and he hoped he was one step ahead, always a little unsure of himself, but acting as if he were not.

The perfect ass.

His flaw was underestimating David.

He walked into his office, a cubicle, really.

"I need the Delta 9-4-1."

"What for?"

"I don't believe that's any of your business." David flipped open his notepad and rattled off timelines.

"Also Operation Full Sweep." He gave him exact times and dates.

"I need the forms first." He snapped his fingers, making David want to leap across the cubicle and choke the fool.

"Just give me the information, Cooperton, I don't have all day."

Cooperton leaned back in the chair, folding his hands behind his head. "Then, no dice. You know that. I have to have the authorized requests first."

People started rising up for a look-see over the dividers. David ignored them and leaned down in his face, and spoke just loud enough for the eavesdroppers to hear. "Let's get this straight, Mike, I have clearance to read them, you don't. I need those files for my boss, need I remind you who that is? And if I don't bring them to her within the next"—he glanced at his watch—"fifteen minutes, my head's on a platter."

Mike smirked. "Not my problem."

"It is, because I'll make certain yours will be next."

Mike's features flattened before he shored them up and sent him a sour look. "You'll have to predate a form, then."

"Gee, you think? Just print them."

The files printed, spitting facedown into a manila file. David stood guard over it till it was done and without a look at Mike, he left.

"Asshole," Mike muttered.

David stepped back inside, stared him down till Mike nervously said, "What?"

He left, smiling as he walked back to the office. He was right. A perfect asshole.

General McGill hung up the phone, resisting the urge to throw the damn thing across his office. He'd met a road block in the name of a CIA paper pusher who was so afraid of dropping the ball he wouldn't toss it. He had the country's highest security clearance, for God's sake, and he wasn't about to let some maggot in a suit get in his way. He rose, reaching for his cover, intent on making a personal appearance and flashing his three stars.

Don't fuck with me, he thought. *I'll eat you alive.* This would be a waste of an afternoon to get to Langley. He grabbed his briefcase and was about to tell his secretary his agenda when Staff Sergeant Walker double timed into the offices. The young man was destined for a stellar career, he thought.

"You need to speak with me?"

"Yes, sir, privately please."

They returned to his offices. "This can't wait?"

"I wouldn't let it, sir." Walker opened a file and spread photos on the desk.

"I asked NSA for anything happening in Hong Kong, sir. In the last hours, they got these from an anonymous e-mail."

"Anonymous?"

"NSA wouldn't give it up. I can find out who it is and they knew it, however, the dates on the photos"—he pointed to the lower right—"were this past week. The same time Lucien Zarek's ship made port in Hong Kong."

"Is Zarek in them?"

"No, sir."

McGill put on his glasses, his gaze moving over each photograph. "They're taken at the same level."

"I noticed that, too, which says to me the camera was hidden, possibly on someone."

"Who?"

Walker just shook his head. "That's Alejandro Carrión, confirmed from DEA. But this man, smiling at the woman, is a Serbian scientist." Walker went on to point out two more. "I'm afraid they are a collection of physicists, munitions experts, and a couple chemists."

McGill looked up. "Oh, hell."

"Yes, sir."

"And the woman? She looks like she's with Carrión."

"I thought so, too. The photos were sent in a stream, sir, all connected as if still on a roll of movie film. There was this one." He pointed to the edge of one that showed others in the room. "I enhanced it." He slid it out from the stack.

"The shooter is holding or dancing with the women. Too close to get a really clear look at her." They both knew that women beautiful enough to make men pant were the easiest way to get close to a man, or make a link to one as dangerous as Carrión. "So the man doing the surveillance was interested in the woman as well as the rest of the guests. Correct?"

"I would say so, sir, but it's the coupling of the scientists that has me thinking they were there to put together the missiles. Or refit them for their needs."

"Who do we have on the watch list that's smart enough to put together the missiles?"

"These guys, to start." Walker pointed to two men in the photos. "And they haven't been seen for a few days, sir, since this picture."

"NSA said the missile parts weren't off-loaded."

"That doesn't mean they couldn't be assembled *on* the ship, sir. With the launchers. That hull is the size of a football field. Airtight, climate controlled for the coffee it usually stores."

That made the theory all the more plausible.

"Good work, Staff Sergeant, outstanding."

"Scoggins was a tremendous help, sir. His division

was tracking communications traffic. And do you remember the M18s stolen last month, sir?"

McGill scowled. "God damn right I do, good Marines died."

"DEA has the weapons."

"How?"

"It seems that Killian Moore bought them back from Zarek and turned them over, sir."

"Moore? His name was smeared by the DEA, why would he help them?"

"I don't know, sir, but it's obvious some of them still trust him. He used counterfeit cash from seizures for the purchase, which DEA provided. The thing is, sir, no one could find out who'd taken the weapons, or get near them. Then Moore arrives in Colombia and bang, he's got a meeting with Zarek. From what we can get from DEA, he asked *specifically* for those rifles and got them."

"You've been busy, Walker."

Walker flashed him a smile and dove into it again. McGill sat, listening.

"I'm thinking since he was railroaded, I mean, charged, that his cover wasn't blown from the last incident. To the cartel, he was still undercover. He could have given them any excuse for being gone so long, hiding out or even prison."

"Did the DEA actually say they were working on this with Moore?"

"No, sir, they weren't. Moore contacted them, and drew them in. Arresting Zarek wasn't in the deal. For reasons Moore would not explain, he wanted Zarek loose."

"Well, dammit, we need to find out why."

"Might have something to do with the CIA."

The shit just keeps getting deeper, McGill thought, studying the pictures. "And the reason is?"

"The calls, sir. To Moore's satellite phone."

McGill's gaze snapped up. "Say again, Marine."

Walker frowned and took a step back. "Scoggins, sir, he learned that someone in CIA secure SatCom has been tapping on Moore's frequency for days. Then it just stopped."

"Why wasn't I told?"

"Sir?" The sergeant frowned. "Forgive me, I don't understand. I assumed you knew. Scoggins gave the report to Captain Hammit two days ago."

McGill muttered a curse, then hit the button on his intercom. "Corporal, Captain Hammit, my office, asap." Jesus. We had a link and he let it go? "Staff Sergeant Walker, I want all Intel that you and Scoggins gathered on my desk in thirty minutes. If anyone gives you flack, tell them to take it up with me. Clear?"

"Yes, sir."

McGill looked at his watch. "We have less than eight hours before our satellite crosses the arena. Hop any bird you can, Sergeant. If that ship is moving, we are running out of time."

"Yes, sir."

McGill pulled one of the photos out from the pile and pointed. "There is a reflection in a mirror. See if you can enhance this. I want to know who the shooter is. And find out the identity of this woman. All these men are very interested in her and I want to know if it's just her face and body, or something else." It was the *something else* he was dreading.

"Well, sir, she is beautiful and sexy and if I may say, sir—"

"Don't. I have eyes and that's just about the best way to distract a bunch of drug dealers and weapons specialists, don't you think?"

A knock made them both look up and Captain Hammit entered.

"That will be all for now, Staff Sergeant."

The captain snapped to attention before the general's desk.

"You want to tell me why you let a viable link on the ground in a time of crisis get tossed?"

"Sir?"

"Any information is not deemed at your discretion, Captain. Dragon One is the only team on the ground and close to this missile transfer."

Captain Hammit paled measurably and if anyone in the Pentagon didn't know what a pissed-off three-star general sounded like, they did now.

David taped the printout under his desk drawer. He couldn't get it out, but he'd read it. Some things were making sense. The archives had it all, along with an order to destroy the files in three days. Why three, he didn't know, but under his drawer was Alexa Gavlin's personal file and mission Intel on Lucien Zarek. There were no memos or reports as of nearly sixty days ago. She'd been missing for weeks without contact, that much he'd learned, and there was no telling what went on, but Price chose to record the barest details. Gavlin herself was more detail oriented, most coming from her computer in her apartment that was seized by CIA officers in Cali. She was sent to learn if Zarek was dealing in larger weapons. She'd reported progress and her suspicions, her contacts and verification of information she'd gathered. Her contact was Santiago, now dead. His body had been discovered in bad decay. David had seen the photo on Price's desk nearly five weeks ago. It was gross.

David pounced on Santiago's files, and found that his personal accounts had taken a major leap around the time of his death. The million dollar kind. If that didn't clue Price in that he'd been compromised, she was ignoring it or was a part of it. An agent didn't make that kind of money, and it was Santiago's legal personal account, so David had to assume it wasn't part of the operation. There was no information on it. What Gavlin had done about it, or if she knew, was pure speculation. But it wasn't looking good for the home team. Her reports ceased nearly sixty days ago.

Then there was Killian Moore. He would have never suspected Price would go outside the Company until he'd traced the satellite communications numbers to Moore's Dragon One team. Specialists in retrievals, highly trained, and Price had hired them. David had copies of the check. Which was damn near a year's pay for him and as yet, uncashed. What couldn't she trust to operatives in her own stable? They were loyal to the core. Whereas Moore, well, he didn't exactly have a stellar reputation since the DEA mess in Colombia. He'd walked out of the Marine Corps claiming his innocence, but could do nothing about it.

He'd been set up. A rookie agent could read through the Intel. However, he knew most of it didn't get into the report, and comparing Gavlin's small part as a relay and the ambush that cost eight men their lives, David realized what Price chose not to let out into the open.

Moore had been betrayed by his own.

That, David could do something about; the reason he had the archives file, yet he suspected the real McCoy was in Price's safe. Getting it was impossible. But with the timelines and locations during the DEA Op, it's a wonder Moore and Gavlin hadn't crossed paths then. David was betting that's how Price got Moore's team to go after her. Naming her the traitor. It was what was left out of the file that made it appear to be true.

David knew Price had been lying for weeks.

She'd said Roister had Gavlin's file. David went after it. No one needed the files Delta 9-4-1. The agent was deceased. A star on the wall. Proof would help.

There were no disks in the CIA, only hard drives and printers. Making copies was easy, getting them out would be tough. Security was all about keeping stuff inside.

His clearance would get him nowhere.

He had a copy stuffed in his wallet. He had to get her access codes to top secret Intel and print it, or find a way to get it to someone who could do something. He glanced at the clock.

He wanted to get home, to check his computer to see if he had made a patch to Moore's com link. He was praying they were as smart as the rumors made them out to be.

Hong Kong
Dragon One CP
Day 26

The sun was up and Max was cooking when a delivery arrived. Riley, ever cautious, scanned it for mechanics till Logan came up, read the label and took it, zipping it open.

"Clue us in." Sam leaned over the counter, snatching a slice of bacon.

"One of the chips that Alexa took out of the missile parts, I sent it off to a pal of mine. He could give me schematics on it, and what it can do, and anything else that's useful."

"I was hoping it was a *Playboy,*" Sam groused.

Logan went to his computer lab station equipped with a web camera and dialed. The screen flashed as the number linked with another computer. A blond-haired man with a scar over his left eyebrow smiled back.

"Well, hell, Chambliss. I'm getting traffic on you guys. Keeping your nose clean?" Nolan Deets was an NSA cryptologist. One of hundreds and Logan's college roomie. He worked on secure information in a single room and information passed to him was highly classified.

"Not exactly, but we're trying. I need a favor."

Deets tapped keys and went secure. "You got it. Shoot."

"I'm getting a signal. It's encrypted and very slow, and low frequency. The encryption program isn't recognizing it, plus I'd need to know why it's directed to my terminal."

Deets worked his keyboard magic, hit the last key with gusto. "Someone's tracking you through the Satellite Communications phone link."

"That's hard to believe. You helped me write this program."

"Anything is possible. I spend all day trying to get ahead of the latest hackers. Just a sec." He tapped keys, then shifted to another screen, going to town. "Tune up your frequency."

Logan typed and the noise came faster and louder.

"Run the decryption now."

Logan opened a second program and ran it through the filter.

"Jesus, its old Morris code," Deets said.

"No wonder the program didn't recognize it."

Sam moved in close, leaning toward the speaker. "It's a warning." Logan glanced at him. "I was a Boy Scout." Sam grabbed a piece of paper and wrote briefly. "It's the same message over and over. 'Dragon One. All Intel compromised. Queen sweeping house. Secure Delta 9-4-1 and confirm.'"

"What the hell is Delta 9-4-1 and who's sending it? And how the hell did they get this frequency?"

The NSA agent worked his keyboard. "David Lorimer. He's got your Sat numbers and he's transmitting from his apartment. He's tapped into a TV dish network and hopping off their satellite, clever little bastard. We should hire him."

"How could this Lorimer know any of this, it's classified."

"Because that's Price's assistant," came from somewhere behind.

The men turned. Alexa stood in the doorway, barefoot and wearing jeans and a T-shirt.

"Price is covering her tracks." She moved closer and took the paper from Sam. "And Delta 9-4-1 is me."

Lucien's ship was dead in the water between Taiwan and the northern Philippine islands.

It was as if everything went to a standstill, except with Chinese MSS investigating the accident at Fujian. Typical Chinese cover-up, Killian thought, sitting in a stuffed chair with a stack of folders on his lap. He sifted through each one, trying to answer the big question: who was buying the missiles and where were they targeted.

The target could be anywhere within a three thousand kilometer range, which was about eighteen hundred miles. A medium range missile launched in Taiwan could reach anywhere on China's coastline, as far inland as Beijing or to Australia or Okinawa.

Or Outer Mongolia for all they knew.

He didn't doubt they were racing against a ticking clock.

Even as the thought burst through his mind, he remembered Price in his backyard, cold, efficient, and giving him a deadline. Why the twenty-eight day mark?

"Logan," he said softly, "what happens in two days?"

Logan turned from the screen, frowning and removing his glasses. "Nothing. Not even a moon cycle, a festival. Just another day. Why?"

"Price put a timeline on us, and there has to be a good reason. She had to know of the weapons, the buyers, something. We're close, despite the setbacks. Something is scheduled and I'm betting it's a sale."

"Or a launch," Alexa muttered, curling on her side on the sofa and drifting back to sleep.

Logan and Killian exchanged a glance, amused. "If she's right, that means that Price knew the missiles were hot and loaded, and sent Alexa in as a patsy."

Killian frowned.

Logan spun the chair. "If in twenty-eight days the missiles were set to launch, then how could Price know about it and not tell anyone? NMCC or NSA don't have any intelligence on this. At least not that I can access. But you hear stuff, trash, and it's always got some clue in it and I'm not getting any."

"So, you think maybe Price helped Zarek. I don't think so." He shook his head. "She's s bitch, but not a traitor."

"Says you."

"She blackmails me to get me in this, then when it doesn't go her way she tries to wipe the slate clean. She knows we are on to her because of Pritchard, so she's covering her tracks. It doesn't make any difference to me, Franco . . . Gordon is dead and my reputation went with him. What's your point?"

"She had to know Gordon was alive and she's the kind of person who likes holding all the cards, and then drawing them up later to use for one reason or another.

I'm betting she knew you'd find Gordon and clean up her problem. I think this Lorimer guy is digging. He had to be if he got the SatCom link. There're millions of them out there and he found ours, a secure link?"

"Say that's all true, what's it do for us?"

"Lorimer could be a good backup. If Price's part isn't exposed, she wins and we go down in flames."

Killian shook his head. "He's a glorified secretary." He wouldn't get his hopes up, his record was spoiled, and he'd never get it back. Franco was dead, and Killian had no one to blame but himself. He would have liked to have dragged the bastard back in irons, but without fingerprint or dental records, Gordon was a ghost.

Logan shook his head, fed up. "It's like talking to dirt with you, ya know?"

"What do you want, Logan? To respond? Be careful. Lorimer could be working for Price."

He looked back at the files, flipping through Alexa's personal report. He'd read it a dozen times, but it was sanitized. He'd have to ask her about a few things, most he knew already. In the file photo she looked cheerleader-cute, a childlike innocence she didn't have anymore.

He glanced at the list of stats, height, weight, markings. The scar on her thigh wasn't listed, nor the ones on the back of her throat from being staked to the ground during the Ops. His gaze flicked to the full body picture, then to her ankle.

He sat up. "Alexa?" he called, nudging her awake.

She rolled to her back, yawned and opened her eyes. "Can't a spy get some rest?"

He shifted to the edge of the sofa and slid his hand warmly over her foot. "Your file says that your tattoo is a falcon."

"Yeah, it's been a lot of things. The Company insisted it be removed, I refused and settled for changing it." She told him how it had first been two angels, to honor her parents.

"But now it's a dragon."

She was awake and focused. "What are you getting at?"

"When did you have it done?"

She frowned softly. "About three years ago."

"It looks refreshed. Recently."

Alexa sat up, curling her leg to the side. She pushed her hair behind her ear for a better look. "I need a mirror."

Killian retrieved one from the bathroom and she propped it so she could see the reflection.

"I thought it was the drugs playing tricks on me."

"Say again?" Killian felt the bite in the back of his throat when he knew they'd discovered something vital.

She looked up. "There are five claws. It's always had four."

He wasn't going to ask her if she was sure. "Logan, let me see the X-ray."

"I told you I didn't find anything, and I have a shot of her leg from calf to toes." Logan grabbed the envelope, holding each one up till he found the right one. "See. It's just a fifth claw. Could the artist have done that intentionally?"

"No." She met Killian's gaze, a realization hitting her. "Oh, man. The tapping sound, it was a tattoo needle."

He frowned.

"I've had this done four times. I know the sound, dammit, and I should have recognized it sooner." That it was locked under a chemically erased memory didn't make a damn bit of difference now.

"Are you saying that whatever Zarek put in you is *in* the tattoo?"

Alexa looked up, panic in her eyes. "In the claw of a Chinese dragon."

Eighteen

The Pentagon
"The Tank"

"General McGill, are you honestly telling us that there are missiles being assembled inside a ship?"

"We believe so, yes, they were loaded, but never off-loaded."

"Do you have any witnesses, confirmation from inside?"

"We're working on that."

"We'd know that if we knew who the buyer was. And the target," an admiral said. "Who's to say they will be launched now?"

"We have to assume they will be soon," McGill shot back. "Our people on the ground say that Moore has been in the area. What he's working on, we don't know, but he's a private citizen. A retrieval expert. However, DEA reports that he was feeding them excellent Intel on Carrión and the Hong Kong drug triads within the last ten days."

"What is Chinese MSS saying?"

"A lot. They haven't deployed ships, but submarines

are a factor and in the water. And their jets are on constant alert." Like a finger on a trigger, McGill thought.

The admiral looked at the other members. "Christ, they're nuclear."

"We believe that a few members of MSS might be involved, but they aren't speaking of it in detail, of course. The only thing we have recently is a training accident in Fujian, several troops were killed with an MSS colonel." He flipped to notes. "Qain Pong. Pong's a hardliner, linked to several deaths, but never charged."

"A cleanup man. That's in house, and not our concern," the admiral said. "Besides, MSS gets their feathers up when it concerns money and everything else is fair game, including torture for state secrets."

"Our satellite confirms the encounter. Thermals show people on the ground for no more than ten minutes, then tracked something leaving fast. But identity is unconfirmed. Suspected startled geese." His tone was sour with doubt.

"Do you believe that?"

"Personally, no. Moore has his own jet, and a chopper that could make the distance and fly under radar." With Sam Wyatt at the stick, it could go upside down, he thought.

"Where is Moore now?"

"On a hilltop in Hong Kong."

"Doing?"

"Nothing, Admiral, all is relatively quiet." Which really meant they had no other Intel.

"And Carrión?"

"He's disappeared."

"Convenient."

He relayed the other aspects; the pictures, flashing each on a large screen. After he laid it out, and the lights switched back on, he turned to the director of the CIA. "Care to add to this, Director?"

"I've not been aware of this, but I will be. The party guests are all familiar, scientists, cartel . . ."

"Can you identify the woman?"

The director glanced, then sighed hard. "She's ours. Missing for several weeks, we thought she was dead. For obvious reasons, I can't say more, but if she's there with Moore, then the weapons are a definite, and a problem."

Day 27

Logan took photos of her tattoo, enhanced it one hundred times, yet found only a fifth claw. "Nothing, I don't see any reason for it except artist rendition."

"Logan, this is mine, I know what's been there for three years, and this didn't have a fifth."

Killian rubbed his thumb over it, her foot in his lap. "Feels grainy on the claw. Riley, grab the infrared lights."

He kept staring at her ankle.

"I didn't know you had a foot fetish." He was stroking her heel.

Killian glanced up, wiggled his brows, then Riley handed over the infrared scope. They cut the lights and he shined it. "There's something there, but it's not clear enough and too damn small."

"Try fluorescents." Riley handed over another lamp, a seven-inch stick.

Killian shined the blue glowing light. "Bingo. Logan." Logan came with his camera, taking several shots and within five minutes he had them loaded, on the screen, enhancing and focusing.

"They're numbers," Logan said. "But for what?"

"Arming codes for the missiles?" Max suggested.

"Why? Zarek could transport them," Alexa said. "Or just memorize them."

"True, but Franco said he was searched a lot."

"Not his brain. Besides, the Colombian police came to his compound and did a search almost weekly," Alexa said. "Searched the coffee warehouse, too. Zarek owned the city, and paid for information or had someone on the inside because he knew a day before each raid and moved his stash. He stored it in the jungle, probably underground. I couldn't get close enough to a location to find it. I'm almost certain he switched it around."

Max joined in. "That still doesn't answer why he put numbers on her. Why not tattoo it on himself, or send e-mail? He used a remailer before." Alexa confirmed with a nod. "He could have hidden it anywhere on that ship."

"Zarek is paranoid. He changed the combinations on locks and alarms every morning. Changed his routine. That's why he's so hard to catch."

"Paranoia tells me he'd had a way he could keep tabs on you after dumping you in the cane field," Riley said.

"Well, that wasn't hard, I was doing exactly what he wanted," she groused. "He watched, closed off the city to me and any contacts. No money or passports, he knew I'd go to Consuelo or Enrique. Like you did," she said to Killian. "He sent Santiago's picture out into the open and the CIA learned of it." She held Killian's gaze for a moment, remembering the ambush in the streets, the CIA and Casta firing at them. They'd come a long way since, she thought, reaching for the only man, the only person she trusted. "He used me for his game. I just didn't know it."

He grasped her hand, smiling a little to himself. "I think Zarek did it because of a broken heart."

Alexa made a face.

"He's in love with you and felt betrayed."

"I did betray him. For the good of the U.S.A."

"But he let his emotions take hold. You made him love you—no, hear me out. You're beautiful, Alexa, exciting, what man wouldn't fall for you if you gave them the time of day. You said Zarek would screw a whore, but treated you like a queen. Clearly his mind separates women into two groups. You played him, your job, sure, but not to him. So when he learned he was being manipulated—"

"—which I still don't know how."

"Not important now, but he turned it around and played a game with you. Using you to transport the numbers, whatever they are, and it kept him in the clear."

"I figured that, some payback. But not a broken heart, just pure anger at being taken."

"I don't think so. He could have just killed you and gone about his way. He kept you around for this reason."

"They aren't arming codes," Logan said into the conversation. The group turned to look at him. "There are only eight figures, six are digits, two letters, that's not an arming sequence." Logan looked up, frustrated. "And I can't tell you what they are. They could be a checking account, for all I know."

Alexa's shoulders drooped.

"Franco said Zarek needed to get them out for the deal." Killian rose. "Keep the Sat link open for now. The rest of us need to pack up and secure the jet."

"You in a rush?"

"We're on a timeline, remember, twenty-eight days, we've used up twenty-seven of them as of this morning. Zarek's ship is dead in the water, and if our speculations are true, and we could be chasing a dark horse, then the minute it moves, some country is going to get hit."

"We can't warn anyone."

"Yes, we can. We have to, we don't have the firepower to blow up a ship loaded with ballistic missiles. Logan, send a message to your pal in NSA. Our government might not be in our corner right now, but I'll bet you a grand they are watching this."

His gaze followed the SUV as it headed down the curving drive. Three gone, three left. He signaled, and his team moved up the hillside, locked and loaded. They took it slow, aware of who they were dealing with and found the area rigged with mines, and flash grenades. Smart, he thought, and signaled his man to come close.

"Cut these, check motion sensors and cameras, too."

He signaled and the eight men spread out moving up to the helipad.

They set the charges, then shifted back into the dark, waiting for their commander to let it rip. Through night vision goggles, he watched the house. They were no different from his team, guns for hire. Except they had a moral conscience. The team leader prided himself on lacking that deterrent.

For a half a million, he'd kill his own mother.

Killian moved back and forth from the rooms to the gear displayed on the table, loading it into black bags and hard-sided cases. Alexa helped, reaching for the electronics.

"I wouldn't. Riley is picky about who handles that. Even I don't."

"Ooh, never piss off an Irishman I always say." She

laid it back down. "What about the computers? Those will take some time to break down."

Killian frowned. "You're right, we better start that first." He called for Logan.

"He went out to the trucks for the containers," she said.

"It shouldn't take that long." Frowning, Killian checked inside first. "Stay put."

She frowned. Something was up. Killian had been so confident about the security here. "I don't think so." She grabbed a gun off the table, and loaded it.

"Alexa."

"Don't start treating me like a girl, Killian. You take left, I'll take the right."

Killian sighed. Arguing with her would just waste time. He went to find out what was keeping Logan. "He probably just needs some extra hands."

She glanced. "Then why are you armed." Alexa moved cautiously toward the back of the house, the bedrooms, checking each one, the closets, then turned back toward the living room.

On the other side of the house, Killian moved to the entryway. The doors were double wide and arched, made of carved rosewood and tough as brick. He didn't see any movement beyond the frosted glass panels flanking both sides of the doors, and walked slowly to the right down the service hall toward the garages. There were three, all connected, and he opened the door, all lights off, and flattened to the wall. The back of the SUV was open.

Where was Logan?

He eased closer, a sick feeling burning in his stomach. He checked behind, left, right, then under the truck. He saw a pair of feet hanging out the back of the truck. He moved swiftly.

"Logan! Aw, jeez."

The man was facedown in the SUV, his left side bleeding. He rolled him over. And the man came up swinging.

"It's me, it's me! Christ."

Logan touched the cut on the back of his head. "There are six at least, black Ops clothing, semiautomatics. Mercs probably. They didn't even trip the God damn sensors!" Logan grabbed a blanket and stuffed it against his bleeding side. Killian reached to help, but Logan waved him off. "No, it's a knife cut, not too deep."

"Can you move?"

"Yes. God dammit. I didn't hear them. Some SEAL I am, huh?"

Killian helped him up anyway, then turned back to the main house. "Alexa!"

"I'm here. I'm okay."

He came around the hall from the garage into the foyer and saw her. "We've got company."

She shifted to look out the windows, crouching. "Get down!" she shouted and dropped as the windows imploded. Glass sprayed, a second later two men dangling from ropes swung into the house from the roof.

Killian fired, taking one out. He dangled lifelessly from the nylon rope. Then glass shattered behind him, and two men came through the frosted panels at the front door like a battalion, riddling the place with bullets, never aiming.

Killian dove, hitting the floor hard and rolling behind a chair. He popped up and fired, clipping one in the thigh. In his line of vision, he saw Logan slumped against the wall and he finished the job. The second one was already past the foyer, moving around toward Killian's position. He could smell him, hear him breathe, and kept himself tucked till a boot crunched on glass.

He popped up fast and sharp, hitting the man in the

throat, the chest and just because it pissed him off, the nuts. He was dead before he hit the deck.

"Nicely done. Come out or she's dead."

Killian checked his ammo. "Logan, you okay?"

"Fuck, yeah, yeah, who are these guys?"

Killian sighted across the distance. A single man held Alexa against him, her head in a lock so she couldn't look up, and a gun at her temple.

"My employer needs her alive." The Aussie accent was heavy. "I don't."

The man had her aligned with him. Killian couldn't shoot without hitting Alexa. Two more men stepped over the ledge of broken glass. Killian rose up to plant a bullet in one—dead center of his face, then his chest.

"I'll hunt you." Two more to kill, he thought.

Alexa's captor glanced at his fallen comrades, then said, "In what?" He inclined his head ever so slightly and the man to his right lifted his arm, and pointedly pressed a detonator.

Yards behind them on the helipad, the chopper exploded. The fuel ignited, setting off a rapid burst of heat Killian could feel from here. Her captor didn't budge. Yet Alexa fought him.

"Behave, bitch. He doesn't need your head." The team backed toward the shattered windows.

"Killian!" Alexa said, her fight making him work to take her. "If he has me, he has the numbers."

He knew that, ignoring the fear in her face, his gaze on her captor. She was still in the line of fire.

"Shoot!" Alexa fought like a wild animal, driving her elbow into the man's stomach, latching her teeth onto his arm.

He barely grunted, and behind the mask, Killian saw the man smile.

"He won't, love," he said, his face close to her ear.

"Because of you." From inside the mask, a long pink tongue slithered out to lick the side of her face.

Alexa jerked her head away. "I'm begging you, millions will die. Shoot!"

Killian swung to the left, putting a bullet in one guard. In reflex, he riddled the sofa with bullets as her captor dragged her. He straddled the concrete sill now.

"If he launches, it could start a war. Shoot! Shoot *me*!"

God, he couldn't.

Soldiers of fortune tapped off shots to keep Killian back and he watched as if in slow motion, the man's arms around her waist, her hair flying wildly and blocking her face as she struggled, kicking, throwing her head back into the man's chin and making his steps falter.

She grabbed the concrete window frame, her hands bleeding instantly. "Killian, you have to do it! You know you do! Millions will die. Please. Shoot!" She spread her arms wide. "*Shoot me.* I'm just one woman!"

"But you're *my* woman!"

For a brief moment, Alexa met his gaze, then as if tossing a rag doll, the merc heaved her out the shattered window. Her scream rose up from the hillside, and Killian raced around the shredded furniture. "Alexa!"

The merc stepped completely through the window, then turned.

They both fired. Killian twice, the merc once. The merc flinched, taking both shots, but cracking off a second. Killian felt the bullet rip through his shoulder, pain snapping at him like a whip, yet he kept moving toward the window, firing at the merc's back. "Alexa!"

He emptied his weapons into the shadows, then heard the fast slide of nylon cord. They're rapelling down the hill, he thought as he fell, blood pumping onto the floor with each heartbeat.

Oh, Jesus. Alexa.

NMCC

Walker ran, pushing people aside, apologizing, then racing toward The Tank. He rapped and a colonel answered, scowling. "You cannot enter here, Staff Sergeant."

"I'm aware, sir, but—"

General McGill turned. "Let him in."

Walker entered the inner sanctum, all eyes on him as he approached the general. "Sir, we have satellite."

The general frowned, looked at his watch. "How?"

"I bounced it off a weather bird, sir, and we got this." Walker handed him the thermal imaging.

The general stared. "One hell of an explosion."

"It's Moore's CP, sir. A chopper lifted off moments after the blast, near the water." He pointed out the frames. "Then swung to this, a cruiser. Three people lowered, then it headed up the coast. Another chopper picked up the passengers."

Tag team escape, great. "Where is it going?"

"Toward Zarek's ship."

"Any survivors?"

"Thermals are hot, but fading, sir."

Bodies going cold, McGill thought, his features tightening. Moore was their one ace and now he could be dead.

Walker leaned closer to say, "Sir, Chinese subs are headed to the area, and fighter jets from Hainan went on full alert."

Good God. McGill smothered his emotions. "Keep me appraised." He looked at the table lined with enough brass and politicians to start their own country. "We have a critical situation," he began.

*   *   *

Alexa rolled down the hillside, and someone stopped her, grabbing her off the ground, and two men carried her to a chopper that was just revving up.

They tossed her in without consideration.

"Drug the Shelia," the leader said, jamming a green medical cloth under his shirt. He let his arm bleed and fell back against the wall of the chopper and smacked the floor three times to signal takeoff. What was left of his team struggled to hold her down and secure her wrists.

Alexa wouldn't make it easy and sank her teeth into black cloth, clamping hard. The man howled like a girl. She held on, her jaw hurting, skin breaking beneath her teeth till he smacked her off. She hit the deck, her head slamming hard.

I'm so sick of being kidnapped. I quit.

She pushed herself up, glared at her attacker. The leader flipped out a cigarette, then pulled off his mask. Alexa met his gaze as the needle slid into her skin. A vague image stayed in her mind as the drugs knocked her out.

"Jesus, she's a fighter." They released her and she slumped to her side.

"Wouldn't you like a piece of that ass."

"Maybe we can when he's done with her, you think," one man said.

The leader snarled, and shoved him. "Christ, you're a pig. We get the money and get lost. If he doesn't pay, we kill him."

"And her."

"She's nothing."

"You know what this is about?"

"No, and I don't care." He turned his gaze out the window toward the horizon.

* * *

Killian heard footsteps and rolled to aim.

"Whoa, whoa, Killian, it's me, Riley."

Riley, Max, and Sam came in armed and scoping the area. "Jesus, what the hell happened?" Max was lifting Logan onto what was left of the sofa.

"They have her, God dammit," Killian said, dropping into a chair.

Sam came in last. "I'm going to kill them. Did you see what the fucker did to my chopper! My chopper!"

"We saw the blast and turned back," Riley said as he pulled out medical equipment and tore open packages. "They must have been waiting for us to separate to get in like this." He applied them to Logan's side.

Killian sat up as Max checked the wound. "The back looks nasty, but no bullet."

Clutching the wad of gauze to his shoulder, Killian forced himself to stand. "Patch it up. We need to move."

"They got the computers," Logan said, leaning up to look. "Dammit." The systems were in a shambles on the floor. "I backed it up. What I had was on disk with me, in the back of the truck."

Thank God. Killian drew one easy breath. "Tell me you put a marker on her."

"No, I figured all of us could protect her."

"Apparently not. Christ. This is a major cluster fuck." Killian yanked off the mask of a dead man, then searched him. "No ID, no markings, black Ops gear. Mercs. I should have seen it coming. No one works for Zarek without lots of cash exchanging hands."

"Will you sit and let me fix that!" Max said. Killian obeyed, and Max started cleaning his shoulder.

On the sofa, Logan lay still as Riley stitched inside his wound, then outside. Without anesthesia. "I hate doing your job," he groused, but kept working. "At least it's a clean cut."

"Do a quick patch till we can get on the jet," Killian ordered. "No telling if they'll come back."

Sam was walking the post with a dead man's rifle, grousing to himself over his chopper. It was still burning. He stepped out a window, and moved into the dark. Seconds later, he returned with ropes. "They climbed up," Sam said, tossing the ropes on the floor. "They cut the flash grenade triggers and took them with them."

"They came in from the roof. Trained, one was Australian. That could mean ex–Royal Marines," Logan said.

"I don't care if they're MI-6!" Killian barked. "They have her and the numbers. We don't know what the hell they are, and they do."

"We can track the chopper, but we have to get to the jet." Logan tried to get up.

"Not yet, dammit." Riley ordered Logan to remain still as he put in the last stitch in his side. "Your head doesn't look so good either." He cut the thread and bandaged him tightly.

Logan was up and moving, listing to one side as he stared at his precious computer systems. "Killian, let's call this one in."

Killian didn't comment on that. "Do a sweep of the house. We need to get in the air asap."

Price strode into the office and stopped at his desk. "Hand it over, David."

He lifted his gaze. "I beg your pardon."

"The files, I want them. You don't have the clearance for that and you knew it. What are you trying to do?"

"Nothing, ma'am, except my job."

"That does not include reading classified documents, lying to Archives and tracing my calls in a secure room. Did you think it would go unnoticed?"

"No, ma'am, I was hoping it didn't." Her brows shot up and David said, "Someone would wonder why, connect, and follow up, trace me, investigate and it would all lead back to you."

Behind her, Fasio entered the office, clearing his throat. He was one of Price's strongarms. "The director is on the floor, and wants to see you."

"Tell him I'll be there in a moment."

"No, ma'am, he said now."

David tried not to smirk.

She held his gaze for a very long time. "You have no idea what you're getting into." Price spun around, and left.

David dropped into his chair, rubbing his chest and feeling his heart beat against the bone. Good God. He looked around. "What to do, what to do," he muttered, then ducked under his desk, pulling the files, then gathered what he could. He'd speak to the director. If he didn't do something, then Price would shuffle him off to jail and no one would question her.

He left the offices. It was now or never.

General McGill wanted to shake the woman. "Your agent turned up in the arena, with Moore, and you have no Intel from her?"

"She refused to contact me. We believed she had crossed over."

The director arched a brow and leaned forward. "She's been spotted in Colombia and Hong Kong, yet you gave her no backup?"

"No, she didn't need it from this end, she was compromised and should have come in; that she didn't . . . speaks for itself."

"No, it doesn't. And frankly, Lania, abandoning our

NOCs in the field is not our policy. We do everything to get them out alive first."

"Yes, but if they commit treason, then we let contact die until we can recover."

"Treason? Gavlin's record gives absolutely no indication she could be bought. What gave you reason to believe this?"

"Her disappearance with Zarek for the same length of time, the death of her relay contact Santiago, then her reemergence without contact to the station."

"No one, Lania? I believe the shots fired at her at the CIA station might have something to do with that," the director said.

McGill waited for her to squirm. She didn't, only lowering her gaze briefly. "What was her assignment?"

Coolly, she turned her gaze on the general. "Track Lucien Zarek, get into his operation and learn all she could. Which she did, then she vanished for several weeks. I sent Moore after her because he could get in deep into the cartels and we didn't have time for an undercover setup."

"Why not? What's the rush?"

"We feared Zarek was dealing larger weapons."

"He is."

She didn't look surprised.

"Right now they are on their way somewhere in Southeast Asia."

The director continued to grill her and McGill had to hand it to the woman. She was a cool customer, and had an answer for everything.

The director jotted a note, then looked at her. "You called the Professor, and now he's dead."

She didn't respond.

"And Chinese intelligence have our listening equipment and reason to accuse the U.S. of spying."

"They spy, we spy."

"There is only one reason you'd call him, Lania. And to my knowledge, no one authorized it."

McGill knew this just went heavy duty. A sanctioned assassination. On one of her own. The question was, why?

Outside David walked past a conference room and through the misted glass saw General McGill. He'd been there for nearly an hour with the director, questioning Price and probably getting nowhere. He purposely dropped his stolen papers, and they slid across the slick floor. He started gathering them, people walking past him, only one asking if he needed help. He listened but couldn't hear anything beyond murmurs.

Gathering the papers neatly, David couldn't stall any longer and just as he was straightening, he heard footsteps. When he looked up, Fasio and Preston were coming toward him. *Oh, shit. She's getting me out of the way so I can't contradict her story.*

He rose, shuffling papers, and when he hoped they'd enter the conference room, they stopped in front of him.

David felt his Adam's apple bob. "She's in there."

Fasio took the papers. Preston grabbed his arms.

"You shouldn't have snooped in her business, Lorimer."

David saw his life circling the rim. The door opened. He met Price's gaze. She looked so smug.

"I told you to gag him," she snapped.

"You can't do this," David said. "I'm not the problem, you are."

The general glanced between the men and Price. She flicked a hand, and the men dragged David down the hall.

"What is that about?" McGill asked, the director coming up behind him.

"In-house nuisance, nothing to concern yourself."

David heard that. "Director! General McGill! I need to speak with you!"

Price ordered him gagged and Fasio snapped out a cloth.

David shouted, "Dragon One has Gavlin!"

General McGill looked at Price, then the director, before he strode up to the young man. The two men tried to gag him, but he fought them.

"Leave us."

The guards glanced at Price, but the director stepped forward. "Do as he says."

They let him go and stepped back, but didn't leave.

"Who are you?"

"David Lorimer, sir, Deputy Director Price's assistant."

McGill looked down the hall at Lania Price. The line of pure bullshit she'd just handed him had smelled bad from the first word, now it was rank. He glanced, reached for a door, then ushered the young man inside. Before he shut the door, he said to his aide-de-camp, "No one gets in, Marine."

The Marine Lieutenant stood at parade rest in front of the door, staring down the CIA attack dogs.

Behind closed doors, McGill looked at Lorimer and recognized the heat of determination. "You have five minutes."

David took a cleansing breath and started.

Nineteen

Dragon Six spewed jet wash as it rose into the sky over Hong Kong.

Inside the aircraft, Killian let Logan repair his shoulder so the stitches would stay and shoot him up with a steroid. He didn't have time for painkillers; he needed all his brain cells functioning.

Riley was at navigation, watching radar and thermals. China had hundreds of satellites and they were using and abusing them to get what they needed.

"I got it, I got it! Moving fast to the ship."

"The ship is stationary?" Killian moved in for a look-see.

"For now. The only way they can get her on that ship is to lower her by pulley or land." He glanced at the weather screen. "The sea is too rough to land, going to be one hell of a ride down."

Killian wanted to worry, to think about what Alexa must be going through, but he couldn't. He couldn't afford the luxury, and he'd already let his heart distract him. A few months ago he would have wounded her to get to the man behind her. While he couldn't stomach putting a bullet in her, even to save her, they were paying for that now. The woman definitely had him twisted ten ways to Tuesday.

He glanced at Logan who was sitting at his computers anchored to the wall of the jet like a com center. If his fingers weren't stitching up or healing them, Logan was happy to have them on a keyboard. "We still getting the signal from Lorimer?"

"Yes, but no confirmation he received mine."

"Sam, ETA to the ship?"

"Forty minutes. I'm going low. Chinese are in the water."

"Shit. What?"

"Subs, I think, could be whales." Sam tapped the flight deck radar as if that would change the readout.

"Be careful, the Chinese navy could think we're spy planes and shoot us out of the sky. And this is our one chance."

"You're so motivating, Mustang, anyone tell you that?" Max said, readying gear at the far end of the craft. There was a lot more open space without the chopper inside. Sam was still pissed about that.

Several minutes later Sam said, "Chopper in sight, it's leaving the ship's arena. Orders, Killian?"

"You can't shoot it down, Sam, Alexa could be still in it, we don't know if they dropped her."

"The ship is moving now."

"Heading?"

"Northwest."

Killian scowled and moved back to look at the screens. "There's nothing there but open sea."

Riley turned his head to meet his gaze. "Except the Amianan Islands."

Killian's features pulled taut. There were a couple uncharted islands, south of Bashi Channel. Ruled by the Philippines, but virtually uninhabited. "Get NMCC on the wire, CenCom or FMF lant. Hell, anyone."

Logan started tapping, then a loud long tone broke through the roar of the engines. "Killian, they're already calling us."

In the Chinese operations command, the room was thick with activity. Technicians awaited orders. Generals conferred. The tracking systems were spread across three walls and two rows deep with screen tracking radar, whalers, and society. China watched everyone, including their own.

But a thin wiry general sat calmly in a chair, observing it all. The *Red Emperor* had far too many incidents connected to it to be explained away and nothing was simple to him. While money had stalled investigations, commands bought for a price, and betrayals against the state, Colonel Lim Tua wasn't as accepting as his fellow officers.

Some wished to stay clear of the United States and Japan, let them work and live as they wished. Others wanted to bring all to their way of thinking. For himself, the general was in the middle. Western decadence was easily ridiculed, yet nearly every household possessed something they'd created. Everyone wanted the prosperity the Americans possessed.

However, Lucien Zarek had a valuable trade agreement with China, as did many Colombian exporters. This agreement made several of his superiors turn their heads when Zarek wanted something. Lim Tua followed the ship's movement across open water, then frowned, and stood sharply, drawing attention as he moved to the maps.

While technology was faster, he preferred the old ways, and grabbed a ruler, then plotted the course of the ship. He was certain somewhere, an American was doing the same thing.

I know where you are going, he thought and turned away, then picked up a phone.

"MSS, now."

CIA listening post, Taiwan Straits
Off the west coast of China
Two hours later

Ringler was about to kill the Orcs in Middle Earth when his receiver started buzzing. He dropped the game control and swung to the screen, slipping on the headset.

"Eyeball to command. Go ahead."

"This is Air Force General Richard Ashton, Alpha Indigo 778."

He tapped in the codes to confirm. NMCC. Whoa. "Yes, sir."

"The *Red Emperor* is in your waters."

"Yes, sir, sitting duck, and under her are two Chinese subs. A helicopter just delivered a large package to the ship, sir."

In NMCC the general cursed and said, "You didn't think to tell us?"

"Sir, I sent the information already this morning." He repeated the transmission.

Beside Ashton, General McGill straightened. He turned his head to look directly at the woman who sat in a chair, her hands folded and two armed guards beside her. *What a bitch,* McGill thought.

"This Intel is hours old!" Ashton blasted.

"Ring up New Zealand, I want film on this and I want it two days ago!" McGill looked at Walker. "Moore?"

"American military and embassy diplomats went into the house and found only dead bodies and blood."

Try to explain that to the Hong Kong police, he thought.

"Still sending the message, sir." Walker was at the keyboard, the generals hovering like expectant fathers.

"You can't involve a civilian, Mike," General Ashton said.

"I can and I will, because of her we've been out of the loop on the seriousness of this, and we need him. Now."

"Sir?" Walker twisted in the chair. "Sir, you have a phone call."

"Take a message."

"He insists, sir, and he outranks me."

McGill frowned and looked at the young man who'd been invaluable. "Colonel D.B. Wakeland, Wing Commander, sir, MCAS Futenma, Okinawa, sir."

McGill hurried to the com center, and put on the headset. "Patch it through and scramble this," he said with a glance at Price.

"DB, this had better be good."

"I got an odd call, sir, Killian Moore. He was one of my—"

"We know, we have a tight situation here, can he be trusted?"

"Damn right he can. He says he's in the air. SSN's moving to Amianan Islands. Gavlin is hostage and had the following numbers on her. Tattooed if you can believe that." He rattled off numbers and McGill scribbled on the desk.

"Anything else?"

"He said he wasn't waiting for a go-ahead."

"To do what?"

"Retrieve Gavlin."

"How many men does he have?"

"At last count, one wounded, one pilot and three able-bodied."

"He expects to stop this with three men? That'd be ludicrous."

"You've never met Killian Moore, have you, sir?"

"Can we give him another team?"

"My men are ready, sir, ETA to location estimated at under five hours."

"Not good enough. Scramble your fighters. Thank you, D.B., we're trying to contact him now."

D.B. gave him the channel to Dragon Six.

McGill hung up, transcribed the numbers to paper, then wiped them off the desk. Before he moved away, Walker touched the general, and he looked back. "Yes?"

"Sir, those numbers, I know what they are."

"Come with me, Sergeant. You, take over." Another man slipped into the chair. He paused before Price. "Bring her."

Dragon Six
Over the East China Sea

"Killian, you got your wish!" Riley held out the headset. "It worked."

Killian pulled the strap on his load-bearing vest, and moved forward in the aircraft.

"Someone must love you, man." They all knew it was risky breaking into secure channels.

"Thank God for Wakeland," he said and slipped on the headset.

"Dragon Six, this is NMCC, General McGill."

"Yes, sir."

"A bird tells me you are on top of this, Major."

"We're trying, sir."

"Just how do you plan to accomplish this with three men?"

Wakeland was damn thorough. "Improvise, sir, adapt. Get in, get her, destroy missiles and get out." On what, Killian didn't know. They might be swimming to Okinawa for all they knew.

"The numbers you sent . . ."

Killian's heart did a quick leap of anticipation. "Yes, sir." He flipped the switch so the team could hear the conversation.

"They're satellite location codes."

"Sir?"

"They are the precise geographic locations of a satellite as it passes overhead, Marine. For the Hawkeye."

Killian's chest tightened. Oh, Christ, they were in trouble.

"Are you aware—"

"I am, sir."

A top secret spy satellite. "Area of observation, sir?"

"Just about the entire Asian theater."

"How did Zarek get them?"

"I'll explain another time, son. Can you confirm WMDs on *Red Emperor*?"

"Affirmative, sir. Russian components, unassembled at the time."

"We have sighting in Hong Kong of Serbian scientists. The party you attended?"

Killian's gaze shot to Logan. The man grinned. "Deets."

"Go ahead, sir."

"Our theory is that they are redesigning them for longer range. Are you aware of a target?"

Killian glanced at Logan. "Commander Chambliss believes it's Korean."

There was a long pause. Killian knew they were cursing a blue streak back in the U.S. Not only were there Americans sitting on the border with South Koreans, it was an ally and bombing it demanded retaliation into North Korea. That would bring China to North Korea's defense, then possibly Russia, while the United States and her democratic allies would rally for South Korea. A world war, he thought.

"You're the only one in the air at the right time. We can't get a Recon or SEAL team to you for five hours, and we lose sight on a bird in an hour. It won't pick you back up till it's too late. All we can do is watch on the Hawkeye."

"How long do we have?"

"Less than six hours tops, then we will have to destroy the *Red Emperor* and the island."

Killian pinched the bridge of his nose. Alexa would die. "All I can say is, keep watching, you'll know when we succeed." He cut the line and looked at his men.

"We have to HALO in or they'll know we're coming." Max was already suiting up.

"She will and that's all that matters," Killian said. "Sam, take us up."

Dragon Six rose, the black jet climbing fast.

NMCC

A hundred feet underground, the Air Force general and his Marine counterpart took a seat at a long conference table, watching the large screens track Dragon Six over Chinese air space. McGill watched the clock.

Hawkeye was untraceable, and monitored Chinese Intel and military movement.

The small screen before him tickered with intelligence relative to the situation. Some movement, alert status in China, and Korea and Taiwan. The Taiwan Straits post was an eye to the Asian theater. He didn't doubt the Chinese knew it was there and listened.

The Air Force was in command. It was their systems analysts and officers that ran the Emergency Actions Messaging. From NMCC they had a global view of all operations in the world, an eye on their friends and foes. McGill had convinced General Ashton that his theory was right, despite the unconfirmed facts. Till he spoke to Moore.

Then Ashton and McGill watched the satellite images, and were helpless.

Everything rested on Dragon One and their skills.

Amianan Islands

Alexa woke with her face in the sand and her body drenched in sweat. She blinked and pushed up, every inch of her aching. She was in a shack, tin walls and roof, and it was like being baked in foil. Looking around, she felt the tackiness of blood on the back of her head. The last thing she remembered was the drugs on the chopper and the Aussie bastard smiling at her.

She pushed her hands through her hair, breaking the dried blood and wishing she wore a watch. Climbing to her feet, she tried the door. Someone on the other side barked and hit back hard. The sharp noise rattled her teeth. She kicked it, pounding on it and screaming to be let out. No one answered this time.

It was pitch-black except for light coming from where the roof and wall connected.

Still daylight. But not for long.

She dropped to the ground, thinking *been here, didn't like it.*

Hurry Killian. We don't have much time.

* * *

Jumping out of a speeding aircraft definitely had its drawbacks, Killian thought. Freezing cold, breathing bottled air, a twenty-thousand-foot drop onto a hostile target and the tangible suspicion that the leap into the jet-black night might be the last one he took.

And he'd never see Alexa again. His chest tightened for a split second, then eased. Gripping the steel frame of the cockpit door with one hand, Killian watched the altitude readout for the jump. High Altitude, Low Opening. Insertion and extraction.

Wearing a helmet and oxygen, Sam glanced at his chart, then the dials. "ETA two minutes."

Killian nodded and checked his watch, setting the time lapse till they were out of range except for radio. His brows drawn, he did some quick calculations between aircraft speed, wind speed, bail, and the acceleration of their free fall to target. Accuracy was essential. It was a one time shot. A do or die moment.

On oxygen like the rest, Killian slipped the mike from inside the mask, then pried off the headset and handed it over to Logan. He resituated the throat mike, two disk sensors wired on either side of his voice box on a black nylon strip around his throat. Replacing the receiver wire leading to his ear, he moved to the aircraft door.

"Lock and load, ladies." He scarcely spoke, voice vibration carrying his words to Max and Riley. The pair looked up, their features hidden in black camouflage paint and oxygen masks.

"Time to crash the party," Max said and held up one finger, indicating the minutes remaining until the jump. As they performed an equipment check on each other, someone made a crack about the wisdom of jumping out of a perfectly good airplane at twenty thousand feet, at night, into unfamiliar territory.

Adrenaline pumped through his veins until Killian

felt like a stallion in a hard charge and despite the frigid temperatures, he was sweating. It all came down to this, he thought, a leap from a speeding aircraft.

The belly of the plane suddenly knocked against a wind draft as he snapped on a fresh cylinder and read-justed the black oxygen mask over his nose and mouth. Inhaling the bottled air, he drew the black thermal hood down over his head, the throat mike and the mask, shifting oval eyeholes into place before tucking the free edge in the high neck of his jumpsuit. Grabbing his helmet, he pulled hard at the fiberglass sides to position the specially poured armor over his head.

Equipped with a white helmet and oxygen mask for the cabin decompression when the door opened, Logan gave Killian the heads up for the jump. All conversation ceased as he flipped the helmet's transparent black windshield down over his eyes. Seconds later, Logan twisted the latch on the aircraft door. Riley and Max levered open the hatch, the hard suck of air pulling on their eardrums.

Icy wind filled the cabin, whipping around them like slashing blades. Violent, daring. Killian shivered on instinct, yet the close-fitting jumpsuit insulated his body better than his grandmother's afghan. Yawning to pop his eardrums, he rechecked the placement of his oxygen and the Bravo-Seven night vision goggles Velcro-strapped against his chest before he stepped to the hatch. His boots on the edge, he positioned his hands on the frame to give himself a hard push to clear the craft. Wind shrieked around him like the howl of a banshee. Below, lay endless sky, risk, an uncertain fate. For more than just his friends and Alexa.

Logan reached to crack the cylindrical Chem-Lite attached to his rip ring, then pointed unnecessarily to the two domed lights alongside the hatch.

Killian waited for the green light, growled, "Semper fi," then leaped, free falling twenty thousand feet.

The wind shear drove them upward, biting into their matte black jumpsuits. Killian heard only the beat of his heart, his breathing, and the whistle of his body rushing through the air toward the rapidly approaching ground. Always one hell of a rush, he thought, scanning the sea through the lens of his windshield. For an instant, he focused on his target, no more than a faint refracting blur thousands of feet below. Out of visual range, the island looked barren, but the closer he fell, the more he could see buildings and mountains.

And the ship.

Walker paced with Scoggins outside the door. Clearance was by special order and getting a message in to the general was tougher than trying to stop a sneeze. He'd been waiting for a half hour, and needed to whiz after all the coffee.

They had bad information, well, not bad, but different. He glanced at the clock. They weren't going to make it.

Lucien Zarek waited patiently, watching the people moving around the island like ants over a mound. Behind him three men waited.

"Zarek, we need them now."

"You'll get them as soon as I get mine." Behind him a laptop showed his Grand Cayman accounts. After another minute the ping finally sounded and he turned, looking at the total. "Very good." He typed in his access and confirmed, then shut the page down. He looked at the Australian standing near the door. "Bring her."

"If you'll excuse me, gentlemen." He handed over a slip of paper. "This is a portion of what you paid for."

One man snatched it and ran from the building, rushing toward the site. Lucien faced the rest. They didn't look too pleased considering he'd just delivered a weapon that had given him more trouble than the American ATF. "I'll have the rest in an hour."

"We don't have hours!"

He stared at the squat, round man. He was older, almost doddering, and therefore lacked suspicion. He supposed it was good for their cause, whatever it was. "Yes, we do. Trust me." Lucien gestured to the door. "Leave."

Without a choice, the men departed, scientists and the buyers, and he looked out the window as his new man brought her toward the building. He noticed her expression, her recognition of the men walking past her. Dunford pushed her into the room. Wisely, he'd bound her wrists.

"Hello, my love." Zarek poured a glass of water and moved toward her. Dirty and disheveled, she was still lovely.

"You bastard! What have you done?"

"Provided a service." He held out the glass. "Thirsty?"

She said nothing, but her green eyes spoke volumes. She wanted to kill him herself. The thought actually made his groin go rock-hard. "No?" He drank the water slowly, taunting her. It was a hundred degrees at least in the shack.

"China, Korea, the U.S., Australia, they're watching all the time, you know that. They've seen your ship."

"But that's it. Seeing. It's nothing more than people living out their lives. Peacefully."

Alexa's brow furrowed as she looked out the window. From the air, she'd bet it looked like a village, nothing more than fishermen or squatters. The old man from the jet, the one she'd helped with his overhead luggage and was at the party—ordered people around. The short geeky man from the ship followed him like a trained dog.

Right under my nose were all the answers.

She looked back at Lucien. "You're a gun dealer, are you that blind? Someone is on your butt all the time."

"And for a while it was you, wasn't it?" He leaned and tried to kiss her.

She jerked back and came in contact with the mercenary. "Cane will kill you."

"Can't. He's dead," came from behind.

She whipped around. He couldn't be. She'd know it. In her heart, she'd know. "Don't count on that." Slowly she looked at Lucien. "I'm going to kill you, Lucien."

"You'll try, I know." Lucien inclined his head and Dunford grasped her arms, pulling her toward a door.

Alexa dug in her heels.

Lucien opened the door and with an elegant wave, gestured inside. Alexa's eyes widened at the sight of the long steel table. Her gaze whipped to his.

"We have some things to retrieve."

"No, you don't. There is nothing there. We checked."

"Really?"

Dunford scooped her up and Alexa's insides locked as he walked to the table. She fought, twisting till he fell with her. She scrambled back and jammed both feet into his chest. He toppled backwards for only a second.

"Ahh, I love a fight." He lunged, and her foot connected to his chin, then she swung her leg to get the momentum to stand. With her hands secured, her balance faltered and she stumbled.

Behind her, Lucien moved up fast, jabbing her with

a needle. She twisted. "I'm really sick of you people sticking me like I'm some voodoo doll!"

He caught her limp body.

Lucien and Dunford laid her on the table.

Things are going downhill, she thought. She couldn't feel her shoulders, nor her back on the steel table. Then she couldn't feel anything. The narcotics wasn't enough to take her under. That would probably have been better, she thought when the Aussie moved up beside the table and strapped down her wrists and ankles. Alexa tried to bring her arm up to fight back, but it wouldn't move. Nothing would. Panic bolted through her. Paralyzed, able to hear, move her eyes, swallow, and breathe, but nothing more. Then they raised the lower portion of the table and a dozen really bad scenarios skated through her mind, terrifying her. Showing up in a porn film seemed like a treat right now.

Lucien swept his hand up her jean covered leg, his smile creepy and sly. "You're afraid, love? Don't be. I would never really hurt you." He bent and kissed her.

Alexa tried to bite him, but couldn't move her mouth. With his teeth, he tugged on her lower lip, gave her a sensual smile that said he had plans for her when this was over, then smoothed his hand over her belly and under the waist of her jeans. All she felt was the sick pressure and helplessness.

Then he glanced at Dunford and said, "Let's be quick."

Killian hit the ground, released the parachute harness, and rolled it quickly as he ran to the stand of palm trees. There was barely anything to use for cover, and they were a half a mile from the site. Max moved up behind him. Riley to his right. They removed their helmets and oxygen masks, stripped out of the jumpsuits and buried them with the chutes. In pale desert cammies splashed with green, they blended in with the terrain.

Riley radioed Sam. "Dragon Six, we're on the ground." He handed Killian the mike.

"Activity to the north side," Sam said. "Ship has been unloaded."

That was fast. "Roger that. You need to get out of there, Dragon Six." That the Chinese had them on radar was a given.

"We have clearance to land in Guam. Will keep in contact."

Riley switched off the radio and stowed it.

Killian sighted through field glasses, spotting movement on the shore. The sun was still above the horizon. He preferred darkness but they were on the clock with this. NMCC didn't think the terrorists would wait for nightfall.

He checked his watch. "Man, this is cutting it close."

"The odds aren't that great, either."

"Three former Marines against God knows how many terrorists and a couple ballistic missiles?" Max said. "Sounds like pretty good odds to me."

"Ooh-rah." They moved out, double-time into danger.

Alexa struggled only in her mind. Her body refused to cooperate, and her solitary weapon was her eyes.

Lucien moved closer. "You're angry."

You think?

"This won't take long."

Alexa couldn't see past her legs, nor could she turn her head; her direct line of vision was all she had. Dunford's hand slid under the sheet, a vile grin shaping his mouth. *I'll kill you first.*

Across her field of vision Lucien's arm stretched, a gun in his hand. He pointed it at Dunford's head. "Touch her again and you die."

Dunford retreated, giving him a nasty look. Lucien looked behind himself and gestured. A small man came into her view. Alexa instantly recognized him. He looked at her sadly, then slipped on rubber gloves.

Then he lifted his hand, the razor's edge of a scalpel winking in the light.

At three points, Killian, Max and Riley observed the camp. He recognized a few from the party. His attention went to the short fat man who'd hurried under the camouflage netting. The launchers were under there, he deduced, then touched the throat mike. "Finn, what's your visual?"

Riley was on the shore side, lying behind a truck. "Fifteen, maybe twenty with firepower. At least five are doing something in a group. I can only see from the waist down under the netting, but it looks like they are working on the launchers."

"Missiles, your nine, Mustang," Max said.

Killian swung the field glasses to his left and focused on the forklift. The pier was short, and not tall enough to reach the side of the cargo ship. It was going to start listing at low tide, so they couldn't use it as an escape. It would take hours for that ship to get underway. Yet there were several other boats, at least one sixty-foot pleasure cruiser. The money, he thought, but the advantage of cargo ships that size is that they could stack freight on the decks and in her belly. The side had hatches like opening the mouth of a whale for Jonah.

The forklift staggered forward slowly, the heavy ballistic missile cradled in its arms like a child. Men formed a line, raising the netting and letting the lift roll underneath.

Thermal lined netting. The perfect shield against satellites. He pressed the throat mike. "That confirms why they couldn't see it on satellite."

"You see the size of that? It's been shaved down. Just a little bigger than a Shahab-3." A *Shooting Star* or a *Silkworm,* a medium range ballistic missile Saddam Hussein used on the U.S. forces, and his own people.

"We can't know the range of something like that. Nine hundred miles, fifteen hundred? And did you see the fat dude. The Korean fur trader from the party."

"I saw. Next time we get a face recognition program."

"Man, I hope the big kahuna can see this." NMCC.

"And do nothing," Riley popped in.

"That's why we're here." Max and Riley had their orders. They knew what they could and couldn't do alone. Avoiding contact with anyone was essential. They were three against about forty.

"Let's load the party favors. Then I'm going for Looker. Rendezvous, my six in ten."

"Roger that."

From here on, Killian and his men used only hand signals. Killian wanted to check every area for Alexa right now, but he had to stop the missile launch. The hard grind of an engine grabbed at his memory and he stilled, sighting.

The launcher was moving up and down, left and right. *They're testing for coordinates without the missile.* Once the missiles were loaded, they had no more than an hour's time before they were ready to fire. He slid down on his stomach, low-crawling to the next cluster of cover, the rifle up out of the sand and his elbows digging in. Killian moved slowly, waiting for men to pass, then hustling yards behind them on the edge to avoid detection.

He couldn't see Max or Riley yet knew they'd be setting C-4 charges and claymores to stop anyone from fleeing to the boats. If anyone of them got close enough, they'd set charges on the missiles. They might not do much damage but they'd stop the launch. Or they'd all be blown to hell.

Killian slid to his knees, hunching over a rock, then rose slowly to his feet. He headed north, getting as close to the activity as he could. At one point, he walked like he owned the joint to the next building, stooped, set a charge, then backed away.

He glimpsed Max on the far end, and caught his signal. He didn't speak, pointed two fingers at his eyes, then the building, then held up three fingers.

I see in there, three figures.

"Looker?" he said into the lip mike. Max slashed at his throat, then gestured to his eyes. *Negative, cannot see.*

Suddenly Max dropped out of sight as a man passed in front of his position, stopped, looked around, then took a leak on Max's hiding spot. Killian would have laughed if he had time. Pushing forward, he moved close to the small building. It was unguarded, and he knelt at the rear, tapped the steel wall, then with his knife, cut through the wire stringing the slats together. It was empty.

A shoe remained behind and Killian's heart clenched. Alexa's. "Found signs," he said, setting a charge at the west. "I need a location."

"I'm behind the truck," Riley said and Killian caught a glimpse of him putting a charge under the gas tank.

"I'm inside the tent."

"Shit, Drac!"

"It's cool." Max Renfield moved to the table of food,

grabbing a ready-made sandwich and a bottle of water. No one paid him any attention. He'd left his helmet in the trees, and since he was dressed in desert cammies like most of the terrorists, he blended in well enough. But he wasn't stupid, he wouldn't risk more.

"You, there."

He looked at the fat Korean man, chewing, and behaving with disrespect, like a merc might. "Yeah?"

"Move this, we don't need it."

Max jammed the rest of the sandwich in his mouth and went to the old man, pulling the box aside and out of the way. The old man pushed him back and continued to tap on a laptop that was connected to the missile's guidance system. He got a decent look at the works. Then he cracked the water bottle open and drank as he left, then slipped casually behind the trees and a stack of foul-smelling trash.

"Mustang, you're right, they did rebuild it. It's got a plotted course and he took out the self-destruct. More bad news, Logan was right, it's headed for South Korea."

Killian thought of all those young men standing watch on the border. The people who'd die. Oh, hell. The arms negotiations. The Secretary of Sate was there and members of the UN.

"We don't have time or opportunity to disarm it. We find Looker, blow what we can, and get the hell out of here. Hopefully Wakeland is the shoot-from-the-hip guy I remembered." Killian had to move fast; once he got Alexa, all hell would break loose. "Dump as many party favors as you can on those things."

Alexa could see the scalpel cut into her ankle, but couldn't feel it. The man was careful and precise, peeling back a bit of skin, then with surgical tweezers, removed something. Lucien instantly took it, sprayed it with water, then held it up. It was a small slip of transparent film so thin only the light refraction made it visible.

Lucien looked at her. "This is worth twenty-five million dollars. Do you know what it is? No? It's your Hawkeye."

What the hell is a Hawkeye?

He held it on the tweezers, staring at it, then pulled out his cell phone. "I have the prize." A pause and then, "No, allow me the pleasure of bringing it to you." He took a step away, then looked back at the doctor. "Let's give her back her memory, shall we? Just a little." The doctor pushed a needle into her arm.

But he didn't have to, Alexa already felt it slipping back.

And the first thing that hit her made her stomach coil.

She'd killed Santiago.

Twenty

Minus 60 minutes
Day 28

"General!" Walker called out when he saw him walk toward the restroom. The guard stepped in front of him, warning him he'd use force, if necessary. But McGill came to him immediately, frowning as he pushed through the secure doors.

"Release him." He gestured the staff sergeant to the side.

"Sir, we have a big problem."

McGill sighed. "Let me have it."

"The codes, they aren't the right ones."

"That's excellent news."

Walker shook his head. "They were the right codes *yesterday*. I'm afraid they were retasked on the twenty-eighth day, sir. This morning."

McGill knew without a doubt that Price let the codes out into the open. While governments could manage to get them for satellites, a way of watching each other, there was always a bird in the air passing over. Hawkeye roamed freely on a course set by intelligence traffic. It had points to cover and was retasked with a new trajectory every twenty-eight days to avoid detection. Never the same sweep pattern twice.

Now terrorists had the vital information and were about to use it to strike somewhere in Asia. Possibly Korea, but Okinawa or mainland Japan could be targets. His eyes flared as the realization hit him.

The Arms negotiations. Secretary of State, the UN delegation.

McGill rushed to get them on a jet and out of harm's way.

Lucien didn't leave and watched her face as the realization returned. She wouldn't get it all at once, but it was a delicious pleasure to see the terror on her face.

A debt paid for the wounds he still felt in his soul.

"Oh, God," she muttered, mentally trying to hurry the effects along. The feeling in her face came first, the pain in her ankle next.

"Yes, little fox. Santiago was good enough to sell me the codes. There is a spy satellite up there and those rich men"—he inclined his head toward the walls and the activity beyond—"they're using it while your people are thinking they don't have anything to worry about, I'd gather. These"—he held up the transparent sliver—"are fresh. And will help them in their cause. Didn't you notice that nothing moved except at night hours? All about the same time?" he gloated. "The Americans couldn't look. And Pong made sure the Chinese didn't either."

"If you think the U.S. has one lousy satellite there, you're wrong. And China has hundreds."

"Not right this moment, they don't." Lucien looked at his watch. "In another fifteen minutes, this will be all over."

He didn't know Pong was dead. It gave her hope that on the Chinese end, he was found out.

Lucien bent, kissed her, and this time she bit him. Instead of hitting her for that, he threw his head back and laughed, swiping at the blood on his lips. "I'll miss your fire." He left her alone with Dunford.

The instant the door closed, the man moved between her legs, spreading them. "I've been waiting for this," he muttered, taking his time opening his belt buckle, his breathing increasing as he lowered his zipper.

God help me, she thought. He flipped out a knife, prepared to cut off her clothing. She jerked on the restraints. "Touch me and I'll kill you!"

"Aw, honey, let me do that."

Alexa's head jerked to the side. Killian.

Dunford threw the knife and missed, then reached for his gun. Killian lifted his rifle to his shoulder and fired. Two shots. The first hit him in the heart, exploding it inside his chest, the second pierced his forehead and splattered his brains on the wall behind him.

The doctor froze for a moment, then darted to the window. Killian followed him with the barrel.

"Killian, no!"

He lowered the rifle, scowled at her.

"He's innocent, Zarek forced him." The doctor slid to the floor, relieved.

Hurrying to her side, Killian kept an eye on the doors and windows as he unstrapped her. Briefly, he hugged her.

"Come on, baby, we have about two minutes." He lifted her off the table.

"We have to contact someone, the codes, he took new ones out of my tattoo. They're for a Hawkeye."

He shook his head. "He has them already."

"No, he said they were fresh, that the U.S. would

think all was fine." Alexa grabbed gauze and tied it around her bleeding ankle. "They were retasked this morning."

"Hell, then the numbers in the claw were a decoy." He nearly carried her to the door, wincing at the pain in his shoulder.

"Price did this. She gave the codes to Santiago to be used as a lure to see who'd buy them. They weren't any good till today."

His features pulled taut. "They're retasked every twenty-eight days."

"Santiago sold them to Zarek and he put them out to the highest bidder."

"Well, that guy is out there now."

"What do we do?"

"We blow the charges and get into the water. Fighter jets are going to level this place," he looked at his watch, "in less than twelve minutes."

"We can't let them launch."

"We'll think of something. Are you okay to run? It's gonna get hairy." He handed her his side arm.

"How many men do you have?"

"Riley and Max." She gave him that very female "men are so dumb" look and he grinned. His heart did a jig finding her alive as he cupped the back of her head and kissed her hard and quick. They edged toward the door, and Killian touched his throat mike.

"I have Looker, we're coming out." He checked the area, then stepped out, moving along the building.

"Mustang, the missiles!"

Killian heard the grinding of gears, and looked. The missiles were rising, the extension cab pushing them past the webbing and shifting for coordinates.

"Oh, my God, they're going to fire!"

"Light us up," Killian said. "Now! Now! Now!"

Alexa and Killian ran across the sand as the first

charge detonated. Fuel barrels shot into the sky. Boats shattered in a spray of wood and machine parts. Screams of the dying were muffled as men scrambled, firing into the smoke. One platform tipped to the side, the wheels burning, and flames licking up the fuselage.

The Korean shouted orders and the second missile rose.

"It's not stopping them!" Alexa watched in horror as the huge ballistic missile pointed toward the sky.

"Finn, get to my six, my six, asap." Killian had one last shot.

General Lim Tua watched the satellite image, his gaze shifting to the four fighter jets streaking across the sky from Hainan Air Base. Mentally he saluted his comrades who would give their lives to stop a war.

"Mustang to Dragon Six," crackled through the radio and Sam bolted into the cockpit, grabbing the headset.

"Dragon Six, good to know you're still alive."

"Patch me to Futnema to Wakeland. We have nine minutes."

Logan slid into the copilot's seat and picked up the radio handset.

"We have to get to the water," Killian said. A stream of bullets thunked into the sand at their feet as they raced across the sand. A hot spray of fire scorched the treetops and Killian threw Alexa to the ground and shielded her. When the dust settled, he rolled to his back.

"Killian." She pointed. "It's Zarek, about twenty yards away."

Killian found Zarek's position, then handed her a detonator. "Give him a surprise."

Alexa slammed it. The explosion rocked the ground and behind Zarek the cache of weapons blew to hell. Zarek stumbled forward, fell to his knees, then after a moment, climbed back up, firing again.

Time stalled. Engines whined, and the worst happened. Ignition. White smoke billowed, cloaking Zarek. Alexa looked up as the cone of the missile pierced the smoke.

Then in a tremendous roar, it launched.

The F-18 Hornets were in the air, waiting for the command. Inside the cockpit, Silver Eagle Executive Officer Major Dave "Archangel" Goodwin flew at Mach 2 from MCAS Futenma, Okinawa toward the Philippines. His radio signaled, the words clear and short.

"American fighter jet. This is People's Republic J-7 attack jet. You are in Chinese airspace. Turn back or you will be fired upon." The accent was thick, but Archangel understood.

"China J-7, be advised, terrorist's missile in the area set to launch. We have it covered. Please retreat."

But the Chinese pilot repeated the message. Over and over.

"Great. Stubborn commies."

The rapid beep of his radar locked on them, the sound filling the tight cockpit.

"Incoming! We having incoming," his weapons officer shouted. "Ballistic missile is hot."

"Give me a lock."

The beep went to a steady tone. "We don't have

enough to take that out," the weapons officer said behind him.

"China J-7, fire! Fire!" The American pilot flipped up a red cap and hit. The pair of stinger missiles raced toward the ballistic missile headed for the South Korean coast. His load dropped, the F-18 Hornet gained altitude.

In the Chinese jet, the captain fired, both pilots peeling away to get out of the explosion's path. And both praying to God and Buddha they were on target.

On the ground, Alexa and Killian watched the missile cut through the sky, high and hot, white smoke trailing in the dusky light.

She gripped his hand. "Oh, Killian . . . all those people."

"Come on, Marines," he muttered, looking through the binoculars. "Do your thing."

He saw two jets cross each other in the sky, let loose the payload, then pull a sharp G-3 turnaway from the missile. "The Chinese are up there, too. Take cover, wildcat."

The Chinese and American missiles hit the five ton SSN. The explosion went out in a wave, a snap of fire and debris that looked like a starburst of orange fire and gray smoke. It lit the darkness, could be seen for miles.

McGill and half the senior staff held their collective breath. The Hawkeye focused down, blinking with each flash and getting closer to the damage.

"We have a hit, we have a hit."

"Thank God," McGill said, sagging into his chair.

"Sir, what about Dragon One? Do you think they got out in time?"

"I don't know, son."

Walker rubbed his face. "It's just not fair."

"Terrorists never are."

Men ran for cover, terrorists screaming orders no one would follow.

Alexa almost couldn't believe her eyes. They were like flies, four F-18s swooping from the right. Three more jets coming in from the left. They fired at the fast-climbing missile, then like a team, shot toward the sky as the debris fractured across the heavens. On the ground, bodies littered the beach, the fat Korean facedown in the sand near the launcher.

Killian grabbed Alexa's hand. "We have to get to the water. It's our only chance." He'd give the F-18s two minutes to reposition and drop.

She ran behind him, explosions radiating a two hundred degree heat blast over the shore in waves.

"Little fox!"

She stopped.

Killian stumbled and turned back. "Alexa!"

Lucien came toward her, a machine gun in his hands. His face was splattered with blood, his arm bleeding, but still he came. Alexa dropped and fired.

Killian skidded to the ground beside her. "Woman! You're damn certifiable!"

"He doesn't get to live," she said and fired again, the bullet eating the flesh of his thigh. Zarek only staggered. She shot again, wanting it to be an agonizing death.

Above them, missile debris hurtled through the sky.

"Get down!" He yanked her flat to the ground. Chunks of metal plunked to the sand.

Alexa pushed Killian back and fired at Zarek, hitting him in the throat. His head snapped back with the force, just in time for him to see the huge twisted fuselage before it landed on him.

The sharp edges sliced through Zarek's body, severing limbs, shrapnel spraying Alexa and Killian. A piece caught him in the chin, her on the shoulder, and he covered her body with his.

Alexa opened her eyes, spitting sand, and Killian rolled off her. Alexa pushed up on all fours, then scrambled back. "Oh, God." She turned her face into Killian's chest and he looked over her head.

"Man, that's nasty."

Lucien Zarek's head lay a couple feet away, smashed nearly flat.

The jets swooped in, riddling the sand with bullets in straight long lines. Alexa flinched in his arms. "Come on, we have to get moving, they'll blanket this place."

"A clean sweep? God, our timing just so stinks."

They ran.

Jets plowed past overhead, the roar deafening and shaking the ground as Killian and Alexa splashed into the water. Then it hit. Napalm. The impact sent a percussion wave across the island that threw her forward into the ocean. Killian was right behind her. A wave pulled them under, the fiery glow visible from under the water. Killian pushed his arms through the water, fighting the current. Alexa was beside him. They surfaced.

Fire billowed like blooming flowers, curling in thick rolls toward the sky. The Chinese had their hand in it,

J-7 attack jets dropping a half-dozen bombs on the island. The earth shivered, water rippled to whitecap waves.

Killian touched his throat mike. "Finn, Drac, come back!" They waited, floating, and got nothing. "Finn, Drac, you out there?"

"Okay, that was fun," Max's voice came over the mike. "Are they okay?"

Killian, a wounded bloody mess, nodded.

They heard splashing, turned to see Max swim toward them, Riley a few feet to his right. They treaded water, smiling.

"God bless international relationships," Riley said, watching as the Chinese aircraft headed home.

Killian wiped water off his face, boat wreckage rolling past them. "I guess we should have spared a boat."

Alexa grabbed onto the wood and looked at the team. "You guys are my heroes."

Killian leaned on the wood, making it bob, and kissed her. "You're mine."

"Good God, he's going soft," Max said. "Get a room."

"I'd settle for a boat right now."

Alexa touched the side of his face, smearing the blood on his chin. "Yeah, and then a bed."

Killian grinned, holding onto the plank and kissing the woman he fought to love.

CIA Headquarters
Langley, Virginia
Four days later

To the far right of the panel flanked by two armed guards, Lania Price ground her teeth. Alexa could tell by her jumping jawline. She relished the final moments of the inquiry. Besides, she wouldn't have missed the chance to see Lania in a baggy jumpsuit with her feet and hands shackled.

"Thank you for your statement, Officer Gavlin. Your clarification in this is most helpful. And we truly regret that you suffered."

Alexa nodded to the director and pushed back from the table and stood.

"You're certain you won't consider returning to duty?"

"No, sir, my decision is final. I'm done."

"This agency and this country owe you and Dragon One a debt we cannot repay."

Alexa stilled, her gaze sweeping over the men and woman assembled. "Yes, you can, and I'm collecting right now."

The director looked shocked for a moment. McGill only grinned.

"I want Killian Moore's record expunged. Gordon Psalt was the DEA mole, he had his face surgically altered and fingerprints destroyed. He's dead."

"We have only your word on that."

"You doubt me now, Director?"

The director's features tightened with shame.

"Will you do as I ask?"

"Moore is too old to be reinstated," McGill said.

"General, you don't pay him enough to get him back in the Marines."

She smiled beautifully and McGill admired her strength.

"But he deserves to have the truth be told to people who matter. Like his CO, and his father."

"I will see to it personally by morning, Officer Gavlin. I swear it."

Alexa eyed the director. "You'll forgive me if I wait to see it happen, sir."

McGill laughed, offered his hand. "Give him my best, will you?"

She shook his hand, nodded, then headed to the doors.

McGill looked at the director and murmured, "You're losing big, this time, Randal."

The director's lips curved ever so slightly in a rare smile. "Perhaps."

Alexa stopped before Lania, meeting her gaze. "A firing squad would be a compassionate sentence."

"Bitter? Alexa, that's not like you."

"You don't know me, Lania, you never did."

Lania snickered. "I made you. You have nothing, no home, no address, no identity."

Alexa slapped her face. Lania turned her head slowly and met her gaze. Behind Alexa, McGill held back the director.

Lania kept her dignity, her chin up. "What I did, I did for the good of the country."

"Really. Which one?"

Lania made a sour face.

Alexa glanced back and met the director's gaze. "I'll be watching you. All of you." She left the large conference room, and was halfway down the hall when a young man stepped out.

"I'm David Lorimer, ma'am."

She walked up to him, lightly kissed his cheek, and whispered, "Thank you, David. You saved a lot of lives. Including mine." He flushed and nodded, and Alexa continued, leaving behind her old life and stepping into a whole new adventure.

* * *

Alexa stood in the Craw Daddy restaurant in New Orleans.

The ceiling was low slung and if Alexa hadn't been outside and knew it was once a big house, she'd have noticed it inside. The walls were gone, but the old plantation style was still there. It was a joint, where you kicked off your shoes, ate, and drank beer and made friends. The air was hopping with Cajun music and the scents of crawfish and jambalaya. Her mouth watered and she inched her way between the crowd toward the bar. Waitresses moved around the place with trays in a dance that defied logic. She stopped one, asking for Killian.

The girl, dark-skinned with a blinding smile said, "You must be Alexa. Boss is in the back, up one floor with the boys." The girl frowned a bit. "You be all right with all those men, girl?"

"I'll be fine, but if the testosterone starts dripping through the rafters, come up there with a hose."

The waitress grinned. "Say hey to Riley for me, tell him Jasmine said so."

Alexa was sure Riley would love to know he had a fan club, and headed to the upper floor. She knocked and the noise was slightly less than it was downstairs. The door opened, and a man with short dark hair and a sexy goatee answered. Sebastian Fontenot, she assumed. It was his house, his restaurant.

"The lady's here fellas," he called out over his shoulder. He kissed her cheek, sliding his arm around her waist and guiding her through the upper floor of the house.

Alexa sighed and leaned into him.

Sebastian frowned slightly and squeezed her a bit. "Tough day." She just nodded, feeling comforted. "You're safe here, *bébé,* trust me."

Trust. It was the one thing she'd have to give these men and they were the first people who didn't let her down.

"Get your hands off my woman, Coonass."

Alexa straightened. Sebastian left her side as she just stared at Killian. In a dark T-shirt and worn jeans that really showed off his body, he simply looked delicious. She wanted to fling herself into his arms and take him somewhere dark and private and show him what he meant to her.

"Well?"

"I'm done."

"Ooh-rah!" He grinned, rushing to her and scooping her into his arms. He kissed her wildly, and she was feeling him up and down before she realized they had an audience.

"Does this go on a lot?" Sebastian asked and the team snickered.

They parted, and Alexa touched his face briefly before looking at the guys. "Hi."

They all hopped up to greet her, and Alexa felt like a queen with so many handsome knights around. A girl could get used to all this, she thought, then slipped her hand in her pocket and held out an envelope to Killian. He frowned questioningly.

"Your past."

His features tightened and even though the team was trying hard not to look like they were listening, they were. Killian took the envelope and opened it. He frowned at the disk, holding it up.

"That's the truth of the DEA joint mission, Price's notes and letters on it."

Killian's gaze lifted slowly to hers. "Alexa, my only chance to get a clean slate was to get the data off the deputy director's personal office PC. How'd you get this?"

"The director owed me."

"You blackmailed him?"

"Threatened lightly." She went up on her toes to kiss him and quickly ran her tongue over the swell of his lips. She felt him come apart a little, and it did her heart good that she could bring this big man to his knees so easily. Killian pocketed the disk and slipped his arms around her waist and squeezed. He didn't say thank you, he didn't need to; she'd given him back his freedom. Just as he gave her hers.

"If you two can pry yourselves apart . . . we've been having a discussion," Riley said. "We took a vote."

She frowned at the team. "Vote, for what? Who has to go downstairs for more food?" She gestured to the coffee table lined with platters, which Max was vigorously sampling.

"The tribe has spoken."

When she just stared, Killian said, "You know, like *Survivor.* On TV?"

She gave him a patient look. "Honey, I haven't seen American television since—" She frowned. "I can't remember."

The group groaned. Max tried to explain what they meant. "We voted you in."

She was touched. "In? To the team?"

"Yeah, sure," Riley said.

"You all agreed?" She got a collective nod. "I'm not sure I want to be on this team." They all stilled, freezing in their movements.

"Why the hell not?" Logan said, looking offended.

"Well, for starters, you tried to put a bullet in my head."

"Hey, Price was behind that."

"I would have never done it." Killian's deep voice rumbled near her ear, and sent shivers down her spine.

"I know that, *now*. But I've spent over a dozen years doing the same thing. I'm not sure I want to do it again, for anyone."

"Pay's better," Sam said.

"There are lots of breaks in between," Riley coaxed, looking like a little boy offering to share his cookies.

She was touched to have so many care about her and lifted her gaze to Killian's, her eyes a little teary. "I'm tired, Killian, really tired. I'd like to know how the rest of the world lives. I want to wake up and not have to watch my back. I want a place of my own, and junk mail and crabgrass and to bitch about the schools in my area. I've never done that. For heaven's sake, everything I own is in the back of that car parked outside." Her voice fractured, tears welling.

The guys gave her sympathetic looks and before she got ticked, Killian led her out to the porch off the back of the house. He closed the doors for privacy and took her into his arms. Alexa cried quietly for the first time in a while.

"It's okay, baby, I understand."

"I don't think you do."

"Do I get points for effort?"

"Yeah."

She tipped her head back and Killian groaned, wiping at the trail of tears. It broke his heart. "I'm in love with you," he said.

She smiled brightly. "Yeah, I know."

"That's it . . . I know?"

"I love you, too, Killian." He kissed her. "But . . ." He frowned. "I need something more right now, just for me."

"I can give you junk mail and crabgrass, a backyard to sunbathe in. Even babies if you want."

Her eyes flew wide. "Oh, jeez, don't *even* go there."

"Okay, sure, not yet."

Alexa met his gaze, loving his vivid blue eyes and the naked truth she saw there.

"I can give you the excitement you had before, too."

"And if I don't want it?"

She'll get bored, he thought. "Then I'll make sure I'm giving you exactly what you want."

"What about you? What do you want?"

"You. Twenty-four seven. In my life. In my bed, every night, every morning. I want to know you're staying with me, that you can make a commitment to me, because I'm ready to make one with you."

Alexa swallowed. No man had ever said that to her. No man had wanted her for more than a week, for what information she was delivering, or the fun they could have in between.

"Sign on with us. We could use your expertise and I can't tell you how many times we needed a woman with us."

"That'll just make you look legit."

"Yeah, maybe, but I can promise you one thing . . . I'll watch your back, wildcat; you won't have to look over your shoulder, I'll be there, always."

Alexa felt a flood of tears building up inside her. Like a child her lip quivered. Like a woman who needed his love, her soul opened. And like a spy, she didn't bother to listen to the dangers of giving up her heart to this man, she just did it. "I love you, Killian Moore."

"That's good enough for now." He kissed her, and she felt his smile against her mouth. "You know I want to propose to you."

A giddy tingling swept over her skin and she ached to say yes. "If you do, I'll lock you in handcuffs again."

He chuckled darkly. "Now there's a kinky thought."

Then he crushed her to him, his big warm hands bunching in her clothes as if she'd escape him again. His kiss devoured her, passion spreading over them, wrapping them in their own world, and shielding them from danger.

Well . . . for now.

And we don't think you will want to miss
PERFECT WEAPON
by Amy J. Fetzer,
coming in March 2006 from Brava.

The anticipation of her pizza made her antsy. Eating was better than reliving her quick, short, nightmare and Sydney couldn't shake the image of Corporal Tanner's death from her mind. She needed to be busy since for three years her focus had been her job in the Cradle, but with her data destroyed, all she had to show for a billion-dollar project was her notes. She read over the crumpled printout, even more certain of her results, then tossed it on the counter and gathered her supplies to make a scented oil for her bath. The hobby was playtime, and like cooking it always helped her relax. It was just a different kind of chemistry, in its simplest form. And it didn't threaten to kill anything except bad vibes. Popping in a Nora Jones CD, she stirred the double boiler, then added lavender essential oils to the mix. She was getting out the bottles and funnels when the knock at the back door startled her.

She glanced at the clock, shocked to see she'd been at it for a half hour, then wiped her hands, turned off the burner, and hurried to the back door. On the way, she grabbed her jar of house cash, plastering on a smile for Ricky. He's grown some, she thought before she opened the door. Bracing it against her butt, she fished in the cash jar, her head down. The scent of cheese and pepperoni made her mouth water.

"That smells great, Ricky, how much do I owe you?"

"More than you know."

Her head jerked up, shock rounding her eyes. Oh, God. The Marine.

The jar slipped from her hands, shattering on the floor. He pushed his way inside, shoving the pizza box on the counter as she turned to run. Jack clamped a hand over her mouth and yanked her back against his chest.

"Not a word, got it?" He pressed the gun to her side.

She nodded and he kicked the door shut and let her go. Instantly, she reached for a weapon, her electric chopper, and threw it at him.

Jack jerked out of the way, glaring at her. "That was stupid." She tossed a kitchen chair in his path, but he kept coming. "I don't want to hurt you."

"Then why are you here—with a gun? What did you do to Ricky?" She kept backing up, sweeping figurines and frames off the shelves.

"He's fine, gone." He ducked as a book sailed past his head. "Jesus, lady." He lunged, grabbed her arm, shaking her. In her pretty face, he saw fear, like he had on the mountain and something in him settled. He'd get little cooperation if she was terrified, and dragging her with him, he moved, turned on all the appliances he could, then in the living room, did the same with the TV. He tuned it to MTV and cranked up the volume.

"Why are you doing that?"

"Your place is likely bugged."

Hell, yes, and she hoped NSA was listening and running to her rescue.

"Sit." He pointed to the sofa and, reluctantly, she obeyed. Jack moved to the window, looking out without disturbing the curtains.

"What do you want?" *Hurry up, Combs.*

"Answers, and you're going to give them to me."

"Like hell I am."

He gave her a deadly look. "You think you have a choice?"

"How far do you think you'll get? There's surveillance out there."

"Not anymore."

Sydney paled. Did he kill them? He looked furious enough right now.

"You've got a lot of eyes watching you. Who are you to warrant so much protection?"

"Nobody."

"Your degree isn't in lying, is it, *Doctor* Hale?" He faced her. "Why were you on the mountain?"

"Why were *you*?"

"I was thinning the deer herd for DNR, Fish and Game. Your turn." She didn't respond, looking like a mutinous schoolgirl in a Johns Hopkins sweatshirt and blue jeans.

"What went down on that mountain?"

Death, she thought. *Only death.*

"Whose blood was on you? Because it wasn't yours."

Her features slackened and sadness spilled over them. Jack frowned, an uneasy feeling sweeping through him, magnified when her eyes teared up a little. But he didn't have time for sympathy. The noise would bring the agent here. Jack knew they had to get lost, now.

"Put on your shoes, get a coat."

She looked up. "No way." God, she didn't want to go anywhere with this man.

He found one, threw it at her. "I can take you without shoes, Doc, but it's damn cold out there. But I *will* take you."

Sydney jammed her feet into her loafers, shrugged into her jacket. Where was the NSA? Why weren't they in here, slamming this guy to the ground and cuffing him by now?

He gripped her arm, and moved with her to the back door.

She dug her heels in, hoping to stall. "You're not a real Marine. Kidnapping isn't in the Marine code of honor."

"It is today. And I'm not keeping you, Doc. I need answers. Fork over, and you're free."

"If I don't?"

He met her gaze and Syd saw only cold determination. "That wouldn't be wise."

She spied the printout. "It will only get worse for you."

More than his men murdered? "I have a right to the truth."

"How do you figure?" She twisted, backing up against the counter. Her hand closed over the printout, the noise in the house muffling the crinkle of paper.

"I saved your life, Doctor Hale, and that got men killed."

"Terrorists, yeah."

"No, *my* men."

Sydney blinked owlishly. He'd said he had friends in the woods. "W-what do you mean? What happened?"

He didn't answer, pushing her out her back door and huddled like lovers, he ushered her toward his truck.

Syd recognized it from the state park. He opened the cab on the driver's side and forced her in. Sydney kept going, shoving her notes down the front of her jeans and grabbing the passenger door latch. No one came to help. No NSA, no police and Syd knew, she was on her own.

She was half out when he caught the neck of her jacket, jerking her back. "You won't win, Dr. Hale," he said close to her ear. "And I don't want to hurt you. Give it up."